D0122800

DESPERATE MEASURES

Also by Fern Michaels

Published by Ballantine Books

ALL SHE CAN BE

CINDERS TO SATIN

FOR ALL THEIR LIVES

FREE SPIRIT

SEASONS OF HER LIFE

TENDER WARRIOR

TO TASTE THE WINE

VALENTINA

VIXEN IN VELVET

The Captive Series

CAPTIVE EMBRACES

CAPTIVE INNOCENCE

CAPTIVE PASSIONS

CAPTIVE SPLENDORS

CAPTIVE SECRETS

The Texas Series

TEXAS HEAT

TEXAS RICH

TEXAS FURY

TEXAS SUNRISE

The "Sins" Series

SINS OF OMISSION

SINS OF THE FLESH

DESPERATE MEASURES

Fern Michaels

BALLANTINE BOOKS • New York

Published in the United States by Ballantine Books, a division of Random House, Inc., New York, and simultaneously in Canada by Random House of Canada Limited, Toronto.

Library of Congress Cataloging-in-Publication Data

Michaels, Fern.

Desperate measures / Fern Michaels.

p. cm.

ISBN 0-345-38440-7

1. Man-woman relationships—United States—Fiction. 2. Married people—United States—Fiction. I. Title.

PS3563.I27D47 1994

813'.54—dc20 94-27157

CIP

Manufactured in the United States of America

First Edition: July 1994

10 9 8 7 6 5 4 3 2 1

DESPERATE MEASURES

Prologue

This was the best day of his life.

He thought about other days in his life, bad days, terrible days, and then the days that were not so bad, that were bearable, livable.

Maddie Stern said she would marry him. He thought it would never happen, just the way he had thought his uncle would never find him. But it had happened. He would have someone forever and ever. Someone who would love him unconditionally, someone to share with, to grow old with, to parent with. Someone named Maddie Stern.

If it were possible to walk on air, Pete Sorenson would have been three feet off the ground as he walked down the jetway to board the shuttle for Boston's Logan Airport. His very tallness hinted that his shadow would be forthcoming. His dark eyes, heavy brow-line, and sinful double row of eyelashes were in stark contrast to his sandy hair.

He was antsy, wired up. Once, he'd had sixteen cups of coffee and a few colas in a six-hour span, and felt the way he was feeling now. And of course he felt guilty. That was it, guilt. Guilt was terrible, it made you do weird things, made you lie and concoct elaborate cover-ups. Not that he was doing something he shouldn't be doing. *Oh yeah,* a voice inside him needled, *then how come you waited till Maddie left for her buying trip to make this jaunt to Boston to see Annie?* Because, he responded to his inner self, I wanted to spend as much time as possible with Maddie. Now that she's away, I won't be cheating on her. *Terrible word, Sorenson, cheating.* Maddie doesn't understand about my friendship with Annie, he continued with his defense. Once she gets to know Annie, she'll feel differently.

He buckled in, listening with half an ear to the stewardess drone on about lifesaving measures, a brief spread open on his lap. He should be paying attention to everything, but his mind wandered to how surprised Annie would be when he popped in unannounced to sweep her away to dinner. Annie was going to be so happy for him.

He'd wanted to tell her weeks ago, when Maddie accepted his proposal, but he wanted to hug her acceptance to him, and so waited to share it until he felt the time was right. Annie would understand. Annie was perfect. A more than perfect friend, the best goddamn friend in the whole, entire world; a more than perfect lawyer; a perfect person in every sense of the word. She had morals, ethics, and the uncanny ability of always having the right answers to all his problems. She always had just the right words, the right expression on her face. Annie was goddamn, fucking perfect, and he wouldn't have it any other way. Somehow, someway, he had to make Maddie see how important Annie was in his life.

Pete leaned back in his seat and let his memories take over. He forgot about the brief in his lap, forgot about Maddie, his uncle, everything but Annie Gabriel. When he sensed commotion around him, he opened his eyes and unbuckled his seat belt.

Boston.

Annie.

Outside the terminal, Pete hailed a cab. Twenty minutes later he was poking his head into Annie's office. "Hey, lady, I find myself in need of a dinner companion. Whataya say, just you and me," he said, leering.

"Pete!" Annie was off her chair and in his arms a moment later. "God, it's good to see you. What are you doing here? Oh, who cares what you're doing here? I'm so glad to see you. Yes to dinner. You're lookin' good," she said, laughing.

Pete eyed her: slim, curly hair, clear complexion, and the oh-so-perfect business suit she favored. Maddie's hair was always in wild disarray and she favored loose-flowing clothing. She called her wardrobe funky and trendy. She always wore three-inch-long earrings that clanked and jangled. Annie, he noticed, wore little pearl drops. "And you," he replied, "look good enough to eat. Dennis must be doing something right," he added, referring to Annie's man of the hour and his old law school roommate.

Annie grinned. "Or something."

"Can you leave now? I want us to have a couple of drinks before dinner. I've got a lot to tell you. Would you mind terribly if we excluded Dennis? I want you to myself this evening."

"No problem. Dennis has night court. Give me a few minutes. There's fresh coffee. Your favorite," she said, beaming.

"Vanilla hazelnut with a dash of cinnamon."

"There's some real cream in the fridge. You know where the kitchen is. Don't you dare eat any of those cookies or doughnuts that are on the table."

"Wouldn't think of it," Pete said, then marched into the kitchen, where he eyed the doughnuts warily. They weren't really doughnuts, they were the holes from doughnuts. He crunched down four.

Pete looked around the kitchen. It was hard to believe Annie had worked for this firm seven years, starting the day after they graduated law school. What was even more remarkable was they'd maintained their friendship, visiting each other once a month, calling once a week and dropping each other funny cards in the mail. Once in a while, if one or the other was out of town or tied up with a bone-crunching case, they missed the monthly meeting, but then they always managed to squeeze in an extra visit. They had that rare kind of friendship that neither party wanted to give up or let fade away.

Pete closed his eyes as he sipped his coffee. He tried to imagine Annie's response to his news. Would she squeal and say, "You sly devil"? Or would she look at him with those wide eyes of hers and say, "Still waters run deep"? On the other hand, she was capable of slapping him on his back so hard he'd move forward a foot. He was prepared to tell her that when he and Maddie got around to having children, he was going to name his first daughter after her. Annie would get all misty-eyed and choke up, and he'd preen and beam his pleasure. Maddie would agree, he was sure of it.

"I'm ready, Mr. Sorenson," Annie said, entering the room with a Chanel bag over her shoulder, his last year's Christmas present to her. "You ate those doughnuts after you promised not to."

"I did not," Pete lied.

"Then how come you have sugar all over your lips?"

"Well, Miss Smartass, I was smelling them. I guess I got too close," Pete managed to say with a straight face.

"Where are we going?"

"Someplace dark and intimate. Someplace where there's soft music and good food and liquor. Someplace where the bill is so high we have to wash dishes."

"God, what are we celebrating? Did you win a lottery or something?"

"Better," Pete said smartly.

"What could be better than winning a lottery?" Annie asked.

"Something."

"Wait a minute, I have to get my briefcase. I can't seem to walk straight unless I'm carrying it." She left the kitchen, returning with a stuffed, battered case. It looked like his own.

"I've missed you, Annie," Pete said, throwing his arm around her shoulders as they left the office. "Why don't you quit this firm and come to New York?"

"Because, as you know, this firm gave me my first job," she replied. "I owe them. Also, I like it here, and there's a good chance I might make partner next year. And on top of that, it's too expensive to live in New York. I'd just be turning in one set of problems for another. Are you staying over or taking the last shuttle?"

"Gotta get back tonight. I have to plead a motion at eight tomorrow morning. Let's go to Bonderos."

He hailed a cab, opened the door for Annie, admired her legs. He hardly ever got to see Maddie's legs, with the long, flowing skirts she wore.

"Bonderos is good," Annie said, settling herself comfortably. "It's awfully expensive, though."

"Annie, stop putting a price on everything. You're worth it. If this town had something better than Bonderos, I'd take you there. Nothing is too good for you. I mean that, Annie. However, there is nothing to compare to *your* lasagna. No restaurant anywhere can make anything half as good. You should sell your recipe."

"Why do I have this feeling you're buttering me up for something?"

"You have a suspicious nature?" Pete guffawed. "I'm here to share. With you, because you are my best friend. My buddy, my pal, my compadre."

Annie had been trying to get a grip on Pete's ebullient mood. Perhaps, she thought, he was overworked. "You've been working around the clock, Pete," she said. "Why don't you take some time off?"

"Can't. I have a handle on everything except the traveling. I'm sick of it."

"You're making money, aren't you? Dennis said—and this is a direct quote—'Pete's making it hand over fist and he's got to be a millionaire several times over.' How does he know that, Pete, and is it true?" Annie asked.

"Well, most of it's true," Pete said defensively. What the hell right did Dennis have discussing his business with Annie? "Listen, I bust my ass for the consortium I work for. Don't let Dennis try and convince you it falls off a tree in my backyard. If I'd known you were interested in my finances, I would have mentioned them to you. It's not a secret, for God's sake. I have a job, I do it well, I think, and I make some big bucks. I bank it, and that's the fucking end of it."

"Testy aren't we?"

"I resent Dennis's comments," Pete said sourly. "I bust my ass out there."

Annie fell silent, in deference to Pete's abrupt change of mood. It wasn't until they were seated in the restaurant that she spoke again. She said, "I know you work hard, Pete, and already you have a reputation that can't be beat. They say you're the best acquisitions lawyer in the country. And I'll drink to that as soon as we get waited on."

"Are you putting me on, or is that really what they're saying?" Pete asked, pleased in spite of himself.

The wine steward approached the table, wine list in hand. Pete waved it away. "Dom Pérignon, 1956. One bottle now, one on ice. When the first one is gone, bring the second one."

"Yes, *sir*," the steward said, backing away.

"What *are* we celebrating?" Annie demanded as she calculated the cost of the wine and dinners.

Pete grinned. "Don't tell me I finally impressed you. I thought that was an impossible feat."

Annie grimaced. "No, you aren't impressing me. I think it's terrible that you spend so much money like this, I don't care how much money you have. There's always tomorrow and a rainy day. You, better than anyone, should know things can go from wonderful to downright bad overnight."

"I like your worry and concern. For so long no one cared if I lived or died. That's a bit dramatic, but you know what I mean. I care about you the same way. That's why I can't understand why you won't take a loan from me to help with your student loans. Interest-free, Annie. For God's sake, think of the money you'd save. I know it isn't easy for you. I just want to help. Why won't you let me?"

"Because."

They'd had this argument so many times, he'd lost count. "Because" was the only answer he was going to get.

When the steward returned, Pete tasted the wine, nodded his approval. He was going to tell her the minute they made their toast. The exact moment she swallowed the wine.

"What are we drinking to?" Annie said, holding the fragile wineglass aloft.

Here it was. The moment when he shared his news with his best friend. The best friend who was going to smile from ear to ear, whose eyes would sparkle.

"We are drinking, Annie, to my engagement and my wedding."

He didn't see any of the things he expected to see. Didn't hear the words; at least right away. He watched as Annie drained her glass. He watched her swallow and make a face. Her eyes were watering.

"This wine isn't worth the money you're going to be paying for it. I'm happy for you, Pete. I didn't know you were seeing anyone seriously. When's the wedding?" She held her glass out for a refill.

"Sometime in August."

"August is a nice time of year for a wedding. I'll be away in August," she said flatly.

"Well, you'll just have to change your plans, Annie." Pete grumbled, not at all liking the direction the conversation was taking. "I can't get married if you aren't there."

"I can't, Pete. My parents are buying into a retirement community in Florida and I have to go with them, help them move, handle the closing on their present house and the one they're buying. Everything's been arranged. I can't disappoint my parents."

"Even for me? Jesus, I didn't mean that to sound so selfish-sounding. Then I'll change the date to September."

"September is no good either. I scheduled appointments in

San Francisco for some job openings. I don't think I'll take them if they're offered, but I do want to get some feel for what's out there in case I don't make partner early next year. You'll send me pictures, and I'll send a smashing gift."

"I don't want a smashing gift. I want you at my wedding."

"I'm sorry, Pete."

Pete enunciated each word carefully. "Do you realize this is the first time in over twelve years that you haven't come through for me? Jesus Christ!"

"I'm sorry, Pete."

"No you're not!" Pete said belligerently. "Is this one of those woman things men aren't supposed to be able to figure out? Like Maddie not understanding our friendship. I think Maddie is jealous of you. I told her she has nothing to worry about. Was that the right thing to say, Annie?"

"Since you already said it, I guess it doesn't matter. What does it mean?" she said, looking everywhere but at Pete.

"Mean?"

"Does it mean I shouldn't call you anymore? You know, once you get married? I guess these monthly visits will have to stop too, huh?"

He was missing something here. "You can always call me at the office. You do that a lot anyway. We'll still get together as often as we can. You bring Dennis and I'll bring Maddie," Pete said happily as he envisioned the four of them as lifelong friends.

"It won't be the same," Annie muttered.

"No, I guess it won't. It could be better, though." He didn't believe his own words for a minute.

"I'll always send you a Christmas card. I'll address it to Mr. and Mrs. Pete Sorenson," Annie said flatly.

"Annie, you're angry with me. I can see it in your face and hear it in your voice. What's wrong here? I was happy for you when you said you were seeing Dennis. I'm the first to admit I'm pretty dense when it comes to women, so maybe you need to explain to me what your attitude is all about."

"I think," Annie said, choosing her words carefully, "that you should have told me about Maddie. I thought we didn't have any secrets, yet you chose not to tell me. I suppose my feelings are hurt. You told me about Barney. Those things were important to you, and we shared. Did you tell Maddie about Barney?"

"I wanted to tell you, but I wanted to keep it to myself for just a little while, you know, keep it close to my chest. I was so afraid something would go wrong and I'd feel like a fool. When I couldn't stand it a minute longer I hopped up here. I'm really sorry, Annie. Now I feel like shit."

"And well you should. I'm not sharing anything with you anymore, Pete Sorenson," Annie said childishly. She finished the last of the champagne in her glass. "Well?" she said challengingly. "Did you tell her?"

Pete winced. How well he remembered Maddie's reaction to Barney. She'd trilled with laughter and said, "Tell me you didn't believe that kid. Tell me, Pete, that you weren't that naive. Are you serious or are you putting me on when you say you believed right up until your sixteenth birthday that kid would actually come for you? That's just too funny for words." She'd laughed and laughed until he wanted to blubber the way he had the day Barney made the promise. Instead he'd picked up his coat and left. He hadn't called her for three days, and maybe he never would have spoken to her again, but she called him and apologized. He hated the tickle of amusement in her apology, but in the end, because he loved her, he let it pass.

"Well?" Annie said a second time. "Did you tell Maddie about Barney?"

"She thought it was silly of me. Why are we talking about Barney?"

"You poor fool," Annie said. A moment later she was off the chair and out of the restaurant. By the time Pete slapped some bills on the table and made his way outside, Annie's cab was two blocks away.

Pete waited outside her small apartment all night, but she

didn't return. He called Dennis's apartment, but there was no answer there either.

With nothing else to do, he hailed a cab and told the driver to take him all the way to New York. When he settled back for the long ride ahead of him, he felt as if someone had drained half the blood from his body.

1

Six-year-old Pete did his best not to cry. He scrunched his eyes shut while he drew his puckered lips almost up to his nose. He felt a tear squeeze past eyelashes his mother said hid the most beautiful, the bluest eyes in the whole world. She was never going to say that again. Ever, ever. His eyes hurt, the same way they used to hurt when his dad made a campfire in the backyard and they roasted weenies and marshmallows. He was never going to do that again. Ever, ever. His six-year-old brain couldn't fathom how his eyes could burn like this if there was no smoke and no campfire.

He watched his knees and pressed them down against the edge of his bed, not wanting to see the lady in the blue dress stuff his things into the grocery sacks. She was pretty, but not as pretty as his mom. The other lady, the one watching over the lady in the blue dress, wasn't pretty. She was mean and wore ugly black shoes with shoelaces. As they continued talking, he slipped off the bed and out into the hall, where he stood listening.

"Don't get involved, Harriet. If you do you'll never succeed in this job. He's just a child. Children are resilient, he'll recover. We're going to place him in a good home. He'll have a roof over his head, food in his stomach, and belong to a family."

"Will they love him? Will he adjust? He's so little, Miss Andrews. He's just about to lose his first tooth. How is he going to handle that? What if the Fairy doesn't leave anything under his pillow?" the lady in the blue dress said.

"That's pure rubbish, Harriet. It's a cold, hard world out there, and there's no place in it for Tooth Fairies. It will build character." The voice changed suddenly and grew hateful. "You didn't fill that child's head with wonderful stories of adoption, did you? Nobody adopts six-year-olds, especially one who is all legs and arms with big eyes. People want babies and cuddly toddlers. Six-year-olds don't have a chance. It's cruel to tell them they might be adopted. Did you, Harriet?"

"No, Miss Andrews," Harriet said in a small voice.

"Just remember something, Harriet. Our taxes, yours and mine, are going to pay for this boy's keep. Parents who are too stupid to provide for their families shouldn't be allowed to have children. The boy's parents appear to have been a shiftless lot."

"Oh, no, Miss Andrews, I don't think so," Harriet said spiritedly. "Look at Pete's clothing, it's been mended beautifully. This little house is shabby, but it's sparkling clean. I think they were just poor and fell on a streak of bad luck."

"If that's so, how do you account for that surfboard? I happen to know things like that cost a lot of money. There was hardly any food in the refrigerator, but there's a surfboard. The price tag is still on it. Maybe it was stolen. Maybe we should think about taking it back and getting the money. The boy needs new shoes and a haircut."

"You can't do that, Miss Andrews. The board belongs to young Pete. The rules say his belongings go with him." The edge in her voice made Pete open his eyes. "I can trim his hair, and I'm certain his shoes will last a few more months."

"You're getting involved, Harriet. I can't allow this. Where is that child? Please tell me you didn't give him permission to run off and say all those tearful good-byes that make you cry. I will not tolerate this, Harriet. I told you I wanted him right here where I could see him. He's going to be squealing and crying as it is when we have to remove him from this rat trap. Now, where is he?"

Pete turned and ran, down the hallway and out through the kitchen, pushing the screen door that sounded scary at night when it opened and closed. He ran across the back porch, down the four rotted steps, across the flower beds, through the hedges, over the Lampsons' sprinkler and through their yard until he came to his friend's yard. He bellowed at the top of his lungs, "Barney! Barney!"

"I'm up here, Pete," nine-year-old Barnaby Sims called down from the tree house in his backyard. "Come on up."

Pete scrambled up the rope ladder. "Pull it up, Barney. Don't let them find me. Hurry up, Barney, pull up the ladder," Pete sobbed. Barney responded to the fear in his friend's voice and quickly pulled up the rope ladder. "What's wrong, Pete?" he demanded as he busily stowed the homemade ladder under a wooden milk box that served as a seat and held such good things as bottle caps, a rusty penknife he wasn't allowed to have, some cookies, and his and Pete's prize mice.

"That lady came to take me away. The one with the ugly black shoes. I don't want to go, Barney. Can I hide here? I won't make any noise. You can sneak me food or give me your leftovers. I can take care of Harry and Lily. Can I stay, Barney, can I, huh?"

"Sure," Barney said, sitting down in cross-legged Indian fashion. "Did they see you come here?"

"No, I ran real fast. They put all my stuff in grocery bags. That lady said . . . she said . . . my mom and dad were a . . . shiftless . . . What's that mean, Barney?"

"I don't know, Pete. Probably not something good."

"She said no one will 'dopt me because they want babies and . . . and something else. What's that mean, Barney?"

With nine-year-old wisdom, Barney said, " 'Adopt' means when you get new parents. You can't have a mom and a dad.

That's why you get adopted. They give you a new name and you call the new people Mom and Dad. Like that kid Jerry at school. He's adopted. I bet she lied to you, I bet someone would too adopt you," Barney said loyally as he put his arms around Pete's thin shoulders. "Go ahead and cry, Pete, I won't tell anyone. When you're done crying, we can eat some cookies."

"That lady said she wants to sell my surfboard so I can get new shoes and a haircut. The other lady said she couldn't do that. It's breaking the rules if she sells it. It's mine!" Pete blubbered. "It's the last present my mom and dad gave me. They won't take it, will they, Barney?"

"Damn right it's yours," Barney blustered. "Grown-ups aren't supposed to break the rules. You tell, Pete, if she does, and don't be afraid of her. Nah, they won't take it," he promised, his fingers crossed behind his back.

"She's ugly inside her heart. My mom always said you can tell when someone has an ugly heart. The lady in the blue dress is nice, but she's not allowed to be nice to me," Pete blubbered.

Barney inched closer to his friend. "Pete, I know you're just little, but can't you remember anything about your uncle, where he lives and stuff?"

"No. Would he 'dopt me, Barney?"

"Well, sure. That's why you have relatives. That's what my mom said. I have an uncle Sam and an aunt Doris. They kiss me and pinch my cheeks all the time. They're okay, I guess. There's supposed to be papers. My dad used to keep all kinds of papers in a box that has a key. Did your dad have a box with a key?"

"Nope. My mom had a box. There were only three papers in it and some pictures. When they got married—that paper; when I was born; and when I wore a long white dress and they dipped my head in water—those papers. My mother's necklace that she wore to church on Sunday was in the box too. That lady said it was pitiful. She said there wasn't enough food in the refrigerator either. I wasn't hungry, Barney. If I wasn't hungry that means there was enough, huh?"

"Damn right it was enough. We have lots of food. You should have told her that."

"What's it like when you're dead, Barney?"

Barney had no idea what it was like, but Pete needed to know. "You live on a cloud, way up high, and you can look down and see everyone. You can't get off the cloud, though. You wear long white things and you kind of . . . sort of . . . float around. Everybody smiles and is happy because living on a cloud is the neatest thing."

"Then I want to be dead too."

"No you don't. Little kids can't die. There's . . . there's no room on the cloud. You have to be . . . big . . . grown-up."

Pete thought about Barney's words. "How do you get up there?"

Barney's eyes rolled back in his head. "They have this invisible ladder and you just go up and up and then somebody already on the cloud pulls you up. Neat, huh?"

"Yeah. My mom and dad can see me, huh?"

"Sure."

"I'm not supposed to cry. My dad said big boys don't cry. Do you cry, Barney?"

He wanted to cry right now. "Nah. People make fun of you if you cry. You can cry until you're seven, then you can't cry no more."

"Who said?"

"I said," Barney said firmly.

"You're my best friend, Barney."

"You're my best friend too, Pete."

"Are you going to take real good care of Harry and Lily?"

"Damn right."

"How long can I stay here?"

"Until they find you, I guess. I swear I won't tell, Pete. I think you should be my brother. Let's cut our fingers and mix our blood. That will make it official. You wanna do it?"

"Damn right I do." Pete grinned. "Don't tell your mother I said a bad word."

"I'm no tattletale. Get off the box. Harry and Lily need some air. Those little holes aren't enough. This knife is a little rusty. It's a good thing our moms made us get those shots when we stepped on that rusty wire last month. Don't close your eyes, Pete. You have to look at what we're doing. It's just a little cut."

Pete watched, round-eyed, when Barney pricked his finger, then his own. Together they rubbed their fingers together, smearing the droplets of blood all over their hands. "We're brothers now, Pete. Forever and ever. My blood is the same as yours and yours is the same as mine. When I get big, I'll come and get you."

"How will you know where I am?"

"I'm smart, I'll find you. Do you trust me?"

Pete nodded. He believed Barney implicitly. He ate the cookie Barney handed him. "Tell me what you're going to do when you grow up," Pete said tiredly.

"Okay. Do you want me to make it like a story or do you just want me to tell you what I think I'm going to do?"

"Make it sound good."

"Well, I'm going to grow up, and when I'm eighteen or nineteen I'm going to find you. You'll be sixteen then. I'm going to work in the grocery store and go to college. When you're sixteen I'm going to take you with me, and when it's time for you to go to college, I'm going to pay your bill. When I'm all done and learn everything, I'm going to get my own business. I am going to be a hort-ti-cult-yurist. I'm going to plant flowers and trees and make things beautiful. You're going to be my partner when you get finished in college. When I make lots of money, I'm going to get a fine house. A really fine house with a swimming pool, maybe build it on the water and get a boat. You're going to live with me. Maybe we can build like an apartment on the house so you have your own door, and guess what, your very own bathroom. I want lots of bathrooms. We're going to have lots of money. We'll be able to eat steak and turkey all the time.

Lemon pie too. We'll always have a cookie jar that's full and those chocolate kisses you like so much.

"I might get married. You'll be my best man because you're my brother now."

"I don't want to be best," Pete said sleepily. "I want you to be best."

"It means you're second best. When the man gets married, it means he's the best and then you're next."

"Okay, okay. Do you really and truly promise, Barney?"

"I really and truly promise. You take a nap now, Pete. I have to go to the store for my mom. I'll come back later. Stay here and don't make a sound. I'll climb down the branches."

"Okay, Barney."

On his way back from the store, his mother's groceries secure on the back of his bike, Barney pedaled his bike slowly past Pete's house, certain he would see or hear something he could take back to Pete to make the little guy feel better. What he saw was the police and every mother who lived on Pete's street. He tried not to look. He almost fell off his bike when he saw Bill Dewbury's mother point to him and say something. He kept on pedaling and pretended not to hear the police officer shout, "Son, just a minute."

Barney's heart was pumping as fast as his legs when he rounded the corner onto his own street. He careened up the driveway, leaping off the bike and grabbing for the sack of groceries at the same time. He slammed the bag down on the kitchen table. "I'm going down to the pond, Mom, to do some fishing. I'll be back in time to set the table."

"All right, Barney," his mother called from upstairs.

He wasn't going to the pond, even though he snatched his fishing pole off the hook on the back porch. He was going to head for the pond, then double back and climb back up into the tree house. He had to try and protect his *brother*. He was just a kid and he wasn't sure what he could do, if anything. He had to try. Pete was such a good little boy, his best friend in the whole world. It wasn't fair that his parents died. It wasn't fair that he was going to be taken away. Barney didn't know how he knew, but he did: when Pete got taken away, he would never see him again. His stepfather would probably take the strap to him this evening, but he didn't care. Besides, Dave Watkins wasn't really his father, he was his *step*father. Dave Watkins was a mean, ugly man, as mean and as ugly as the woman with the ugly black shoes Pete had told him about. He hated Dave Watkins.

Barney ran like the wind, down to the pond so it wouldn't be a lie, then back through the yards until he reached his own back-yard. He pitched the fishing pole up into the branches before he shinnied up the tree. He was breathing hard when he lifted the burlap sack that served as a door to enter the little house that his father had built for him when he was little. Each year his father worked on the tree house, improving it. Then he went away. Well, he wasn't going to think about *that* today. Today was Pete's day.

"Pete, wake up. Shhhh, don't make any noise." Pete stirred sleepily and then was instantly awake when he saw Barnaby's face.

"What's wrong?" he asked fearfully.

Barney told him.

"Are they going to put me in jail?"

"They don't put kids in jail, Pete," Barney said. "They're here to make you go with those ladies. It's like a block party in front of your house. We have to be quiet."

"I really love you, Barney, as much as I love Harry and Lily."

"I love you too. Listen to me, Pete. If anything goes wrong and they find us . . . I want you to remember what I said: If they take you away, I'll come get you when you're sixteen."

"Will your stepdad whip you for hiding me up here?" Pete asked.

"Yep. I don't care. I hate him. He's not my father. He hits my mother sometimes. Don't tell anyone I told you that, okay?"

"Sure. I won't tell."

"Do you want to know something, Pete?" Pete's head bobbed up and down. "Do you know what I want to do more than anything in the whole world?"

"Find your dad?"

"Yeah, but after that I want to . . . I want to stick my face right up in Dave Watkins's face and say kiss my ass!"

Pete clamped his hands over his mouth so he wouldn't laugh out loud. Barney did the same. They rolled on the floor, pounding each other on the back, their faces red, tears rolling down their cheeks.

Barney sobered almost immediately when he heard voices in his backyard. He put his finger to his lips when he heard his mother's sweet voice. "Barney went to the pond to fish. He took his fishing pole. He loves to fish. He left about half an hour ago. No, I haven't seen Pete all day. I just want to hug that little boy. It's so sad. Barnaby cried all night. If I see Pete, I'll send him home."

"Okay, so I cried," Barney said quietly. "I knew I was going to miss you, so I cried last night to get it out of the way. I didn't know she heard me. Listen, we need a plan. I'm not letting them take you without a fight."

Pete's eyes lit up. "What kind of plan?"

"Look, the only reason you and I can get up this tree is because we're both part monkey. My mother said that's the reason and mothers don't lie. Those cops and that lady with the ugly shoes can't climb up here. The branches are so big and thick at the top, they can't come at us from one of the other trees. We're kind of safe. Let's see what we have here to use as weapons."

"They'll get a ladder," Pete whimpered.

"Then we'll do what they do in the movies, we'll lean out and push it backward. This is our castle, our domicile. I learned that in school. No one is allowed to invade someone's castle. You don't have a home anymore, so I'm giving you this one. This is your castle, Pete Sorenson. We're gonna defend it."

The standoff, when it came, wasn't anything like the boys expected. The fire department arrived at the same time Dave Watkins came home from work.

"Are you ready?" Barney asked, his voice shaking in fear.

"Yeah." In his hands Pete held a pillow that had been slit down the middle. He was holding the slit closed with both hands. Barney held a can of yellow paint in one hand and a can of black tar they'd used to seal the cracks in the wood. It was almost full, all soft and gooey and dark as licorice. Two more pillows were on the floor, with slits down the middle.

"Get your ass out of that tree house or I'm coming up to get you," Dave Watkins shouted menacingly. "I mean it, Barnaby. You are interfering with the law, and I'm only going to say this once: Come down. Now, I know you're up there, so come down now before I get the strap."

Barney looked at Pete. Both boys shook their heads. Barney stuck his head out between the burlap curtains. Barney's eyes rolled back in his head, then his fist shot in the air. Pete watched bug-eyed when his brother, his best friend in the whole world, yelled at the top of his lungs, "Kiss my ass, Dave Watkins!"

"Yeah," Pete shouted, "kiss his ass!"

"He's coming up the tree," Barney said. "There's a fireman right behind him. He's sticking something in the tree. Get set, go!"

Yellow paint, black tar and feathers rained downward. Dave Watkins slipped and fell backward, knocking the fireman loose.

Pete clapped his hands gleefully. More feathers showered the air. Pete sent the tar can sailing through the air. The yellow paint can followed.

"All right, boys, that's your fun for the day," the fireman said. "Now, let's go down the tree like good, little boys."

"Make me," Pete said.

"Yeah, make him," Barney said.

An hour later Pete and Barney were on the ground.

Violet Sims fussed over both boys as she watched the ambulance attendants lift her husband onto a stretcher. She heard someone say both his legs were broken. She felt like cheering. Instead, she hugged her son and Pete.

Violet stooped down until she was eye level with Pete. "Honey, I want you to be very brave. I know you don't want to go, and if there were any way I could keep you, I would, but I can't. Barney and I love you very much. Time will go fast, and before you know it you'll be all grown up. I know that's hard to believe right now. Do your best, Pete." She kissed him soundly before he was led off by one of the firemen. Tears puddled in his eyes.

"Pete," Barney hissed, "stop crying."

"But you said—"

"I know what I said, but I just changed my mind. You can't cry after six. If they see you cry, they'll think they can get over on you, you hear me? Dry your eyes and be through with it." Then he leaned over and whispered in his friend's ear, "We gave them a hell of a fight. Always remember that."

"Do you think my mom and dad saw what we did, Barney?" Pete whispered back.

"Heck yeah. Bet they're clapping their hands. You be tough now, you hear me? I'll never forget you, you little squirt. I'll make sure Harry and Lily are well taken care of. Go on now," he said gruffly.

"Okay, Barney. Don't forget you're gonna come for me."

"I won't forget, squirt. A promise is a promise."

Up close Helen Andrews looked meaner and uglier, if that was possible, Pete decided. "Where's my surfboard?" he demanded belligerently.

"It's in the car, honey," the lady in the blue dress said.

"You apologize right now to all these police officers and firemen for making them come here to get you out of that disgusting tree," Helen Andrews said nastily.

Pete raised his head to stare up at the social worker. His index finger beckoned her to drop down to his height. She did so. Pete pushed his face up against hers, remembering Barney's words.

When they were eyeball to eyeball, he said, "Kiss my ass!" and immediately danced out of the way. The lady in the blue dress smiled. The fireman turned his head, his eyes dancing in glee. The cop pretended he had a spot on his blue shirt.

Pete climbed in the car and sat down next to his surfboard. "I'm sorry, Mom and Dad. I did it for Barney."

2

Pete Sorenson was almost ten years old before he was able to make a serious attempt at reaching Barney. It wasn't that he didn't think about his blood brother; he did, every day of his life, and he always remembered him in his prayers at night. He simply wasn't permitted to do much of anything but chores, his homework, more chores, and doing his best to survive in a foster home filled with other foster children, all older, all bigger and stronger than he was. It was a rare day when he went to bed with a full stomach, rarer still to go to bed without a bump, bruise, cut, or scrape. His foster parents, a couple name Bernie and Blossom Nelson, said he was incorrigible. The children all knew that the Nelsons didn't even know what the word meant. They also knew that all their foster parents wanted was the money the state paid them for their keep. The money, after the week's menu was planned, went for beer, wine, and bingo. If the food ran out before the next check, they ate peanut butter on bread. The peanut butter came in gallon jars and they never ran out of it. Sometimes they had to cut the mold off the bread.

Pete hated the Nelsons and he hated the other foster-care children. Somedays he even hated himself. He wrote long letters to

Barney that he kept in the back of his geography book, letters full of love and longing, of wanting to belong, that never got mailed because he didn't have an address.

Pete Sorenson dreamed a lot. At first he dreamed about Barney, almost every night. Then he started to dream about his faceless, nameless uncle and how his uncle was going to come for him. When he wearied of those dreams, he dreamed, in a thousand different dreams, of ways to kill Bernie and Blossom Nelson.

He hated the way they smelled. Bernie always had a strange odor coming from his pants, and Blossom smelled like she hadn't changed her underwear. They sweat a lot too, and made terrible noises when they ate. Bernie slurped his coffee and beer. Blossom's two front teeth were missing, so she made whistling sounds when she ate or drank, which was all the time. Pete hated everything about his life. He longed for the day Barney would come for him.

Now, Pete was in the room he shared with three girls, licking his wounds, but a victor nonetheless. One of the older boys, Dick Stevenson, had tried to take his surfboard out of his room. He'd fought like a tiger and told Bernie Nelson he was going to call the social worker and tell her how he was treated. "They'll put you in jail!" he screeched at the fat, balding man. He'd gotten a beating, but that was nothing new. He still had his surfboard, and that was all that mattered.

He lived in Asbury Park now, a long way from where he'd lived in Iselin, around the corner from Barney's house.

Pete didn't realize he'd been holding his breath until he heard the back door close. The room he shared was over the kitchen. That was another thing. Boys were supposed to be with boys and girls with girls, but the Nelsons didn't care. In a way, he didn't care either, since the girls who were his roommates were little and he kind of helped them. They didn't touch his surfboard either. His breath exploded in a loud whoosh. The Nelsons were going to Saturday afternoon bingo at St. Stephen's. He was supposed to clean up the yard, take out the trash, and peel the potatoes for supper. Bernie wanted the fence whitewashed, but Pete wasn't going to do any of those things. He was going down to the beach and try and hitch a ride to Iselin. He wanted to see Barney. He *needed* to see Barney. He wanted to talk to Barney's mother, to ask her if she'd call the lady in the blue dress so he could be sent somewhere else. Barney's mother would help him if she could.

With all the courage he could muster, Pete walked brazenly out the front door and down the walk. Then he ran, as fast as he could, to the beach, where he spent an hour walking up to people and asking them if they lived anywhere near Iselin. It was four o'clock when two young girls said they lived in Rahway and would give him a ride.

When the girls dropped him off an hour later on Green Street, he was so giddy he didn't know what to do. He stood in the middle of the sidewalk flapping his arms up and down until he could get his bearings. It all looked wonderful, and vaguely familiar. He thought he recognized the hardware store, the movie theater. He crossed the street and walked down one of the side streets until he found the street he was looking for. He saw his old house. Tears misted his vision for a moment. An old man was rocking in a chair on the front porch. He looked like he was asleep. A tear trickled down Pete's cheek. He wiped it away. He ran, then, around the corner till he came to Barney's house. He went up the steps to the front porch and rang the bell. A man with a beard, holding a motorcycle helmet in one hand and a beer in the other, opened the door. "Yeah?" he drawled.

"Is Barney here or Mrs. Sims?"

"No. They moved away. I bought this house last year. You the boy's friend?"

"Yes. My name's Pete Sorenson. Do you know where they moved?" he asked, his heart hammering in his chest.

"No kid, they didn't say. Mrs. Sims took the boy and left. You want Dave, he's living over Flip's Bar, last I heard. Don't think they told him where they were going, though."

He wanted to cry. "Did you know Barney?" he whispered.

"Just the last couple of days is all. He looked like a nice kid. He showed me his tree house. Bet you played in it with him."

"Yes, I did." The tears dripped down his cheeks, he couldn't help it. "I have to find him. I need Mrs. Sims to do something for me."

"Look, Pete, come on in. Do you want a soda pop or something?"

"Yes, sir, that would be nice. Thank you."

They sat at the kitchen table and talked man to man. Pete told him his story. The man listened, his beer forgotten. "That's down right shitful!" he said when Pete was finished. "What's going to happen to you when you go back?"

Pete shrugged, and then he stood up and lifted up his T-shirt.

"Jesus Christ, you're only nine years old!" the man sputtered. "Now listen, you stay right here. My brother's a cop. I'm gonna call him. He'll know what to do. Don't be afraid, Pete. Cops are good people. He'll know how to get hold of the lady in the blue dress. I want you to trust me. Listen, there's lots of food in the fridge. Help yourself. Just stay here. I want your promise."

"Okay, I promise," Pete said wearily. "What's your name?"

"Duke."

Pete nodded. "I like that name. What's your brother's name?"

"Nathaniel. We call him Nat."

At seven o'clock Pete was reunited with Harriet Wardlaw from Child Welfare. He told his story a third time, and then showed the whipping marks on his back. He let her hug him because she smelled so sweet and clean, the way his mother used to smell. He cried again. The cop offered him a handkerchief.

Pete was treated to a large bowl of ice cream while a flurry of phone calls were made in the living room.

"Okay, slick, this is how it's going down," the biker said, ruffling Pete's hair. "I'm going to give you the ride of your life on my Harley. Nat and Miss Wardlaw are going to be right behind us. You and the others are leaving Bernie and Blossom's abode. For good. They'll be hauled up on charges. We'll try and find your friend Barney for you. My brother said he'd do that on his off time. We're not making any promises, though. Miss Wardlaw is also going to try and find your uncle. Again, no promises. Is this okay with you?"

"Where am I going to go?"

"Don't know that yet. Hopefully, it will be someplace good."

It *was* the ride of his life. He loved every second of it. He particularly loved the way the Harley roared into Bernie's backyard, the one he hadn't cleaned, and then swerved right next to the back steps. "Yo, Bernie!" Duke bellowed as Pete slid off the seat.

"What the hell!" Bernie Nelson said, coming out to the small back porch. "Who are you? Get the fuck off my property. You!" he shouted, reaching for Pete. "Are going to feel the back of my hand!"

"Wanna bet?" Duke drawled as he stepped off the bike. He reached for Bernie's shirt, which was missing two buttons, and yanked him from the third porch step onto the ground. "You were saying, lard-ass . . . Ah, I see, you only talk big around little kids, eh?"

"What's going on here, Bernie?" Blossom said, trundling out to the back porch, the children behind her.

A blue Ford Mustang came to a halt behind Duke's motorcycle. Harriet Wardlaw got out, walked over to the Nelsons and handed them a folded paper. "I'm taking the children," she said. "All of them. Get their things. Now!"

To one of the little girls, she said, "What did you have for dinner tonight?"

"Mashed potatoes," the girl replied in a voice that was barely audible.

"What else, honey?"

"That's all," the little girl said.

A second and then a third car pulled to the curb, and finally a patrol car that said Asbury Park Police came to a stop.

"How about McDonald's for everyone?" Duke boomed. "As much as you can eat! They're giving prizes this week."

"Who the hell are you?" Bernie blustered.

"I'm an architect. I just happened to be at the right place at the right time today. I think you might say this is a case of divine providence. But this guy, the one with the gun, is my brother, who just happens to be a cop. You of course know Miss Wardlaw. The men behind her are your town's finest, as you will find out shortly."

Harriet Wardlaw turned to Pete and asked quietly, "Where's your surfboard?"

Pete smiled. "You remember my surfboard?"

"Honey, I remember everything about you. Hurry up, I don't want you here a minute longer."

Pete ran into the house to get his things. He was back on the porch in under seven minutes. For the first time in a long time, he felt happy.

Months later Pete received a letter in the mail. It was from Nathaniel Bickmore, Duke's brother. He said he'd been unable to locate Mrs. Sims and Barney. He thought Mrs. Sims crossed over the state line to get away from David Watkins, and probably changed her name so he couldn't find her and Barney. "I'll do my best and keep on it in my spare time," he wrote. "We're doing our best to try and find your uncle, too. I just wanted you to know we haven't forgotten you. Duke said to say hello." It was signed, "Your friend, Nathaniel."

Pete was in his new home, a pleasant enough place, with an older couple who were childless. He had his own room, with a small-screen television and a portable radio. He had his very own desk and a set of encyclopedias. His foster parents were Hiram and Etty Penshaw. They were stern and unsmiling, neither kind nor unkind. It was basically a house of silence. Etty read all the time. Hiram puttered in his workshop after he put in his time at his job. The food was good and plentiful, and there was always dessert. Pete even got an allowance of fifty cents a week. He'd saved almost all of it. If he knew where Barney was, he could go to a phone booth and call him. He had new clothes that actually fit him and were ironed. He looked like everyone else at school.

He still didn't have any friends, but that was by his own choice. He didn't want to make friends and then have his guts ripped out again. Every night he prayed for Barney. He wondered if Barney prayed for him or if he'd forgotten about him.

Pete was twelve when Nathaniel said he thought he had a lead on his uncle. It didn't lead to anything. When he was fourteen, Mr. Penshaw died and Mrs. Penshaw decided to move to Georgia with her sister. Harriet Wardlaw was called again and Pete was placed in a third foster home. Etty shook his hand, handed him an envelope, and then walked away. There was a hundred dollars in crisp twenty-dollar denominations in the envelope.

Pete moved in with the Krugers and knew right away it wasn't going to work out, because the Krugers had a son of their own, Dwight, who was a year younger than Pete. They had wanted the state money so they could lavish material things on Dwight. He lasted exactly seven months before he told Otis Kruger to kiss his ass standing up.

The Menalis family wasn't much better, but he managed to last there for a year and a half. He was about to utter his favorite expression to Avrim Menalis when Nathaniel Bickmore arrived in person, to tell Pete he believed he'd found his uncle. A meeting was arranged for the following day.

Pete drank a gallon of coffee at the fast food restaurant he worked in after school. He didn't want to go home, so he worked an extra shift, daydreaming about the meeting. Nathaniel hadn't said anything substantial about the man who he thought was his uncle. Maybe he was finally going to belong to someone again. Maybe his uncle would love him.

Avrim Menalis and his son Nevil arrived at the restaurant just as Pete finished serving a group of teenagers who were out past their curfew. Nevil looked mean, like he had a burr in his shorts. His father's eyes looked like cold steel.

"We'd like some food here," Nevil said, his voice surly, his eyes contemptuous. Because he lived in their house, Pete showed respect to the boy, who was his own age. In his opinion, Nevil would never amount to anything. His marks in school were either low D's or F's. He had great difficulty reading whole sentences, and his vocabulary was mostly guttural grunts. His father said Nevil didn't need a lot of book learning because he was going to work in the family's meat packing business in Jersey City. All you needed was a strong back, powerful legs, and hands capable of removing a side of beef from a steel hook.

Pete took pride in his appearance. He was well over six feet tall, and he'd put on a good amount of weight. He not only looked healthy, he was healthy. He worked out in the mini gym in back of the restaurant, which his boss, Josh Philbin, used early in the morning. He was excelling in school and was always on the honor roll. He'd saved money, with which he hoped to use to buy a secondhand car. He knew now he could make it on his own if he had to. Josh had taken him under his wing and even offered him a room in his own house if things with the Menalis family ever got out of hand. The offer was a security cushion for Pete, but he knew he'd probably never accept it. Staying with the Menalis family and working off his keep was a point of honor with him.

In just a few months he'd be ready for college. He'd filled out all the forms, applied for aid, and sent in his money along with his applications, using Josh Philbin's address for his return mail.

"What would you like, Nevil?" Pete asked courteously.

"Whatever's free. Three burgers, fries, two milk shakes, double order of onion rings. What'ya want, Pop?"

"If it's free, I'll have the same thing," the older Menalis said slyly.

Pete stared at father and son. He had several options. He could give it to them free and then pay Josh for the food. He could just give it to them and say nothing. Or he could tell Nevil and his father . . . what?

"It's not free, Nevil, and you know it. I have to account for everything at the end of the night. Mr. Philbin keeps a tight inventory. Do you still want the food?" He knew they'd say yes and then stiff him. They'd just get up and walk out. Nevil was forever bragging about doing it in other places. Sometimes he'd say the food was overdone, underdone, or there was a bug in it. After he ate everything.

Now, Pete tallied up the check in his hand and said, "Pay me now and I'll order the food."

Maybe he took a stand because of the hope, the dream, that tomorrow the man he was going to meet would really be his uncle and he'd be out of there.

Nevil was sloppy fat like his father, their bellies hanging out over their belt buckles. Nevil struggled now to get out of the booth. Pete backed up a step and then another step. The teenagers stopped eating long enough to watch. "You insulted us, Petey. I don't like it when you insult my old man."

"Then don't call your father your old man. Show him some respect. Do you want the food or not?"

"Sit down, Nevil. He's right." Avrim laid a ten dollar bill on the table. Pete wasn't sure, but he thought he saw respect in the older man's face. "I said sit down, Nevil."

"Jeez, Pop, those kids are going to tell everyone I backed down from this smarty-pants tomorrow."

"So live with it, Nevil, and don't ever call me your old man again."

"You wait, smart boy, your ass is gonna go in a sling," Nevil spat. "You wait and see what I do to that fancy surfboard of yours. You just wait!"

Pete walked back to the kitchen. The cook, a middle-aged man with tired eyes, too many kids, and an equally tired wife, said, "You handled that real good. Josh is going to be real proud of you. I'd get that surfboard out of their house if I was you."

"I took it out a long time ago," Pete replied. "Josh is keeping it for me. Josh keeps all my stuff. The only thing I have at their house is some clothes. Old stuff. He took a knife to my clothes not too long ago."

"You shoulda left, Pete. Josh said he'd take you in."

"It's okay, Skeeter. It's just a few more months. Maybe sooner if tomorrow works out."

It was eleven-thirty when Pete took a last minute check of the restaurant, turned on the alarm, and left by the back door. He was barely in the alley when he was jumped from behind. Taken off balance, he went down and was immediately jerked erect, his assailant behind him. Two people, he decided; one with a knee in his back, an arm around his neck choking him. He was pummeled from the front, kicked in the ribs and groin. He was shoved forward, landing in trash he'd taken out earlier, before his assailants fled. He felt his eye squeeze shut and knew his nose was broken. His face felt twice its normal size. Warm blood trickled down his neck. He thought he was going to die. Right then he *wanted* to die.

Who was going to find him? It was dark as pitch in the alley. They wouldn't find him till morning. Maybe by then he really would be dead. And who would care? Who would give a good rat's ass if he died? No one. Not one damn soul walking the earth. "Well, I goddamn well care," he muttered. He belonged in a hospital, that much he knew. People there would take care of him, make him well. If he didn't die.

He tried to crawl, mewling like a newborn puppy, to the back entrance. If he could just get to the door and open it, the alarm would go off and the police would come. So would Josh. Maybe even Skeeter. They'd take him to the hospital, and a nurse who smelled sweet and clean, the way his mother used to smell, would take care of him. She'd smile at him, touch his forehead and tell him everything was going to be all right. He'd believe her too. Nurses and mothers didn't lie.

Pete knew he blacked out twice before he made it to the back door. Every crawling step was pure torture. He knew some of his ribs were broken and there seemed to be something wrong with his left knee. Still he struggled. When the bells, whistles, and siren went off in the restaurant, his first thought was he'd died and gone to heaven. He started to call his mother and then he blacked out.

When Pete woke again, he knew he was in the hospital. It hurt to breathe. Everyone seemed to be talking at once. Josh Philbin was cursing, using words Pete had never heard before. "You take care of him, I don't give a shit what it costs. Get him one of those special nurses to sit with him." Then he heard Skeeter's voice, but couldn't hear what he was saying. Later, when they took him to a room, he heard Harriet Wardlaw talking to Josh, but again he couldn't hear what they were saying.

He knew he was going to cry, and he didn't care. He felt a cool cloth touch his cheeks. "It's okay to cry, son," a kindly voice said quietly. "There's no one here but you and me. My name is Maryann and I'm your nurse. Is there anyone you want me to call?"

He thought he said Barney, but he wasn't sure. Where was Barney right now? What was he doing? Barney would never have taken the beating he'd taken. Did that mean he was a coward? They'd come up behind him, pinned him. There was no way he could have fought back. That alone had to make *them* the cowards, because they hadn't taken him on in a fair fight. He thought he said, "Oh shit." He heard a chuckle and a voice say, "That sums it up pretty good. You need to sleep now. There's a lot of people out there in the waiting room who care about you. Tomorrow you can see them."

This time he knew he spoke aloud. "Who?"

"Mr. Philbin, a police officer named Nathaniel, his brother, that nice Miss Wardlaw, Mr. Skeeter, and the two police officers who found you. That's seven people. Sometimes patients come in here and there's no one waiting to find out how they are. Sleep now."

When Pete woke the following day, he was aware of two things immediately. The first was that he was in intense pain.

The second was his room. There were flowers everywhere. One arrangement would have made him laugh if he'd been able to laugh. The florist had taken pains to make the arrangement look like a hamburger with a milk shake and fries on a tray. There were balloons tied to a plastic football, and violets in a cup that had a picture of a basketball on the side. A giant teddy bear with red balloons tied to his paw was on the dresser. Flowers of all colors lined the windowsill.

The doctors came then, one after the other. He was going to live, they said cheerfully. He was going to be in pain for a few days, and on crutches for six weeks or so, but he would live with that too. You're young, they told him. The young heal rapidly. This last was said so carefully, Pete cringed.

"You have visitors, lots of visitors," his nurse said.

Pete opened his eyes. He wanted her to look like his mother, but she didn't. Maryann had gray hair and dimples. She was plump and she smelled like Noxzema. A grandmother? He asked. She nodded. A grandmother was almost as good as a mother. He waited for her to smile. She did when she gave him four little pills. "It will ease some of the pain. We don't want you to depend on them. We'll give them a few minutes to take effect, and then I'll show in your visitors."

He could barely distinguish them, but he recognized all the different voices. He was told not to talk, they would talk to him. And they did. They told him how much they cared, how sorry they were that such a thing could happen to a nice person like him. "I'm going to kick some ass, I can tell you that," Josh Philbin said. "I'll find the SOB that did this to you. Skeeter here has some ideas, and the police are out there doing their job."

"You're not going back there, Pete," Harriet Wardlaw said. "I checked with the courts, and it's been agreed that you can spend the last months before college with Mr. Philbin and his wife."

He wanted to ask about his uncle. Was the meeting still on or was it canceled? Harriet Wardlaw held up her hand. "Pete, I told Mr. Sorenson we should wait a few days. I want you bright-eyed and bushy-tailed when you meet him. Is that okay? Raise your hand if it is." Pete's hand fluttered. What was a few more days? If he looked anything like he felt, he might scare off this person who could prove to be his uncle. He fell asleep in the middle of his thought. His visitors tiptoed from the room promising to return the following day.

He dreamed. Of a faraway place called Bell's Beach. The waves were monster high and his father was riding his new surfboard. Christening it, he shouted. His mother was standing on the beach with him, holding his hand. Her eyes were full of love and kindness. Her hair was blowing about her face. How pretty she was. He told her she was prettier than an angel, and she smiled.

"C'mon, Pete, let's build a sand castle," Barney called from the water's edge.

"Look, Mom, Barney came back. He said he'd come back for me and he did. He kept his promise. Jeez, he looks the same. I'm almost as big as Barney, huh, Mom? Why'd he wait so long, Mom?"

"I don't know, honey. Maybe his mother needed him to take care of her and he couldn't leave."

"You left, Mom. I would have taken care of you. Barney would have helped me. Do you like it up on the cloud? Do you watch me, do you miss me?"

"Oh, sweetie, of course Dad and I miss you. We watch over you all the time."

He jerked his hand free. "That's a crock and you know it. If you watch over me, then how come that jerk Nevil beat me up? I knew it was him, I could smell him. He had that scuzzball friend of his with him. They smell the same. Barney lied to me. Everyone lied to me. You don't live on a cloud with Dad. I'm not stupid. Everyone thinks I'm stupid. I believed Barney, and then he left me too. I hate him for that. I'm not going to look for him anymore. Go back on your cloud with Dad. Look, he won't even talk to me. He's on the wave on my *surfboard. I carried that everywhere they sent me. I had to fight to keep it. Really fight. They wanted to sell it so I could get a haircut and new shoes, but the lady in the blue dress wouldn't let them. You should have come down off your cloud and . . . and . . . go away, take Barney with you."*

"I love you, honey. Barney loves you too. Someday you'll understand that there are things we can't control or change. Dad and I are very proud of you, Pete. Kiss me good-bye. Dad and I have to go now."

"Don't leave me again, Mom. Tell Dad I want him to stay."

"Goooooddd-byyyyye, Pete," his mother called as she walked across the water to get on the surfboard with his dad. She blew him a kiss. His dad blew him a kiss too.

"Don't take the surfboard, Dad."

"I won't, son. I just christened it for you."

"Hey, Barney, are you going away too?" he asked angrily.

"Yeah, I gotta go too."

"How come?"

" 'Cause my mom said so. You gotta do what your mom says. I'm gonna come back for you, Pete, just the way I promised. I swear on my mom."

"Kiss my ass, Barney!" he screamed. "The day you come and get me is the day I'll kiss your *ass. I'm big now so you can't lie to me anymore."*

"I'm not lying. I promise."

"You're a liar! You promised to come and get me when I was sixteen. I'm seventeen and a half. You damn well lied. I hate you, Barney Sims. I hate your guts!"

Pete woke, the scream dying on his lips.

"Bad dreams are terrible, but they don't mean anything," the grandmotherly voice said softly. "Shhh, go back to sleep." He felt a cool hand on his brow. His anxiety eased and he drifted into a peaceful sleep.

On Friday, late in the afternoon, Pete was sitting in a wheelchair in the solarium when Nathaniel Bickmore, Harriet Wardlaw, and the man who might be his uncle appeared.

"You look like my dad," Pete blurted, as the man and Harriet sat down, and Nathaniel left. He did, it wasn't wishful thinking on his part. The man's salt and pepper hair was closely clipped, as was his mustache. His dark eyes, the color of chocolate licorice, were keen and piercing. Pete's heart almost stopped beating when the man stared at him, hard, with not a trace of a smile.

"Is this your father the way you remember him?" The man asked him, holding out a photograph. "He was eighteen or nineteen when this picture was taken."

He had polish on his nails, Pete noticed. He stared at the picture for a long time. "My dad had a bad scar on his neck. This looks like my dad."

"Which side of his neck?" the man asked.

"The left side. He said he fell over a barbed-wire fence and had to have nine stitches. It was down from his ear. A little part of his ear was crooked."

"He had eleven stitches," the man said. "I had to ride him to the vet to get the stitches. The regular doctor was too far away, and my bike was rusty with a bad wheel. The accident was my fault. My father just about skinned me alive."

They talked for a long time, with Leo Sorenson doing most of the talking. He told Pete things about his father he never knew. Interesting things, things he wished he'd known as he was growing up. Leo's voice sounded sad most of the time he was talking. The sadness wasn't lost on Pete.

"I think, when you're up and around, that you and I will go to the cemetery and say our good-byes. I understand you weren't allowed to attend the funeral or burial. We'll go together."

The voice was so brisk and professional-sounding, Pete knew the trip was as good as accomplished. It had to mean this man really was his uncle. He really did have a relative. Nothing was said about him going to live with Leo, though. He nodded and waited.

"I've only heard good things about you, Peter. Glowing reports. You turned out well."

He sounds, Pete thought, surprised. "Thank you, sir."

"Call me Leo. I imagine it'll be hard for you to call me Uncle now, at this stage. You're practically a man. I understand you're off to college in the fall. How'd you like to go to Harvard? How'd you do on your SATs?"

"I had a composite 1480, sir."

"I can get you in. You want to go. I'll pay the bill. No aid. You can let me know in a few days."

"Okay, sir. Leo."

Pete's eyes started to burn. This wasn't the way it was supposed to be. There were supposed to be hugs. Then some handshakes and a couple of claps on the back. Maybe some talk about going home together, things they'd do together now that they knew one another.

"I'm an attorney. Did you ever think about law as a career?"

"No. I thought . . . I think engineering is what's best for me."

"Engineers are a dime a dozen. Anyone can be an engineer. Law is where it's at. Big money. Hard work, though. Your father used to say he was going to be a lawyer, but he didn't want to go to law school. He dropped out of college too. He had dreams. I'm sorry they didn't work out for him. Think about the law. Sorenson and Sorenson. I like the way that sounds. No money in engineering. . . . Is there anything you need, Peter?"

"No, sir."

"Did anyone say when you'd be getting out of here?"

"No, sir . . . Sir?"

"Yes, Peter."

"How come you never . . . shouldn't you have known . . . What I mean is, weren't you ever curious? . . . I think you should have known about me," Pete said flatly.

"It does sound terrible, doesn't it? One would think there should have been warning bells, something proclaiming your birth. There wasn't." What there was, he didn't say, until later, much later.

It all sounded like a lie to Pete.

"Why do I have this feeling you don't believe me?" Leo asked quietly.

Pete wanted to ask him if he had a guilty conscience, but he didn't. "I don't know why that is, sir. We looked for you for a long time."

"In the beginning, when your parents first got married, they moved around a lot. Your father wasn't much for calling or writing. It's another way of saying he didn't want to be bothered with me. At least that's how I perceived it at the time. I think," Leo said choosing his words carefully, "that if you try, we might come to like one another. If nothing else, respect on both sides will suffice. Is it a deal?"

It wasn't as though he had a bushelful of choices. "Yes, sir," he said, nodding.

"Good. I think we should shoot for discharge on Tuesday. I'll hire a nurse for you and take you home myself. I'll have my driver pick up your things. I'm sorry I didn't know about you sooner. I would never allow my brother's son to be shifted from pillar to post. I'll do my best to make it up to you."

A second later he was gone.

"Oh, Pete, isn't it wonderful? Now you have a family," Harriet Wardlaw said happily. She clapped her hands in glee.

"He didn't act like . . . I don't think he likes me. I don't think he liked my dad very much either. He's just going to do his duty. I'm not sure I want to go with him. Maybe I should just stay with Josh until it's time to leave for college. He wants me to be a lawyer like him. I thought it would be different. I thought he'd say we'd go to a ball game or fishing or *something.*"

"Pete, your uncle never got married. I don't think he knows much about kids. He's a wealthy man, or so I'm told. He's also one of the finest attorneys in the state. I checked him out real good. You both need time. If you meet each other halfway, I'm sure things will work out. I am so happy for you, Pete. I'm only sorry it's taken us so long to find him. I wish we'd been able to find Barney. That seems to be a lost cause, I'm afraid to say."

"It's okay, Miss Wardlaw. When Barney is ready, he'll find me somehow. I know it."

"You have such high hopes, and now you're disappointed, aren't you?"

Pete nodded, his eyes miserable. "He's not what I expected. He's nothing like my dad. I wonder if he liked my mother? He didn't even mention her."

"He told Nathaniel they lost track of each other. It happens in the best of families, Pete. Look, I'm not saying you have to go with him if you don't want to. It's all up to you. Whatever you decide is okay with me. We want whatever is best for you."

"I appreciate everything you've done for me," Pete replied. "Nathaniel too. I'll think about everything. I promise."

"Time to get you back to your room," Miss Wardlaw said. "It's getting chilly in here. Oh, Pete, I'm so happy for you."

"Thanks, Miss Wardlaw, for everything."

"It was my pleasure, Pete. I wish all my cases ended up this well. I'll see you over the weekend. You have a lot of thinking to do. Think it through, Pete, and do whatever is best for you. Only you, Pete. Are we clear on that?"

"You bet."

He liked it when she pecked him on his cheek. He was reminded of his mother all over again. "Miss Wardlaw, what's that stuff you wear? It smells . . . like my mom used to smell."

"Why, thank you, Pete. That's one of the nicest things anyone ever said to me. It's Lily of the Valley talcum powder. When I was a little girl, my mother had this wonderful garden and there were rows and rows of the little flowers. They grow on a stem and look like little bells. They're as pretty as they smell. The whole garden used to smell so wonderful. I guess it reminds me of back home, of being a little girl. So long ago," she said sadly.

"But it's a nice memory," Pete said.

3

Pete settled back in the limousine, his leg stretched out so it could rest on the seat opposite him. Leo Sorenson sat next to him.

They were almost to Ridgewood when Pete came to the conclusion his uncle was not a talkative man. It was okay, he didn't feel much like talking. He closed his eyes and tried to imagine what his uncle's house looked like, what his life was like and what part he would play in it. Miss Wardlaw had said Leo's house was on an estate that sat back from the road, almost a mile, and protected by twelve-foot-high iron gates. Supposedly there was even a small guardhouse where people had to be announced before the gate was opened. She knew this, she said, because she'd gone there to talk to Leo. She'd gone on to say there was a housekeeper, a cook, a butler, two full-time gardeners, and a chauffeur. There's an Olympic-size pool, a tennis court, and a guest house with eight rooms. "Not too shabby, Pete," she'd concluded, smiling.

Not too shabby at all. But was he going to fit in? Would Leo care about him, or was he simply doing his duty? Everything worked two ways, both parties had to make an effort, and he was prepared to make the ultimate effort by accepting Leo's help. He was prepared to give up engineering and do what his uncle wanted. So many people had gone to bat for him, and all of them thought Leo's offer was just what he needed. His eyelid twitched when he thought about words like indebtedness, obligation, and loyalty. But he couldn't say no to Harriet Wardlaw, Nathaniel, and Duke. Even Josh Philbin and Skeeter said they thought he'd be a hell of a Harvard man.

This was supposed to be a good day. A wonderful day. The kind of day he'd dreamed about for years when he was shuffled from one place to another. It was supposed to be right up there with the day Barney would come and get him. He knew now Barney was never going to appear. He accepted it, but it didn't stop him from fantasizing. What would Barney say about all this? Go for it, Pete, was what he'd say.

What kind of brother was Leo Sorenson? Obviously, one who didn't care about his brother and his brother's family. Pete's eye twitched again.

His uncle spoke, softly. Pete's eye twitched again. "There's a pool on the property. Perhaps you'd like to invite your friends up for a barbecue. I could hire a band and you can dance poolside. I understand you young people are into things like that. When your leg is better, of course."

"I can't swim. There was never any time for fun activities, and I really don't have any friends. I always had to work and do chores. It's a nice gesture, though. Maybe before I leave for college you could ask Miss Wardlaw and Nathaniel for dinner. Josh and Skeeter too. They have wives. Duke . . . Duke might come too. I'd like to say good-bye to them." He felt his uncle's body stiffen. His voice when he spoke was equally stiff.

"If that's what you want. You made your decision, then, about college?"

"Yes. I'll go to Harvard, if they'll have me, but isn't it too late?"

"It's never too late. I think you need to change the way you think, Peter. I said I could get you in, and I can. I never make promises I can't fulfill. It's a lesson in your life you need to learn."

"Will I get my dorm deposit back from Villanova?" I'll change the way I think, Peter thought; think positive. Barney will come someday.

"I'll see to it. You'll like Harvard, and then Harvard Law. Hallowed halls and all. I see the makings of a very fine attorney in you. A very rich, fine attorney."

"I don't know if I want to be rich," Pete muttered.

"Of course you want to be rich. Only a fool would say otherwise. Remember this, money can help buy happiness, and certainly health. You need to know how to handle money. You use it to make sure you stay healthy, you use it to surround yourself with things that make you smile. I tried to teach that to your father, but he refused to buy into it. He preferred to dream about money instead of earning it. Maybe if he'd listened, he—"

"Don't talk about my dad."

"All right, Peter, I won't."

"Are you healthy and happy?" Pete asked.

"Reasonably so. I want for nothing. It's a wonderful feeling."

"Harvard is expensive."

"Very much so, but that's not a concern. Getting you the finest education is our only concern. I had to work my way through school. You need a goal, and you need to work toward that goal and not let anything interfere. That's why I'm so successful today."

"He said modestly," Pete muttered out of the corner of his mouth.

Leo laughed. "Touché, Peter." Then he asked, "What kind of car would you like?"

"I have my eye on a Toyota. I just need another hundred dollars, but if I get my dorm deposit back, I can get it. The man is holding it for me. Josh said it's in tip-top shape."

"Save your money. I thought I'd get you a convertible. A new car. This way I won't worry about you breaking down somewhere."

Pete felt pleased, not about the car—who wouldn't like a brand-new convertible?—it was the worry that pleased him. Someone was finally going to worry about him. "That's very nice of you."

"What color? Red? Girls like red. I can have it delivered this afternoon if you like."

Everything was immediate with this man. "I haven't had time to take my driving test."

"We can do that tomorrow. You can take the test on an automatic. And I also bought you a new wardrobe." This last was said almost shyly.

In spite of himself, Pete was interested. He liked clothes. He wondered how his uncle knew his size, and then he stopped wondering. This man who was his uncle was a doer, a mover and a shaker. "Thank you. What kind?"

"The works. I called Calvin Klein, Ralph Lauren, and Armani and told them to send one of everything. Miss Wardlaw was kind enough to give me the sizes. We even got you a tux."

"Jeez," was all Pete could say.

Leo beamed. "I have a cabin cruiser down at Belmar. I'd like it if you took a Coast Guard course this summer. It sleeps eight. Nice boat, but I don't go on it much."

"Why is that . . . Leo?"

"Lack of time, getting other people's schedules set with mine. For some reason it never seems to work out. The boat just sits there. Perhaps you and I can use it. They tell me young people like to water ski. Do you?"

"I never tried. First I'll have to learn how to swim."

"We'll get you an instructor as soon as your leg is better. Did I forget anything?" Leo asked anxiously.

"It doesn't seem so."

"That's good, because we're home. Now you can see everything for yourself. Welcome to your new home, Peter."

Pete rolled down the window as the limo sailed through the open gates. His jaw dropped and his eyes almost bugged out of his head. The house was huge, red brick with ivy embedded in the mortar, rather like a fairy-tale house full of peaks and crisscross windowpanes. There was so much lawn, and it was greener than emeralds. There were flowers everywhere and shrubs that looked like they were trimmed with manicure scissors. "Barney would love this," he said.

"Who's Barney?" Leo asked.

"Barney is someone I used to know," Pete said flatly. "How many people live here? Why do you need a six-car garage?"

"The housekeeper and myself are the only ones who actually live in the house. Everyone else goes home at night. The garage came with the house. It is full, though. I like antique cars. I drive them once in a while. When I first bought them, I told myself I was buying them as an investment. You know, in case I ever fell on hard times. If that happens, I could sell them and be comfortable. The insurance is outrageous. Now I look on them as acquisitions."

"Yes, sir."

"Are you up to walking a bit? If so, I can show you the pool and the tennis courts. The flower gardens in the back are well worth seeing."

"I'd like that. I can maneuver with the crutches pretty good. . . . What's that building by the pool?"

"It's a cabana. It has a kitchen, bathroom, a wet bar, and a big-screen television. For parties."

"Do you have many parties?" Pete asked curiously, moving awkwardly on the crutches.

"No. I guess I should explain that. This place," he said, waving his arm about, "is a retreat, a sanctuary. My own private place. I rarely, if ever, invite anyone here. I make sure everything is maintained, because if you don't take care of things, they . . . decay. And, no, I do not even know how to play tennis. They tell me the court is one of the best. You can take lessons."

"The guest house looks just like the big house," Pete said, pausing to rest for a moment. "Does anyone live in it? You could rent it out and use the money to pay for the insurance."

Leo laughed. "No, no one lives in it. I had it built. I'm not sure why anymore. Probably because the property is a little over twelve acres and I thought it would look nice. Everything more or less goes together. I like things to look nice, be of a piece, if you know what I mean."

Pete didn't know, but he nodded anyway. "Did you ever see my dad's house?"

"No, I didn't. It was my understanding it was a rental house."

"Yeah, it wasn't ours. We just lived in it. It wasn't as big as your cabana."

"I'm sorry about that, Peter."

He really is, Pete thought, setting off awkwardly again.

Leo now noticed the difficulty Pete was having with the crutches. "There will be other days when you can meander around," he said. "I think you should go in and rest for a while. You might want to soak your leg in the Jacuzzi. It's very restful. I had it installed over the weekend for you. The doctor said it would help."

Pete nodded. Just how much money did this man have? he wondered.

"I have an elevator." Leo grinned.

"No kidding!"

"Good thing too, or you might not be able to get up the stairs. It came with the house. I happen to love it."

"Yeah. I will too. Thank you for everything," Pete said.

Leo shrugged. "It's my pleasure, Peter."

He means that too, Pete realized.

Everything was beautiful, rich, and elegant. The only thing missing, the most important thing of all, was any personal sign that a real flesh and blood person lived in the house.

Leo left him at the door to his room. He placed a fatherly hand on his shoulder for a moment. "I'm going back to the city. I'll be home for dinner. We usually eat around seven-thirty. Is that too late for you?"

"No, sir. Seven-thirty is fine."

"If you want anything, just ask Millie or Albert. That's what they're here for. Rest your leg."

"I will."

He was in his room. The door was shut. He turned the little latch and locked himself in. He leaned his crutches up against the wall and hopped around *his* room. All he could do was shake his head from side to side. The room was *huge,* and carpeted in an ankle-deep pile that was apple-green. It looked new, unused. The Jets could have skirmished on it. The desk was *huge.* The bed was *huge.* The chair and ottoman next to the fireplace was *huge,* almost as big as a couch. He could hardly wait to bounce on it. One whole wall was given over to closet space, half the doors mirrored, the other half louvered. Standing on one foot, he opened the door and gasped. He wouldn't have been at all surprised to see a conveyor belt come to life. Jackets and pants hung together and had little matching tags, which meant, he assumed, which jacket went with which pants. Shirts every color of the rainbow hung next to them. Sweat suits, winter wear, and then summer wear were next. There wasn't a crease or a wrinkle in anything.

Behind the mirrored section, skinny oak shelves held sweaters, all with designer labels. Every make and model of sneakers were lined up neatly next to six pairs of fine leather shoes. Dock-Siders, sandals, and scuba fins were next. Above that a wet suit. Golf clubs and three tennis rackets leaned into the corner next to his surfboard. All of them had his name emblazoned on the tags. Cans and cans of tennis and golf balls were in the box on the floor. Fastened to the back of the door was a tie rack and a belt rack. Both were full. Six pieces of French luggage were on the top shelf.

Pete turned, hopped over to the double dresser and opened the drawers, one at a time. Underwear, compliments of Calvin Klein, socks with a polo player on the side, T-shirts by the dozen, of every color, shorts with the same polo player on the hem, casual sweaters, sweatshirts, pajamas, every article known to man. Dozens of each. On the top of the dresser was a shaving set, a bottle of men's aftershave and one of cologne. He only shaved once a week. A silver comb and brush with his initials on the back. A portable radio he could barely lift was next to a picture of his mother and father. He didn't want to look at it now, so he turned it over facedown. Later he would think about the picture.

He continued to inspect his new room. On the wall opposite the closet was an entertainment center complete with big-screen television, stereo, and tape player.

He inspected the desk, the chair behind it. He frowned when he saw a tag on the chair that said it was ergonomically designed. Whatever the hell that meant. Later he would look it up in his brand-new *Random House Dictionary* that sat on his desk right next to his brand-new *Random House Encyclopedia.* Centered on the desk was a Gucci wallet with five hundred dollars in twenty-dollar denominations in it, a Gucci watch with a stark black face, and a Gucci key ring with one key on it. The key to the house.

The key made everything official. He finally belonged to someone. Leo was his family. Leo had gone to great lengths to do all these things. He remembered the Jacuzzi.

Pete hopped over to the bathroom, reached inside and turned on the light. He gasped. It was something out of Arabian Nights. It was all shiny black with gold accents. He blinked. Was this a guy's bathroom? Obviously his uncle thought so. He could see himself in the floor, on the wall tile, in the mirror over the triple sink. A black toilet and another toilet without a seat stared up at him. He experimented and grinned. The sunken Jacuzzi was black and gold marble with three steps leading up to it and then three steps leading down into the water. All he had to do was press three buttons and he would have light and music at the same time, the whirlpool would activate, and the temperature would rise to 104. A shower with a bench in it was larger than two normal-size bathrooms. Recessed lighting made everything sparkle. He wondered if the fixtures were gold or gold-plated. He decided he didn't care one way or the other.

He hopped back to the living room, stopping long enough to pick up the picture of his parents before he made his way over to the deep white chair next to the fireplace. He took one second to appreciate the fact that there was a fireplace in his room, a fire neatly laid for use in October, when he wouldn't be here.

It was all so goddamn, fucking perfect.

Pete snuggled into the chair and stared at the picture in his hands. Obviously it had been a snapshot his uncle had enlarged. He was so grateful, he cried. And cried.

Two days later Pete walked down to the gatehouse to accept a special delivery letter addressed to him. It was his acceptance letter to Harvard University. For the guard's benefit, he let out a whoop of something that sounded like joy.

The following days passed in a blur for Pete. He took his driver's test and passed. He wasn't at all surprised when a man from the motor vehicle station came to the estate and gave him his test in the back courtyard. A tennis instructor showed up and shared the fine points of tennis. The day after that, a golf pro arrived, showed him how to handle the clubs, and set up a schedule that wouldn't interfere with his tennis lessons. A lifeguard from the country club taught him to swim in two days. He felt silly as hell floating around the huge pool with two Clorox bottles tied to his arms, but he didn't drown, which was the point. Leo was offering the basics in everything he chose to pursue. The Coast Guard course was offered to him on an individual basis and was also done at home, three days a week for two weeks. He passed with flying colors.

Just about all his bruises and cuts were healed. He was able to put his full weight on his leg now, and a few more therapy sessions, also at home, would allow the doctor to pronounce him A-Okay.

He had breakfast and dinner with his uncle every day. Once or twice a week they played chess. Sometimes they watched a television program together and ate popcorn.

They weren't bonding, and they both knew it, but they tried, and then they tried harder.

And then summer was over and he was packing to leave for Harvard.

The six pieces of French luggage were stowed in the backseat and in the trunk next to his surfboard. His trunk with his bedding and pillows had been sent on by Albert the butler days ago. All that remained was to say thank you, good-bye, and yes I'll call once a week and I'll be home for the holidays and thank you again, sir, for being so kind to me.

At the last minute, though, he couldn't just stick out his hand. Instead he wrapped his arms around his uncle, who immediately stiffened.

His eyes burning, Pete stepped back and muttered something that sounded like, "Thank you for this opportunity, I'll make you proud of me." He felt something being pushed into his hand. A bank book. Now he was going to have to say thank you all over again. He nodded, muttered the words, and climbed behind the wheel. At the gatehouse he looked at the numbers stamped inside: $25,000.

He was on his way.

4

Where did the years go? Pete wondered. He craned his neck, his eyes searching the busy library. One minute he was settling into his dorm, and the next he was graduating. One deep breath later he was in law school, and now he was in his final year. He'd take the bar and go out into the world to make his fortune. If Leo had anything to do with it, it *would be* a fortune.

Pete was in Harvard's main library waiting for his best buddy in the whole world. Waiting for the person who'd made him stick with the law, giving up her own precious free time to tutor him, encouraging him, cursing him, cajoling and anything else she could think of to make him want to finish.

"I hate quitters," she'd said once. Hell, he hated quitters too. Her methods worked, which was why he was here, waiting for her. He knew he'd pass the bar, that wasn't what was bothering him. Annie Gabriel was what was bothering him. How was he going to make it on the outside without Annie pushing and shoving him? Which didn't say a whole hell of a lot for him. Was he so weak he needed a woman to prod him along?

Oh, he hated the law! Maybe practicing would be better than school, though.

Ruth Ann Gabriel, Annie to her friends, was one of a kind. Not only was she graduating from this prestigious law school at the top of the class, she'd passed the CPA exam the first time out, all four parts. She'd ace the bar too. She was petite, blond, pretty in a plain sort of way, and she was so goddamn fearless, he wanted to shake her and tell her what the world was *really* like. The only time he'd ever seen anything closely resembling fear in her eyes was when she talked about all the financial aid she was going to have to pay back. "It will take half my pay for ten years to pay it all off," she'd said.

When they separated on graduation day, he was going back to New York to work at Leo's law firm. Annie had a job offer in Boston with a decent firm. Pete had asked Leo if he could use her in his office, and Leo had come back with such a generous offer it made his head spin. When he presented the offer to Annie, however, she'd looked at him with such pity in her eyes, he'd cringed. "If I can't make it on my own," she said, "then this isn't where I belong. Thanks for the offer, though." And that had been the end of that.

Pete was certain there was no one in the world who was kinder, gentler, more piss-assed obnoxious than Annie Gabriel, and he loved her. "We're not going to get involved," she'd said early on. "I have things to do, places to go. Relationships get in the way. I need to see what I'm made of." She'd gone on to say, "And a sexual relationship always ruins a friendship."

Once he'd hit on Annie after a moot court session. They'd gone back to her room and opened a bottle of wine. She drank most of it and was tipsy when he was ready to leave. She'd leaned against him and whispered, "I love you so much, Pete Sorenson." He'd kissed her, clumsily at first, and then . . . she'd pushed him away and said, "Go home, Pete." He'd tried to kiss her again, but she clamped her lips shut and opened the door. He would never forget the tears streaming down her cheeks. "I'm drunk," she said as she pushed him out the door. "Don't pay attention to anything I say."

He'd walked for hours trying to figure out what it all meant. When he returned to his own room, he decided he would never understand women.

"Your problem, Sorenson," Mark Ritter had said, "is you love her, but you aren't *in* love with her. Maybe she feels the same way and doesn't know how to handle it."

"Don't you have to love someone before you're *in* love?" Pete asked.

"How the hell do I know?" Ritter said. "I just love 'em and fuck 'em and go on about my business. I don't want any emotional baggage standing in the way of my career. When it's time for me to tie the knot, I'm going to marry some senior partner's nubile daughter."

Pete felt that Mark Ritter was stupid, dense. "What about love?" he asked. "Don't you want to spend your life with someone you love, have a family and look forward to your golden years?"

"In your dreams, Sorenson. You know, you're an asshole if you believe all that crap. Love is for fools. Women suck you dry. Financially and emotionally. I'm not going through that bullshit. Trust me, I'll make sure the nubile daughter is good-looking, with a body to match. I can handle the rest." Pete never felt the same about Mark Ritter after that. In fact he went out of his way to avoid him.

He hadn't dated much while he was in law school; there simply wasn't time for the party scene, and he'd pretty much gotten that out of his system during college days when, like Ritter, he'd had so many one-night stands he lost count of them.

Pete envied Annie for her uncanny ability to live in the moment. To her, anything before the moment was history and didn't bear thinking or talking about. He wished he was more like her. He dwelled on everything, worried to death, dissected it and then worried some more. Maybe it all stemmed from his childhood. Maybe he was fucked up. Hell, yes, he was fucked up.

Where the hell was Annie? She said she'd meet him at eight o'clock, and it was nine now. He wondered if she was sick. But then, Annie never got sick, she simply wouldn't allow her body to carry germs. And then he saw her and knew immediately what the sappy smile on her face meant. He didn't recognize the stirrings he felt as jealousy, but he wanted to throw his book through the window.

"Sorry I'm late," she said, sitting down across the table from him. "Let's get right to it. You look like you're in a daze, Pete. Is something wrong?" Her sappy expression was gone, replaced by a look of genuine concern.

"I was thinking."

"You shouldn't do that, Pete. You're dangerous when you think." She smiled, and he felt better right away. Today she was wearing something that was as blue as her eyes. A little gold pin was on the collar. He'd never seen it before. He knew everything Annie owned, which wasn't much. She wore just the right amount of makeup, kept her pale hair short; "wash and wear" she called it. She always looked professional. She's beautiful, Pete thought. "You look pretty this morning," he said.

"Thanks, but don't think that compliment is going to make me go easy on you. Just two more months, Pete, and we're outta here."

"I'm going to miss you, Annie."

"Me or the security blanket I represent?" Annie said warily.

"Both. Annie?"

"Yes."

"Why didn't you and I . . . that night when we had the wine after moot court . . . what is it about me that . . ."

"Pete, you're my best friend. I don't think I will ever have a friend like you. I hope . . . I mean, if we'd gotten involved, two months from now we'd wave good-bye to one another and send Christmas cards for a few years and then we'd forget each other. I don't want that. I care about you too much. Sometimes I actually feel like you're a part of me," Annie said carefully, her eyes averted.

"Yeah, yeah, I feel that way too. So why—"

"We needed to get to this place. Now, when we walk away two months from now, if it's meant to be, it will be. I don't know how else to explain it. Are you following me here?"

Pete nodded. "Annie, did I ever tell you about Barney?"

"No. Are you telling me there's something about you I don't know? Who's Barney?"

Pete told her. "I believed, right up to the day I turned sixteen, that Barney was going to come for me. I honest to God believed it. There are no words to tell you how I felt when midnight passed and Barney was a no-show. In my gut I still hope . . . want . . ."

"Oh, Pete, how awful for you. Children have a way of . . . I'm sure Barney meant every word he said, and if circumstances were right he would have kept his promise. You don't know for a fact that he never tried to find you. Did you really tell that man to kiss your ass? At six years old?"

"Damn right I did. With gusto. I was sticking up for Barney. I still think about Barney. Someday I'm going to try and find him. I need to know if he tried to find me. It's like there's a piece of my life that's missing. If that sounds stupid . . ."

"It doesn't sound stupid at all. Memories are so wonderful. Especially yours. I had such an . . . ordinary childhood. Nothing ever happened. Actually, it was downright boring. I was this terrible-looking ugly duckling. None of the girls wanted to be seen with me. I guess that's why I'm such a reader. It was all I did."

"And look at you now!" Pete said proudly.

Annie reached across the table to take Pete's hand in hers. "Promise me, Pete, that we'll always be friends. Promise me that we won't go that Christmas-card route. I'll always be here for you. I swear on . . . on Barney."

Pete nodded. "I swear too . . . on Barney."

"Since we're, ah . . . sharing," he continued, "was that sappy expression on your face when you came in anything to do with you getting laid last night?"

"Pete!" Annie hissed.

"Well, does it?"

"None of your damn business."

"I thought we were each other's business. I want an answer."

"Up yours, Pete," Annie said, clearly flustered.

"And I thought you were saving yourself for me." He realized he meant the words the moment he uttered them. Annie looked like she realized it too.

"You aren't exactly a monk, Pete. I seem to recall some of your . . . escapades, the ones you felt the need to share with me. Look at me, Pete Sorenson. Are you judging me?"

"Hell no. Ah, Annie . . . I've had this fantasy for so long about us . . . and how it would be."

"Fantasy?"

Pete's head jerked upward. He'd never heard her voice sound so cold and brittle. "Well, yeah. Fantasy is as good a word as any. You made it clear you wouldn't . . . you didn't . . . What the hell is happening here, Annie?"

Annie was on her feet, the blue dress fussing about her knees as she gathered up her books. Her eyes spewed sparks. "Fuck you, Pete Sorenson," she snarled.

"Annie, wait. Jesus Christ, I didn't mean that the way you took it. Annie, wait. Goddamn it, I try to do what you want and you kick me in the gut."

Pete followed her outside, Annie's shoes slapping on the concrete as she tried to run from him. "I was out of line," he said. "I'm sorry. It'll never happen again. Annie, I would never, ever hurt you. You know that. I'm . . . What I am is . . . jealous. Yeah, I'm jealous. I wanted to be the one to put that sappy expression on your face. Me, not some guy I don't know. . . . Or do I know him? Forget it, forget I said that. It's none of my business."

Annie turned. "For every action, Pete, there is a reaction. I reacted. Look, I can't—won't—go to bed with you because . . . because I care about you. If I need a bodily release, I can find it anywhere. Why are you looking at me like that? You guys talk like that all the time. I won't . . . I will not muck up our friendship. If you think so little of it, then maybe you and I should just . . . go our separate ways. I'm sorry for my part in this. I have to get to class."

"Are we studying tonight?"

"I don't know," Annie called over her shoulder.

He was more confused than ever. Love was love. Love. In love. Love. Out of love. This confused, euphoric, gut-wrenching feeling had to be some kind of love. Son of a bitch. He remembered a feeling that was similar the day Barney said he'd come for him. That was love. When Leo came for him, that was a kind of love too. The first time he had sex, he thought it was a kind of love. "Shit!" he said succinctly. He jammed his hands in his pockets. "So fuck you too, Annie Gabriel," he muttered as he turned and walked in the opposite direction.

Back in his apartment, Pete paced, up and down, over and around. Damn Annie Gabriel. He couldn't let it go on like this. God, the look on her face, it was so terrible, he'd made it back just in time to puke up his guts. He had to make things right with Annie. The only problem was, he didn't know how. In a fit of something he couldn't define, he called his uncle Leo. He blurted out the past hour's happenings. "I want to do something, but I don't know what. Do you have any ideas, any advice?" he asked hopefully.

"I have an idea, Peter. I'll need thirty minutes or so. I just need to know one thing, can you manage a few days off, your friend too?"

"How many days is a few? Annie won't have a problem. It's me, I'm not the quick study she is. Four, tops."

"Sounds good to me. Five would be better, though. I'll get back to you in half an hour or so."

Pete waited. He paced again, up and down, over and around. When the phone rang forty minutes later, he caught it in midring. "Yeah," he bellowed.

"I have it all set up. Pick up your friend and take a cab to

Logan Airport. There's a charter waiting for you. Your destination is Paris. Your hotel has been booked. First-class all the way, Pete. Your pilot will have all the details. Sometimes you need to do something completely . . . what I mean is, you need to act on impulse on occasion. I'm happy to be of help. I think it sounds like both of you need some getaway time before those hallowed halls close in around you."

"Paris as in France?" Pete said, his jaw dropping.

"That's the only one I know. Have a good time, Peter."

"Yes, sir, I will, sir," Pete said, but he was talking to a dead phone. Jesus Christ, Paris, France with Annie. His fist shot in the air. Pack a bag or not pack a bag. Hell no, he'd charge everything on the Visa card Leo gave him that he'd never used. He'd buy Annie a Paris creation.

"Yeahhhhh."

Fifteen minutes later Pete was in the back of Annie's classroom. He tiptoed down the aisle to her seat and hissed, "Come with me right now. *Now*, Annie."

Annie didn't question the order. She gathered up her books and followed Pete from the room. "What's wrong?" she asked fearfully.

"Look, don't ask any questions, just follow me. Nothing is wrong. That's all you need to know."

An hour later Annie squealed, "What do you mean we're going to Paris? Paris, France?" she said when they were in his car, heading to the airport. "I don't believe this! You're out of your mind!"

"Haven't you ever done anything wild and adventurous, Annie?"

"Well, yeah, when I was a little girl I always wanted to go to Paris. . . ."

"Well, you're in luck. We're going to Paris!"

"Oh God, I don't have any clothes. Not even a toothbrush." Pete flashed his Visa card. Annie howled with glee.

"I bet there's champagne onboard, a gourmet meal and a

movie," Pete said. "We're both on overload. We need this. We deserve it."

"It must be nice to be rich. How much is this costing?"

"I have no idea, but Leo never springs for anything unless he can afford it. I expect in the end this will be my graduation present. Neat, huh?"

"I could get real used to this," Annie said when they were in the plane, looking around at the plush seats, at the two stewards who would serve them. They were the only passengers. "God," was all she could say. "Wait a minute, I can't go, I don't have my passport with me," Annie said, tears forming in her eyes.

"Voilà!" Pete held it up. "I stopped by your pad and your roommate found it for me," Pete said, handing it over. "A passport that's never been used," he fretted.

"You know, I got it thinking, 'Someday . . .' This is someday," she said happily. "Oh, Pete, this is so wonderful. I can't believe it. How long will we be there?"

"Three days, four, longer if you think we can get away with it. Let's take it one day at a time."

"Is there a payback for this? You know what I mean?" Annie asked carefully.

"If you mean are we going to sleep together, the answer is no. I know Dennis is the man of the hour. I have no woman of the hour, so this is just a trip that we're going to enjoy together. Annie, I can't think of a single soul I would rather see Paris with than you. We're gonna have a great time."

"We damn well better, because I know I'm never going to get back there again. I just know it's costing a fortune," she grumbled.

"Do we care? I mean we care, but Leo . . . Leo is very generous. Sometimes people need to give, and sometimes other people need to accept. You know, I never touched that money Leo gave me every semester. A few hundred, but that was it. I liked earning my own money.

"Now look, we are not going to think about classes, Dennis,

or anything but this trip. We can handle this. We are going to have the time of our lives and rack up some wonderful memories. Is it a deal, Annie?"

"Oh, yes, Pete. How can I thank you for this?"

"Just smile, Annie, that's all I want."

"I can handle that."

"This is some spread, huh?" Pete said, pointing to the elaborate array of food the steward had brought. "I wonder how Leo managed this all on such short notice."

"Magic," Annie said. "Plus some big bucks. I love it, just love it," she said, pointing to the lobster tail on her plate. "Is caviar any good? Oh, who cares, I'm going to eat it anyway."

Pete smiled. He was happier than a pig in a mud slide.

On arrival they were met by a friend of Leo's from the American embassy. They whizzed through customs and were in a limo headed for the Paris Ritz.

"I read about this hotel, Annie," Pete whispered. "Some Egyptian owns it. He owns that expensive store in England, Harrods. It's supposed to be elegant and comfortable. Is that possible? The rooms are named after famous guests like Coco Chanel, Marcel Prost, and Edward the Seventh. Great restaurants too. We have an itinerary. Leo thought of everything. He got one of those fax machines. He thinks it's a toy. He faxes all day long. I guess that's how he did all this."

"So what does our itinerary say?" Annie asked a while later when she looked around the suite of rooms assigned to her. Everywhere she turned there were fresh flowers and baskets of scrumptious fruit. Champagne was chilling in a bucket. "I can't believe hotels have satin bedspreads," she said in awe.

"My room is just like this," Pete said. "We can take the fruit and champagne and have a picnic. You love picnics. Let's see, it says we're taking a boat trip on the Seine, we're going to see a circus. This might surprise you, Annie, but I've never seen a circus."

"You are now." Annie giggled. "What else?"

"There's an aquarium on the list, biking, ice cream. It says here ice cream is not just ice cream. The place to go is Berthillon's. They have thirty flavors. Leo likes ice cream, so this has to mean he's sampled those thirty flavors. Butter-Chaumont is a park, picturesque, it says, in the downbeat Nineteenth Arrondissement of northeast Paris. It has a lake, waterfall, and clifftop folly or belvedere, whatever that is. God, this list is endless. I don't see how we can do all these things. Listen, Annie, we're both adventuresome, let's rent some bikes and go off on our own. We'll do the ice cream things because I know Leo is going to quiz me on the flavors. We'll eat when we feel like it. I don't like tours, and I don't think you do either. You game?"

"You bet. I need to get some knockabout clothes, though, so maybe we better hit some shops."

Pete burst out laughing. "Take a look in the closet. The hotel must have sent them up earlier. I've pretty much got one of everything, even a tux. Leo is big on tuxes. Shoes too. Boggled my mind."

Annie was already opening her closet, oohing and ahing. "I don't understand any of this. How does your uncle know my size? Lord, these clothes must have cost a fortune."

"I bet he radioed ahead or something. Even I know you're a size seven. I'm just across the hall from you. I'm going to take a shower and put on some of these fancy duds, and then I think we should go somewhere and get a drink and make some plans."

"Hmmm," was all Annie said as she fingered the material on a Donna Karan jacket. She had to think of something nice to do for Pete's uncle. The only problem was, what did you give a man who had everything, and the money to buy more of everything? Maybe she could donate some money to the SPCA in his name. She had to do something. She couldn't simply accept such a grand vacation and not make some kind of attempt to show her appreciation. Later, she'd talk to Pete about it.

It was four of the most wonderful days of Pete's life. Annie proved to be the enjoyable companion he knew she would be. In a way, he looked at everything through her eyes. He knew that with Leo's help, he'd given Annie a memory she would treasure for the rest of her life. It didn't bother him a bit that he was going to owe Leo. Big-time.

Because he was a romantic at heart, Pete capped off every evening with an ice cream cone from Berthillon's and a huge bouquet of flowers from a flower stall along the Champs-Elysées. Annie said she was going to keep one flower from every bunch and press it into her Memory Sampler. Pete felt his chest puff out.

And then it was time to say good-bye to Paris. Annie found herself crying as they pedaled along the bike route they'd pedaled every day. She was still crying as she licked a banana ice cream cone, and she cried harder when Pete bought all the flowers from the flower-stall owner, who smiled indulgently and said something in French that sounded like "young lovers."

When they boarded the plane, Annie was still crying, weeping, actually. Pete himself felt misty-eyed.

"I want to say something . . . meaningful," Annie said, "but don't have the words. Thanks, Pete. It hardly seems adequate."

"It'll do," Pete said gruffly.

Annie did something then that was so impulsive, so unlike her, Pete could only stand like a cigar-stone Indian and stare at her. She kissed him. With her mouth open, her tongue caressing his closed lips. Then he said something incredibly stupid. "Stop that or you'll be sorry."

"Oh yeah?" Annie drawled.

"Yeah," Pete said hoarsely.

"If that's the way you feel about it, okay," Annie said tartly.

"It's not the way I feel about it, it's just that you can't tease . . . flirt . . . do things like that unless you mean to carry them through." Jesus, he sounded like some stuffy schoolteacher lecturing his son on his first date.

"Smartass. How do you know I wouldn't follow through? Too late now, Sorenson, you had your chance and you muffed it. It would have been a great fireworks display to end a wonderful trip. Sex on an airplane. Wow! Eat your heart out." She smiled, but there was no smile in her eyes.

Annie felt like the walking wounded when she entered her small apartment. Childishly, she crossed her fingers, hoping her roommate was out. She needed to stretch out in a warm bubble bath and think. She'd never been this tired in her life. In the last five days, if she had eight full hours of sleep, it was a lot. Couple that with jet lag both ways and she was about down for the count. How she'd hung on this long was beyond her.

Ah, good, Marie wasn't home. There was a note on the kitchen table saying she wouldn't be back till Monday afternoon. "Hmmm," Annie thought groggily as she made her way to the bathroom the size of a closet. The tub was old, with claw feet, and painted bright blue on the outside. The toilet was green, the miniature sink a brown egg color. The landlord had tried to work a miracle and failed miserably. The nicest thing in the room was the gaily braided rug, which matched a shower curtain so wild in color it made one snap to attention.

The water gushed into the tub, the old-fashioned stopper on the chain secure in the drain. Bath salts were added, almost half a jar. Bubbles and steam wafted upward as Annie stripped down to the buff. She marveled again at the costly clothing she'd been wearing the past few days. She'd wanted to leave them behind, thinking somehow they were only on loan, but Pete squelched that kind of thinking. He himself had jammed the designer clothes into two string bags they'd picked up on a shopping trip.

"Ah, to be rich," she sighed as she slipped down into the steaming wetness. Ohh, it smelled so good. She did love the scent of gardenia. It was her one weakness, buying sweet-smelling bath salts and body talcum to match. She wadded up a thick terry towel and leaned back so it would cushion her neck.

Now she could think about Pete and the trip. Pete alone. Pete, period. She'd all but thrown herself at him, and he'd pushed her away. Which just went to prove, she supposed, that her thinking in regard to him was right.

Pete had baggage he needed to sort through before he could enter into any kind of a relationship. She knew she was the type to want commitment, unconditional love, and in her heart she knew Pete wasn't capable, at this point in time, of giving her what she wanted and needed. Pete knew it too; that was the part that bothered her. Would he ever realize she loved him with all her heart? She decided the answer was no. The only way he would realize it was if she took him by the shoulders, looked into his eyes and said, "Pete, I love you and want to marry you." Pete needed words, and they both needed freedom, for now, to see what life was all about. If they kept the friendship alive that they'd started so warily, the day might come when Pete would say the words to her. Until then, she was going to have to live with the decision not to muck up their friendship or even clutter it up with careless words and a quick roll in the sack.

She wondered now if she'd been giving off some mixed signals that Pete didn't know how to deal with. Like that business with Dennis, and then again on the plane, where she'd literally thrown herself at him. Damn, she worked so hard at keeping their friendship on an even path. Now she'd gone and screwed it up. Because it was the right time to, she told herself. She'd been tired, happy, and it just seemed right to her. But not to Pete. Was it ever going to be the right time with Pete? Was she destined to go through life being his best buddy?

Enter Dennis. Dennis was someone to date. Someone to sleep with when the need arose. She had to admit she rather liked the look on Pete's face when he saw her with Dennis. She couldn't help but wonder what her own face looked like when she saw him with Carolyn Withers. She didn't like waking up with Dennis next to her. Didn't like eating breakfast with Dennis. She always felt disloyal, like she was cheating on Pete. Dennis was *someone.* She'd been up front with Dennis because that was the kind of person she was. She'd told him she had no intention of getting married until she was at least forty and established in her career. Dennis said he felt the same way. Once a week sex was what they had. A truly sorry state of affairs.

Annie Gabriel did something then that she swore she would never do where Pete Sorenson was concerned—she cried, she sobbed, she blubbered until she couldn't keep her eyes open. She staggered from the tub and wrapped herself in a warm, tattered and frayed robe her parents had given her when she was fourteen. It was a comfortable old friend. She nuzzled the sleeve as she curled up in bed.

She thought about Pete and Barney. Why, she didn't know. Maybe because she'd never had a close friend like Barney. Right now she wished she had a friend, the kind you can call at any time of the day or night for consolation.

She'd told Pete she had a boring, uneventful childhood. In a way, it was true, and in a way it wasn't. Her family was unlike Pete's early family. So many times she'd wished for togetherness, but it hadn't happened. Now, when she thought about it, there simply hadn't been time for togetherness. After school she went to dancing class and from there to a gym class. She was dropped off at home at five-thirty just as the tutor arrived. She was tutored in everything, even though she didn't need it or want it. "You are going to amount to something someday, Ruth Ann. The only way that can happen is if you're well-rounded and educated." She'd wanted to snap at her mother and say that to be well-rounded you needed friends, but she would have gotten a lecture about bad habits, going astray, and peer pressure. She'd taken piano lessons, singing lessons, had sung in the choir, attended Bible class, and then the early French and Spanish classes. By the time she was twelve she could speak both languages fluently.

High school had been the same: school, two part-time jobs to save for college, baby-sitting on the weekends. She hadn't gone to one dance, one prom, had one date, or even gone to a football game. "Well-rounded my butt," she snorted. "I was a misfit. And I wore glasses and braces until the end of my senior year."

And then it was off to college, where she'd met Pete. Her first real friend. Lord, how she loved him; so much, she ached at times. Tears burned her eyes. She swiped at them with the sleeve of her robe. If there was one thing she was grateful for, it was all the lessons, all the tutoring, the good study habits, for they enabled her to breeze through her own classes and help Pete with his. It wasn't that he was dumb; far from it. He simply lacked discipline and was uninterested in the details of the law. He'd remedied that, though. As long as he had a notepad and his list of lists, he was okay.

Pete was going to be successful someday, and she was grateful she had a part along the way.

"I want you to love me, Pete," she said aloud. "I want us to share our lives. I can't think of anything more wonderful than having your babies, of talking to you about our cases after the kids are in bed. I want us to read the funnies to the kids on Sunday mornings. I want us to picnic together, I want us to depend on one another, to love each other unconditionally. I want to take care of you and want you to take care of me. I want a family with lots of little Petes. If we ever get married, I want to name our second son Barney. If you only loved me a little, half as much as I love you . . . my life would be so wonderful. So very wonderful."

Annie cleared her throat. It wasn't going to happen, so why was she torturing herself? She whimpered as she curled into the fetal position. A moment later she was asleep.

It was a new day. Time had a way of marching on. It would never stand still for the Annie Gabriels of this world. Maybe for the Pete and Leo Sorensons of this world. Her world was going to be whatever *she* made of it.

"So there," she muttered. "You cried your first and last tear for Pete Sorenson. So there."

• • •

They were sitting on the steps of Annie's apartment building after the graduation ceremony. He didn't want to let her go. Goodbyes were so terrible. It didn't matter that she would be only an hour away by plane. What mattered was they finished what they came to do. Now, both of them were going to take their places in the world. Pete felt like crying.

"Listen, I have a present for you," he said hoarsely. He handed over a card with two five-hundred-dollar bills in it. "It's for your dress suit for court. You know, one of those knock-'em-dead suits all the female barristers wear. Don't even think about not taking it. Think of it as a tool of our trade. The Blackstone bust is . . . a mate to one I bought myself. I figured I was going to have to be reminded from time to time what this crap is all about.

"And Annie, I have all this money left over. You know, I've told you, I barely touched the money Leo gave me each year. I can lend it to you to pay off your loans. Two percent interest. Actually, I don't want any interest at all, but I know you. I won't bug you like a bank if you miss a month. It's yours, Annie."

"That's so generous of you, Pete, but I can't accept it. I've got some character building to do. I'll be fine. If I ever find myself in a bind, I'll be sure to call you. I have a present for you too. It's not much. More a memento." She withdrew a small package from her purse and handed it over.

Pete grinned. "A pocket watch."

"Yes and no. I didn't have enough money for the watch part, so I got the case. I owe you the watch. I put a picture of us in it."

"I'll treasure it, Annie. This is right up there with my surfboard. Thanks."

"Don't hold your breath waiting for the watch part."

"Wouldn't think of it."

"It's time to go, Pete. My dad is picking me up. It's been . . . great. I'll miss you."

"Me too. I mean I'll miss you too. Leo is waiting for me. We're always going to be friends, right?"

"Always. Forever and ever. I love you, Pete Sorenson."

"Forever and ever is a long time. I love you too, Annie Gabriel."

" 'Bye, Pete."

" 'Bye, Annie."

He still felt like crying. So cry, he told himself. He was blowing his nose when Leo walked up to him and offered his hand. Pete shook it vigorously.

"Congratulations, Pete."

"Thank you, Leo. Thank you for everything."

"Still hate the law?"

"I don't hate it, but I don't love it either. Let's just say I'm not fond of it. I'm not sure I would have liked engineering either. What I would really like to do is be a beach bum."

"You and half the world. I'm proud of you, Peter. I'm giving you a month's vacation. I thought you might like to see the Orient." Leo handed him a ticket. "If you'd rather go to Australia, turn it in and change it. We do a lot of business in the Orient. It's your call, Peter."

"I'll take the Orient. I'm not ready for Australia yet. Someday."

"Yes, someday." Pete thought his uncle's voice sounded sad.

"Let's go, Peter. We have some celebrating to do. It isn't every day I have a nephew graduating from Harvard. Well done, Peter. Well done indeed."

"I'm ready to celebrate, Leo," Pete replied.

"Then let's do it."

5

Pete felt himself at loose ends. He'd just finished up a job and had four days to kill, four days to catch up on paperwork. Paperwork his paralegal couldn't handle. He should be doing something, or at least looking forward to doing something. But what?

Leo was away on a business trip. For some reason, every single guy Pete knew had gotten married during the five years since he'd left college, so there was no one to hang out with at night. He didn't have a lady at the moment, but he did have a little black book with dozens of numbers. He knew he could just make a call and have a dinner date and even sex if he picked the right number.

Or, he could drive to Boston. See Annie. Fly to Boston. He would get there quicker. See Annie. Yeah, seeing Annie was at the top of the list. Should he call first or surprise her? Always call first, Sorenson, he thought. Annie's a big girl now, and involved. He'd always thought he'd be the one to get involved first. Why hadn't he? *Because, you dumb schmuck, you thought Annie would . . . yessss . . . that Annie would see you were the one for her.* Ah, but are you, Sorenson? Can you see yourself getting it on with Annie? *Oh, yeahhhh.* Then how come you didn't after that Paris trip? *Because I was fucking stupid, that's why.* He'd thought she was being nice, thanking him for taking her on the trip, that Annie's kiss had been impulsive. But Annie wasn't an impulse person. He didn't want her to regret it later. How in the damn hell do you know she'd regret it later? he asked himself now. Because she *said* so. She *said* she didn't want to screw up their friendship. She *said* that and a lot of other things. He cared about her too much to put her in that kind of position.

Isn't that her decision? Who appointed you God, Sorenson? You don't love Annie. If you did, you wouldn't be able to eat or sleep. You'd want to spend every waking moment with her. You'd get light-headed and start to look sappy, and other people would notice. Question, Sorenson: If Annie Gabriel worked here in the city, would you spend more time with her? *Hell yes.* I rest my case.

Love starts off as a friendship and grows. Forget that business about eye contact across a crowded room, that only happens in fiction. Love is something that has to develop. Love is knowing the other person inside and out. Your problem, Sorenson, is you're not ready to commit to anything. Why is that?

He hated these talks with himself. He'd fly to Boston, and if Annie were busy, he'd meander over to Harvard and talk with a few of his old law professors. Yeah, yeah, that's what he'd do if Annie were busy.

In fact, Annie was in court, and his law professors were busy with prior commitments. He called Dennis and made a date for lunch after leaving a message for Annie.

It was a warm day, great for walking. He preferred to walk with someone, but since Annie was in court, he headed for the park to drink in some sunshine and do a bit of daydreaming until it was time to meet Dennis for lunch.

It took him a full five minutes to find an unoccupied bench. He watched the children scamper about, their mothers close by. God, once he'd been that young, but he wasn't carefree like these youngsters with their balls and bicycles. He thought about Barney, and wondered where he was and what he was doing at this very second.

Barney.

Someday, somehow, he was going to find Barney and . . . and tell him that when things were darkest, when it looked like he was never going to get out from under, thinking about him and what he'd say and how he'd react was what got him through, so that he was able to take his place in the grown-up world called society. He needed to tell him that Duke and Nathaniel tried to find him.

"You changed my life, Barney," Pete murmured. He looked around to see if anyone was paying attention to him. It didn't appear that anyone noticed him at all. Still, better not to *talk* to Barney, better to think about Barney. In the end it was the same, because Barney never answered back.

Jesus, Barney, I've got you tied up to Einstein, Socrates, and the President. It's like you have all the answers. Why is that? Yeah, you were a couple of years older than me. Maybe it was because you had guts. I swear to God, Barney, I think it's because you told Dave Watkins to kiss your ass. I say that too, but only in moments when all else seems to fail. I don't say it any old time. I'm selective, like you were.

You know something, Barney? You changed my life. I know I told you this so many times, but saying it makes me feel good. Talking to you, thinking about you, makes me take a step back so I can think twice, wonder what you'd do or say in a particular situation. As a kid, I thought you knew everything, that you had all the answers. I bet you still do.

Aloud, Pete said, "Jesus, Barney, I wish you were here." A second later he was back in his think mode, when two women wheeling baby carriages approached his bench.

I bet you're married now and have a kid. I know you're the best father in the world. I bet you take care of your mom too. Just the way I'd take care of mine if she were here.

About you coming for me on my sixteenth birthday—I forgive you. I never said that before. I know if there was a way for you to keep that promise, you would have, just as I would have.

I have money now, Barney. Lots of money. I'm almost ashamed to tell you how much. If you aren't in business as a horticulturist, I could set you up. We could go to ball games and have barbecues. I swear to God, Barney, I'd give it all up if you'd just come back into my life. I need a good friend, a buddy, a pal. Annie's all those things, like you were. I wish I could talk to you about Annie. Sometimes she eats at my soul and I don't know what to do about it. Do you think that's love? What the fuck is love anyway?

Pete looked at his watch. Time to move his feet. He squared his shoulders at the same moment a soccer ball whacked him in the back, moving him two steps forward.

"Gimme my ball, mister," a child of six or so bellowed.

"Yeah, give him his ball," a second, older-appearing child said belligerently.

"I'm sorry, mister," the first child said.

"I know that, son, here you go," Pete said, holding out the ball. The second boy stared at him.

He was back in Iselin, New Jersey, and he was staring at himself and Barney. He grinned. "That was some kick."

"Don't you be talking to him, Sam, he's a stranger," the older boy said.

"He's right, son," Pete called over his shoulder. "Always listen to your friend."

"I'm not his friend, I'm his brother," the boy shot back.

Pete stopped and turned. "All the more reason for you to listen to him," he said, his eyes on the boy named Sam.

Two drinks into lunch made Pete realize he didn't like his old roommate Dennis at all. He was a know-it-all, my-way-is-best type. Why hadn't he seen that side of him when they were in law school? Because he was so damn busy spending all his time at

Annie's, he thought, so Dennis could bring his dates back to their apartment, that's why.

What the hell did Annie see in him?

"So, Pete, how's it *really* going? The legal scuttlebutt is you're going to be a legend in your own time. The know-it-alls are taking bets. Five years they say." Pete heard the envy in Dennis's voice and chose to ignore it.

"Well, I'm busting my ass, if that counts. I'm traveling three weeks out of every month. I know just about every hotel in the world, and the stewardesses call me by name. If that's the stuff legends are made of, then maybe so."

The envy was still in Dennis's voice when he said, "Those in the know are saying you walked away with five hundred thou for a real estate deal you worked out in Gstaad. True or false?"

"Put a one in front of the five and you'll be on the money," Pete lied. *You deserve the lie, Dennis. I'd never even dream of asking you how much money you make.*

"Jesus! I guess it pays to be connected. I'm gonna be slaving away for the rest of my life, and when I die, I probably won't have that much socked away."

Pete finished his beer and signaled for a refill. Dennis was drinking a vodka gimlet.

"So, Pete, what's your game plan? If you're earning the kind of money you claim, what are you going to do with it? You *say* you're busting your ass, so that doesn't leave time to spend it. I don't get it," Dennis said, slurring his words slightly.

There was no way he was going to tell this son of a bitch that he donated hundreds of thousands of dollars to orphanages all over the country, Pete thought. There was no way he was going to tell him he was doing his best to provide for his own future and a rainy day. Dennis would never understand. Dennis wouldn't care either. Dennis lived for the moment. Spend, spend, was Dennis's credo. *Jesus, Annie, what have you gotten yourself into?*

"Well?" Dennis snapped.

"I just sock it away and let it earn interest. Why, are you thinking of hitting me up for a loan?" Pete asked irritably.

"Are you offering?"

"No," Pete said curtly.

"Annie told me you offered her a loan to pay off her student loans and she refused. She has pride. So do I. We'll make it on our own. We don't need you to lord it over us."

"What's this *we* stuff? Is that how you look at it, I'm lording something over you? Kiss my ass, Dennis. I thought we were friends. I value friends and work damn hard to keep them. You know what? You aren't worth a good spit. What Annie sees in you is beyond me. I'll get the check, since I invited you."

He paid the check at the front of the restaurant and was outside a moment later. He drew deep, ragged breaths. What was *that* all about? Whatever it was, he wasn't ever going to allow it to happen again.

Pete hailed a cab to the courthouse. He'd watch Annie in action. Maybe he'd pick up a few pointers. Annie was the best.

He settled himself in the back of Judge Leland's courtroom. She looked good. Damn good. Annie was wearing a navy-blue suit with a high-necked, white silk blouse. A single strand of pearls looked to be her only jewelry. He felt something tug at his heart.

When court adjourned at four-thirty, Pete walked up to the railing and said, "Hey, counselor, how about a drink? Looks like you're going to win this one."

Her smile was the prettiest thing he'd ever seen. "Pete, how nice to see you. I love it when you just pop in. Are you here to visit, or just passing through?"

"Well, I was going to invite you and Dennis for dinner, but he and I had lunch and I blew any thoughts of that happening."

Annie frowned as she snapped the lock on her briefcase. "I swear this thing gets heavier every day. Pretty soon I'm going to need a dolly to carry it. What happened, did Dennis get on his high horse, or did you say something out of line? You're good at that, Pete."

"Let's walk, it's beautiful out. Give me the bag," he said, reaching for Annie's briefcase. She willingly handed it over.

When they were outside, walking, Pete asked, "What's with you two? Have things changed since last month when we talked?"

"Nope. Things are the same. Dennis . . . Dennis wants it all now. Look, I'm not being disloyal, Dennis tells anyone who will listen that he has no patience. He wants the best cases, the highest fees, and he wants to be able to spend money . . . the way you do. He has never gotten over that Paris trip." She shrugged.

"Are you two going to end up together?"

He didn't realize he was holding his breath until Annie said, "Who knows? If it doesn't work, it wasn't meant to be. We're for now."

"I want to know something, Annie. I want you to tell me the truth. Do you love Dennis?"

"Do I ask you about the women you go out with? There are some things, Pete, that are very personal and private."

"I'm not *involved* with anyone. Besides, I'd tell you the moment it happened. Well?"

"I like him. Dennis can be very charming. He can even be considerate when he puts his mind to it. He's a very good attorney, Pete. He'll make it if he develops a little patience. But to really answer your question, no, I'm not *in* love with him. I don't think he's in love with me either. Like I said, we're for now, Pete, it's that simple. And I resent you asking me."

"Someone has to look out for you. Sometimes, Annie, you don't have enough sense to come in out of the rain."

"Damn it, Pete, I resent that too. Keep up this line of talk and you'll be going back to New York minus *two* friends."

That should have been enough to shut him up, but it wasn't. "I worry about you."

"Well, don't. I've been taking care of myself for a long time. As you can see, I'm doing just fine."

And she was, that was the part that bothered him.

"We're here," Pete said, holding open the door to a dimly lit bar the local attorneys favored. He felt a pang of something he couldn't define when several attorneys, some male, some female, stopped Annie to chat or just touch her arm in passing. Everyone liked her. And why the hell shouldn't they? She was the nicest person to ever walk the earth.

"I want a cold beer and something hot to nibble on," Annie said after they sat down.

"I'll have the same, except you do the nibbling."

Annie ordered potato skins stuffed with cheese and bacon bits. He knew he'd eat four of the six that would be brought out.

"So, out with it," she said testily.

"With what?"

"With whatever it is Dennis is going to throw at me. I like to be prepared. What did you do?"

Not what did Dennis do, what did *he* do? "I realized this afternoon that I don't like Dennis. I don't think I ever liked him. You asked for it, so I'm telling you the truth. He had the gall to ask me what I do and what I plan to do with all the money I earn. His envy was palpable. There seems to be a lot of scuttlebutt going around about the kind of money I earn. And he was on his way to getting sloshed over lunch. What kind of attorney gets drunk at lunch?"

"When you aren't in the big leagues, it's easy to fall into that jealousy trap. God, Pete, you know the kind of hours we put in, the billable hours hanging over our heads. There's no excuse for Dennis drinking at lunch, though. I think this is a first. This is just my opinion, but I think he's jealous of you."

"So, I'm jealous of him. He has you."

"You had your chance, Pete, you turned me down," Annie said lightly.

"Bad timing," Pete said just as lightly. It wasn't right, didn't *feel* right.

"I'm curious about something, though. Friend to friend, and I feel comfortable asking you, what *are* you going to do with all that money you earn? I can't even begin to comprehend the numbers that buzz and abound."

"You really want to know?"

"That's why I asked."

"Provide for my future. For the future of the children I hope to have someday, and for their children and their grandchildren. I want to know I've provided for generations of my blood for years to come. I don't ever want what happened to me to happen to them. I want a family, Annie. Lots of children. I want everything I never had. But first I want to earn it. Me. I don't want someone giving it to me. Why do you think I'm busting my ass?"

"You need a life, Pete. You know those proverbial roses everyone talks about? You need to stop and smell them from time to time. What good is all that going to do you if you drop dead at forty-five?"

"Five more years, Annie, and it will all be locked into place. I have the trusts all set up, and the insurance is in place to pay death taxes—not that I plan on dropping dead, but it's needed. Then I'm going to Bell's Beach. I'm going to be a beach bum."

"What about the wife and kiddies?" Annie asked sourly.

"They'll be with me, living off the land and going bare-assed naked, no shoes."

"You're nuts. You can't live off the land . . . beach. Nothing grows on the beach."

"I'm a city boy. So I need a few lessons on how to survive and become a beach bum. I'm gonna do it, Annie. You wait and see."

"When I come to visit you, should I wear leaves and burlap or a string bikini? What will the little woman say?"

"She'll say, 'Did you bring the latest issue of *Cosmo*?' " Pete guffawed. Annie doubled over, laughing.

They paused while the food was placed on the table. Then Pete asked, "How about you, Annie, has your game plan changed?"

"Nope. Sometimes," she said, leaning over the table, her eyes dreamy, "I think . . . dreams are just that, dreams. I want a house with a nice kitchen, you know, the stuff all in a row with a window over the sink. I'm gonna put little red pots on the sill full of herbs, and when I cook, I'll just pick off a stem. I want shiny pots with copper bottoms. What I'd *really* like is to have a fireplace in the kitchen, and a rocking chair with a thick, padded seat cover. I can't decide if I want a cat or a dog to cuddle with. Maybe two rocking chairs for my . . . for . . . you know, when I get married. He probably won't have a lot of time to sit and rock with me. Maybe Sunday mornings. Sunday mornings are good. I could live with that. That's in the beginning, until I have kids. I'd like four, but the chances of that are about slim to none. I'd like two boys and two girls. A boy first, so the others can have an older brother. I think that's important. You've heard this a hundred times, Pete, why am I telling you again?"

"Because I love hearing it. Go on," Pete said, digging into Annie's potato skins.

"I want maple trees that give off a lot of shade. I'm gonna hang a tire from one of the limbs. A little boy on the street I lived on had one. I wanted to swing on that tire so bad, but my mother wouldn't let me. She said it was a dirty old thing and my clothes would get all dirty. As if I cared. Then she got sick and was in bed with a really bad cold. It was in the winter. After I took up her tea, I put on my coat and ran down the street, and man, I played on that old tire for over an hour. I only went home because I was freezing. I didn't get dirty either. I never told my mother. It was one of the best days of my life.

"Raking leaves, planting spring flowers, mowing the lawn, those are all going to be family projects," she continued. "We're going to carve the pumpkins together, cook Thanksgiving dinners together, and go out for the Christmas tree together. We're going to be a family and do everything together. The day I get married is the day I'm going to start saving for college for the kids.

"I'm never going to give up my career. I don't mind putting

it on hold while I have babies, but after that I think I might open up a little family practice and do it out of the garage I remodel into an office.

"I'm going to love my husband to death. Not really, but I am going to . . . make sure he never falls out of love with me, because I simply do not believe in divorce. Maybe that's not realistic of me, but it's how I feel. Like you, Pete, I want to belong, to have my very own family. I want us to get dressed up on Sundays and go to church. I want to teach my kids about values, honesty, and caring about the other person. I want them to love me so that when it's my turn to go to that . . . that place at the end of our lives, there's someone to grieve for me. For a little while. I want them to remember me and say things like, 'Do you remember when Mom did this or that or Mom said this or that?' I want to be someone's mom and someone's wife. Do you think I want too much, Pete?"

"Hell no. Will you make chicken soup for your husband if he's sick? What if you're working, will you take a day off?"

"Absolutely. My husband won't be helpless, but if he's sick, then it will be my job to take care of him. I'd expect him to do the same."

"You didn't say anything about your budget," Pete said fretfully.

Annie laughed. "You know all this. You can probably tell me all about my budget, and stop eating all my skins."

"So tell me about your budget."

Suddenly, Annie wanted to cry. She didn't want to share all her dreams with Pete. It was Pete she wanted to marry, Pete she wanted to grow old with, Pete she wanted to take care of, Pete she wanted to be part of her life, Pete's kids she wanted.

"You look like you're gonna cry, Annie. I only ate four. I saved two for you. You never eat more than two. Don't tell me, I know, it must be that time of the month. So what about the budget?"

Annie stuck out her tongue and made a face. Men were so . . . "I'm going to have a budget. So much for groceries, so much for clothing, so much for utilities. I'm going to keep envelopes like my mother did. Each envelope was for something, and she kept them in the kitchen cabinet by the telephone. I'm going to start out that way, but it's going to require a lot of trips to the bank. My mother dealt in cash, whereas I'll be writing checks. I just want to see what that's like. I'm even going to have an envelope for the paper boy. Then, at the end of the month, if I've managed to save some money, it will go into a separate bank account for when the kids start college. I'm going to have a water bottle for change too. I'm going to keep it in my closet. My mother did that and saved for years. She managed to save twenty-two hundred dollars, and she gave it all to me when I left for college. I didn't want to take it, but I did. I was so careful, too, of what I spent it on. It took them so long to save it.

"If I work, I'd like us to live off my salary if we can, and bank my husband's money. This is all so far out in left field, Pete. It's probably never gonna happen."

"Sum it up, Annie," Pete said gruffly.

Annie leaned back in her chair. He looked so intense, unlike the way he usually looked when they did the budget thing. She felt something prick at her heart. She felt the urge to cry again, to pound him to a pulp. She wanted to scream, *Tell me what you think, tell me if you care for me, tell me if there's even a remote chance that someday we'll be together.*

"Well?"

"Sharing and caring. That's all I want out of a marriage. If I can have that, the rest will fall into place."

"Listen, if I can't find someone to . . . you know, go to Bell's Beach with, will you . . . you know, give it all up and go with me?"

She grimaced. "Well, sure, Pete. Every girl likes to be second best. In a heartbeat."

"Is that the truth or a lie? I need to know."

"It's whatever you want it to be, Pete."

And that's all he was going to get from Annie Gabriel.

"You louse, you ate five of those. You said you didn't want

any." She snatched the last one from his fingers and popped it in her mouth. "So there," she mumbled around the potato skin.

"You free this evening?"

"I have to go over today's testimony. If you have nothing to do, you can come back to the apartment and I'll fix some dinner around nine or so, if you can hold out that long."

"What will you fix?" Pete asked craftily.

"Pepper steak with sun-dried tomatoes, and those freeze-dried Japanese mushrooms you like. Wild rice. Banana cream pie. Frozen, of course."

"Of course. I accept. What about Dennis?"

"What about him?"

"Will he be there?"

"Pete, Dennis has his own apartment, I have mine. We do not share. He has his life, I have mine. I do not ask permission to do anything, nor does he ask my permission. It's not as though we're engaged, for heaven's sake."

"Do you think you might?"

"What? Get engaged?"

"Yes."

"I don't know."

And that was the end of that.

6

Rain slashed against the apartment windows. It sounded ominous and ugly to Annie's ear. She moved, and Dennis stirred slightly. She wanted to get up and go into the living room where she could think, but she was afraid Dennis would wake up and the discussion they'd had after a very satisfying round of lovemaking would continue. Maybe if she did it in degrees and then kind of slid off the bed he wouldn't notice. He *looked* dead, but Dennis had a way of sleeping with one eye and ear open.

Annie strained to see the digital clock on the night table on her side of the bed. Now, though, because of their bedroom calisthenics, she was on the opposite side of the bed. She sighed wearily. Suddenly her life was a mess. She moved, waited, moved again. She looked at her bed partner. Where Pete had dark hair and dark eyes, Dennis was blond and blue-eyed. He was as tall as Pete, thinner, though. Dennis didn't have time for squash and jogging, he was too busy trying to fatten his bank account. He worked eighteen hours a day, sometimes more. His bank account was healthy, but not robust. She moved again, waited, moved again. Dennis wanted to move in with her, had talked about nothing else since they'd seen Pete, nearly a year ago now. He argued that they could share the rent and utilities and they'd both save that way. She'd said no. He'd grumbled and brought up Pete. Dennis always brought up Pete in moments when things didn't go his way.

Dennis moved, mumbled something in his sleep that sounded like he was arguing with a judge. An ugly look pasted itself on his face. Annie sucked in her breath.

"Why don't we make this legal?" he'd said when they finished making love. "Why don't we get married?" She almost jumped out of her skin. Marriage to Dennis wasn't something she ever thought about, and it wasn't on her horizon either. She didn't love Dennis. She was more than fond of him, and their sexual encounters were wild and healthy; often they made love for hours on end. He was snoring now, lightly. She moved, waited, moved again, until she was at the edge of the bed. He looked vulnerable, like a little boy. She couldn't begin to imagine Dennis as a little boy. She thought of him as born grown-up, shrewd and calculating. He had a small measure of ethics, but not anywhere near what she had. She was honest, he was semihonest. She wouldn't ever, under any circumstances, sell a client short. Dennis, on the other hand, was only interested in the retainer, the billable hours he could pad, and what was in it for him in the end. He was not above coercing a grateful client into giving him a bonus.

So, what was she doing in bed with someone she didn't really even like? Would she *consider* marrying Dennis? Not in a million years. Time to tell Dennis it had been nice while it lasted, and thanks but no thanks. It would be different if she hadn't made her feelings known from the beginning. Dennis had agreed, and now he was breaking the rules. Time to move on.

She was on the floor now, looking up at Dennis, who was still snoring, louder than before. That meant he was in a deep sleep and it was okay to move out into the living room.

Annie knew she wasn't going to sleep anymore, so she went into the kitchen and fixed herself a cup of herbal tea. While it steeped she fired up a cigarette. Life was a bitch, and then you died. She thought about Pete then because he was never far from her thoughts. She hadn't seen him in almost a year. She couldn't believe it. She talked to him regularly, though. All he did was travel, living out of a suitcase and banking his money. It had to be a very unsatisfactory life. She felt the need to stroll down Memory Lane, but Memory Lane had a way of making her cry. She wouldn't cry over Pete Sorenson or Dennis or any other man. She gulped at the tea, burned her tongue, said, "Oh shit!" just as the phone rang. She reached for it and caught it on the first ring. "Yes," she whispered around her burned tongue.

"Annie, it's Pete. Whataya doin'?"

Annie stood up and closed the kitchen door. "What do you think I'm doing at three o'clock in the morning?" By God, she wouldn't tell him she was thinking about him, she just wouldn't. "I just burned my tongue."

"At three o'clock in the morning?"

"Yes, at three o'clock in the morning," Annie mumbled. "I couldn't sleep. Where are you?"

"Bangkok. I want to marry you, Annie."

Annie's eyes started to water. He was drunk, she could hear it in his voice. She said so.

"Maybe a little bit," he said. "Jesus, I hate this country."

"You hate everything, Pete," Annie snapped. "You hate the law, you hate traveling, you hate foreign countries. Is there anything you *like*?" She carried it a step further and said, "I hate it when you call me in the middle of the night with a snootful."

"I like you. I really like you. I don't like that . . . Dennis."

"Ask me if I care, Pete. What time is it over there?"

"My watch says it's three o'clock. Twelve-hour difference. You should know that, Annie."

"I should know a lot of things, but I don't. Why are you drunk at three in the afternoon?"

"It's my day off, and sightseeing is no fun alone. Remember when Leo sent us to Paris? We had fun, didn't we, Annie?"

Annie relented. "Yes, we did," she said softly. "For the most part we always had fun. I miss that."

"Don't you and Dennis have fun?" Pete asked craftily.

"That's none of your business, Pete." This was like a bad romance novel.

"Are you going to marry me, Annie? I asked you, but you didn't answer me. Why didn't you answer me?"

"Because you're drunk. Ask me when you're sober and in person. Down on one knee. The whole nine yards, flowers in one hand and gumdrops in the other."

"Why? I had to get drunk so I could ask you now."

"Why do you want to marry me?" Annie said, holding her breath for his reply.

"Because I do. I want a family, lots of kids to love. You said you wanted the same things. We go together. It was always you and me, me and you. Well?"

"Dennis asked me to marry him this evening, Pete." There was silence on the other end of the line for so long, Annie thought he'd hung up.

"Oh yeah. Tell him to kiss your ass. He's not good enough for you. He doesn't have an ethical bone in his body, and I know you don't love him." He was slurring his words so badly Annie could only make out half of what he said. "You gonna do it?"

"Do what? Get married?"

Pete roared with laughter. "No. Tell him to kiss your ass. It's a great feeling when you tell some crud to do that. Barney taught me that. When should we get married?"

"When you're sober and you ask me."

There was another silence, this one longer. "If I'm sober and ask you, will you?"

"When you ask me, you'll know my answer. I hate it when you get drunk, Pete."

"I hate it too. There's nothing else to do."

"Soak up some local culture," Annie said.

"I want a family so bad. I want to belong, Annie. I want the house, the kids, the ball games, the swimming meets, the dog shit, the dog, sitting up all night when one of the kids is sick, barbecues—I want that, Annie. Time is going by too fast. I think that's what made me . . . I want that, Annie."

She wanted exactly the same things.

"I'd never stop you if you wanted to keep on working, have a career. . . . Well?"

"Ask me when you're sober, Pete."

"Damn right I will. Will tomorrow be soon enough?"

"Yeah, tomorrow will be fine, Pete."

"Are you still my best girl, my buddy? Do you think about me when I'm away, Annie? Wha'd you have for dinner tonight? Jesus, I miss seeing you! How about coming over here? You'd love Thailand. The shopping is great."

"I miss you too, Pete. And no, I can't fly to Thailand, no matter how great the shopping is."

"Why, Annie?"

"Because."

"I hate because answers. I always answer you. Because why?"

"Because I said so," Annie snapped.

"Are you going to call up Dennis now and tell him? I want you to do it now, Annie. Soon as we hang up."

Something snapped in Annie. "Kiss my ass, Pete." It was the worst thing in the world to say, especially to Pete. She'd never uttered his end-all solution to everything. She replaced the phone and then she cried, sniffling into the sleeve of her old, comfortable robe. It seemed to her she'd waited all her life to hear Pete ask her to marry him, but he was asking her for all the wrong reasons. Tomorrow, today actually, he said he would call her and propose all over again. "Yeah, yeah, and they got ice water in hell," she muttered. Sober, Pete would never call. Would he even remember this call? She doubted it. It was funny, Pete rarely had more than two drinks when they were out. He always said he didn't like the feeling of being out of control.

She finished the herbal tea, cold now. Why today? Why did

Dennis propose today? She wished she'd kept a diary so she could write in it. Two proposals, one from a drunk and one from a man who wanted to ride on her coattails, a man with little or no ethics. Love and happy ever after were for other people, not the Annie Gabriels of the world.

She waited all day, glued to the phone, willing it to ring, snapping at Dennis when his physical presence blocked the phone. Not a single person called her. She sent Dennis home at dusk, telling him she was getting a migraine. It wasn't a lie, it was something she'd wished on herself for thinking Pete meant what he'd said. She sat up all night, and still the phone didn't ring. And on Monday she didn't stray from her office, and checked hourly with the receptionist to make sure no overseas calls had come in for her. She did the same thing on Tuesday and Wednesday.

"Kiss my ass, Pete Sorenson," she blubbered in the lavatory as she reapplied her makeup for the seventh or was it the eighth time.

Finally, on Wednesday evening, Annie knew for certain Pete was not going to call.

She was so devastated with the realization, she stumbled and almost fell on her way to her bedroom. She sobbed, great racking sounds that made her shoulders shake while her knees turned to mush.

When the hard, gasping sounds died down to whimpers and she was exhausted, Annie murmured into her pillow, "I just wanted to belong to you, Pete. I know people shouldn't belong to one another, but it's how I feel, how I wanted you to feel."

It seemed to Annie as she closed her weary, heavy eyes that it was the end of the world.

Pete Sorenson woke with the Queen Mother of all hangovers. Now he knew what Annie felt like when she got one of her migraines. How the hell did she stand it? She was Annie, that's how.

The phone call to Annie rode to the surface of his mind. He groaned. Pete Sorenson, last one out of the gate. One stinking, fucking day too late. Dennis, the bastard, had beat him to it. "Call me when you're sober and ask me," Annie had said. Well, not likely, toots, he thought. He didn't need to have his nose rubbed into her lover Dennis's proposal. If she wanted Dennis, he was all hers. Dennis wasn't going to fit into that life and that goddamn budget of hers.

I want those things. Me. Not that stupid Dennis. He's a chrome-and-glass, condo person. He doesn't care about yards and herbs on the windowsill, and he hates fireplaces because they're drafty and you have to sweep up the ashes. He probably doesn't even own a sweat suit, and he wouldn't know what a garage was if he fell into one. He doesn't have junk. He doesn't accumulate things. Jesus, Annie, he wouldn't sit in a rocker unless you gave him his weight in gold.

"You know what, Annie, kiss my ass," Pete bellowed at the top of his lungs.

"And another thing, don't ask me to file your divorce papers a year from now when he ends up in jail."

Goddamn it, how could Annie accept Dennis's proposal? Or did she accept it? She'd said he asked her. He wished he could remember everything she'd said. All he could *really* remember was she hadn't said yes to *him*. If she *really* loved him, she would have said yes as soon as he'd asked her.

He felt alone. He wished he was little again so he could cry. He wished for Barney, the way he always did when things went awry.

The years loomed ahead of him. He grieved and didn't know what or who he was grieving for. Probably himself, he thought as he made his way to the bathroom.

"All I want," he bellowed under the needle-sharp spray of the shower, "is to have a family and belong to someone. Is that too goddamn much to ask?" Hell yes it was, otherwise Annie would have said yes.

"You just broke my heart, Annie Gabriel. I don't know if I can ever forgive that.

"I just don't know."

He saw her across a crowded room. Just the way it happened in the movies. The only difference was, this was a trendy bar called Swoozies, and he was half snookered. His eyes weren't exactly crossed, it was more that he'd had two drinks on an empty stomach and he was stressed out, but not so stressed out that he wasn't aware that he was staring at his destiny.

Pete blinked. She was so beautiful it almost hurt to stare at her. He moved slightly from the crunch of people around him to get a better look at his destiny. She was dressed like a Gypsy, in a wild colored outfit with loose sleeves and a skirt that probably swirled when she walked. He didn't know how he knew this, he just knew it. He stooped over to see what was on her feet, and wasn't surprised at all to see she was wearing bright red suede boots. But it was her dark eyes and dark, wild mane of hair that brought his gaze front and center. They were laughing eyes, and they were staring at him. He stared back. He imagined he could hear her silver earrings tinkling. She must like silver. It was around her neck and on her arms. He had to meet her, *now.*

He needed to know if she was some lawyer's date or if she just stopped for a drink and the buffet, which was free. She might be a student at Marymount, which was directly across the street. But when he narrowed his eyes, he decided she was too old to be a student; old meaning she was in her thirties. A woman who looked like she was comfortable with her identity. Suddenly he felt confused and wasn't sure why. "I think," he said to the attorney standing next to him, "I just saw my destiny. I'm thirty-five," he said, a silly smile on his face.

"Yeah, yeah, where have I heard that one before?" His companion laughed. "Which one, and hell, I'm thirty-seven."

Pete stared at the woman in the buffet line, willing her to turn to look at him again so he could smile at her, maybe hit on her. If she'd noticed him once and smiled, she might do it a second time. What could she do but turn away if she wasn't interested? He continued to stare at her intently, certain she would feel his eyes boring into her. A moment later she turned and bit into a chicken leg. Their eyes met for one brief second before she sunk her teeth into the chicken leg a second time.

Swoozies was jamming, thanks to the gathering of attorneys to wish one of their own well on his making partner. He couldn't even remember what the guy's name was. Lloyd something-or-other, he thought.

His destiny was holding her plate aloft the way the waitresses did when they wove their way through crowds. She was laughing at something the girl next to her said, crinkling her eyes. She moved like a gypsy, swinging her skirt and hair; flashing her bracelets. A moment later she was out of his line of vision. God, he had to find her.

Pete set his drink down on the bar, fought the crowds, snatched a chicken leg from one of his buddies' plates and continued to shoulder his way across the room. Then he saw her, leaning against the wall. Even from the distance he could see four chicken legs on her plate. It didn't seem to him that she was here to flirt, to be hit on, or to drink. She was here to eat, and she was enjoying the chicken. Hell, it was good chicken and it was free.

She didn't look poor or struggling. She was dressed well, trendy, and she carried a Chanel bag on her shoulder. She must just be hungry. He liked healthy appetites.

He was close enough to her now to speak. She smelled wonderful, like spring after a rain, or maybe it was a summer meadow with flowers in bloom. Not that he ever tramped through a summer meadow full of flowers.

He waved his chicken leg and looked around helplessly. "All the plates were gone."

"That's a problem. Be glad all the food wasn't gone," she said, laughing. "Put it on my plate."

He did as instructed. If she'd said take off for the moon, he would have sailed through the open door. "Pete Sorenson." He grinned. *She's perfect and I'm falling in love. Now, this minute.*

"Maddie Stern, and this is my friend Janice." For the first time, he noticed the woman with her. He smiled and nodded, then turned his attention back to Maddie. She said, "You look like an attorney, so you must be one."

"Are you saying we have a *look*?" She had a sense of humor. God, you have just answered all my prayers.

"Pretty much so. You know what Shakespeare said, don't you?" Not bothering to wait for his reply, she said, "First we kill all the lawyers. That's what he said." Her eyes defied him not to laugh.

"Are those your sentiments?" he said, pretending mock horror.

"Well . . ." she drawled.

"Do you have any idea how difficult law school is? It's like being a medical intern, you never sleep. Taking the bar is horrendous. Not too many people pass the first time around. It's almost as bad as the CPA exam. I'm a good attorney," he said stiffly. *Don't let her be mocking me out. Please, God, this is the woman I was destined to meet and . . . marry. I know it. I know it, God.*

Maddie laughed. "I'm sure you are. I was just teasing."

"I guess that means you aren't a lawyer." Teasing. Wonderful.

"No. I'm a buyer at Bloomingdale's, and Janny is a stockbroker with Merrill Lynch."

Pete smiled. "Commendable professions." A career woman. The other one too. Maddie Stern. What a positively beautiful name. Maddie Sorenson would sound even better. He wondered just how drunk he was.

"What kind of law do you practice?" Maddie asked.

"I'm an acquisitions attorney. It's kind of complicated. I work for a consortium that's headed up by my uncle's legal firm. What that means is, I buy up property and then sell it for the consortium."

"How exciting. And lucrative." Maddie smiled.

She's impressed, and she's flirting with me, Pete thought happily. "I feel," he said brazenly, "like you're my destiny. Do you feel anything?" He was so sure of his feelings at the moment for this beautiful creature, he was never going to let her get away from him. Instant love.

Maddie frowned, her brows wrinkling. "I feel," she said stretching out her words, "like I could eat four more chicken legs." She laughed at the expression on Pete's face. "I was just kidding."

"No you weren't," he said huffily. "I don't like it when people say things and then say they don't mean them." Shit, now he'd gone and done it.

"I hate that too. So does Janny," Maddie said solemnly.

"Would you girls like to go out to dinner with me? There's just so many chicken legs you can eat, and besides, the platter is empty. They stop filling it after six-thirty." He held his breath, his fingers crossed at his side while awaiting her response.

"We'd be delighted," Maddie said, speaking for both of them.

"You will?" He was stunned. She was interested. He could tell by her laughing eyes. Hot damn.

Janny grinned. "We eat a lot."

Pete laughed. "So do I."

"I think someone wants this section of the wall to lean on," Maddie said, leading the way through the crowd.

It was stifling outside when Pete hailed a cab. "How about the Russian Tea Room?"

"Sounds wonderful to me," Maddie said.

And it was wonderful, Pete thought later when he noticed that Janny was gone. He did like tactful young women. He couldn't help but wonder if Maddie had given her some kind of sign that she should leave. Because he was dumb when it came to women, he admitted to himself.

Maddie smiled and the room brightened. "I'm not really interested in the stock market, and how will I get to know you, really get to know you, if a third party is babbling about stocks and bonds? I don't think I've ever had this much champagne at one time. Isn't it frightfully expensive?"

Pete waved his hand to show what he thought about the price of champagne. "We can order as much as you like, maybe even a bottle to take with us. I'm having a wonderful time." Jesus, he sounded like a sixteen-year-old sophomore out on his first date.

"I'm having a wonderful time too. It was nice of you to invite Janny and me to share dinner with you. Two strangers . . ." She leaned over slightly and cupped her chin in her hands. "Tell me all about Peter Sorenson. Everything."

He was drunk on his feelings and the champagne he'd consumed, and he talked and talked. About everything and anything. She asked questions, lots and lots of questions, about his business, his uncle, his apartment, his cars. He was, after all, talking about himself. She said she wanted to know *everything.* She was *so* interested in him, he felt his body go from warm to hot. All over. He mentioned it, and she laughed.

Pete finished the last of his champagne. He reached for Maddie's hands. "Do you know what I'd like to do right now, this very minute?"

"Tell me," Maddie purred.

"I'd like to make love to you, slow, agonizing love that would go on all night long. That's *exactly* what I'd like to do. I never met anyone like you. You're so . . . vibrant, so alive. I never saw red suede boots before," he blurted. "You remind me of a Gypsy, the way you dress, and all that . . . that wonderful wild-looking hair. I'd like to bury my face in it. What would you like?" he said, a sappy expression on his face.

"Do you really want to know?"

"Ab-soo-lutely."

"I'd like to rip your clothes off, rake my nails down your bare chest, yank at your hair and have you take me standing up in front of a mirror. Now. This minute."

"Jesus. That sounds . . . wild. Does that mean you don't like making slow, lazy love for hours and hours? In front of a mirror, huh?"

"Uh-huh. I guess inside I am kind of wild. Slow, lazy love is nice, but it seems like a waste of time. I like the moment, you know, go with *the* moment. If you do that, you don't have time for slow, lazy lovemaking. It doesn't really matter now anyway. We just met, and I'm not the kind of girl who does things like that on a first date, and this isn't really a first date anyway."

"I know that," Pete said huffily. "It was all hypothetical."

"Not with me it wasn't. I really feel like doing what I said," Maddie cooed.

He wished Barney was in the men's room so he could ask him what he should do now. Barney always had all the answers. This woman was confusing the hell out of him.

"I think we should call it a night," Pete said, flustered.

"I think you're right. This was a wonderful evening. I enjoyed it tremendously, especially all the talk. I love to talk. Are we going to see each other again?" she asked boldly.

"I would like that very much. I think you are my destiny. I told that to some lawyer at Swoozies and he laughed in my face. Am I your destiny?"

"I wouldn't be a bit surprised."

Arm in arm, they left the restaurant. At Maddie's apartment he made a date to see her for dinner on Friday evening. He sang all the way home. At the top of his lungs. Lustily. With gusto. Ever so happily.

It wasn't until he was almost asleep that he realized he hadn't kissed Maddie good night. He should have done that. He wanted to do it. Why hadn't he? Probably because he sensed the wild-haired, wildly dressed Gypsy known as Maddie Stern didn't kiss on a first date either. Ahhhh.

Maddie Stern stared at herself in the mirror. "Damn, this doesn't look right either," she muttered as she ripped at the clothes on her back. The pile of clothing on the bed gave testament to how important this third date with Pete Sorenson was. *Attorney-at-law.* You really stepped into it this time, Maddie. Bigtime. A great guy, nice-looking, great dresser, super job, rich. Maybe super rich. Maybe even mega bucks rich.

She thought about the men she'd dated this past year. Not that there were that many. One of the buyers in men's wear, a window dresser from Saks, and a guy whose testosterone hadn't developed fully. All nice guys. No sparks. No money. Sloppy dressers. No bank accounts. They all liked to split the dinner checks. No cars, public transportation; buses instead of taxis.

"God, it's so much easier to fall in love with a rich guy. Not bad, Maddie Stern. And guess what," she told her reflection in the mirror, "you ain't never going back to the Bronx. Never ever."

She was back in her closet, rummaging for something special for tonight's date. She should have bought something new, one of those knock 'em dead outfits the slick magazines talked about. Well, she was always pretty good at mixing and matching when her charge was tapped to the max. "I think I'll go western tonight," she muttered as she pulled a rust-colored, gored skirt from the hanger. She had just the right belt, heavy silver, three-inch-wide sectioned circles with inlays of topaz stones. Perfecto. A deep gold, suede vest that was two shades lighter than her boots. Her blouse had wide sleeves and was a subdued Indian print with matching headband. She'd tie the band around her forehead with the ends trailing down the sides. A slight fringe bang, silver hoops in her ears. *Voilà!* A knock 'em dead outfit.

Pete arrived promptly at seven. Maddie gave him a minute to drink in her outfit before she stepped into his arms to nuzzle there for a moment. She smiled when she heard him suck in his breath. He kissed her lightly before he loosened her hold on him. "No more of that or we won't be leaving here for a long time."

Maddie chuckled. "Would that be so bad? I love spontaneous happenings. I'm a bit of a serendipity person myself."

"I love the anticipation of something. We are going out," he said firmly. "We have reservations. You look gorgeous."

"And you look handsome. Cashmere, eh," she said, fingering the material in his jacket. Tonight he was wearing his Finsheims, of which he said he had eight pairs; trousers so well-tailored she knew they were custom made; a white button-down shirt with his initials on the cuff. She knew the cuff links and tie clasp were solid gold. She knew about gold, about material, shoes, and everything it took to put a person together. She worked for Bloomingdale's, after all. She even knew that his belt was crocodile. There was a fortune on his back. Her own outfit paled in comparison. She'd gone to Jersey one Saturday to a store called Mickey Finn and bought everything she was wearing for seventy-nine dollars. Everything was marked down two or three times. If she'd paid full price, her outfit, including the boots, would have cost her $575.

"I'm ready, counselor," she said, slinging a small suede purse over her shoulder.

The restaurant was uptown, trendy and brightly lighted. "Best food in town, for the moment," Pete said after he ordered drinks.

The drinks were wonderful, the dinner excellent, the dessert to die for, the after-dinner drinks marvelous. Now it was time for after-dinner talk. The let's get to *really* know each other talk every couple had soon after meeting.

"I'm surprised you and Janny don't share an apartment. You could save quite a bit of money that way, or don't you believe in saving?" Pete asked curiously.

"At first we talked about it, but we're both private people. We each need our own space. We're both very capable, responsible people. We had to be to get to where we are now. Foster homes will do that to you," she said wryly. "Sometimes being alone makes me feel vulnerable. I do get lonely from time to time, but then I call Janny or another friend and it passes.

"I put myself through college, got a good job. For a while I worked two jobs and weekends, worked my way up to the position of buyer. To answer your question, yes, I save money. Not a lot, because of the high rent, but I do manage to put something away every week. Personally speaking, I don't think that's too shabby."

"What about your family? Do you have aunts or uncles, cousins?"

"Not a one. Are you sure you want to hear this? It's not very interesting."

"I want to know *everything* there is to know about you, Maddie Stern," Pete said quietly. "I was . . . I was in foster homes too."

"I was three when my mother died. My father came in one day and said mother was sick, and before he could get her to the hospital, she died. He did his best to take care of me. For a while he left me with neighbors and friends while he worked. He always made dinner, though. To this day I hate macaroni and cheese. It was the only thing he knew how to make except for cereal and peanut butter and jelly. He always tucked me in at night, always read me stories, and he would use different voices for the characters in the stories. Sometimes he made up stories as he went along. I remember laughing and giggling a lot with my father. Sometimes . . . sometimes if I try real hard, I think I can smell his aftershave lotion. I always got a whiff of it when he kissed me good night. He gave the best bear hugs.

"I think I was six when he met this woman named Belle. She pretended to love me when my father was around. When he wasn't around I went to bed dirty with only a sandwich for supper. My socks were always dirty, and when I was seven the lady next door showed me how to wash out my panties at night. Belle was . . . slovenly and she reeked of strange smells. I hated to be around her.

"When I was twelve my father died. It was the same year Marty Kelly kissed me on the cheek. After the funeral, Belle packed my bags and said, 'Kid, I'm not your mother, and the way I see it, it's time for you to leave here. The foster care people are coming by to pick you up. You can call me once in a while, but don't make a habit of it.' I stayed in some kind of dormitory for a while and then a couple took me in.

"It was bearable because I met Janny and we had summers together.

"I was sixteen before I got smart enough to start asking questions. My father had a hundred-thousand-dollar life insurance policy, but Belle got it all. I called her and she said, and this is a direct quote, 'Tough noogies, kid, it's all gone.' "

Pete was off his chair and then she was in his arms. The other diners looked discreetly away as he crooned to her, "You'll never have to worry about anything again as long as I'm around. I'm going to take care of you forever and ever. That's a promise, Maddie."

It was what Maddie wanted to hear, needed to hear. She knew in that one, exquisite moment that her future was secure.

"Now it's your turn. Tell me all about Pete Sorenson. From the day you were born," Maddie said, her eyes crinkling up at the corners.

It took him almost an hour to tell her.

"Did you leave anything out?" she teased.

Did he? He hadn't told her about Barney. The only person he'd ever told about Barney was Annie. He'd mentioned him to Leo, but not in any great detail. "Well, do you want to hear the kid stuff?"

"Of course. I want to know everything." She smiled intimately at him and then raised her eyebrows and openly leered at him. He laughed.

"I had this friend named Barney. We were best buddies. He was a couple of years older than me, but that was okay. He treated me like a buddy, and that was all that was important. He had a terrific tree house we played in. Jesus, I loved that kid. His mom was super too, but she was married to this prick who Barney hated. I think his mom was afraid of the guy, but she did love Barney the way my mom loved me.

"The day the social service people came to get me, I ran over to Barney's tree house and hid. We put up a hell of a fight, but in the end I had to go. Barney and I made a pact, we even cut our fingers with this old rusty knife and said we were blood brothers. Who knew anything about tetanus shots? Certainly not us. We didn't get blood poisoning, so I guess it wasn't that rusty. Anyway, Barney swore he would come and get me when I was sixteen. He'd be older and on his own then. He said he'd never forget me because we were blood brothers. I believed him. It made all those foster homes bearable because I knew Barney would come for me the day I turned sixteen."

Maddie trilled with laughter. "Tell me you didn't believe that kid. Really, Pete. That's the funniest thing I ever heard. I know you were only six, but at six you know a little bit, for heaven's sake. You really believed him! Did you keep a calendar and mark off the days and years? Pete, you are so naive sometimes." She laughed again, a chilling sound that made the fine hairs on the back of Pete's neck stand on end. "What happened on the day of your sixteenth birthday when he didn't show up?" She laughed again.

"I was devastated. I believed him because I wanted to believe him. I believe," he said coolly, "that something happened to prevent him from keeping his promise to me. I will always, until the day I find Barney, believe that. That particular day, that particular incident, was the . . . I will never forget it. Not ever. I think it's time I took you home."

Maddie blinked, reached for his hand. He jerked it away and was on his feet before she could blink a second time. She felt her secure future slip away from her. How stiff he looked. Brittle, actually. Fear ran down her spine. "Pete, wait. I'm sorry. I guess

I . . . I don't know much about little kids, boys in particular. I'm sorry if I . . . what did I do, hurt your feelings? Listen, sixteen is pretty old to . . . Pete, I'm sorry. I'm really sorry."

"I am too, Maddie."

Pete's face was a mask of disappointment when he dropped Maddie off at her apartment. She talked all the way, apologizing for her lack of understanding, begging him to understand, to forgive her.

"Will you call me?" she asked quietly when he turned to leave her.

"I don't know," he said honestly.

He didn't call her, and he was miserable. He did call Annie, just to talk about mundane things. Even Annie failed to cheer him up. He talked to Barney—for hours on end in his apartment, where no one could hear him. He polished his surfboard a dozen times.

He was stubborn, he would never call, no matter how much it hurt. Barney was just too damn important to him. Couldn't she see that? Couldn't she tell by his tone of voice?

And then she called. He knew she was crying, had probably cried buckets. "Pete, I love you so much. I've been so miserable. Can you ever forgive me? I guess I just didn't understand. I do now, though. Please."

Because he loved her, he forgave her.

"Would you have called me, Pete? I need to know."

"No, Maddie, I wouldn't have called."

"That's good, we're being honest with each other. I can handle it if you can. Can you come over now? I need you, Pete Sorenson."

"And I need you, Maddie Stern. I'll be there in fifteen minutes."

When he hung up, he said aloud to his old friend, "What do you think, Barney? It takes a big person to come around. I wouldn't have buckled no matter how much it hurt."

• • •

"Oooh, I feel so good, Pete Sorenson." Maddie stretched, arching her back and at the same time thrusting her knee into Pete's groin. She laughed when he groaned. She felt his instant erection. They had already made love twice. A heartbeat later she was on top of him, her dark hair a waterfall that cascaded down over her face and covered her heaving breasts.

"One of these days you are going to kill me," Pete moaned as he felt himself slide into her, his fingers searching for the dusky nipples beneath the waterfall of her hair.

Maddie stopped her wild gyrating atop him just long enough to suck in her breath and curse his slowness, her wetness, his hardness. Her head reared back, the wild mane of hair behind her. She was aware of Pete's rotating hips, his fingers on the nubs of her breasts. And then she was beneath him in the blink of an eye, her hands guiding him, again cursing his slowness, demanding he satisfy her. "Now," she hissed, her breathing ragged.

"No, no, no," Pete whispered. "My way this time. Shhhh, let me make love to you." His mouth swooped down on hers. "You're the nectar and I'm the bee," he murmured as his tongue wrapped itself around hers.

His hands moved, both of them, one trailing down her hard, flat stomach, the other searching for and finding the dark patch of curls. Maddie stirred on the bed, urging him to search for and find the soft folds of her secret place and the wetness that would caress his hand. She murmured words he couldn't hear, but he sensed the urgency behind them. In turn he whispered the words lovers had been using since time began.

He nuzzled her neck, at the same time inhaling the faint fragrance that remained on her slick skin. He blazed a trail from her throat to her bare breasts, and she trembled with exquisite anticipation. All things moved to the distance, nothing and no one existed beyond this moment and place. The only reality was the way her body reacted to his. Pleasure radiated upward from some hidden well, and he allowed himself to be carried with it, unable to hinder the forward thrust of his own desire, lifting out of space and time into the turbulent waters he was creating in his love.

Greedy hands and fingers drew him closer, so close they were almost one, closer than any secret. As her hands moved over him, Pete was filled with a sense of his own power and exulted in her passion for him. She was so beautiful with her moist, kiss-reddened lips parted seductively, and her languorous, heavy-lidded gaze hinted at a depth of passion that excited him unbearably. Damn, he was hungry for her; he would have liked to spread her beneath him and plunge into her fiery depths, to feel himself become a part of her. Each curve of her body was eloquent; the roundness of her breasts with their dusky pink crests; the slender arc of her hips, which narrowed into long, lean legs; her silky skin gleaming softly with a sheen of desire. He would take her slowly, savoring each inch of her, the way he'd dreamed of since first seeing her, delighting in the pleasure they would share.

When he moved to cover her body with his, it was her turn to protest. "No, let me," she whispered, rolling over on top of him.

As she leaned over him, her cloud of dark hair tumbled around his face, grazing his shoulder and tickling his chest. She smoothed his chest with her fingertips, trailing through the patch of dark curls, exploring the regions that were smooth and hairless, then moving to the flat hardness of his belly. He heard himself gasp as her hand wandered dangerously close to his groin and then flew upward again to his chest. He wanted to applaud her daring, yet he almost laughed when he saw her eyes widen wickedly.

In the time it took his heart to beat once, she was nestled between his legs, purring and licking.

When she lifted her head to look at him, her eyes heavy with desire, he was reminded of a feline who has just discovered the cream crock; the little smile she bestowed upon him was rife with a cat's self-satisfaction. And she was feline, he found himself thinking, sleek and smooth and silent, like a jungle cat, a black panther who has just given chase and was now anticipating the feast. She reached out to touch him again with her silky tongue, this time watching him, aware of his every reaction, relishing the hardness of him and feeling it pulsate in anticipation of her touch. When she closed her mouth around him, a deep throbbing sounded in his chest and rumbled from his lips. Unable to withstand her sensuous onslaught a moment longer, he reached out and pulled her beside him, and this time it was he who took the superior position. Only having her, losing himself within her, would satisfy.

A golden warmth flooded through Maddie as he brought his mouth to hers once again. His movements were smoothly executed as he drew a path from one breast to the other, covering each first with his hands and then with his lips. She clung to the strength of his arms, holding fast as though she were fearful of falling in on herself, never to be found again.

His hands spanned her waist and rounded to her buttocks, lifting her slightly from the bed. Tortuous, teasing explorations of his tongue made her shudder with heightened passion. Her fingers, greedy once again, clutched and pulled at his dark, ruffled hair as though begging him to stop, while her body arched into his, feverishly exposing herself to his maddening mouth. He searched for and found the secret places that pushed her to the brink of release, only to have his worshiping kiss follow another path before returning again to the first.

A yawning ache spread through Maddie, demanding satisfaction, settling at her core and forcing her to seek relief by writhing and thrashing about restlessly. Pete held her there, forcing her to him, adoring her with his hands and lips until she could deny herself no longer. Her body flamed, her back arched, and her world divided in two parts; her need and his lips. And when the tremors ceased and his mouth covered hers once again, she tasted herself there. She was satisfied, yet discontented; had feasted, yet was famished. There was more she wanted, much, much more. She wanted to share with him the release of his own passion, to participate in bringing him to that same wonder.

He urged her onward, assuring her he was ready. Grasping her hips, he lifted her and wound her parted thighs around him. She guided him into her, pulling him forward, driving him downward, knowing that same need within him, a desire of a different, cooler color than before. It was as though once having slaked his thirst, he could now enjoy the flavor. Moving with him, becoming part of him, Maddie fueled his passion and renewed her own. Together they were flung upward; together they found the sun, the moon, and the stars.

He wanted to sleep, needed it, craved it, but Maddie bounded off the bed. Naked, hands on hips, she said, "Move it, Sorenson, we have showers to take and food to prepare."

Pete blinked. He didn't mean to say it because only a fool would utter something like this, but he did. "Was it as good for you as it was for me?"

"Better." She blew him a kiss.

On their eighth date Pete said, "I'm in love with you. Will you marry me?"

They were in Central Park, jogging. Maddie stopped long enough to say, "I thought you'd never ask. Yes, yes, yes."

At the end of the three-mile jog, Maddie fell into Pete's arms. "This has got to be the happiest day of my life."

"Mine too," Pete said gruffly.

"Are we going to have a real wedding, you know, church, gown, attendants, the whole thing? I don't think I can afford anything lavish, Pete. Simple will do it. Maybe a brunch or a breakfast. Will you be embarrassed if it's small? That doesn't mean it will be . . . tacky, just small. Tasteful. God, I always wanted one of those bang-up weddings, you know the kind. Pictures, wonderful dinner, the church, gorgeous gowns. Exquisite flowers; orchids. In the church. Lots of balloons." She made a face to show how far she'd come in her dream of a church wedding.

"Whatever you want, Maddie, and don't worry about the money. Do it up right. Spend whatever you have to. We're only going to do this once, so let's do it right. When do you want me to give you my guest list?"

Spend whatever it takes, she thought. Good Lord. She knew she could spend a fortune without even trying. Don't worry about the money, he said. Well, then she wouldn't worry. "Whenever you have it ready. I only have a dozen or so people to invite. How about you?"

"Twenty, tops. Annie, of course, is at the top of the list."

"Uh-huh," Maddie said.

"Uh-huh. What does uh-huh mean, Maddie?"

"It means," Maddie said carefully, "that I think I'm jealous of Annie Gabriel. You talk about her all the time like she's some . . . some saint, some paragon of something or other."

"Annie's not a saint, but she is very special. So special I couldn't even *think* about getting married unless she were there. When you meet her, you'll know what I'm talking about." Pete decided that he was absolutely, positively, not going to dwell on Maddie's attitude toward Annie. She didn't know her. From the looks of things, she didn't want to get to know her either.

"Are you going to continue your friendship with Annie after we get married?"

"I hadn't thought much about it, Maddie. It's a forever kind of friendship, the kind you have with Janny. Is this going to be a problem?"

"I don't know, Pete, is it?"

"I think," Pete said carefully, "it's only going to be a problem if you turn it into a problem."

"If I told you I wanted you to curtail your friendship with Annie, would you? I'm not saying I would ever ask that of you, but would you?"

Instead of answering her, Pete asked a question of his own. "If I asked you to curtail your friendship with Janny, would you do it? I'm not saying I would ever ask that of you, but would you?"

"Yes, but with terrible misgivings. You?"

"No, Maddie. I guess this is going to be a problem."

"It could be," Maddie said thoughtfully. "I know it's fashionable for men to have women friends and vise versa, but part of me, the selfish part of me, wants you all to myself. You share too much with her. You should be sharing with me."

"Maddie, I've known Annie for almost twelve years. I could never turn my back on her. She got me through law school. I owe her. Big-time."

"When is she going to want to collect, Pete?"

"What do you mean?"

"There's always a payback. When is hers coming due?"

"That's silly, Maddie. Annie isn't like that. She's a kind, warm, generous, unselfish friend. In all the years I've known her, she's always put me first."

"When people are in love, they do that."

Pete sucked in his breath. Suddenly the sunny park, the wonderful moment, was dark and gloomy. "Then why aren't you doing that?" he said quietly.

"What's that supposed to mean?" Maddie asked with an edge in her voice.

"It means . . . Annie always says . . . if you love someone, their happiness comes first. I just happen to agree with the statement. You know my friendship with Annie is important to me. You should be willing to accept it. Instead, I suspect you're waiting for me to say I'll give up that friendship. I won't, Maddie."

"Even if I say it's important to me?"

"It doesn't concern you. It would never occur to me to ask you to give up something that was established before I met you. I had a miserable childhood, Maddie. Friends are very important to me because I don't make them easily and when I do they're my friends for life."

Maddie laughed, a trilling sound. The same kind of laughter he remembered when he'd told her about Barney. "I was just testing you, Mr. Sorenson. Of course I'd never ask you to give up a friendship. We're two of a kind, you and me. We know about friendships." She smiled then and kissed him lightly on the lips. The smile didn't reach her eyes, though. Something rumbled throughout Pete's body. Gas, he thought in dismay. Three hot dogs would do that.

They walked back to Pete's apartment, licking ice cream cones on the way. The bad time was over, but not forgotten.

"I have an idea," Maddie said. "Let's take a shower together. You soap me up, I'll soap you up."

"And?" Pete teased.

"Then I'm going to lick you all over just the way I'm licking this ice cream cone."

Pete grinned. "Promises, promises."

"Oh yeah, race you the rest of the way."

Nikes slapped at the hot pavement. They were in a dead heat when they careened around the corner to Pete's building. The doorman proclaimed them duel winners.

When they finally ran naked from the shower, they were like a raging brushfire, out of control. They were wild animals trapped in the heat and flames that only a bodily release could extinguish.

Afterward, Pete groaned, to Maddie's delight. She snuggled into the crook of his arm. "Pete, do you think our lovemaking will always be so wild and wonderful, even when we get older?" she whispered.

"Absolutely," Pete said drowsily.

"Promise me," she whispered again.

Pete's eyes snapped open. Everything with Maddie had to be a promise. "I promise." He thought about Barney again and his promise.

"Okay." A moment later she was asleep, her breathing little puffing sounds against his arm. He closed his eyes and willed himself to sleep.

Lovemaking was always like this, wild and intense. He wondered what it would be like to make slow, lazy love for hours at a time. Was it his fault, or was it Maddie's, or was it both their faults because they wanted instant gratification?

The sun was setting when they woke.

Pete swung his legs over the bed. They had a routine of sorts now, after months of togetherness. They always made love after a run or a jog, showered, and then he cooked a meal for the two of them. If they weren't too stuffed from Pete's culinary expertise, they either watched television or took in a movie, then made love again. It was almost a habit, or if not a habit, then a settled routine. And wasn't that the same thing? he often wondered.

He loved Maddie. He really did. It was so wonderful to belong to someone emotionally. He thought about Barney then because he always thought about Barney. Barney was part of the settled routine. He wanted to talk about him to Maddie, but he didn't want to hear that strange laughter again.

"So," Maddie said from the bathroom doorway, "what gastronomical, culinary delight are you going to prepare for us this evening, Mr. Sorenson?"

He almost said shit on a shingle. What the hell was wrong with him? "How about my super-duper chili, which is so hot we have to keep the fire extinguisher on the table?" he said with forced cheerfulness.

"That sounds better than my ragout and noodles. After we're married, I'm going uptown and take a cooking course. It will have to be at night. I can't have you doing all the cooking. How will that look?"

"Like you don't know how to cook?" Pete said briskly as he headed for a second shower.

"I'll change the bed while you shower. I know how you like to sleep on crisp, clean sheets. This bed," she chuckled, "looks like a bunch of chickens have been scratching around on it. Do you want me to chop the onions and peppers afterward?"

"After you take your shower."

"That's what I meant, Pete. I love working with you in the kitchen. Everything is so homey and . . . and I missed all that. Pete, is anything wrong? You seem kind of quiet. Is it that discussion we had about your friend?"

"My friend has a name, and yeah, it's still bothering me a bit."

"Good, you're being honest. I like that. I swear, Pete, I will never stand in the way of your friendship. I detest jealousy, and yes, I'm jealous and it's obvious I have to work on that and I will. That's my promise to you."

"That's good enough for me. I guarantee, you are going to love Annie. I wouldn't be surprised if you two become best friends. Wouldn't it be great if I could find Barney? God, my life would be perfect if that happened."

"Life's funny, Pete. One of these days you might be walking down Madison Avenue and you'll bump into him. Stranger things have happened," she said, giving the pillowcase a vicious yank. Feathers sailed upward. "You need to get foam rubber, Pete."

"Take my Bloomingdale's charge and order some. Better yet, get them on your discount," Pete called over his shoulder. Maddie stared after him a full minute before she pulled off the second pillowcase. Like I really have time to shop for pillows, she thought. Maybe she could get her assistant to order some. She would do whatever had to be done to put a smile on Pete's face. She buried her face in the pillow and muttered, "I hope he never finds that Barney. Annie what's-her-name is going to be hard enough to deal with. Add a Barney and it would be all downhill." Selfish tears burned her eyes. She just wanted him to want and need her. She didn't need anyone else, so why did he?

"Your turn," Pete called from the bathroom.

Maddie bundled up the bedding and carried it to the front hall.

Pete was already in the kitchen browning frozen meat when Maddie joined him. With weeks of long practice, she set about getting the chopping board, the wicked-looking knife to chop with, and the vegetables ready.

"I already washed the peppers," Pete said. Maddie nodded. She just dumped the stuff in the refrigerator or tossed the whole plastic bag in the vegetable bin. This way when the stuff got rotten, she just tossed out the bag.

"Are we having dessert?"

"I have some frozen cake and frozen pie. It says 'Belgian Apple' on the box. It looks like it has a lot of syrup and crushed nuts on the top. Cool Whip should make it go down real easy."

"That's so sinful. Move over, I'll slide it in the oven."

While they waited for the dinner to cook, Maddie sat in her nest of pillows on the floor, irritation rivering through her. Damn, Pete always made such a production of rummaging for the tape. It was the only one they ever watched, and it was right on top of the pile. Still, he had to make this . . . ritual. And it *was* a ritual, of finding the tape, leering at her, smacking his hands in glee that they were going to watch the stupid tape for the hundredth time, maybe it was the two hundredth time. She knew the dialogue by heart, knew the exact sequence of scenes. Who in their right mind watched *Invasion of the Body Snatchers*? She felt like screaming when Pete said, "Shall we watch the original or the remake?"

"The one with Donald Sutherland." For the life of her, she couldn't remember if it was the original or the remake, and she didn't give a hoot either. Why couldn't they just once watch something light and funny? Because, Maddie, she told herself, you pretended to like it to make points with Pete, and now you're stuck. You're also stuck pretending you like Bob Marley. Too late to fess up now.

She knew to the minute how long the movie was, how long it took the chili to cook, how long it would take the pie to bake.

The moment the opening credits were over, Maddie plastered herself against Pete and squealed at the same time he did. Pete laughed in delight. A ritual. "God, I love this movie."

"I know," Maddie said, forcing a laugh.

When it was over, Pete rewound the tape for the next time and placed it back in the video cabinet. "Let's check on our food." He popped in the Bob Marley tape on his way to the kitchen. She smiled when Pete sang along with the singer.

"Why *do* we eat this stuff?" Maddie gasped. She reached for her tall glass of milk, which was supposed to ease a burning tongue.

"Because it's *good*," Pete said, slurping from his own glass of milk. He continued to eat the red-hot chili. "It is good, isn't it?"

"I'll let you know tomorrow if my insides burn out. I love it," she said, wiping at her eyes. She did love it, but the aftermath always left her weak for days.

They had their pie and coffee in the living room as they watched the Sunday night movie.

At eleven o'clock, when it was time to go to bed, Maddie said, "It was a wonderful day, Pete. Probably the best day of my life. I can't wait to be Mrs. Peter Sorenson. Are you aware we didn't talk about it at all?"

Of course he was aware. He'd been waiting all evening for her to say something. To bring out the calendar and choose a date. "I thought maybe you wanted to think about it, maybe talk to Janny or something, and then we'd settle down to work out the details."

"When are you going to tell your friend Annie?" Maddie asked, fluffing up the pillows.

"Maybe I'll go up next week, or maybe the end of this week if I can free up my calendar. It's not something I want to tell her over the phone. I want her to see how happy I am. That will be important to her."

" 'Night, Pete," Maddie said, kissing him on the cheek. "I love you, and thanks for giving me such a wonderful day. I'll treasure it always."

Pete drifted into sleep, knowing, like Maddie, he would treasure this day for the rest of his life too.

Maddie lay awake for a long time. She diddled with the idea of getting up and going into the kitchen for something to ease her heartburn, but she didn't move. If she did get up, she could close the draperies. But if she did that, she'd have to get up early to open them so Pete could see the sun come up. She'd wanted to fuss about the drapes, but like the movie, the chili, and Bob Marley, she hadn't wanted to rock her own little security boat.

It occurred to her then, as it had many times over the past months, that she was being dishonest with Pete, pretending to like and love certain things so he would believe they had so much in common. The truth was, they had nothing in common, not really. Sex today pretty much proved that.

And yet, she loved Pete. She really wanted to marry him. She'd managed, so far, to stall talks about children. She didn't want kids. It wasn't that she didn't like children; she did. She didn't want to be tied down, didn't want to have to go through nine months with a fat belly, didn't want to be called Mommy. Children were for other people. She simply wasn't parent material, whereas Pete was. If there was guilt anywhere in regard to Pete, this was it. Pete wanted lots of kids. He'd play ball with them, hike with them, teach them to swim, go to all their plays at school and be an all-around pal and father. She'd be left alone unless she participated, and she didn't like any of those things.

She loved Pete, she really did. He was so generous, so kind, so endearing. And why not? When you had the kind of money he had, it was easy to be kind, generous, and endearing, because you didn't have to worry about money. At times she thought he was a millionaire several times over. She'd tried to tease and trick him into telling her, but he'd clammed up and would only say she'd never want for anything. He was backing her at the store, which proved to her that he had more money than he could spend.

She remembered the first time she'd set eyes on him at Swoozies. She'd been staring at his suit, the cut of it, the way it fit him, and trying to figure out what it cost. She knew for certain it wasn't an off-the-rack suit. Now she knew he had them custom made in Hong Kong and they cost less than she thought. He had suits from England too, custom-made, as were his shoes. She herself didn't own anything that was custom-made. That would change soon.

Maddie smiled in the darkness. And Pete thought their eye contact was kismet or something just as corny. She had to do something about her heartburn. Maybe she could hide Pete's chilies. If she never ate chili again, it wouldn't bother her.

In the kitchen she dropped two Alka-Seltzer tablets in a glass of water and waited for it to stop fizzing. She guzzled it, burped, then burped again. She drank a second glass and waited for it to work.

Maybe she should sleep on the couch. The nights she stayed over, she never got any rest. Pete was all over the bed, throwing out his legs, flinging his arms every which way. And when he wasn't doing that, he was snoring so loud the shades rattled. After they were married she was going to suggest twin-double beds. Dark circles and a certain irritability would convince him they each needed their rest. Yes, the couch would be the ideal place to spend the rest of the night. She would crawl back into bed with Pete before dawn. Thank God he was such a sound sleeper.

She loved him. She really did.

Pete whistled happily as he towel-dried his hair. Today was going to be one of those never-to-be forgotten days. If he had anything to do with it.

He'd had the idea for a Maddie day as he was dozing off. He'd gotten so excited, he reached for the pad next to the bed to make his list. And an impressive list it was. Wake Maddie up, head for the Battery to watch the sun come up. Water and sun at the same time. He knew in his gut Maddie had never watched the sun come up. Then a long walk, breakfast at the Regency, and from there to the Plaza, where they'd make arrangements for their wedding. On to Bergdorf for Maddie to choose a wedding gown. Lunch at Lutèce. Another walk. Then Central Park with a fuzzy yellow blanket, where they'd cuddle under some tree and talk about everything under the sun. Having children, pets, their dream house, food, clothes, business, what colleges the children would go to. Retirement. What kind of his and hers rocking chairs for their front porch, wicker or oak rockers. Their travel plans for retirement. Starting off with a round-the-world trip.

He had so much love stored in him, love that had to come out. Sharing it with Maddie was the dream of his life.

"So, tell me, Barney, what do you think? Jesus, I wish you were here. I'd like to hear what you think of Maddie. I've never been in love before. It's an awesome feeling. There are days when all I do is think about Maddie. Sometimes I can't eat or sleep. Sometimes I get this sick feeling in my stomach, that same awful feeling as when they took me away. The only thing that kept me going was knowing you were gonna take care of me, that we were going to be buddies for all our lives. Some shrink would probably love to get inside my head if I ever told him how I talk to you. I'm not nuts. Jesus, I just want to belong to someone. I want to be able to count on someone no matter what. You know, the way I counted on you, and the way I counted on . . . Annie. It comforts me to talk to you the way it comforts me when I talk to Annie.

"I need to talk to Maddie about Annie. She doesn't understand how close we are. She doesn't understand about you either. I'm not sure if I should press it or roll with it. I could use some advice, but since you aren't here, I guess I'll just kind of roll with it.

"I gotta tell you something, Barney. You know what hurts the most? The fact that you aren't here to be my best man. I'd kill for you to be here. I mean that. I never made a best friend. I know a hundred guys I can ask to stand up for me, but it isn't the same. Time to sign off if I want to pick Maddie up and get to the FDR Drive to watch the sun come up.

"Signing off, Barney," Pete said, flipping a smart salute.

So what if he talked to an invisible person? You do what you have to do to keep going, and it pleased him to have conversations with an old friend. It was changing, though. Before, the conversations meant he was under stress. Now the conversations took place at any old time.

Twenty minutes later Pete let himself into Maddie's apartment. He headed straight for the bedroom, where he took a minute to stare at the sleeping woman who was soon going to be his wife. Jesus, she was beautiful, with her hair fanned out around the pillow. How soft and vulnerable she looked in sleep. And she loves me, he thought. She wants to marry me. She wants to belong to me just the way I want to belong to her. She wants to grow old with me.

A pair.

A set.

Us.

Pete tapped her on the rump. "Hey, sleepyhead, wake up. I have a Maddie day all planned. You have fifteen minutes to get dressed."

"Pete. C'mere," she said sleepily, holding out her arms.

"Nope, come on, we're going to do things today. Us things. Things for you and me. C'mon, Maddie, up and at 'em." When she still didn't move, he said, "We're going shopping!"

"For what?" Maddie asked, swinging her legs over the side of the bed.

"The biggest diamond Tiffany has for sale. Move it, Maddie. You have time for a three-minute shower. No time for makeup. You're beautiful enough without it. The clock is ticking, honey."

Munching bagels and cream cheese they picked up from the Korean deli around the corner, they took the FDR Drive to the Battery, parked the car in a lot, and raced to the park overlooking the harbor and the Statue of Liberty in time to watch the sun creep up.

"Our first sunrise together, Maddie. I love sunrises. It's such a great way to start a day. Sunsets are great too, because the long day is over and you can look back and say I did this or I did that and tomorrow is another new day."

Maddie smiled. "You're a sentimental softie. Guess that's why I love you so much."

Pete kissed her. All his emotions, all his longings, went into the kiss, and Maddie responded to it in kind. "I love you, Maddie, so very much. Every day I thank God I went to that guy's making-partner party at Swoozies. I almost didn't go. I can't even remember what his name is."

"It doesn't matter now," Maddie replied. "What-ifs don't count. We're here, we're together, and that's all that counts. We're going to be happy, aren't we, Pete?"

"Damn right we are. I'm going to work at it twenty-four hours a day. We'll probably have arguments, we'll probably have a few knockdown, drag-out fights along the way too. I want us to agree, right now, that we will never go to bed angry with each other. Can you promise me that, Maddie?"

"I want that too. I can't imagine anything worse than you on your side of the bed and me on mine and then waking up and not talking to one another. I promise. What do you think about separated beds?"

"There's nothing to think about. No way. Married people are supposed to sleep together. I think I'd take that as a rejection if you wanted separate beds. You don't, do you?"

"No, of course not. I just asked a question."

"You scared me there for a minute," Pete said happily. "Listen, it's a beautiful morning. Let's walk. I can come back later and pick up the car. You game, Maddie?"

"Sure. Where to?"

"The Regency."

"That's a long walk, Pete."

He grinned. "So we'd better get started."

In fact, they took a cab partway uptown, at Maddie's insistence. Famished, they ate without talking. They were on their third cup of coffee when Pete said, "What colleges do you think we should . . . you know, prepare for?"

Maddie's stare was blank. "For our children," Pete explained.

"You want to plan for . . . for colleges now?"

"I think it's worth a discussion, don't you? We do want children, don't we? I know I do, and you said you do too. So, we should sort of, kind of, talk about it."

"Well, yes, but I thought . . . a couple of years . . . we need to get some stability to our lives. A couple of years," she repeated.

"That's fine. But you need to plan now. We never really said how many kids . . . what kind of dogs we're going to get. I kind of like cats too. . . . I'd like three kids, maybe four."

"Pete, I'll be pregnant forever. That's thirty-six months of pregnancy for four, twenty-seven for three. For God's sake, think about me. I don't have that many childbearing years left, and I will not even think about having a child after forty. Now, if that upsets you, I'm sorry. This is my body we're talking about here."

Pete's jaw dropped when he saw the way Maddie's lips were trembling. If she gave her napkin one more twist, it would be in shreds. He felt like every kind of wretch for making his girl so upset. "Maddie, please, don't be upset. I didn't mean . . . we can . . . I didn't think . . ."

"I know," Maddie said softly. "One child when we're in a position to . . . to give of our time . . . I don't know exactly when that will be. If this is a problem, we should discuss it now. Having your baby is . . . is . . . Have I spoiled things now?" she cried wretchedly.

"Oh, honey, of course not. We have time . . . so I was being selfish. You're right, it is your body, and we . . . we'll go over this again when . . . when the time is right."

"Let's get out of here into some warm sunshine," Maddie said, standing up and reaching for his hand. She smiled. "If you only knew how very much I love you, Pete Sorenson. Telling you is one thing, but knowing it and feeling it is something else. Please, I don't want us to be upset over this. Children, a child, are in our future. We both need to leave footprints, and what better way than a child of our love? I need you to understand, Pete."

Pete nodded because he didn't trust himself to speak. Outside in the sunshine he looked around. It was the same sun in the same cloudless sky as when they entered, but it seemed less bright, less warm. In fact he felt chilled.

"Where to now, oh fearless leader?" Maddie said lightly. She reached up to tweak his cheek before she favored him with a megawatt smile.

"The Plaza. I thought . . . think it would be nice to have our reception there."

"The Plaza!" Maddie squealed. "Pete, really, we can have it at the Plaza?"

He wanted to say, Didn't I just say that? He was still smarting with Maddie's decision. *What do you have to say to that, Barney? The love of my life isn't crazy to have my kids.* He forced a smile to his lips. "Yes, we can have it at the Plaza. I knew you'd like that."

"I can hardly believe it. Come on, walk faster, Pete, I can't wait to see and talk to them. Can I pick out anything or do we go for a package deal?"

"Whatever you want, Maddie," Pete said quietly.

"I want, I want, I want."

In spite of himself, Pete laughed. She was like a child in a candy store with a pocket full of money. Either you loved unconditionally or you didn't love at all. And he loved. God, how he loved.

It was after eleven when a dazed Maddie, clinging to Pete's arm, exited the Plaza. "I thought it might be expensive, but I didn't think it would be *that* expensive. Maybe we should rethink this, Pete. Lord, I get weak in the knees just thinking about that deposit check you wrote out. You didn't even blink. There are other places just as nice as the Plaza. I think we need to rethink this, Pete. It's so much money. We're basically paying for the name of the hotel."

"It's a done deed, Maddie. I never go back on my word. We're stuck with the Plaza. I think it's what we both want."

"If you say so, but someplace else is okay too. What now?"

"Now, we're going to Bergdorf so we can pick out a wedding gown for you."

"No, no, I can't let you do that. I have to pay for that. The girl pays for the gown, Pete."

"Even when the guy insists on it?" he said playfully.

"Yes, I'm afraid so," Maddie said wistfully. "It's wonderful of you to offer. You could, if you don't mind, pay for Janny's dress. She's on a pretty strict budget. Weddings are expensive for the maid-of-honor."

"My pleasure. It was always my understanding that the bride's parents paid for the wedding. Since this bride doesn't have a family, I decided to step in. It's settled, Maddie."

"Well, if it's settled, you can't see it. I mean me in it. It might take a long time for me to pick out a gown. What will you do? This isn't right."

"Of course it is. I'll meander down to the men's department and get some new socks. The washer eats mine. I'll give you an hour and a half."

"How much . . . there are other stores, bridal stores . . . Bergdorf is frightfully expensive. I might be able to get a deal at Bloomingdale's."

"Buy what you want. Everything you want and need. I want to do this for you, Maddie. I want to give you everything. Don't be chintzy now. You get the best, the most beautiful gown they have. Okay?"

"Okay. I promise I'll be done in exactly an hour and a half. How should I . . . ?"

"Here," Pete said, holding out his charge card. "There's no limit on it, so use it till it melts."

"You are the most wonderful, the sweetest, the kindest man I have ever met. I love you."

He must really be all those things, Pete thought. Annie had said the same thing to him hundreds of times. She'd also said he was stubborn, lazy, and a know-it-all.

Maddie was sipping a cup of tea when Pete walked into the bridal salon nearly an hour and a half later. "I'm finished. Ten minutes early."

"And . . ."

"I got the most beautiful, the most gorgeous, the most exquisite gown. It was frightfully expensive," she said quietly.

"Okay," Pete said, signing his name with a flourish. His eyes widened slightly at the total amount on the charge slip. "Let's go, pretty lady, we're doing lunch at Lutèce. I made a reservation. By the way, I bought two dozen pairs of socks."

"Really?" Maddie giggled. "What color?"

"Black."

Maddie gasped. "All twenty-four pairs?"

"Yep. The washer eats them every week. This way I don't have to worry about matching them. Don't women do the same thing when they buy stockings?"

"I guess you could. I wear panty hose, so it doesn't exactly work that way. Thank you, Pete, for everything. You are being so generous. I don't quite know what to say."

"Thank you is enough. I love doing things for you, Maddie, because I love you, and when you love someone you want them to be happy. You do whatever it is that makes them happy. Come on now, Lutèce awaits us and our appetites."

The rest of the day passed in a happy blur. It was six o'clock when Pete dropped Maddie off at her apartment building to shower and dress for dinner at Bouley. He handed over the fuzzy yellow blanket they'd bought at Bloomingdale's. "I'll pick you up at seven-thirty."

Maddie reached up and kissed him lightly on the lips. "Pete, this was one of the nicest days of my life. Thank you for being you. Thank you for loving me, thank you for making me part of your life. And we're going to talk again, real soon, about babies and our future. I promise."

Pete beamed. "That's good enough for me. Think about adopting too. I love kids, Maddie. You need to know that."

"I know, Pete. See you at seven-thirty. I'll be the girl in the lobby with the smile in her eyes, on her lips, and in her heart. Will you recognize me?"

"Anywhere, anytime. I love you, Maddie."

"I love you too, Pete."

Did I step into it or what? was all Maddie could think about on the ride up to her apartment in the elevator.

It was ten-thirty when, arm in arm, Pete and Maddie left the restaurant. "Those prices were outrageous, Pete," Maddie grumbled. "However, I loved every minute of it. That dessert was so sinful I'll need a week of penance. Listen, I have an idea, it's a gorgeous night, let's walk uptown to Fairy Tales. I know it's a hike, but we need to walk off that dinner. If my legs give out, we can hail a taxi. We really haven't meandered through the store together. You've been listening to me for so long going on and on about it that you must be curious by now."

"I didn't want to . . . interfere. It's your baby, Maddie."

Maddie stopped dead in her tracks. "I don't believe I heard what I just heard. Without you there would be no Fairy Tales. It's *ours*, Pete."

"No, Maddie, Fairy Tales is yours. I'm just the money man. I wanted to do it for you."

"It's a dream, Pete, that I thought would never, ever happen. I've never owned anything in my life. It seems all I've done for years and years is to kick and scratch just to make it from one month to the next. Dreams are so important. Without them, you might as well pack it in. I'm so glad I didn't give up on mine. Thanks to you, it's all going to be a reality. I will never be able to thank you, Pete."

"I don't need thanks. I want you to be a success."

"I hope I can justify your faith in me. Pete, what if it doesn't work? What if I made mistakes, what if my suppliers don't come through for me? What if—"

"Nothing is going to happen, Maddie. Your biggest selling point when this was on the drawing board was your belief in yourself. You sold me, and trust me when I tell you I am a hard sell. There is no way this can fail. I feel it in my bones, just the way I feel it when I'm about to close a deal. It's that old gut feeling. It hasn't failed me yet."

"I can't wait for you to see everything. It is a fairy tale come to life. I'm going to walk you through it. If you have the same kind of imagination I do, you'll be able to see it." She squeezed his arm.

Pete's left arm shot out. A cab slid to the curb. "Then let's get there quicker so I can get a gander."

Twenty minutes later they were standing by the door, the key in Maddie's hand. "Are you ready?" she demanded breathlessly. "Oh, Pete, every time I come here I get goose bumps and my heart starts to pound. You don't know how important this is to me. I tell you it is, but I don't have the right words to . . . It's almost as if it's *my life.*"

Pete gripped her shoulders and turned her toward him. "Maddie, there's room here for me, isn't there? You are so intense when you talk about this. Sometimes you scare me. I mean it."

"Oh, Pete, no. We're a team, you and me. This is what I'm going to be doing, it's not who I am. You will always be part of my life, that life we'll hold special at the end of the day. That will be our time. Long, wonderful Sundays, and after the store gets settled, I'll take Mondays off and we can have two-day weekends. Everything is going to be perfect for us—the business and our lives. Trust me, Pete, I'm going to work at it twenty-four hours a day. I don't ever want you to have regrets. That's so important to me, Pete. That you have no regrets." She squeezed his arm and turned back to the door. "Ready?"

"Ready."

"God, my very own key to my very own business," Maddie chortled as she swung the door wide open. "So, what do you think?" she said, snapping on the light.

Pete looked around at Maddie's cluttered domain. She was right, it was her domain. Layers of sawdust swirled around his ankles. He saw hanging wires, exposed pipes with caps on the ends. As far as he could see, it was one huge room. "Nice," he mumbled.

Maddie laughed. "It's not nice at all. Follow me and I'll mark off the sections with my shoe. I want to show you where everything is going to go. This is the Cinderella section, this is the magic section—Aladdin. That's going to be super. Here's Snow White and her buddies. See this cubby here, this small section, it's going to be my seasonal section. We're going to start off with Halloween. Listen to this, Pete," she said, excitement ringing in her voice, "I'm getting sizes two, four, and six of every costume. By that I mean all the fairy-tale characters. Not a lot, because even though we have a few months, my ladies can't give me quantity, so it's going to be on a first-come basis. Next year I'll have hundreds of orders. I just know it. The costumes are so exquisite, I couldn't believe it when I saw them. Hand-stitched, everything is first-rate quality. None of that sleazy material the usual Halloween costumes are made of. We're also getting orange satin pumpkin treat bags in different sizes. They have a plastic insert and a cap that looks like a real pumpkin top. The stem is green satin. Fifty bucks a piece."

"Fifty bucks!" he said. "Kids carry pillowcases to put their candy in. I saw that on the news one year when they were doing a Halloween special of some kind. Fifty bucks," he repeated, his voice tinged with awe. "How much is your cost?"

"It takes an hour and a half to stitch one up. That's five fifty-five. Ten cents for the insert, a dollar and a half for the material and shipping. Roughly nine bucks."

"Jesus. What about the costumes?"

"Take a deep breath, Pete. Remember, they're one of a kind. Handmade. Full of detail and extras that make the costume. Two hundred dollars. In some cases, depending on the costume, more. Believe it or not, the more outrageous the cost, the more people think they have to have it." She shrugged. "There won't be any left. What I need and will have trouble getting is more women to sew."

"Pay them more, Maddie. Jesus, maybe you do have a gold mine here."

"I keep telling you that, Pete. I'm going to pay more after I get my first delivery. It's all taken care of. You should see what I have planned for Christmas. Priceless items. The shopping bags are works of art. Savers, if you know what I mean. Come January you'll see women carrying them all over the city. They aren't throwaways. Isn't it exciting, Pete? I swear to God, I've never been this happy. And I owe it all to you."

"Do you think you'll be this happy the day we get married?"

"Hmmm. What'd you say, Pete?" Maddie asked as she ducked under a gaggle of hanging wires to head toward the back of the store, where the supply room and kitchen were partially partitioned off.

"I said I'm glad you're so happy," Pete said gruffly.

"There's nothing in the world to compare to this, Pete. Nothing."

Pete sneezed, once, twice, three times. "Time to leave, Maddie."

"You're right. Thanks for coming with me, Pete. I wish I could sleep here. I wish I could be here every minute of the day. I think I will sleep here the night before the grand opening. I won't sleep at home because I'll be too excited."

"How about the night before our wedding?"

"Same thing," Maddie said breezily.

He didn't think it was the same thing at all. He was about to say as much, then thought better of it. "I'm ready if you are."

Pete watched as Maddie locked the double Dutch doors. Her long, slender fingers caressed the shiny brass lock and door handle. It was almost as if she were caressing part of his body. Somehow . . . he felt cheated.

"Shit," he said, and stomped his feet to rid them of the Sheetrock dust.

9

"Forty-five days is a long time, Pete. I'm really going to miss you," Maddie murmured sleepily.

"That's the down side, Maddie. Think about the up side. Fifty-one days from today we'll be married." His voice was just as sleepy sounding as Maddie's.

"Umm. You'll call regularly, won't you?" Maddie said, wrapping her legs around his. "Someday, I want the two of us to travel to all those places you go to on business. I want to see it all with you."

"Ha! Before you know it, you'll be traveling as much as I do. Once you open Fairy Tales, you'll be big-time and a frequent flyer. Then, Miss Big-Time, I want you to tell me how much sightseeing you do when you're on a business trip. As I see it, we'll be ships passing in the night." His voice changed, became worried, sounding pensive.

Maddie bolted upright. "Don't say that, Pete. I'll never let that happen. I'll be able to juggle being a wife and a fledgling entrepreneur. It's going to take a year, maybe two, for the business to get off the ground. Are you having second thoughts? Do you think I'm making a mistake?"

"Of course not. You're going to be a huge success. You are, after all, one of Bloomingdale's head buyers. I feel it in my gut."

Maddie stroked Pete's arm. She smiled when he shivered. God, how she loved this man. "If I am a success, it's because of you and what you've done. Half rent on Madison Avenue. All those contacts you have. But most important, you believe in me. I hope I don't disappoint you, Pete. Lord, what if I fail, what if I'm wrong and this city doesn't need a pricey, top-of-the-line children's store? What if . . . what if . . ."

"Too late now. Your rent is paid for three months, the renovations are under way, your stock is ordered. You can't back out. Trust me, honey, New York is ready for Fairy Tales. I've got your publicity locked up tight. Maddie Stern, I don't want to hear another word about this. Kiss me now or forever hold your peace."

"You are delicious, Pete. You taste better than a root beer stick." They tussled and the worrisome moment was over. "I just hope you have enough stock," Pete said, sliding out of bed.

"I have more than enough, Pete. I wish you didn't have to leave. This is perfect. Do you think you might be able to speed up your return?"

"If you moved in with me or I moved in with you, I wouldn't have to leave right now." He held up a wagging finger. "You said we both needed our space. I'll do my best to expedite business. I'd hate like hell to miss your grand opening. I'll call every chance I get."

"Forty-five days sounds like forever. You'd better hurry or you'll be late."

Pete turned and leaned over the bed. "Maddie, I love you more than life itself. It's trips like this one coming up that made it possible for me to help you open your own business."

"I know, Pete. Take your shower and I'll make coffee."

"Okay, Mrs.-soon-to-be Peter Sorenson. You gonna grind the beans?" he said, smacking her rump on his way to the shower.

"You bet. Genuine cream to go with it. A bran muffin with

lots of butter. A real cholesterol killer. When we're married, you aren't going to eat like that anymore. You get tofu for breakfast and seaweed for lunch."

"I know this great divorce lawyer . . ."

He sang lustily, his voice booming out of the steaming bathroom, a ditty about love and commitment whose words he made up as he went along. Jesus, he was happy. He'd finally found the woman of his dreams, and miracle of miracles, she'd agreed to marry him.

World-traveled, he'd met all kinds of women, but none of them made him feel the way Maddie did. She loved unconditionally. She was warm and gentle, and when she looked at him, he saw the love in her eyes. They were going to have a house in Connecticut, a summer place in the Hamptons, a dozen kids and two dozen grandchildren. They were going to grow old together and rock in wicker chairs on a big old front porch. He'd get one of those tractor lawn mowers so Maddie could sit on it with him when he mowed the grass on weekends. He was finally going to belong to someone.

Of course, he hadn't discussed this at any great length with Maddie. He assumed because he wanted it the same way Annie wanted it, that all women basically wanted the same thing, and Maddie fell into the category of all women. Maddie had said yes, children were on her road map; she hadn't said when, though. He'd give her a year, maybe a year and a half, and she'd be ready for what he referred to as "the works."

All he needed was the time, the hour, magic. That's what he needed, a goddamn bushel basket full of magic. In order to have all that, he was going to have to work his ass off; not that he wasn't doing that right now. Jesus, maybe he'd have to work harder, put in more hours. The children would have to be miracle births if he didn't put a clamp on his business travel.

Until he met Maddie Stern, he'd been a workaholic, spending more time abroad than he did at home. Annie was becoming a stranger to him. He frowned. He couldn't let that happen. Being an acquisitions attorney meant he had to move when his clients said move. He hated the beeper he wore, hated the cellular phone in his car, hated leaving Maddie's phone number with his clients.

He was about to complete the Windsor knot in his tie when he stopped and looked at his reflection in the mirror. He leaned closer. "Is that disillusionment I see in your face, Sorenson?" he asked his reflection. "Because if it is, think about your bank balance, think about the Rover you own outright along with the Beemer, think about the deposit on the Stamford house, think about Fairy Tales, think about those custom-made suits and shoes you wear, think about the expensive presents you lavish on Maddie. Think about *that*, Sorenson, and wipe that look off your face.

"Maddie," he bellowed.

She was a whirlwind coming through the door, the coffee cup in her hand. She offered it to him as though it were a prize, and in a way it was. She made wonderful coffee. Pete loved it. "What is it, what's wrong?"

"Maddie, would you still love and marry me if I was a plumber or a trash collector?"

"Pete Sorenson," Maddie said in an awed voice, "of course. I love *you*. If you don't believe that, then there's no hope for us. You do . . . believe me, don't you?"

Maddie stared hard at the man who would one day be her husband. He was far from handsome, more on the plain side, well-built, with the clearest gray eyes she'd ever seen. So often she told him they were the color of mourning doves. His sandy hair was thinning on top, to his dismay. He said his nose was too beaked to go with his angular face, his jaw jutted forward too much, he fretted, and his ears could stand to be pinned back. She loved every inch of him. Now, she said so, again.

Pete smiled. "Maddie, I will always love you. Into eternity, and if that sounds corny, I'm sorry."

"It doesn't sound corny at all. I feel the same way. Are you going to give me your itinerary?" she said briskly.

"No can do, honey. I'm going to be on the move. These guys like to play host and put me up at different places, sometimes in apartments and condos they own. I can tell you pretty much what city I'm going to be in. I'll call every chance I get."

"I get nervous, Pete, not knowing how to reach you when you're away. I can handle two weeks, but forty-five days . . ."

"You're going to be so busy with Fairy Tales," Pete said gulping at his coffee, "you won't have time to miss me. Don't forget, if you have time, buzz up to Stamford and take a look at the house. If you like it and can see us living in it, give them a check to bind it. I have the down-payment money set aside."

"Oooh, imagine me . . . us, living with all those rich people in Stamford. We'll fit in, won't we Pete?"

"I'm sure we will. I think it's a Maddie house. The master bedroom has a fireplace, and the master bath has a Jacuzzi. It's us, honey. The kitchen is great, the kind you said you always wanted. Lots of windows, a free-hanging exhaust system, cedar beams, real brick on the floor, with crocks of flowers. You're gonna love it, Maddie."

"It's outrageously expensive." She frowned.

"Maddie, I want you to have it, but if you can't see us growing as a family in it, if you don't like it, that's different. The finances are *my* concern. Now come on, give me a big kiss and I'm out of here."

"I called downstairs. They're holding a cab for you," Maddie said, leaning into him. She kissed him, mashing herself against him. She grinned when he groaned. "Call," she said, shooing him out the door.

"Don't forget, you have a root canal appointment three weeks from today, and that crazy cat of yours has to go for his checkup next week." He was still rattling off appointments she needed to keep when he sprinted out the door. She heard him say, as she slid the bolt home, "You are a total airhead when it comes to keeping appointments." And he was right, she was.

She missed him already, and he was still in the elevator. She resisted the crazy urge to run after him, to beg him to stay.

This wasn't like her. She wasn't a clinger. If anything, she was more independent than most of her peers. Until she met Pete eight months ago, she was content to go through life as a career woman. Meeting Pete changed everything. God, all that money!

Back in her cozy red and white kitchen, Maddie poured the remains of her coffee into an oversize mug. She scraped the butter from Pete's muffin and munched contentedly. She sighed deeply. It was all so perfect, this life of hers. She really had it all these days, unlike so many of her friends, who were scrambling to get to the top of their chosen professions and to find a man who would take care of them. She'd really stepped into her own private pot of gold.

"Ooooh, that tickles and feels soooo good." Maddie laughed when her cat Tillie wrapped herself around her bare feet. "He's gone, Tillie. Need I remind you that you need to make more of an effort to get along with Pete. He's here to stay. He brings you fresh salmon. I only give you tuna and Meow Mix. Purr, Tillie, I love it when you do that." She reached down to scratch the fat yellow cat behind its ears. She was rewarded with loud purring.

Maddie slid from the chair to her hands and knees. She scooped up the fur ball and held her close as Tillie purred. "I have this awful feeling, Tillie, that something is going to go wrong. Everything is so perfect, it can't be real. Sometimes I think I'm dreaming and I'll wake up and Fairy Tales is just that, a fairy tale. I've never felt this way before. Women's intuition. You know, like your cat sense." Tillie continued to purr until warm tears touched her, then she leaped from Maddie's arms and parked herself by the refrigerator door.

"Okay, okay, I'm entitled to a good cry once in a while." Maddie hiccuped. Tillie sat patiently by the refrigerator, waiting for her breakfast.

Maddie spooned so much salmon into the cat's dish it spilled over the sides. Tillie watched these strange goings-on as if to say, *Don't think I'm eating off the floor. Besides, you're giving me too much.* Maddie snorted at the finicky cat before she carried the remains of her coffee to the bathroom.

It was still warm and steamy from Pete's shower. She sniffed and smiled. The room smelled just like him, all woodsy and manly. She touched the thick towel hanging on the rack. Pete liked blue towels, the bath-sheet kind. She'd gotten six at Bloomingdale's with her thirty percent discount. She should have bought more, but washing them in her compact washer-dryer was an all-day job.

An hour later Maddie was back in the kitchen with her appointment book spread open in front of her. She looked at the miniature calendar at the top of the page. The forty-five days loomed ahead of her. It might be a good idea to call some friends now and set up some social evenings. She dialed, gave her friend Janice's extension, and sat back to wait. The moment she heard her friend's voice, she started to babble, ending with, "So how are my ten shares of Coca-Cola doing?"

"The same thing they were doing when you called last week. You sound funny, is something wrong?"

"No . . . yes. Not really. Pete left a little while ago. For forty-five days. I started to miss him before he was out the door."

"Where'd he go this time? You need to put a leash on him, Maddie." Janice laughed.

"He promised to cut his travel in half after we got married. By the way, the bridal shop called yesterday. They want you to go in for a fitting next Tuesday. I told them it would have to be on your lunch hour, and they said okay. Give them a call, okay? The other thing I called about is, how would you like to drive up to Stamford and look at a house this weekend? Pete gave me the keys to his car. The Beemer," she crowed.

"The weekend starts tomorrow, Maddie. Do you mean tomorrow or Sunday? I thought we were going to paint the woodwork at Fairy Tales."

Who but a lifelong friend would give up her weekend to paint woodwork? Maddie thought. "We can do that next weekend if you're free. Let's go tomorrow and make a day of it. I'll treat to dinner, and you can try and sell me some stock. How's it going?"

"Merrill Lynch isn't real fond of women brokers. I'm here on probation, thanks to a friend of a friend. I need some rich clients. Like Pete."

"What about all the names I gave you from Bloomingdale's?"

"They're afraid to invest. I've been following this stock called Unitec. It's a bargain at two bucks."

Maddie felt bad for her friend, and a moment later it occured to her that she might be able to help.

"So, what time tomorrow?"

"Tenish. We can stay overnight if you want."

"I'll leave it up to you. How's Fairy Tales coming?"

"They're putting the new ceiling up as we speak, and the floor is scheduled to go down tomorrow. The hopscotch floor is so bright it boggles your mind. The cubby departments go in next week. Saturday will be a good time to match up the paints with the floor. If they're off even a bit in the color, they won't look right. I want this to be perfect, a one-of-a-kind store. Someday, I hope to have a chain of them, and then I can invest all my profits with you."

"On that happy thought, I'll leave you. I have to go to a meeting. I'll come by around nine-thirty. Scruffy clothes, right?"

"Right."

Maddie sighed. She always felt good when she spoke to her friend Janice. Janice was real, a part of her youth, part of her old life.

On her walk over to the corner of Third Avenue and Forty-sixth Street, Maddie ran her bank balance over in her mind. Money was going out faster than it was coming in. The high rent she was going to be paying every month petrified her, even though Pete's negotiation with the landlord, who was a friend, had reduced it. The decorations, the built-ins, were custom-made. Possibly another mistake. But Pete seemed to have money to burn, so why was she worrying?

In the beginning, her plan was to open a little children's store that sold one-of-a-kind clothing, mostly handmade. When she'd told Pete about it, he'd moved like a whirling dervish, arranging things, taking charge, giving her input every hour of the day. It was nothing for him to call her from Germany in the middle of the night with an idea for Fairy Tales, saying it was the kid in him and when possible he wanted to work in the store on Saturdays so he could play with the toys and the children.

As she waited for a traffic light to change, she winced when she thought about the loan the Small Business Administration had denied her. Pete had jumped right in and offered the financing, a loan so large she still couldn't comprehend the numbers. When she incorporated, she'd offered, hesitantly, to put the business in both names, but Pete had said no, this was her business and the loan was a straightforward business deal. With lawyers and everything. Plus bills from said lawyers. The clock was already ticking, and she was nervous. Pete just smiled confidently, saying he believed in her and what she was trying to do. *"Fairy Tales Can Come True."* She planned to play the song, sung by Frank Sinatra, in the background once the store opened.

Maddie felt a rush of goose bumps on her arms when she reached the entrance to her three-thousand square feet of store space. The new door was up. A pristine white Dutch door. She giggled. A Dutch door on Madison Avenue. Mother Goose, Cinderella . . .

She'd gotten the idea for Fairy Tales years ago when she visited California. Quite by chance, on her way to Stallion Springs to visit a friend, she'd stopped in a quaint bookstore in Tehachapi. She remembered how stunned she was to see a circle of children gathered around a burning fireplace, mothers in chairs sipping herbal teas, while a woman named Chelley Kitzmiller read fairy tales to the children. She'd walked around the store on tiptoe, marveling at the little compartments where adults browsed and older children played with toys geared to the learning process. Little racks of handmade ruffled smocks for serious crafts were tacked on a pegboard. Everything was for sale, from books to smocks to lace-edged socks and pinafores.

Miss Chelley, as the children called her, said her bookstore was a gathering place. A homey place for friends and neighbors and first-time customers. The only problem, Miss Chelley said, was that she no longer had any first-time customers. Repeat customers made for success. Maddie had carried that scene, that conversation, around with her for years, knowing someday she'd put it all to good use.

In a way, it was a dream of hers to own something of her own, to be solely responsible for the success or failure of her own business. She crossed her fingers that her homey, comfortable, upscale, pricey store would be a success.

Maddie walked around her cluttered domain, tramping in sawdust and Sheetrock dust, marveling at the hanging wires, the exposed pipes for the plumbing, the new windows that had grids in them now, à la Hansel and Gretel. She brushed at the Sheetrock dust building up in the fine hairs on her arms. She had to get out of here before she choked to death. The catalogs, the order blanks, her thick file with the names of various tradespeople under her arm, she left the store, but not before she stood back to admire the double Dutch doors.

And it was all hers.

"This house is gorgeous," Maddie said, her voice tinged with awe. "This . . . this is . . ."

"Ritzy." Janice giggled. "I love Tudors. If the key is in the mailbox like the realtor said, then this is the house. I wonder how much it costs. Did Pete tell you?"

"Seven hundred fifty big ones. It's so . . . *big.* I'll need a gardener, maybe two." Her voice was full of elation.

"Take a look around this neighborhood," Janice said. "Everything is pruned and mowed to perfection. The chances of a bunch of husbands creating this look is about one in a million. Two gardeners," Janice concluded positively.

Maddie reached into the wooden mailbox for the key, then held it up. "This is it."

"Maddie, do you have any idea how very lucky you are? You have a sweet guy who loves you, a guy who is helping you financially with your business and now this house. This is a long way from the Bronx, Maddie."

"Janny," Maddie said, using the childhood nickname she'd given her friend in kindergarten, "I'm scared, but in some cockamamy way, I'm elated too. Yesterday when Pete left, I had this awful feeling something was going to go wrong. I haven't been able to shake it off."

"Oh, Maddie, I think it's the forty-five days that's bothering you. Pete's trips are usually shorter. A month and a half is a long time. What could possibly go wrong? Nothing, that's what!"

Janice stepped into a tiled foyer. "Maddie, this is soooo gorgeous." She moved beyond, to the sunken living room, and gasped. "Look at the fireplace! It goes all the way to the ceiling." Her eyes popping, she said, "You can stand up inside the opening. I bet you could roast a whole pig in there."

"It's going to take so much furniture. I love buying furniture. I'll be able to shop for days. Pete said I can buy whatever I want. Money's no object. Can you believe that, Janny? I can't wait to move out of that crummy apartment on Forty-ninth Street. Still, I do love Manhattan."

"This is so perfect," Janny said, only half listening. "Pete's going to want to entertain. So will you once you start dealing with all those people you're doing business with. I would kill for this, Maddie. God, you are so lucky. Let's look at the kitchen. I love kitchens."

"That's because you're a good cook. I'm lucky I can boil eggs and water. I'm a whiz at opening cans and boxes, though," Maddie said ruefully. "I'm going to get a cook and a housekeeper."

"Just think, you'll get off the train, your housekeeper will pick you up at the train station, you'll waltz in here, she'll have a drink waiting and your dinner all set out. She'll do all the laundry, the dusting, and all that junk. All you'll have to worry about is keeping Pete happy and running Fairy Tales. It's the perfect scenario. Everyone lives happily ever after, just like in a fairy tale."

"Do you think Pete will balk at a cook, housekeeper, and two gardeners?"

"That's Pete's problem. He's the provider," Janny said airily.

"The commute is going to be a killer. Retailing is a killer too," Maddie said, her eyes wild.

Janice ignored her comments. "Jeez, would you look at this kitchen. I've never seen anything like it, even in magazines."

"A contractor built it for himself. His wife left him and ran off with the electrician who wired the house. Pete told me that. The house has never been lived in. Everything is custom-made."

"Maddie, loosen up and think about how you're going to make love to Pete in front of that gorgeous fireplace. Lord, the carpet alone is thicker than a down comforter. These cabinets are cherrywood. This center island is beautiful, and those cedar beams . . . oh, Maddie, you'll be so happy boiling water. Look at those Tiffany lamps hanging over the bar area! The wrap-around window in the breakfast room is gorgeous. You need to get colored place mats, the kind with fringes. Cottage curtains with the same color tiebacks as the place mats. Why do you suppose the contractor's wife ran off with the electrician? I'd never give this up."

Maddie snorted. "Because she was stupid. The electrician offered her love, and that was more important than this house. She's probably living in the Bronx in a six-floor walk-up."

"This floor is real brick, laid one by one. That costs," the ever practical Janice said. "Picture the kitchen with copper pots that shine and loads of green plants in clay pots. Use your imagination, Maddie."

"I'm going to hire a decorator. I want the *best.* Let's go check out the bathroom and bedrooms. There'd better be one with its own bath for you. We'll decorate it together for when you come up to visit on weekends."

"Oh, Maddie, that's the nicest thing you've ever said to me." Janny hugged her friend. "I'll bring wine and cheese like they do in the movies. We'll always be friends, won't we, Maddie?"

"Of course we will. You're better than a sister, Janny."

"I feel the same way."

Arm in arm the two friends climbed through the deep pile on the stairs to the second floor. "Look, Maddie, you can look down into the living room. It's wonderful," Janny gushed.

"A sunken tub. It has two steps!" Maddie said in awe. "It's a whirlpool. Big enough for four people. My God!" Maddie said.

"This is luxury. You can decorate this bathroom with any color you want. This sandy beige tile will go with any color."

"Six bedrooms, two with fireplaces. White carpet," Maddie said, moving from one room to the next. "Take your pick, Janny."

"This one. Oooh, it has a sunken tub too. Who's going to bring in the firewood?"

"Our butler." Maddie burst out laughing. "You can keep clothes here and everything. That way, you can leave right from the office and take the train here and not have to worry about your things. Maybe our housekeeper will serve us breakfast in bed."

"Now you're getting the hang of it," Janny said, dropping to the floor. She hugged her knees and stared dreamily out the window. "You love Pete, don't you, Maddie?"

Maddie sat down next to her friend. "I still can't believe he loves me. I'm just ordinary. He's so . . . so worldly, so educated, so . . . different."

"Are you putting yourself down, Maddie Stern? Because if you are, I'm going to slap you. It's Pete Sorenson who's the lucky one to have found you. Don't you ever forget it either," Janny said loyally.

"Okay, I won't. You're a good friend, Janny."

"Now that we have that all sorted out, let's check the garden, the pool, that four-car garage with the apartment on top, and then go get some lunch. Does it have a pool house?"

"Pete said it does. It has indoor plumbing so you don't have to come into the house to use the bathroom. Since neither you nor I know how to swim, I suggest we gloss over the pool area."

"We're going to learn to swim. All you have to do is tie Clorox bottles to your upper arms and you can swim." Janny giggled. "I saw that on television."

"After you learn, I'll give it a try. I could really go for a big, juicy hamburger with lots and lots of onions and a slice of tomato. A big plate of greasy french fries and a strawberry sundae for dessert."

"You are a kind friend, Maddie. I'll leave the tip."

"We have to stop by the realtor, drop off the key and leave a binder check. I guess I have to sign on the dotted line or something like that."

"I'm happy for you, Maddie. You deserve this and more," Janny said, hugging her friend.

A light, misty rain was falling when Maddie dropped off Pete's car at the underground garage. Steam rose from the sidewalk. It seemed cooler in Connecticut. That would be a plus in the summer. The only problem was, she'd be spending her days here in the city.

Tillie greeted her the moment she opened the door. In the blink of an eye the cat was in her arms, nuzzling her neck and purring loudly. "Missed me, huh? Well, how about some salmon and some nice warm milk. I'll put a scoop of ice cream in it, and we'll never tell Dr. Lowe we did it, okay? She thinks cats shouldn't have milk or ice cream. What does she know, she's just a vet," Maddie said, cuddling the cat. She rambled on and on as she prepared Tillie's dinner.

While the cat ate, Maddie made a pot of coffee. She was pouring the cream into her cup when the phone rang.

"Pete!" she cried happily. "Where are you? . . . Tokyo! Did you walk down the Ginza? . . . Is it warm there? It's sweltering here . . . Tillie misses you, but not as much as I do . . . I love the house. I can probably get used to a live-in housekeeper and cook. We need two gardeners. I don't have a green thumb . . . I love you too, Pete. I'm counting the days too . . . Janny went with me. She's going to help me paint the woodwork at Fairy Tales next weekend . . . No, I won't forget my gum surgery . . . What kind of present?" She laughed. "You're tormenting me, Pete . . . No, I absolutely will not kiss Tillie for you. No, no, no . . . Oh, all right, but only because I can't say no to you. When will you call me again? . . . 'Night, Pete. I know it's morning there, but it's eight o'clock here. I love you."

Maddie blew Tillie a kiss. The cat hissed at her before prancing into the living room.

Maddie sat down at the table and drank her coffee. A shower was going to feel real good, maybe a glass of wine, and then twelve solid hours of sleep.

"Mrs. Pete Sorenson. Mrs. Peter Sorenson. Madelyn Marie Sorenson. Mrs. Maddie Sorenson," she trilled on her way to the shower. How wonderful it sounded. How positively wonderful.

10

"I'm miserable," Maddie said on Sunday afternoon, after her gum surgery. "My face looks like one of those blow-up whatchamacallits. God, Janny, what if the swelling doesn't go down by tomorrow? Pete hasn't called in four days."

"You're whining, Maddie. By tomorrow the swelling will be gone. Stop worrying. You can take two more aspirin and in thirty minutes you can take another pain pill. Maybe we should go out for a walk. The city is quiet. How about an ice cream cone? I could go for one," Janny said brightly.

"Maybe after I take the pain pill. I feel like I've been rode hard and put up wet. I heard that on a western show on TV last week. It sums up how I feel," Maddie grumbled. "I should have had the damn tooth pulled."

"Think in terms of three thousand dollars for a bridge you have to take in and out. Think of the appointments you'll have to keep before you get that bridge. A day or so of pain, in my opinion, is the way to go."

"I like it better when you talk about stocks and bonds. What do you have now in your portfolio?"

"Some of this and some of that. Little bits and pieces. Hey,

I'm a working girl paying the rent, dry cleaning, and buying food. My investments are small and stable. I splurged and used my vacation money to buy Unitec. I now have a thousand shares. I bought seven hundred fifty at fifty cents. If it goes to ten, like I think it will, I'll be rich. I'll have enough to buy myself a little house somewhere in Jersey. I might even have enough to buy a used car, maybe a new one. It will give me enough to start a search for my mother. I know it's going to go up. Just like I know the swelling is going to go down on your face by tomorrow."

"Come on, Maddie," Janice said, "take your pain pill early and let's go out for a walk. I can't wait to get a macadamia-nut-crunch ice cream cone. With sprinkles. My treat."

The streets were blistering hot when the two friends exited Maddie's building. They walked around the corner to the small convenience store owned by a pudgy Korean woman who lived in Maddie's building.

"Macadamia-nut-crunch. Double dip on a wafer cone," Janny said happily.

"Vanilla. Single dip on a wafer cone," Maddie muttered.

"It's blissful in here. We should stay and eat it here. By the time we step onto the sidewalk these cones will be dripping all over us," Janny said.

"It was your idea," Maddie replied, accepting her cone. "Remember how fast we used to lick them when they were melting? You were faster than a streak of lightning." She moved toward the door, held it open for Janny to follow her.

Janny shouldered past two men directly in her path. Maddie stepped aside, saw the black car with the visored driver and two passengers in the backseat as the car slowed in front of the store.

"Do you mind?" Janny snapped as she was jolted backward.

Maddie's tongue was stuck in a groove she'd made in the dripping ice cream. She eyed the occupants of the car before she stepped around her friend. She saw it all, the panic on the men's faces next to her, the snout of the black gun, the mean little eyes of the man holding the gun. She saw a second gun a heartbeat later. Without thinking, she spun around, shoved at the convenience store door, dropping her ice cream cone in order to push Janny to the ground.

Janny's screams rang in her ears as bullets smashed into the men and through the plate-glass window. She saw the Korean woman's fearful face before her own face smashed into the floor. She smelled ripe fruit, shoe polish, and licorice. Fear made her roll over. She felt rather than saw Janny scramble over her, shrieking, or maybe it was Mrs. Ky shrieking. She thought her heart would pound itself right out of her chest.

Both young women cowered back against a metal rack of Lay's potato chips. Everywhere she looked she saw blood. She forced herself to look at the two prone men in the doorway. "Call the police!" she screeched. "Now! Do it now, Mrs. Ky! Nine-one-one! Hurry!"

"Oh my God!" Janny said, smashing herself against the metal rack. She felt it digging into her back, but didn't care. "We were almost killed. If you hadn't shoved me out of the way we'd be dead. Dead! Do you hear me, Maddie, we'd be dead! Now I owe you for that too!"

"Shut up, Janny. You would have done the same thing for me. I saw the guns. I didn't know bullets made such big holes. I never saw so much blood."

"Oh my God, it's all over my clothes. Yours too. We have to throw away these clothes," Janny babbled shrilly.

Behind the counter Mrs. Ky was crying into her hands. Maddie forced herself to inch away from the potato chip rack toward Mrs. Ky. For the first time she saw the little cakes on the rack, Twinkies, Ring-Dings and Sno Balls. She liked all of them. Anything with sugar was her favorite. She smelled the overripe fruit and licorice again and wondered where it came from. Maybe a cleaning solution, since no fruit was sold in the store. Later on she would ask. She was in shock, she thought, as she stumbled to her feet.

Behind the counter with her arms wrapped around Mrs. Ky, Maddie stared at the bodies in the doorway.

"This is murder," Janny gasped. "We witnessed a murder! Merrill Lynch isn't going to like this. We'll be on the front page of tomorrow's paper. Think about your store, Maddie. You'll get all those looky-looks. Oh, God!" Whatever else she was about to say was cut short when a police car screeched to the curb. A second police car followed, and then a third with an ambulance, its siren blasting, double parking next to the first police car.

The women huddled together in fear as the police swooped into the small store.

"Someone tell me what happened," a uniformed officer said gently.

Maddie spoke haltingly. "We were leaving. . . . This car . . . was going slow, the window was down. . . . It was so hot, I remember thinking . . . I can't remember what I thought. . . . I think the two . . . the two men were coming into the store. . . . I saw the gun . . . two guns. . . . I dropped my ice cream and . . ."

"She pushed me out of the way and saved my life," Janny said hysterically.

"Did you see the person with the gun?"

"Very clearly," Maddie said. The moment the words were out of her mouth she was sorry. Her life was changing, right here in front of her eyes.

"What about you, miss?" the officer said, addressing Janny.

"I saw him. He had lots of hair. It all happened so fast. Blood splattered everywhere. I thought the broken glass was going to gouge us."

"Ma'am," the officer said to Mrs. Ky, "did you see anything?"

"No, I see nothing. I see nothing outside, only two mens fall down. Much blood. Too much blood. My husband go home to sleep. We open all night. He much tired. Is okay if I go fetch him?"

"Not right this minute. We have to take your statements. I

want you to stay right where you are until Detective Nester gets here. Try and remember everything you saw, the minutes before it happened, when it was over, everything, no matter how unimportant it might seem to you."

"Who can think at a time like this?" Janny cried.

"It's going to be all right, Mrs. Ky," Maddie said. "They'll let you fetch your husband soon. They have to . . . to do all these things. This," she said, remembering words she'd read in newspaper articles, "is a crime scene now. We can't move. They have to make chalk marks and put up a yellow tape or . . . or something. Why don't we make some fresh coffee for the officers. It's something to do," she concluded lamely.

"It's a dumb idea," Janny muttered. "They're . . . stiffs now. When someone gets killed like this, they call them stiffs."

"Are they gangsters?" Mrs. Ky whispered.

Maddie looked at Janny. Gangsters meant crime families and underworld figures. "Oh God," she said.

"It was a rub out," Janny said hysterically. "They saw us. We saw them. We should have lied. Why didn't we lie?"

"We aren't liars, that's why. You're supposed to tell the truth when something like this happens. Well, you are," Maddie said defensively when she saw the look of disbelief on her friend's face.

"We're dead meat!" Janny said dramatically.

"Stop it this instant, Janny. You're scaring Mrs. Ky to death. I mean, you're scaring her witless."

A man in plainclothes entered the store. "Ladies, I'm Detective Nester. Is there a back door?" he asked. "I'd like us to go outside and talk."

Maddie's first thought was, He's so ordinary looking. How could someone so ordinary handle this mess? Then she looked at his eyes and changed her mind. Sandy hair, brown eyes, no distinguishing marks on his face, mustache. A little character there, she thought. Someone ironed his shirts; there was a crease in the sleeves. He was hot and sweaty, but he was still wearing a tie. He towered over them, six-feet-four, maybe -five. He looked like he either worked out or ran. Like Pete. "Do you run?" she asked, and didn't know why she'd asked such a silly question.

"Five miles every morning." He didn't seem to think it was a strange question at all. "After you, ladies."

The hot, humid air slapped at them when they walked out to the walled-in space behind the small store. Maddie's jaw started to throb. She leaned up against a trash can, Janny on her right, Mrs. Ky on her left.

"Now, tell me everything," Nester said quietly.

They were all dripping sweat when the detective ushered them back inside the store. Maddie almost collapsed with the blast of cold air. She asked for aspirin and gulped down four of them. The bodies were gone.

Nester motioned to two of the uniformed cops. "Sanders, you take Mrs. Ky to her apartment, bring the husband back. Seal off this store entirely. You and Mendel stay here until you're relieved."

"What about us?" Janny asked.

"I have to take you downtown. You agreed to look at the mug books. We'll bring you back."

"Can't we change our clothes?" Janny asked. "Look at us . . . I want to take a shower. Maddie's in a lot of pain. . . . Can't we do it tomorrow?"

Maddie shook her head. "I can't do it tomorrow. I'm having my grand opening. Look," she said to the detective, "Janny's right, we need to . . . change our clothes. You can have one of the officers wait for us while we change." The detective nodded when he heard the stubbornness in her tone.

A crowd was gathered outside when a young officer named Melas escorted the girls around the corner to Maddie's apartment.

Tillie greeted them at the door, arched her back and hissed her disapproval at the officer's shiny black shoes. "She doesn't like men," Maddie said tightly. She bent down to pick up the angry cat and marched to her room, Janny trailing behind her. She closed the door and started to rip at her clothes. "They go in the trash. I'm never going to wear them again."

"Blood doesn't come out," Janny said, by now having regained her usual composure. "Sometimes with seltzer it will, or is that club soda?" Janny's clothes landed on top of Maddie's. "You take a shower first. I'll find us some clothes to wear." She looked at the answering machine. "Shit! I bet Pete called while we were out." She pressed the message button. She closed her eyes when she heard Pete's warm, dear voice.

"Hi, honey. Guess you're not home. Stupid me, it's Sunday afternoon. Bet you're at the store with Janny or out seeing a movie. I miss you. If I eat one more wonton, I'm going to explode. Everything is going great on this end. I just wanted to call and wish you luck tomorrow. I know you'll be beating off customers with a stick. Make lots of money so I can quit and you can support me. I'll try and call tomorrow night to see how the grand opening went. I love you, Maddie. I can't believe I found you in New York with all those thousands of people. I can't wait to see you. I dream about you every night. Hiss at Tillie for me. Tell her I miss her too, and say hello to Janny. Love you, Maddie."

Tears dripped down Maddie's cheek. "I love you too, Pete," she muttered. She was still crying when Janny came out of the bathroom wrapped in one of Pete's blue fluffy towels.

"Your turn," Janny said. "Was it Pete? Guess so by the tears on your face."

"We'll get through this," Maddie said, then took her turn in the shower.

While the water pelted her, however, Maddie cried again. She needed to talk to Pete. Pete was a lawyer, but then so was his uncle, Leo Sorenson. When they got back from the police station, she'd call him to see if he knew how to reach Pete. She felt better almost immediately.

For hours they looked through mug books and drank bitter, black coffee that tasted like farmyard mud. At seven o'clock they ate a dry corned beef sandwich and two pickles, compliments of the NYPD.

"One more hour, Detective, then I'm calling it quits," Maddie said at eleven o'clock. "I have a store to open tomorrow."

"That goes for me too," Janny grumbled. "Maybe the men were from out of town or something."

"Keep looking, ladies," Nester said quietly. "This might surprise you, but I haven't seen my kids in two days. I leave before they get up and get home after they're asleep."

At twenty minutes past eleven Maddie's eyebrows shot backward to meet her hairline. She nudged Janny and pointed.

"It's him," Janny squealed. "Look, here's the other one. Look at all that hair. I knew he had a lot of hair. Maybe it's a wig or one of those pieces men glue on their heads. They call them rugs or . . . something."

Nester leaned over to peer at the pictures. "Big-time, ladies. Real big-time."

"What does that mean?" Maddie asked nervously.

"Hoods. They have a godfather that protects them."

"Who's going to protect us?" Maddie demanded hotly.

Nester's face showed disgust. "The police, that's who."

"Against a crime family, the underworld?" Janny said. "Those people kill people *in prison.* If you think I'm going to . . . to finger . . . crooks, you have another thought coming. That sandwich and coffee doesn't buy you anything. Not with me it doesn't," Janny sputtered.

"Ladies, ladies, you watch too much television. You don't seriously expect me to believe you'd let two thugs gun down two innocent people, smash up an innocent woman's store, and not do anything about it, do you?"

"I think Janny is right, Detective Nester. I . . . I really don't want to get involved. We told you who they are, you take it from there."

"It doesn't work that way," Nester said quietly. "If you don't help us, they walk free. They go unpunished. Do you want that to happen?"

"Of course not," Janny said, "but I'm selfish enough not to want to put my life on the line either."

"You'll be under police protection."

"That thought doesn't comfort me very much," Maddie said. "Who were the men who were killed?"

"Underlings," Nester said. He watched Maddie carefully, his instinct warning him her decision would be her friend's decision.

Maddie thought about her life, Pete, and the new store. It would all be disrupted if she did what this man wanted. She thought about the house in Connecticut and making love with Pete in front of the fireplace. "I agree with Janny." She got up, stretched her neck muscles, her eyes on her friend. "I want to go home now," she said firmly.

Janny's eyes thanked her. "Me too." She scurried alongside her friend for support, half expecting the detective to drag them back to their seats.

Nester loosened his tie. He jerked at it and then pulled it over his head. He tossed it on the desk. It was a nice tie, Maddie thought. He was nice too. That and a dime wouldn't get her a cup of coffee anywhere in the world.

Maddie surprised herself when she asked about Mrs. Ky. Janny, her eyes round, stared at Maddie.

"Are you asking me if she'll be safe?" Nester said. "I don't know. She said she didn't see anything. I believe her, you believe her, but will *they* believe her? That alone should be reason enough to make you do your civic duty."

Maddie frowned. "Look, we had the bad luck to be in the wrong place at the wrong time. We told you who the men are. I'm not going to let you ruin my life. It's your job to protect Mrs. Ky. Us too," she added as an afterthought. "You won't do that, will you, unless we agree to do what you want? Well, isn't that right?"

"No, it isn't right. We'll do everything we can, but we aren't a baby-sitting service."

"Exactly where does that leave us?" Janny demanded.

"It means whatever you want it to mean," Nester said quietly. "Protective custody isn't so bad. We put you up in a nice hotel, pay for all your meals, give you twenty-four-hour bodyguards. After the indictment and the arraignment, we wait for the trial. Your testimony will put those bastards behind bars. You'll be sending a message that this city, that innocent people, won't put up with this kind of thing. It's so close to home, ladies, it has to make you think."

"I am thinking," Maddie said. "What happens to us after you give us the red carpet treatment? After the trial? How long will you protect us? Day, weeks, months? Years?" she asked.

"As long as it takes," Nester said.

11

By the time Maddie and Janny reached Fairy Tales, Maddie thought she would jump out of her skin. Janny, she noticed, had a noticeable tic over her left eye.

The smell of fresh paint, wallpaper, and new merchandise assailed her nostrils as she opened the shutters on the front window. Janny turned on the lights, bathing the fairy-tale room in a soft, mellow glow that mixed with the warm August sunshine. Maddie turned on the air-conditioning.

"There's not a single thing to do except say hello when the first customer walks through the door," Janny said. "I'll make coffee and you call Pete's uncle. We have a whole hour before you unlock the door. You could call Detective Nester to see if there's any . . . news. They might have caught the guys by now."

The rainbow-colored caftan Maddie had on swished nervously as she headed to the little office at the back of the store. She was on hold when she heard the front door tinkle. She heard Janny drop the basket of the percolator into the sink. A moment later she saw a flash of ginger-colored pants running to the front of the store. "It's Detective Nester," she heard Janny call over her shoulder.

Maddie listened intently to the person on the line for a moment. "I'd like to leave a message," she said. "Tell Mr. Sorenson that Madelyn Stern, Pete's fiancée, called, and I would appreciate it if he'd call me at the store or at home after six." She left both numbers. Why was she surprised to hear that the elder Sorenson was in court? After all, he was an attorney, and attorneys hung out in court most of the time. "Damn!"

Maddie walked to the front of the store, where Janny was deep in conversation with Detective Nester. She smiled when she heard Janny explain how a particular game was played. Nester was giving her his undivided attention. "I'll buy one," he said.

"The store isn't open yet," Maddie said stupidly.

"I wanted to beat the crowds. My wife told me about this store. She can't wait to get here to spend my money. I think you're overpriced," he said mildly. "Pretty upscale area. Guess the rent is high. My wife explained to me about markups. So, have you ladies thought about what we talked about last evening?"

Maddie blinked. "Yes and no. We're frightened, but I guess you already know that. I don't understand why we have to be scared out of our wits. We didn't do anything wrong, and here we are, looking over our shoulders, afraid to sleep, afraid to go out. It's not right and it's not fair."

"No it isn't, but that's the way it is."

"We pointed out the men. Can't you watch them? You should be able to arrest them without involving us. We need a lawyer. That means we have to pay out a fee, and we didn't do anything wrong. What kind of justice is that?"

"It's the system. I told you, you have to pick them out of a lineup. You can't just say someone did something and have the police rush in willy-nilly and arrest people. They have rights too. You witnessed a crime. It's your duty as a citizen to come forward."

"Who are those men?" Janny demanded.

"The shooters are Bull Balog and John 'the Angel' Naverez. The dead men weren't carrying any ID. We think they're top lieutenants of a New York crime family. If we can't make the arrests stick, they stay free to kill someone else. I guess you didn't see today's paper," Nester said, placing a copy of the Daily News next to the cash register. Maddie recoiled; so did Janny.

"Read the article and call me. I can have Angel and Bull picked up and schedule a lineup after you close up shop. Good luck with your grand opening," Nester said, sticking the gaily wrapped package under his arm.

"Bottom of page two," Nester called over his shoulder. Maddie shivered when he closed the double Dutch doors.

"We should have charged him double," Janny seethed as she ripped the paper open. She read aloud, the color draining from her face. Maddie sat down on the stool behind the counter, her face as white as Janny's.

"This is positively shitful," Janny exploded when she was through reading. "Mrs. Ky described us perfectly. And then saying we live in her building on East Forty-ninth, around the corner from the U.N. building—God! Does Mrs. Ky know your name, Maddie?"

"Not that I know of. I don't go in that often. Every so often I stop for milk or bread, sometimes the paper. Actually, Pete goes in more than I do. He buys canned salmon for Tillie. I'm sure I never told her my name. She's a very shy, sweet little lady. She calls me 'miss.' I've seen her in the elevator from time to time. She does know, if she remembers, I get off at seven. She's . . . higher up." Maddie's face closed up tight. "She knows . . . oh God . . ."

"Now, don't panic," Janny dithered. "She . . . won't tell. After all, she must know the score. No, she won't mention it. What reason would she have to do that? She'll just assume you told the police yourself. The paper doesn't say anything about what floor you live on. We're not going back there tonight, right?"

"Right," Maddie muttered. "Mrs. Ky's English isn't very good. Even if someone asks her, she might not understand. We can go to Pete's apartment. I have a key. We won't even go back for clothes. We'll make do with what we have. We can wear these . . . costumes tomorrow. We can pick up some underwear at an all-night drugstore along with toothbrushes. . . . No, we aren't going back there," Maddie said emphatically.

"Does that mean we're going to go to the lineup?"

"No. Yes. I don't know. Turn on the radio and see if there's any news. We should have listened this morning. Why didn't we?" Maddie asked, her face creased with worry.

"Because we're stupid, that's why," Janny said sourly.

"We're not stupid, Janny." She thought for a minute and came up with one of Pete's favorite phrases. "We're piss-ass scared. Damn it, this isn't fair. Our lives are changing minute to minute, and there's nothing we can do about it. I think . . . I think . . . we'll be safe at Pete's. His place is on Fifty-fourth between First and Second. He's on the ninth floor. We can use the stairs and go in the back way. There has to be a back way. I could use that coffee now."

It was seven o'clock before the women entered Pete's apartment. Two stops, via a cab, at a twenty-four-hour drugstore and at Chase Manhattan to make a night deposit, completed their day.

"For someone who's a bachelor and away a lot," Janny said, "Pete has a well-stocked freezer and cupboard. You name it, it's here. Does he cook?"

"Like a gourmet chef. Listen, they're rehashing the news," Maddie said, sitting down on the sofa, her eyes glued to the huge television screen on the wall.

"This is like being in the movies," Janny said, settling herself next to Maddie. She kicked off her shoes. She bounded off the chair a moment later when she heard Detective Nester's voice say, "Mrs. Ky dialed 911, but was unable to tell us what was wrong. By the time we arrived at the scene, both Mr. and Mrs. Ky were dead."

Janny slid to the floor as Maddie slammed at the seashell centerpiece in the middle of the coffee table. She watched as it shattered on the parquet floor. A moment later Maddie ran to the door to check the locks. She was breathing like a long distance runner when she returned to huddle on the floor next to Janny, who was crying into her sleeve.

"We're next. I know it. They're going to find us. Sure as hell they are. We should take all our money out of the bank and go . . . as far as we can. It's our fault the Kys are dead. How are we going to live with that?" Janny sobbed.

"It is not our fault. How can it be our fault? Maybe it's a little bit our fault . . . no, it isn't. It's Nester's fault. It's the police department's fault. Why didn't they give the Kys protection, like they said they'd give us? It's their fault. She didn't see those men. We were the ones who picked them out of those . . . damn dirty books."

"Maybe it's a warning to us," Janny cried. "The best thing we ever did was to come here. Does the doorman where you live know where Pete lives?"

"No, how could he? Listen, we have to think about this calmly and rationally and make a decision. One we can live with. Damn it, now I'm not going to know if Pete's uncle called. I have to find a way to get hold of Pete. I'll call around the world if I have to. The important thing right now is, we're safe. No one knows about this apartment. No one saw us come in. We were smart enough to get out of the cab a block away. We're starting to think and act like criminals."

"We should dye our hair, cut it, so we don't look like we do—you know what I mean," Janny said. "Maddie, I just had a horrible thought. Do any of the people in the building know about your new store?"

"Everyone," Maddie replied, sitting down with a thump. "Pete put up a notice in the lobby. He was so proud. We joked about it."

"Maddie, what are we going to do?"

"Janny, I don't know. I don't feel like I'm capable enough to make a decision right now. You have a say in it too, you know. All we did was go out for an ice cream cone, and now our lives will never be the same. It's not fair."

"Are you sure the door is locked?" Janny asked.

"Yes. There's no fire escape outside the window either. We're as safe as we can be. Pete has an unlisted number, so no one can call us. For now we're okay."

"What about Fairy Tales?"

"Oh, Janny, I don't know," Maddie wailed. "I just don't know."

12

The luxurious hotel room was starting to close in on him. Pete knew he had an acute case of cabin fever. Usually he was able to shake it off by going for a walk or doing some brisk calisthenics, but today nothing was working. Maddie's roommate Tillie would be a welcome companion at the moment.

Christ, he detested this business. He didn't know how it was possible to be so good at something he hated as much as he hated the practice of law. He hated the travel, loathed hotel rooms.

Where the hell was Maddie? He'd been trying for days to call her, and now the operator was telling him her phone number was disconnected. He hadn't really started to worry until he had the operator try Janny's number and was told that it too was disconnected. The phone number at Fairy Tales was temporarily out of order. What the fuck did *that* mean?

He should have been out of here three days ago, but one of the older Chinese refused to conduct business over the weekend and then said he wasn't free until tomorrow. Four whole days to do nothing but hang out. "Shit!" he said succinctly.

The uneasy feeling he was developing in the pit of his stomach had nothing to do with the bourbon he'd consumed. He was worried and wasn't sure why. Damn it, he needed to talk to Maddie. Needed to hear her voice. He still didn't know how Fairy Tales had done opening day.

Pete leaned back into the fluffy pillows. Nine days till his wedding. He was off schedule now by four days, thanks to Mr. Li Yuen.

No matter what, he was leaving on the twenty-sixth of August. No one was going to disrupt his wedding. No one!

Pete reached for the phone. He dialed a set of numbers and waited. His own voice on his answering machine hummed over the wire. Maddie wasn't there either. He redialed, and smiled when he heard Ruth Ann Gabriel's voice. Annie was his buddy, his pal, his friend, his compadre. He couldn't wait to introduce her to Maddie. He fired up a cigarette before he took another long pull from the bourbon bottle. He was to the three-quarter mark.

"Pete! Is that you? Where in the world are you? You sound like you're thousands of miles away."

He liked the chuckle in her voice, liked the energy she put into everything she did. Annie cared about him. She was better than two sisters. "I'm in Hong Kong. How are you, Annie?"

"Hanging in there, Pete. And you? When are you coming to Boston?"

"Soon. Annie, I need you to do something for me. I hate to ask, but I'm worried about Maddie. Do you think you can hop down to the city and check it out for me?"

"I think you just have pre-wedding jitters. What's got you so uptight?"

He told her.

"Okay, I'll take the shuttle after work—for you, Pete, at least this once. Do you have a number where I can reach you?"

Peter rattled off the Peninsula's number and his room number. He gave her Maddie and Janny's addresses. "Try Fairy Tales too. It's the store Maddie just opened. The operator said the number is temporarily out of order. She's been saying that since yesterday. I'll stay glued to the phone. Listen, stay at my apartment, no sense in you paying for a hotel room, and I'll reimburse you for the air travel. You are one in a million, Annie."

"That's what friends are for, Pete. Are you sure you're going to make it back in time for the wedding?"

"Hell yes, I'm sure. Annie, I'm sick and tired of busting my ass. I want out. I need a life. I need a year—"

"To surf, I know. The grand dream. You want to roast weenies on the beach, make love in the sand, swim in the moonlight, eat cold hot dogs and warm beer for breakfast. Find Barney. I remember it all, Pete."

"One of these days I'm gonna make it to Bell's Beach, and no one is going to stand in my way. And somehow, some way, I am going to find Barney. How about you, Annie? Are you and Dennis ready to tie the knot?" The silence on the other end of the line prompted Pete to repeat his question.

"Dennis told me yesterday, over a lunch of crab and champagne, that he would like a year away from me to be sure I'm the right woman. Something like that. He dumped me. It's okay, Pete, don't feel sorry for me. It's better that it happened now. I'd hate to have to go through a divorce. When I get married, it's forever. You know that."

"That sucks, Annie," Pete said angrily. "Dennis is never going to find anyone better than you. It's his fucking loss, you remember that."

"I have a question. Why don't you and Maddie go to Bell's Beach for your honeymoon? You said you always wanted to go to Australia. It was your dream, Pete. If you don't do it now, you might never do it."

"All we can manage is a long weekend. Fairy Tales, the new store, needs its boss, and I have some business I can't neglect. I'll get there, don't worry. Is business good? I wish you'd leave that schlock outfit and come work for me. We'd make a good team, Annie."

"Yeah, yeah, yeah. Seriously, I appreciate the offer because I know it's sincere, but I'm not ready for the fast track. I have my niche here and I'm comfortable. I have a chance to make partner early next year if I can come up with eighty grand to buy in. I'm thinking about it."

"Annie, it's yours, all you have to do is ask."

"I know that, Pete, it's the asking that's hard. Listen, I have to hang up and wind down things if I want to make that shuttle. Are you sure the super will let me in?"

"Hell yes. I'm going to call as soon as I hang up. Call me as soon as you know something."

After he hung up, Pete looked at the phone, at the empty bourbon bottle. He was just drunk enough to do something stupid like calling Dennis Morris. He acted on his drunkenness. The minute he heard Dennis's voice, Pete blurted, "You stupid son of a bitch, why'd you dump Annie? She's the best thing that ever happened to you!"

"What's it to you, Pete? Listen, I don't owe you any explanation. Just because we were roommates at law school doesn't give you the right to interfere in my personal life, even if Annie is your ex-girlfriend."

"Annie was never my girlfriend and you know it. We're good friends. For God's sake, she's like a sister to me."

"Sister my ass! She's been in love with you since the day we did our first moot court."

"You're crazy," Pete said uneasily.

"And you're John the Baptist. You know it, you just don't want to look it in the eye. I'm tired of living in your shadow. It's always, Pete said this, Pete said that, Pete's going to do this or that."

The uneasiness was growing. "You're off track here, Dennis. We're good friends, we got each other over lots of bad spots. She was always there for me, and I hope I was there for her. There's nothing else."

"Maybe for you there isn't, but try telling that to Annie. Do you know what she did when you told her you were getting married?" When Pete didn't answer immediately, Dennis demanded, "Well, do you?"

"No. We had a few drinks, but that's it."

"Yeah, well she had a few more drinks, okay, and about twenty-five other ones. The bartender called me from Kelly's and told me to come and get her. She was sloppy drunk, crying and moaning. She puked in the cab, on the steps to her apartment, and all over her living room. It was never the same after that. You ask me, it's your fault for being stupid all along about Annie Gabriel."

"Fuck you, Dennis," Pete shouted. He slammed the phone down so hard it slithered off the night table.

He thought about Annie then, because he had to pay attention to what Dennis said. Just because, in his opinion, Dennis was an asshole, didn't mean he didn't know what he was talking about. Was Annie in love with him? He had to admit he didn't know. She called him and he called her. Good friends did that. They stayed in touch, remembered birthdays, sent Christmas plants to one another. Good friends shared experiences and from time to time shared their miseries too. They consoled, congratulated, and . . . smiled through their tears. They loved each other, but they weren't *in* love.

Dennis didn't know what the hell he was talking about, Pete decided abruptly. Annie was a true, loyal friend, and Dennis couldn't handle another man in Annie's life. Well, fuck you, Dennis, Pete railed to himself. It's your problem. He dozed then, hoping he'd dream about Maddie, but it was Annie's smile that beckoned him to Morpheus.

Annie Gabriel stepped out of the car in front of Maddie's building. It was a doorman building, but there wasn't a doorman in sight. She walked around the lobby for a minute or so before she rang for the elevator. It seemed to be stuck on the fifteenth floor.

She headed for the stairs, her legs protesting the long climb. It was an old building with peeling paint and worn carpeting, but she knew the rent was outrageous. She checked the number against the notes she'd taken. Satisfied, she walked down the hall to Maddie's door. A white sheet of paper was taped to it. The message read: DUE TO FAMILY EMERGENCY, I'M OUT OF TOWN. There was no signature. She didn't know if it was Maddie's writing or not. Annie shifted her weight from one foot to the other as she wondered if it was possible to pick the lock. A moment later she had one of her credit cards in her hands. She jiggled it carefully. It probably only works in the movies, she thought, and then the door opened. She stepped inside and immediately backstepped.

Something was wrong here. With the weak hallway light filtering into the apartment, she could see wild disarray. Instinct told her not to venture into the room. She closed the door. Back in the lobby the doorman looked at her suspiciously. "I'm looking for Miss Stern," Annie said. "You weren't here so I went upstairs. Would you happen to know where she's gone?"

The doorman shook his head. "I haven't seen Miss Stern for three or four days."

Annie thanked him and left the building. She walked over to First Avenue and hailed a cab. She gave the driver the address for Fairy Tales.

What she hoped to learn in the dark was a mystery, but she knew Pete would ask if she went to the shop. She knew there would be an alarm system, so she wouldn't be doing any lock picking.

Twenty minutes later she pretended to be a window shopper, peering between the iron bars stretched across the display window. A dim light burned in back of the store, but there wasn't enough light to see anything in detail. There seemed to be no disarray here. Everything seemed normal. Passersby didn't stop or look at her strangely. After all, this was New York City, where no one ever, supposedly, helped one another or made eye contact.

She walked back to the waiting cab with the ticking meter and gave Pete's home address.

The super opened Pete's door for her. She switched on the lights and looked around. "Nice pad," she murmured. She wondered why Pete had never invited her here. Everything was leather and comfortable. The decorator, whoever he or she was, had used neutral tones to play up the largeness of the room. It was a two-bedroom with an eat-in kitchen and a formal dining room. An honest-to-God fireplace took up one wall of the living room. A giant-size television was set up on the opposite wall. When did Pete have time to watch television or build a fire?

The apartment, at first glance, looked unused and unlived in. She frowned when she walked into the kitchen and saw coffee cups and leftover coffee in the pot. In the bedroom, the king-size bed was unmade, a liquor bottle on the nightstand, plus two cups that looked like they held cocoa. She leaned over to smell the pillows. Two different scents. Not aftershave; Silence. She had a sample bottle. She couldn't identify the second scent other than the fact that it was light and flowery, definitely not aftershave or hair shampoo. Maddie and her friend Janny, whom Pete had mentioned. Maybe. It made sense.

Annie placed a call to Pete. He picked up the phone on the second ring. "It's Annie, Pete," she said, trying to make her tone light.

"What's going on, Annie?"

She told him.

"Maddie doesn't have any family," Pete said, "except a stepmother and stepbrother she doesn't get along with. Scratch that. Janny doesn't have any family either, that's why they get along so good. They were foster-home children."

"Pete, when you left here, what did your apartment look like?"

"Probably pretty messy, but Leona comes in twice a week to clean up. Did she screw up?"

"Somebody's been here. Your bed is unmade, and both pillows look like someone slept on them. There are a few cups and a liquor bottle which look like they don't belong in the bedroom."

"No, no, nothing like that. I left from Maddie's. I seem to recall a mess of my clothes in the corner, a pile of cleaning Leona usually drops off on her way home. Is the check on the dining room table?"

"There was nothing on the table, not even dust."

"Then Leona was there after I left."

"Is Leona the type to party with the boss away?" Annie asked cautiously.

Pete snorted. "Leona is sixty-five and has arthritis in both knees. She's miserably married to a no-good so-and-so, and doesn't have time to party. Besides, she doesn't have the key, the super lets her in and then locks up when she leaves. I pay handsomely at Christmas time for that little service. Something is wrong, Annie."

"I admit something doesn't seem quite right. It's entirely possible, Pete, that some sort of emergency came up and that Maddie, and maybe Janny, went off to do whatever . . . was needed." It sounded lame even to her. "What are the chances of you coming home early?"

"Not good. If I leave, this deal falls apart. I'm the cohesive. For some reason, these people like me. I guess they trust me, because they keep requesting me to handle the legal matters. There's no way I can leave right now. As it is, I have to make up four days, so that pretty much means I'm going to be working 'round the clock. Look, go by Fairy Tales in the morning and see what's going on there. Call me as soon as you check it out. Annie, I can't thank you enough. I'll talk to you tomorrow."

For some reason, perhaps to keep him from worrying more than he already was, she'd decided not to tell him she'd already been to the store. She'd go again in the morning. "I know you'd do it for me. 'Night, Pete."

Annie replaced the phone on the little night table next to a picture of Pete and Maddie. She picked it up. How pretty she was. How happy they both looked. Her eyes misted. "Make him happy," she whispered. "Please don't hurt him."

Because it was too early to go to sleep, Annie made the bed, carried the cups and liquor bottle to the kitchen. She washed all the cups before she made a pot of coffee for herself. She realized she was hungry when she looked into the empty refrigerator. The freezer was full, everything frozen rock-solid. She managed to pry loose a bagel and a stick of butter that she placed in the microwave oven to defrost.

Annie kicked off her shoes, unbuttoning her suit jacket as she made her way to the bedroom. Hanging on a hook behind the door was a striped velour robe. It must belong to Pete, she thought, sniffing, recognizing his scent. She slipped her arms into the robe and belted it. For a brief moment she allowed herself to nuzzle the sleeve before she padded back to the kitchen. She poured coffee, picked up her briefcase and went into the living room. She read the paper she'd picked up at the airport and curled up on the sofa. There was no way in this world she was going to torment herself by sleeping in Pete's bed. Once again she found herself wondering why Pete had never invited her here to this apartment. Oh, he'd invited her to New York often enough, booked her at the Carlisle and paid the bill, but never brought her here.

Dennis was right, she was in love with Pete Sorenson. Unrequited love. "You better love him as much as I do, Maddie Stern, that's all I can say," she muttered tearfully as she flipped the pages of the *Times.* She skimmed over an article about the U.S. suing General Motors for selling one of its cars despite knowledge of brake fluid leakage. Let some other lawyer handle that. She wondered if Pete knew Jack Nicklaus won the PBA golf title, and made a mental note to mention it. She skimmed through the *Time's* skimpy crime news, reading that two men were gunned down in cold blood on Sunday afternoon in broad daylight. "That's New York for you," she said. The woman who was an eyewitness to the crime was going to testify. "You do that and you're dead meat." In disgust she tossed the paper on the coffee table and turned on the television set. She watched what Pete called a shoot-'em-up-bang movie, not knowing or caring what she was watching.

Eventually she dozed, her face cuddled into the bulky sleeve of Pete's robe. Her last conscious thought before drifting off was, true love meant you wanted the other person to be happy, even at the cost of your own happiness.

At ten o'clock sharp the following morning, Annie stepped from a cab directly in front of Fairy Tales. She took a moment to admire the pristine whiteness of the double Dutch doors. Maddie had an eye for decorating. From what she'd been able to see last evening, Fairy Tales was a one-of-a-kind enterprise, just the kind of business Pete would be comfortable backing. It wouldn't hurt his bank account at all to be the husband of the owner. Always keep it in the family, was Pete's motto.

Annie walked into the store, her heart leapfrogging in her chest. She wasn't sure why. She looked around, mesmerized by the detail, the unusual merchandise and the childlike atmosphere of the shop. She looked up to see two women heading in her direction. "Hi, I'm looking for Maddie. Is she here?"

"Miss Stern was called away on a family emergency a few days ago," one of the women said. "Can we help you?"

Annie shrugged. "And you are?"

"Maddie's cousins," the second woman said, her gaze sharp and penetrating. "And you?"

"Ruth Ann Gabriel. I'm from Boston. Maddie's fiancé has been trying to reach her, but her phone has been disconnected. I went by her apartment and there was a note on the door. I need to talk with her as soon as possible. If you're her cousins, you must have the number where she can be reached.

"It must be serious," Annie said, looking around, "the family emergency I mean. This shop just opened on Monday." She smiled at the women, who regarded her stonily. They're cops, Annie thought.

"You came all the way from Boston to talk to Maddie?" one of the women said incredulously.

"Boston isn't that far on the shuttle. Pete is very worried. You being Maddie's cousins and all, you must be aware that it was Pete's money that backed this enterprise. I'm an attorney. I think

I might need to see something in writing authorizing you to be in this shop. Better yet, why don't we call Mr. Sorenson in Hong Kong now and straighten this out."

"We aren't authorized . . . Maddie didn't say anything about making calls out of the country," the second woman said. "And the phone has been out of order since yesterday."

"That's no problem, we can call the phone company," Annie said. "The phone company is real good about immediate repairs for business. I have a phone card. We can charge the call to my office or we can make the call collect. Why don't we do that right now," Annie said quietly. "Maybe we should call the police." *Let's see what you have to say to that.* "If you're Maddie's cousins, why aren't you at the family emergency?"

Three women entered the shop and immediately started to ooh and ah over the displays. They motioned to the two women for help. The "cousins" exchanged glances, but moved off to help the customers, leaving Annie alone.

They were cops, she was sure of it. She'd seen the little byplay when she'd entered the store, with one of the women's hands going to her hip in a reflex motion. Obviously, she was used to wearing a holster. A beat cop. Now what? she wondered. "There's something dark and brown here, Pete, and I think I just stepped in it," Annie murmured under her breath.

Annie continued browsing the shop, her eyes blurring when she picked up dainty baby outfits that were so exquisite it boggled her mind, as did the miniature price tags. The labels, Annie thought, were just as exquisite as the garment itself, handmade, created by the person who'd made the outfit. Distinctive.

She knew in her gut the phone wasn't out of order. Maybe she should leave the store, call Pete from a phone booth and have him call the store. The two women looked like they were capable of booting her right out. God, what was going on here?

Annie stepped aside as the five women converged on the wrapping table. She watched as merchandise was wrapped in confetti-colored tissue and then placed in shimmery boxes that matched the tissue. The boxes were then placed in oversized shopping bags with silvery strands of cellophane to add the final touches. A class operation. She winced when the totals appeared on the cash register. Twenty-one hundred dollars between the three women, who were still oohing and ahing.

The moment the door tinkled shut, Annie said, "Well, ladies?"

"We can't give out information and we can't help you," one of them said coolly. "We aren't making any overseas calls until Maddie authorizes it. If you want to call the police, you'll have to do it somewhere else. Now, if you don't mind, we have customers to take care of."

There was nothing for Annie to do but leave. Outside, she hailed a cab and gave Pete's address. Thirty minutes later she was on the phone explaining to Pete exactly what had happened. "I called the phone company, and they said the phone is working. Give me thirty-five minutes or so to get back to the store, and then you call while I'm there. Don't hang up till you speak with me."

Minutes later Annie was back in the cab, her mind whirling. Pete was so upset he was threatening to leave Hong Kong on the next flight. She'd convinced him to wait, to let her have one more try at the store. He'd agreed.

Now she was staring at Fairy Tales from the cab window. She didn't need to get out to see the double Dutch doors were closed and locked, the bars spread across the window. One woman was jiggling the handle of the door while another was trying to peer through the shutters. "I'll just be a minute, wait for me," she said to the driver. She dashed across the street and walked up to the women.

"I don't understand," one of the women said. "The store was open twenty minutes ago."

The woman who was peering through the shutters said, "Maybe they're out of stock. This store was jammed yesterday when I was here. I forgot my credit card and had my things set aside. I said I would pick them up at noon. It's noon!" she snapped.

Annie hopped back in the cab and gave Pete's address for the second time in less than an hour.

Pete paced his hotel room like a caged animal. He snapped and snarled as he lashed out with his foot, kicking everything in sight. He picked up the phone and roared, "Try that number in New York again. Let it ring until I tell you to stop." He counted along with the buzzing sounds on the other end. Thirty-three. "All right, operator, never mind, cancel the call."

"You have a call, Mr. Sorenson, shall I put it through?"

"Yes, damn it."

"Pete, it's Annie. The shop is closed. I'm back at your apartment. What do you want me to do now?"

"I've taken up enough of your time, Annie. I'm going to see about changing my plane ticket. I'll call the police from here. Annie, thanks a million. I owe you. Big-time. I'll call you when I get back to New York." There was an edge to his voice when he said, "Don't forget, you're coming to the wedding."

She didn't answer this, but said instead, "Look, I'm not going to say don't worry. Just use your head. Call me if there's anything I can do."

" 'Bye, Annie. Thanks again."

After he hung up, Pete called the operator again, saying, "I want to make another call to the States. Try both these numbers. Tell whoever answers the phone this is an emergency. I'll stay on the line."

Pete gulped at the scalding coffee in his cup, barely noticing that he was burning his mouth and throat. He continued to pace, the phone receiver glued to his ear. If anyone could get answers, it was his uncle Leo. He was on his third cup of coffee when his uncle's voice boomed over the wire.

"Peter, I hope you have good news."

"Leo, there's a problem. Not here, at home." He told his uncle about Maddie. "I need your help. If you can't get me some answers, then I'm out of here. You'll have to get someone else to finalize. Li Yuen is dragging his feet anyway."

"Peter, the consortium doesn't like talk like that. Now, tell me again, everything you know, and let me see if I can make sense of it."

After Pete told Leo what he knew, his uncle said, "It occurs to me, Peter, that your fiancée might have cold feet and is taking the easy way out. I'm disappointed, Peter, that you didn't see fit to tell me about your marriage before. I didn't even know you were engaged. I thought we were family."

"We are. Maddie wanted . . . wants it simple. Just a few close friends. I was going to tell you when I got back."

"You're running four days behind schedule, Peter. You cannot slough off this deal because you're getting married. You should have allowed for a delay. I don't think I need to remind you we're paying you a fortune for this job. You can't walk out on it. Do we understand each other, Peter?"

"Maddie is more important to me than this deal. I'll do my best, but I'm coming home for my wedding, you need to know that."

"As you know, Pete, the individuals involved in the consortium are powerful people. They like you, respect your business acumen. They have it within their power to break you if you cross them."

"All I do is broker deals," Pete replied. "Anyone can broker a deal."

"I'll see what I can find out about your fiancée and call you back," Leo said coldly. "In the meantime I suggest you get on with the business at hand."

13

Maddie woke with a blinding headache. She rolled over, pulling the pillow on top of her head.

"I thought you were dead," Janny grumbled. "You didn't move at all for the past hour."

"Were you going to check on me?" came the muffled response.

"No, I'm too sick. If you were dead, I was going to kill myself."

Maddie rolled over again and struggled to a sitting position. She cradled her aching head in her hands. "We can get up, dress, eat breakfast, and walk out of this stupid hotel if we want to. Nester couldn't do anything to us. So . . . this is a new, fresh day, and we have to decide what we're going to do. And when we make the decision, we have to stick to it. We cannot backwater. Once we sign those papers, we are committed."

"I can't think till I brush my teeth and have coffee. My mouth tastes like three-day-old dead fish," Janny said inching out of the bed. "I know, I know, we'll decide. I think we both know we don't have any other options, but if you want to talk it to death, that's okay with me."

In the doorway to the bathroom Janny turned and said, "Did we really drink that much last night?"

"Yes," Maddie said. "I have a very clear recollection of doing that."

"Oh God," Janny said, closing the bathroom door.

"Yes, oh God, You are the only person—being—who can help us now," Maddie grated as she got out of bed.

Later, clean and smelling of hotel shampoo and powder, the two women huddled in the room drinking black coffee and smoking cigarettes.

"I guess what I'm trying to say, Janny, is, I'm going to enter the program if . . . if they make us a few promises. Think hard now, what do you want to ask for? I know what I want. I think they'll make some concessions. If we're as important to the government as I think we are, I think they'll bend a little. We certainly have nothing to lose at this point. And we ask to be placed together in the Witness Protection Program." The program, they'd been told, would protect them up until the trial, issuing them fake names and IDs, and then afterward, if necessary.

The government people arrived at noon with bulging briefcases. Nester arrived a few minutes later. He looks tired, Maddie thought. She thought she could still see pity in his eyes.

Marshal Adam Wagoner droned on for forty minutes. Maddie listened intently. William Monroe from the Justice Department added a few words, as did Carl Weinstein from the FBI. When Weinstein finished, he sat back in his chair and motioned to Maddie.

"We understand," she said. "Janny and I have agreed that we will enter the program if you meet three of our conditions."

"No deal," Wagoner said coolly.

Maddie stood up and reached for her purse. "Gentlemen, you need us more than we need you. If we walk out of here now, we won't come back. Yes, we'll probably be killed, but we'll be who we are when we die. Yes, we have the guts to do it, don't think for one minute we don't."

"You can at least listen," Nester said quietly, his comment directed toward the marshal.

"We don't make deals," Wagoner repeated.

"Consider it a request," Janny snapped.

The man from Justice said, "Spit it out."

"I want your word, Mr. Wagoner, that when my fiancé returns home, you will let me speak to him. I know what you said about his uncle. But even if your suspicions are correct, and his uncle is 'connected,' as you put it, I don't believe Pete knows about it. And I'd want to ask him myself anyway. I want to hear it from Pete's own lips. You can arrange a phone call, he can tell me yes or no." Maddie held up a hand to forestall interruption. "Then," she said succinctly, "if Pete wants to join me, you will arrange it.

"Secondly, Janice wants all her Unitec stock transferred to her new name, whatever it turns out to be. We want it done today before we leave.

"Third, we want to be located in the same place. Together."

"Yes to the first two, no to your last request. Decide now," Wagoner said, towering over Maddie.

"But why?" both women cried in unison.

"It's too risky. I'm denying this request for your own protection. Is there anything else?"

"No," Maddie murmured. Janny shook her head.

"That's it, then. Pack your belongings. You'll be leaving here at dusk, possibly a little later." He held out his hand. Both women stepped back, refusing to accept his outstretched hand. "Good luck," he snapped.

Nester remained behind, the guard outside the door.

"I guess your promotion is pretty much guaranteed," Maddie said quietly. He nodded. "Will Wagoner do as he promised?"

"I have to believe he's a man of his word. I think you need to prepare yourself for the fact that Mr. Sorenson might not want to give up his life for you. You need to be realistic, Maddie."

"I know that. I can accept it if I hear it from him. We're both going to try very hard to handle this."

"I wish you both the best of everything," Nester said. "I'll see you at the trial."

"If the trial is successful and you bring down the . . . whatever you call those people, will we be permitted to leave the program? I forgot to ask that question. How could I have forgotten to ask something so important? I need to know that. Janice needs to know."

"If the 'threat area' is safe, I would think you're free to do as you please. That's just my opinion. I wish I could be more help, but the Marshals Service is outside my realm. They don't take kindly to questions. I can call and ask, and they can say they'll get back to me, five years from now. Think of it as your light at the end of the tunnel. It will be something for you to hang on to," Nester said quietly.

"Detective, what's your first name? We should know that, don't you think?"

The detective shuffled his feet and looked embarrassed. "Otis," he mumbled.

"Otis, if Pete goes to the police and asks questions when he returns, what will he be told?"

"I don't know. Orders haven't come down in regard to Pete Sorenson. I'm not lying, Maddie, I really don't know."

"But you know everything. Can't you—"

"No, Maddie, I can't. Look, I'm not your enemy, neither is the marshal or the Justice man or the guy from the FBI. We're a network pledged to keep you and Janny safe. We do whatever it takes. I'll see you around. You ladies are okay."

"Thanks, Otis." Maddie's hand shot out. Nester's eyebrows inched upward with the pressure she exerted. There was respect on his face when he left the room.

"Welcome to the Witness Protection Program, Miss whatever-your-name-is," Maddie said in a choked voice.

"I'm going to miss you, Maddie," Janny sobbed.

"Me too. I mean I'll miss you too. Now look at us, our makeup is all smeared."

Janny eyed their new police guard. "Is it okay if we go into the bathroom to fix our makeup?" The guard nodded.

Inside, Maddie ripped at the wrapper from a fresh roll of toilet tissue. She smoothed it out. With a pen from her purse she scrawled a written message: "If things get bad, put a message in the personal column of *USA Today.* Use the initials FT for Fairy Tales. I'll do the same. Once a month." Maddie looked at Janny, who nodded, then she continued writing: "Each time, give a number of your phone number, every Friday, until you give the whole phone number. I'll do my ad every Thursday until you have mine. After that, once a month." She looked at Janny again before she ripped off a section, threw the wad of paper in the toilet, and flushed it. She scribbled on the remaining paper: "Scratch everything I just wrote. We need phone numbers at phone booths. Same deal, every Friday for you. I'll do Thursday. Every Saturday, after we have a full number, you be at your pay phone and I'll be at mine. Twelve noon."

Janny nodded and scribbled: "That's ten weeks or two and a half months. Let's do the ad every day."

Maddie nodded, turned the paper over and wrote: "Eight hundred numbers mean no charge, no record on a phone bill. How do we pay? They'll check our mail." Janny rolled her eyes and shrugged. Maddie wrote: "I have the feeling I'm going to be watched a lot more carefully than you. You pay for both accounts if you can. If I can, I will. If you give them the initials, they'll know what to look for when we call the ads in. It's worth a try." She scrunched up the paper into small, tight balls before she flushed them down the toilet.

Janny used her index finger to trace words on the mirror. "We're breaking the rules and we haven't even started."

Maddie nodded. Her finger traced the words "I don't care."

Janny wiped the mirror with a damp washcloth.

Both women applied a slash of crimson to their mouths before they returned to the sitting room to finish watching "As the World Turns."

Hours later, sobbing and crying, hanging on to one another, the women hugged and said their good-byes. Tears streaming down her cheeks, Maddie waved wanly to her best friend as she was led away by four U.S. Marshals at seven o'clock. Twenty minutes later four more U.S. Marshals arrived to take Maddie downstairs and out to the waiting car.

Madelyn Marie Stern and Janice Hobart no longer existed.

14

Peter Sorenson stormed through the lobby of his apartment building. He felt like a wounded bulldog. He had jet lag, was hungry, tired, and needed sleep. He dumped his bags in the foyer of his apartment, ripped at his tie and suit jacket as he made his way through the dining room, living room, hall, and into the bedroom. His clothes, as he shed them, went into a pile in the middle of the floor. Seconds later he was in the shower, lathering up.

Jesus, he was tired, more tired than he'd ever been in his life. On top of that, he was sick with worry and fear. He was supposed to get married tomorrow. As he shaved he wondered if Maddie had called the minister to cancel the wedding. He'd have to check that out.

Ten minutes later he was dressed in a cotton Perry Ellis sweater, worn, comfortable jeans, and Dock-Siders. He raged about the apartment for another five minutes before he gathered up his keys, wallet, and headed for the door. His hand was on the phone to call the garage to send up his car when the phone rang, the sound vibrating through his hand. He picked it up on the third ring, hoping it would be Maddie, knowing it was his uncle Leo.

"When did you get in, Peter?" Leo asked, skipping the amenities.

"About fifteen minutes ago, and I'm on my way out. You should have the paperwork first thing in the morning. We'll talk later, Leo. There are no problems." He replaced the receiver, waited for the dial tone before he called the garage. Leo was probably having an anxiety attack, he thought.

He was lucky to find a parking spot directly in front of Maddie's apartment building. His own set of keys in hand, he walked down two steps that led to the building's entrance. The doorman recognized him and held up his hand. He eyed the keys dangling from Pete's fingers. "Sir, Miss Stern is gone."

"I know. I want to look around the apartment. The rent is paid till the first of the month, a month after that if the security deposit wasn't refunded. I have a key," Pete said briskly.

"I guess I can't stop you, then," the door man said quietly.

"No, I guess you can't. Did Miss Stern take her cat?"

"The cat is gone, sir," the doorman said. He was remembering the instructions he'd been given by the police. Do not volunteer anything. He liked Miss Stern, liked this man standing in front of him because he was responsible for putting the smile in Miss Stern's eyes.

"Did she say where she was going?"

"No, sir, she didn't. People are giving their notice right and left," he blurted.

"Oh, why is that?"

"I'm not supposed to talk about this, sir. The management company doesn't want me to talk about it either."

"Talk about what?" Peter grated.

"The double murder, sir."

"Well you just talked about it, so you might as well tell me the rest. I promise not to tell anyone you spoke with me."

"Mr. and Mrs. Ky were murdered in their apartment. They own the little store around the corner. Most of the tenants in the building shop in their store. It happened on the sixteenth, I believe. Ten or eleven days ago," the doorman said, wrinkling his brows as he tried to recall the exact date.

"Do you think that's why Miss Stern moved? Did she move or did she go away?"

"Her phone's disconnected. Her furniture is still in the apartment. I'm not sure, sir. I haven't seen her in quite a while."

"What about her mail?"

"I wouldn't know anything about that, sir."

"Has anyone been around here asking questions about Miss Stern?"

The doorman thought about the police warning, thought about Miss Stern and her possible involvement with the police. He wanted to tell the nice man with the worried eyes that *too many* people had been around asking questions, but his tongue wouldn't work. He shook his head, refusing to make eye contact with the attorney.

Pete waved airily as he headed for the elevator. When he reached Maddie's apartment, he looked for the note Annie spoke of. It was gone. He let himself into the apartment. It was cool and dim, musty-smelling. It looked the same, just empty. He recognized a dead basket of flowers as the ones he'd sent the day before he left. There was hard candy—butterscotch, his favorite—in the candy dish. A flat bowl of little colored stones they'd both been picking up these past months sat on the coffee table. Maddie liked odd things, and the colored stones proved to be a conversation gimmick on many occasions.

The cushions on the sofa had indentations in them. Maddie usually fluffed them up before she went to bed. She must have left in a hurry. Maddie was meticulous about housekeeping. She wasn't much of a cook, but she was the next best thing to a neat freak. At least compared to his own sloppy habits.

The kitchen was tidy. The red coffeepot was filled and waiting, and the canisters were filled with sugar, coffee and flour. She must plan on coming back at some point, Pete thought. If she were going away for good, she'd empty out all the food. He opened the refrigerator and grinned. It was almost as empty as his own. Chinese food containers were closed tightly, Italian foil dishes with cardboard tops, cheese, cold cuts, and bread were tied in Baggies. A bag of bagels and three apples completed the contents. The cabinets held staples and dishes. He picked up the receiver on the wall phone, held it to his ear. Nothing. He replaced it. It would cost more to have the phone reconnected than it would to keep the phone on. What was she thinking of, to disconnect it? He flicked the light switch and was rewarded with yellow light. Why disconnect the phone and not the electricity?

The bedroom was neat and tidy, the bed made, no stray clothing anywhere. The dresser was bare, with a light coating of dust, possibly powder. He yanked at the closet doors and saw clothing and shoes, a shelf with handbags and boxes of scarfs, winter hats, and sweaters. Two of the three suitcases were missing.

The bathroom was bare, nothing on the small vanity. No toothbrush. He opened the drawer to see if his was there. It was gone too. So was his shaving cream and the razor he kept in the drawer. Two towels hung neatly on the rack.

To Pete's inexperienced eye, it didn't seem like Maddie left in a hurry or was harried in any way. He walked over to the little rosewood desk to check it. He'd gotten the antique for her on her birthday. She loved it, would never have left it behind if she didn't plan on coming back. She kept her bills in it, her checkbook, and all her notes for Fairy Tales. There were pens and pencils, but no papers. He started to grieve for his loss.

Maddie loved him. He knew it, believed it. She would never go away and not tell him. Somehow, some way, she would have gotten word to him. Unless . . . she wasn't able to do so. They were supposed to get married tomorrow. He felt an ache start to build within him.

Pete took one last look around. Maddie would never have left the Red Skeleton clown picture behind either. It and the rosewood desk were two of her most prized possessions.

Pete sat down. He felt drained, like a rag doll, limp spaghetti,

Jell-O. All of the above. Because he had nothing else to do, he picked up the remote control to the television and turned it on. It pleased him. She must be coming back. Goddamn it, she had to come back. They had plans, places to go, things to do. They were getting married, for Christ's sake.

He was about to bang on the end of the table when he remembered the pain he felt when he'd done the same thing in Hong Kong. He picked up a brocade pillow from the couch and sent it flying across the room. Dead flowers flew in every direction, three of the petals sailing downward, ever so gracefully, to land on his knees. He felt like crying. And why in the goddamn hell shouldn't he cry? He was human, had feelings just like everyone else. He was supposed to be macho, tough as rawhide, able to weather anything. It was all fucking bullshit. He hurt. He ached. He felt pain unlike anything he'd ever felt before. No, once before . . .

Son, I don't know how to tell you this, but your parents, well . . . they're gone . . . to a better place, I'm sure. . . . You have to be brave . . . big boys don't cry. You're going to make your parents proud someday. How was it possible to make dead people proud of you? He didn't want to be brave. He wanted to bawl, to kick and scream. I want my mom and dad! Do you fucking hear me, I want my mom and dad! His dad was supposed to take him to California in the summer and teach him how to surf. His dad said that someday, when he was really good, they'd go to a place in Australia he'd read about called Bell's Beach. He said giant waves came in there every twenty or so years and it was his dream. My mom's too. I have to be real good, though . . . or I can't go. I never got the chance to even be bad, let alone good. . . .

Pete wiped at his eyes. He wondered what Barney would do in this situation. He was crying. That was good. *Fuck you, magazine writers who say men shouldn't present a weak image.*

Pete closed his eyes, willing his closed lids to conjure up the surfboard in his closet. It was the last present his parents had given him. On his sixth birthday, the year they died. He'd dragged that surfboard with him everywhere. Sometimes he stared at it for hours.

Leo didn't understand about the surfboard, and Pete had never tried to explain. Well, maybe he tried once when his room at the estate was being redone, and Leo wanted to toss it out. "Redone, my ass," Pete grated. "I was never fucking there, so how could it be *my* room?" He'd gone at Leo with all the gusto of a nineteen-year-old, kicking and shoving, gouging and bellowing his head off. He'd used words even Leo hadn't heard before. He didn't get to come home that summer. Instead, Leo sent him on a backpacking trip in Wyoming that was so arduous, grown men buckled and had to be taken back to the camp. He'd made it, though, by plotting Leo's death in a thousand different ways. He'd returned to Leo's palatial estate in New Jersey two days before it was time to return to Harvard to find a Jaguar convertible. Had he been properly grateful? Hell no, he hadn't. He'd told Leo to shove his Jaguar convertible. He'd never taken a second look at it.

He was twenty before he figured out why he didn't like his uncle Leo. To this day he still didn't know if the dream he'd had was real, something buried in his subconscious or just a plain old dream. In the dream he was four, maybe five, and he'd been playing checkers on the back porch with Barney Sims when he heard his parents talking in the kitchen. He'd heard his father say, "I'd rather pick shit with the chickens than ask Leo for a loan." At the time he thought it was the funniest thing he'd ever heard. Barney Sims thought it was funny too. Both of them had clapped their hands over their mouths to keep from laughing aloud. Then it wasn't funny anymore when he heard his father say, "I don't care if we lose this house and the car. I'll get another job. Marie, I love you with all my heart, but I will not ask Leo for money. I might not be able to buy you diamonds and furs, but I'll always make sure I take care of you and Pete. Just say you're with me, and no matter where we are it won't matter because we're together." Pete's eyes almost bugged out of his head when he heard his mother's voice, the voice he loved that had such a warm chuckle in it, say, "I'm with you, Albert, and so is Pete. But right now what's important is, where are we going to get the money for Pete's surfboard? We agreed we'd never promise our boy anything if we couldn't keep that promise." His father said, "I have some ideas on that. For starters, we'll redeem all those pop bottles in the cellar. You can bake and sell your strudels, and I'll do some lawn work for the people on the other side of town. Who knows, I might get a job in the meantime, and we can keep the pop bottles." His mother laughed over that.

In the end, none of that worked out. They got the money for the surfboard when his mother pawned a piece of jewelry, a gold locket crafted to look like a book. There was space for four pictures that turned like pictures of a book. His baby picture was in the locket, his parents' wedding picture, his picture when he went off to kindergarten, and a picture of the three of them. In the little box of mementos Miss Wardlaw gave him after the funeral, he saw the pawn slip for the locket with four tiny little pictures. He'd bawled for days and days. Miss Wardlaw thought it was because of the funeral, which was partly true. Every time he looked at the surfboard, he bawled his eyes out. Even now, to this day, when he opened the closet door and saw the board, his eyes misted over.

"Shit!" Pete said succinctly. A moment later he was on his feet. He didn't have time for trips down Memory Lane.

In the small foyer he caught a glimpse of himself in an ornate mirror. Jesus! He looked like something spawned from black, mucky water. He finger-combed his dark hair. It didn't help. He rubbed at the stubble on his cheeks and chin. He muttered another expletive. He wished he'd brought his shell-rimmed glasses with the tinted lens. At least they'd cover the dark circles and bags under his eyes. "I look," he muttered, "like an undertaker's client who can't make up his mind."

Minutes later he was in his Range Rover, heading for Janny Hobart's apartment. Christ, where were they? Maddie wouldn't take off on him like this. She just damn well fucking wouldn't do it. There was something wrong. He could sense it, feel it. Jesus Christ, he could *smell* it. He thought about the small packet of wedding invitations Maddie had made up for the few friends they were inviting to their wedding. He had one folded in his wallet. He knew the words by heart: *This day I will marry my friend. The one I laugh with, live for, dream with. Love.*

At Janny's apartment building he didn't get past the doorman. "She moved out," was all he was going to get from the bulldog countenance.

Back in the Rover, Pete realized he'd actually gotten more from Janny's doorman than he'd gotten from Maddie's: Janny moved out. Janny's studio apartment was furnished, whereas Maddie owned everything in her apartment. Janny was like family to Maddie. Maybe Maddie was helping Janny relocate or . . . something. Wise up Sorenson, he told himself. That would mean she's scratching her wedding to help a friend. No, Maddie wouldn't do that. Girls didn't cancel weddings. Not his girl. Never his girl.

The Rover ground to a halt, made an illegal U-turn before it speeded up and headed back uptown. The minister would have the straight skinny on what was going on. Surely Maddie had called him. Jesus, what if the man thought the wedding was still on?

Twenty minutes later Pete parked in a No Parking zone. He locked the Rover and sprinted across the street to the parish house. He jabbed at the bell, waited a moment and jabbed at it again. The third time, he kept his finger pressed on the glowing white circle. He thought the bell ring sounded like the beginning sounds of the Our Father. He must be nuts. Perspiration dotted his brow and upper lip. He wiped it away with the sleeve of his shirt. He finger-combed his hair a second time, the index finger of his right hand still pressed to the bell.

Finally the minister came to the door. "Mr. Sorenson, how nice to see you. Does this visit mean the wedding is back on?"

He looks so comforting, Pete thought. His eyes were worry-free, his smile genuine. He was at peace. And why the hell shouldn't he look at peace? Pete thought wildly. All the man did was pray to God all day. He wished that he'd been more religious in the past. "No. I don't know. I need to talk with you, Reverend."

"Certainly, son. Come in to my study. We can talk there. Would you like some coffee or tea? Perhaps a sandwich or a slice of pie?"

How kind and gentle he is, Pete thought. He looks like an overgrown cherub. "Coffee," he said.

The reverend chuckled. "I cultivate this image. It makes my work easier. Now, tell me how I can help you."

"Did Maddie call you, Reverend? Did she cancel the wedding?"

"Several days ago. It didn't sound like Maddie, but then, she was crying. Sobbing actually. I felt so bad. I wanted to go to her. I wanted to go to her or have her come here, but she said something that sounded like—and I'm not really sure this is what she said, but to me it sounded like, 'It isn't wise.' She thanked me for everything and apologized. The call didn't last more than a minute. It took me a few minutes to find her phone number, and I called her right away, but the operator said the number was temporarily disconnected. I then called her maid of honor, and the operator told me the same thing. For some reason, Mr. Sorenson, I don't have your number." His voice turned fretful at this declaration. Pete rattled it off, and the minister copied it down carefully.

The housekeeper, a plain-looking woman with a tie-around white apron, the kind his mother used to wear, set a tray down on the corner of the minister's desk. The mugs were thick, plain white with sturdy handles. A large plate was filled high with plump sugar cookies. His mother used to make sugar cookies that tasted faintly of orange and lemon. He reached for one, bit into it. Identical. "Does your housekeeper make lemon meringue pie, and does it have those little brown sugar beads on the top?" Jesus, did he just say that?

The minister smiled. "Yes, she does. When she isn't looking, I use my finger and lick them all off the pie. My mother used to swat me good for doing that. Martha's pies are the first to go when we have bake sales."

"My mother used to make a little pie for me. I always ate the top first. She made me my own little cakes too. I ate the icing first too. Maddie isn't much of a cook," he said ruefully.

"I'm sure she'll learn, and if you share with her, I'm certain she'll do her best to learn how to bake. What is it, son, what's happened?"

Pete told him, ending with, "It's not like Maddie. I know she didn't get cold feet. She would never let me hang like this. I don't know what to think."

"Have you been to the police?"

"I'm going there when I leave here. Maddie's not in a hospital. At least I don't think so. She did call you. She's with her friend Janny. I'm almost certain of that. First thing Monday I'm going to call Merrill Lynch to see if Janny quit her job."

"Does Madelyn have family here in the city?"

"A stepmother and a stepbrother. She never talks about them. To be honest, I don't even know their last name, though it's not the same as hers. If Maddie found herself in some sort of trouble—and I'm beginning to think that's what happened—she would never go to her stepmother. Janny, yes. They're both gone. I'm holding on to the thought that they're together."

"I'll pray for them, and you too, Mr. Sorenson. I'm afraid it's all I can do. If I hear from Madelyn, I'll call you."

"Thank you, Reverend, and tell your cook these are some of the best cookies I've ever eaten, next to my mother's."

"She'll be pleased to hear that, Mr. Sorenson. If there's anything I can do, please don't hesitate to call."

"Reverend, do I owe you . . . ? Someday I'm going to come back here and talk to you about . . . a friend I had a long time ago."

The reverend nodded. "Come to church on Sunday if you can."

"I'll do my best," Pete said. Outside, he realized he hadn't just given lip service. He meant it. If he could, he'd make services every Sunday from now on.

At the police station, Pete sucked in his breath. He smelled stale sweat, scorched coffee, cheap perfume, and Pine Sol. The six sugar cookies rumbled ominously in his stomach. He marched up to the desk and said, "I want to file two Missing Persons reports."

"Names?" the cop on desk duty said.

Pete cleared his throat. "Madelyn Stern and Janice Hobart."

The officer on duty leaned over his desk before he pushed his glasses up his bony nose. "Wait here, I need a second form. Take a seat."

Instead of sitting down, Pete paced. He stared at hookers dressed in fishnet stockings and spiked-heel shoes. It was true, they chewed gum. He felt a grimace build on his face. He listened to language so ripe, it exploded in his ears and turned them red. He turned from his frantic pacing to bump into a pimp with so much grease in his hair, it was dribbling down onto his thick eyebrows, giving them a glossy shine. He sidestepped the pimp, zeroing in on a conversation between an irate citizen and an officer who was listening intently to his explanation. "Those cruds ripped out my radio, stole my briefcase and were stealing my tires, and you arrest me! What the hell kind of society is this anyway? All I did was try and protect my property. I want a lawyer!"

"Sir, you beat the boy, you banged his head on the car. He has rights too. He's only fourteen."

"Rights my ass. If he's old enough to steal my radio and tires, he's old enough to take a beating. I didn't even see his face when I dragged him away from my car. As soon as I saw he was a kid, I stopped slugging him. What about my fucking rights? Do any of you fucking cops care that I'm sixty-seven years old? If that punk got to me first, I'd be dead. Well, what do you have to say to that?"

"You can make one phone call. Go straight back and take a seat."

"Amen," Pete said, then was ushered upstairs to a quieter office. "I'm Detective Nester," a plainclothes officer said from behind a desk.

"You want to file a Missing Persons report, sir?"

"Pete Sorenson, and yes, I want to file two Missing Persons reports."

Nester took four phone calls and was called away from his desk twice. Pete kept looking at his watch as his fingers drummed on the dusty, littered, detective's desk.

It was nine-thirty, according to the large clock on the wall, when Pete signed his name to both reports. "You aren't going to do anything about this, are you?" he said wearily.

"Why do you say a thing like that?" Nester asked quietly.

"I can see it in your face. It's my business to read people. I'm not saying you won't do the paperwork. I'm saying you aren't going to go out there and beat the bushes. You probably think she dumped me and didn't have the guts to tell me. Well, you're wrong."

Pete fished around in his pocket for his wallet and withdrew the crumpled wedding invitation. "Read that and tell me she dumped me. No, no, you're wrong."

"Do people make up their own sayings, or is this preprinted? You know, they give you a list and you pick one out?" Nester asked curiously.

"No, Maddie worked it out. She said it was exactly how she felt. I feel the same way about her." For one heartbreaking second Pete thought he saw pity in the detective's eyes. Whatever it was, it was gone a moment later.

"We'll be in touch, Mr. Sorenson."

"Sure, and tomorrow is a new day," Pete said, his eyebrows shooting upward in disgust.

"Are you trying to tell me you don't have a high opinion of the police?"

Pete deliberately eyeballed the detective for several seconds. "I feel *very* confident I'll find my fiancée before you will. Do you know why I say that, Detective Nester?"

"No, Mr. Sorenson, I don't."

"Because I'm going to work night and day on this. I'm not going to be bound by rules and regulations and shift work. I won't be sloughed off and I don't have two hundred other cases staring me in the face. I'm a taxpayer and I have every right to expect the best this police department has to offer. Think of me as an extra pair of feet and hands. I won't tire of this, Detective, you need to know that."

"Understood, Mr. Sorenson. We'll be in touch." He held out his hand. As a courtesy, Pete gave him a bone-crushing shake.

Pete felt Nester's eyes boring into his back when he weaved his way around the desks in his search for a path that would take him downstairs and out.

When Nester was certain Pete was gone, he sat down at his desk and called Carl Weinstein at the FBI. The moment the agent identified himself, Nester told him about Peter Sorenson.

"How much of a pimple on our ass is he going to be?"

"Think of it in terms of a boil, Weinstein."

"Listen, I don't know if you heard or not, but Adam Wagoner suffered a major stroke. He was taken to Walter Reed Hospital early yesterday. I don't think he's going to make it. He should have retired ten years ago," Weinstein said callously.

"No, I hadn't heard. What does that do to the promise he made to Miss Stern, that she could communicate with her fiancé?"

"Cancels it right out. You're to say nothing, Nester. Do we understand each other?"

"Yes."

The connection was broken. Nester stared at the black receiver in his hand. "Up yours, Weinstein." He yanked a file from the stack on his desk and slammed it down. He did his best to stare off into space, but Pete Sorenson's face kept getting in the way. "Poor, dumb son of a bitch," he muttered.

• • •

It was barely light when Pete crawled off the couch on Monday morning. He looked at his watch: five-twenty. He was starved and he itched. He padded out to the kitchen, threw a frozen steak under the broiler, then showered and shaved. He entered the kitchen in time to turn the steak. He brewed coffee, shoved frozen dinner rolls in the microwave, then sat down to make what Maddie called his infamous lists. He couldn't do anything without a list. He had lists everywhere, in the bathroom, in the kitchen, in his briefcase, in his hip pocket. He even had a list that listed the lists. His colleagues said he was organized. He called it bad memory.

His address book, the yellow pages, his legal pads, and a stack of pencils glared up at him. At six-ten he made his first phone call, to a colleague who sounded bright and alert, despite the early hour. "How's it going, Pete?" he asked.

Pete told him, then added, "I need a lot of favors, will you pass the word along? And I need the name of the best private dick in business. I owe you dinner and two tickets to the next Rangers game."

"I'll get back to you before I leave for the office." That would be in thirty minutes, since most of the lawyers he knew were out of the house by six-thirty and in their offices by seven, where they toiled till way past the dinner hour. He shook his head when he thought about the comparisons writers made between lawyers and used car salesmen. Every lawyer he knew worked their ass off, just the way he did, for his clients.

Pete checked his steak, punched a few holes in it to make it broil faster. The rolls steamed inside their plastic bag when he removed them from the microwave oven. He spread two inches of blackberry jam on the sourdough rolls and wolfed them down, one after the other. He was on his third cup of coffee when his steak was done, just the way he liked it. Maddie liked hers still on the hoof. He shuddered when he thought of the bloodred meat she drooled over. He spread spicy brown mustard in a thin layer, then a thin layer of ketchup, and last added A.1. steak sauce. He cut it all up, tossed the bone in the garbage, and sat down with his lists.

At exactly six forty-five the colleague was on the phone. "Write fast, Pete, I'm on the run. I've got motions, a deposition, two closings, and I have to somehow convince Judge Pettibone to give me a continuance on the Capricone business. What that means is, I don't get to eat today. Marcia wanted to fool around last night and I fell asleep on her. She isn't talking to me this morning. Ready?"

"Yeah. Why do you do it, Mike?"

"For the bucks, same reason as you do. I fucking hate it. I wish I was a truck driver tooling down the highways of life. Don't think I'm kidding either. Here goes . . ."

Pete wrote steadily, his own brand of shorthand. He thanked his friend. He made calls right up till nine o'clock, when he called a detective named Jakes and made an appointment to meet with him at a deli on First Avenue. His next call was to Annie.

"I need a favor, Annie, a big one. I'm almost afraid to ask you, but here goes: Can you possibly take a leave of absence and come to New York and operate Fairy Tales? I'll make it worth your while, and if they fire you, I'll get you a job paying three times as much as you're making, or you can work for me. I need your answer now, Annie."

"You got it. I'll be there early this evening."

"Annie, I don't know how I can ever repay you. I swear, I'll make it up to you."

"We're friends, Pete. You'd do it for me, wouldn't you?"

"Hell yes."

"Any news?"

"I'm working on it. I filed two Missing Persons reports last night. I'm hiring a private dick. I'm doing everything I can think of. If you have any ideas, I'd like to hear them."

"It almost sounds like . . . like they were . . . this is going to sound silly, but it sounds like they were spirited away by someone."

"I'm beginning to think the same thing. I'll see you this evening."

Jesus, what a friend, he thought after hanging up.

Pete's next call was to his uncle Leo. Unlike all his hardworking lawyer friends, Leo didn't arrive at his office until ten-thirty or so. Pete called the house and was told Leo had an early morning breakfast appointment and would be in the office by ten. Pete was sitting in the waiting room when Leo entered through the huge plate-glass doors.

He looks slick, Pete thought. He felt the urge to finger the material of his uncle's suit. He was blow-drying his hair these days. He'd never noticed before. He also had clear polish on his nails, a manicure. The tie alone cost at least three hundred dollars, but his shoes looked scruffy and unshined. The shoes and the plastic briefcase were so at odds with the rest of Leo's look that Pete winced. Hell, everyone had quirks. He had a few himself.

Leo Sorenson's office was plush. There was no leather anywhere to be seen, not even on the priceless books stacked neatly on the shelf, all cloth-bound. The furniture was deep and comfortable, covered in a rich, textured, nubby material that caressed one's fingertips. The carpet was thick and deep, covering the tips of his shoes and somehow working upward to meet the drapes in a continual flow of eye color. Maddie would call it a symphony of color, but only because of the slashes of brilliant paint on the walls that were framed in stark aluminium. Now, the early morning sun turned the greenery into long-leafed emeralds. Directly in Leo's line of vision, if he was sitting at his desk, was a medium-size fish tank with tropical fish of every color.

If I were a client, Pete thought, as he sat down across from his uncle, this room would intimidate the hell out of me. And it would make me want to put a rubber band around my checkbook.

Leo settled himself in his padded, woolly chair. "To what do I owe this unexpected visit?" he asked carefully, not liking the look on his nephew's face.

"I need . . . a favor. If you don't like the word 'favor,' help is what I need," Pete said quietly.

"Correct me if I'm wrong, Peter, but I believe this is the first time you've ever come to me for . . . help. I've often wondered why you kept yourself so distant from me. I never pried into your affairs. I guess the time is passed when . . . we should have discussed your grudges, if you had any. As you know, I never had a child, didn't know the first thing about raising a boy. If I made mistakes, you didn't say anything. . . . Why are you here, Peter?"

He's nervous, Pete thought. He doesn't like me any more than I like him. Somewhere along the way, after those first years, their true attitudes toward each other had come out. Now, instead of answering his uncle's question, Pete asked one of his own: "Why don't you like me? Is it because I look like my father? I know you two didn't get along. I still have the surfboard," he blurted. He felt childish, suddenly out of his depth.

"I know. I hope you get to use it someday."

"Don't worry, I will." He cleared his throat. "I know you have contacts all over this city, all over the world. I need you to . . . what I would like to ask you is, will you help me find Maddie?"

"I can try, Peter. I only work half days in the summer. Will tomorrow be soon enough?"

"Can't you make some calls today? You're a personal friend of Morgenthau, aren't you?"

"Yes," Leo said carefully.

"I filed Missing Persons reports for Maddie and her friend Janice. The detective I spoke with gave me the impression he wasn't going to bust his ass to go out there and scour the city. I was supposed to get married yesterday. Ask Morgenthau if he can come down on the detective, his name is Nester, and get some push behind him."

"And I could come out of this looking like a fool if it turns out your girlfriend took off and left you high and dry. I don't like to be made a fool of, Peter."

"She didn't leave me high and dry. She just opened a million-dollar business. Why would anyone in their right mind go off and leave that behind? You just don't close the doors and walk away from something like that. She would have left me a note. Maddie is an up-front person. I have this feeling she's been spirited away. Abducted is not out of the question here. She's god-damn gone, and I want her back, her friend too. The cat's gone too."

"She called my office," Leo said, "left her home phone number, and when I tried to return her call, the operator said her phone was disconnected. I was out of town for a few days when the message came in. She called a second time at my home, but I was out for the evening. She left the hotel number, but when I called it, the operator said no one was registered by that name."

Leo rummaged in his desk drawer until he came up with a wad of pink message slips. He licked at his index finger as he flipped through the slips. "See, here it is!" He handed the slip over to Pete, who looked at it, with concern. "And here's my telephone log. See, I returned her call and made a notation that the phone was out of order."

"So she was trying to get in touch with me through you. Now I'm more convinced than ever that something happened to her."

"You might be right, Peter," Leo said thoughtfully. "I'll call Robert this morning. I'm sorry about your wedding." Pete nodded, his mouth a grim, tight line. "Is there anything else, Peter?"

"No. I assume you were satisfied with the deal I put through."

"More than satisfied."

"Then you'll understand if I put any future business on hold for a while. I need to devote all my time to finding Maddie, and I can't do that with business hanging over my head. Besides, I'm burned out. I need a break."

"You take breaks and rest on your laurels when you're sixty-five, not when you're in the prime of your career. Business is business, Peter. A week off, but you're on call. The Midwest deal is heating up. You're needed. We've been working on this deal for three years. With your expertise, we might ace out the Japanese. You do have a contract, Peter."

"It has four months to run and then I'm out. It's time I learned how to use that surfboard. Don't push me on this, Leo. I've given you my blood and sweat for the past seven years. I've made you so much money, you'll never be able to spend it even if you live to be a hundred. Jesus, I don't ever want to have to come into an office on Saturday and Sunday. I'm sick and tired of ninety-hour weeks. Half the time I forget what day it is or what city I'm in. I make lists. Lists, Leo. I can't function without lists. What the hell kind of life is that?"

"A life with lists that gives you a very nice living," Leo replied, chuckling.

15

It was a nasty little apartment off A1A in Fort Lauderdale, Florida. The ancient kitchen was loaded with roaches. The walls were a dingy eggshell color, the floor covered with cracked linoleum. The padding on the kitchen chairs was ripped and held together with gray electrical tape. Bits of dry egg yolk and purple jelly decorated the aluminum ridge around the Formica table. The one window was so grimy, Maddie had to wipe a circle with a wad of toilet tissue to see through it.

Days earlier she'd refused to eat anything that came out of the filthy, ugly refrigerator that was painted pink. At one time it had been blue, and another time a dingy beige. She'd amused herself one day by picking at the peeling paint. That and counting the roaches was her entertainment.

The tiny living room and even smaller bedroom were horrors she didn't want to think about. She'd demanded the marshal guarding her go down to the strip to bring back oversize beach towels because she refused to sit on the furniture, since it smelled of dry urine and decayed food. She absolutely refused to sleep in the sagging bed, with its thin mattress and ugly spread the color of charcoal. The tattered edge gave testimony to the fact that the spread was once a grayish-pink floral pattern. It too smelled of something Maddie couldn't identify until the marshal said it was a marijuana sex smell. She'd bolted from the bedroom, to the marshal's amusement.

She was nervous now, irritable with the lack of sleep and decent food. She felt dirty and knew she smelled, but there was no way she was going to use the filthy tub, which seemed to be growing some kind of fungus.

"Whoever owns this place should be put in jail," Maddie muttered. "I've been here eight days. You said it was only going to be a matter of hours. When are we leaving here?"

"When we're told it's safe to leave. We've been through this a hundred times, Miss Stern."

"It must be a hundred and ten degrees in this place. Look at my hair, it's frizzing up, and we're *inside.* I want to move to a decent place. I don't want to stay here. I want a bath in a clean tub. Is that too damn much to ask? You people didn't tell me it was going to be like this. You said hours, not days. I want out of here. You said I would be given my new identity and taken away within hours. Do you hear me? Listen to me, I'm talking to you," Maddie shrilled.

"Miss Stern, I don't make the rules, I just obey them. You signed on, now you have to live with it. I'm sure it isn't going to be much longer."

"That's what you said yesterday and the day before that and the day before that. I *demand* you take me out of this . . . this fleabag. Oh God, there's a cockroach crawling up my leg. I want out of here," she said, swatting at the roach. "If you don't get me out of here, I swear to God I'll . . . I'll throw one of those kitchen chairs through that damn dirty window. Are you listening? You aren't keeping your promise. You said a few hours. It's now close to a hundred hours. I won't stand for it! You better listen to me," Maddie said, hysteria creeping into her voice. "You have no right to take me out of my environment and put me in this . . . this hellhole. You call somebody, and you call them *now*!"

"It won't do any good, Miss Stern. This is all a process, and you can't hurry up this process. You have to be patient. Now, why don't you sit down and watch television."

Maddie paced, wringing her hands, her eyes taking on a wild look. "Married people spend less time together than we do. Explain that to me." She didn't like the way she sounded, didn't like the edge creeping into her voice. "I feel like killing you and walking out of here," she blurted.

The marshal snorted, but his hands moved upward to touch his shoulder holster. Maddie saw the slight hand movement. Her shoulders slumped. She walked back to the kitchen to stare out of the window.

It was all going wrong. Nothing was the way Nester said it would be. Janny, if she wasn't in the same predicament, was probably following the plan they'd made and placing her ads in the paper and wondering why there were no ads from her. And Pete, where was Pete? What was he thinking, feeling? Did Adam Wagoner keep his promise to tell him where she was? There should have been word by now. Nothing was working out. She might as well be dead. Maddie Stern *was* dead. She tried to square her shoulders but failed miserably. She didn't even have a name anymore. If right now, this minute, she walked out onto the street and tried to buy something, she couldn't. Unless she had cash in her hand. She couldn't rent a car or drive it. Her birth certificate was gone. Maddie Stern didn't exist. Tears dripped down her cheeks.

Maddie stomped her way back to the living room. "You people are not keeping your end of the bargain. I did everything . . . gave up everything. I deserve better, and I damn well demand better. I don't believe anything you say. I'm leaving here, and don't try to stop me. Everything was a lie to get us to agree to go into this damn program."

The marshal stood up. Would he dare attack her? Maddie wondered. A surge of adrenaline rushed through her. She eyed the grimy door with its peeling layers of paint. She was in shape, but then so was the marshal. The two locks might give her a bit of trouble and she could lose seconds. She had to get out of this place, that's all there was to it.

"I can't let you do that," the marshal said, not liking the wild look in her eye. "Look, I'll make a call, sit down and let's discuss this."

"It's too late to discuss this. We've been discussing for eight days. I can't stand it. I don't care. You people lie, you don't keep your word. I don't owe you anything. If you try and stop me, I'm going to scream my head off."

The annoyance and frustration building over the past eight days erupted into anger so hot and scorching, Maddie felt light-headed. She started to mutter and curse under her breath as her pacing became frenzied, her sneaker-clad feet making slapping, shuffling sounds on the imitation wood floor.

She was in the kitchen doorway, her eyes on the round circle she'd cleaned with the toilet tissue that afforded her a view of traffic on A1A. The corroded toaster with its frayed cord and damaged plug drew her to the table. "Watch this, Marshal," Maddie said, picking up the toaster and heaving it toward the clean circle on the dirty window. She laughed when it smashed the glass and sailed through the window. She was smoking now, her smoldering anger no longer subdued as she looked around for something else to heave through the broken window. "What do you think of that Mr. Marshal?"

He bolted forward and wrestled with her, trying to pull her out of the filthy kitchen. "I think you might have hurt someone is what I think," he said as he struggled with her. "The police are going to be here pretty soon. Calm down."

"I told you to take your hands off me!" she shouted, and he backed off as she straightened and glared at him. "There was so goddamn much testosterone from the feds that day, I could god-damn well *smell* it! And this is the fucking result. Get out of my way, Marshal, before I do something we're both going to regret!"

"Miss Stern—"

"Stop calling me Miss Stern. I'm not Miss Stern anymore. You people took away my name. You didn't give me a new name. You promised me, you damn well promised me a new name in twenty-four hours. Did you give it to me? No, you did not. You're liars. My fiancé should be back by now, why hasn't someone brought him to me? Adam Wagoner gave me his word. All you people do is lie to me."

The marshal backed away from Maddie, a look of stunned surprise on his face.

"Gave you his word about what?" the marshal asked.

"He promised he would allow Pete to get in touch with me. Like all your promises, it hasn't materialized, has it?"

"Didn't anyone tell you about Wagoner?" the marshal demanded, a stupid look on his face.

"Tell me what?" Maddie snarled.

"He had a stroke and isn't expected to live. I thought you knew. That's part of the reason you're here. Things got screwed up. Right now we're all in a holding pattern."

"Maybe you are, but I'm not. Get out of my way. If you people are so damn inefficient, you don't have any business trying to protect me. Who in the damn hell is minding the store? Am I stuck here until Mr. Wagoner dies and they appoint a successor?"

"Look, sit down and I'll make a call. I can't let you leave here."

Rage, unlike anything Maddie ever experienced, ripped through her. She lashed out, kicking, screaming, and shrieking at the top of her lungs. The television on its rickety stand fell to the floor, the legs of the spindly table shooting off in the opposite direction. Maddie scrambled for one of them. She waved it menacingly as she danced around the ugly, smelly chair she'd been forced to sit in for days.

"This makes it a little more even now, doesn't it?" she said, waving the table leg wildly. It occurred to her at that moment to wonder why no one called or knocked on the door to see what all the ruckus was about. She realized it was the kind of place no one would investigate unless gunshots were heard or blood oozed from under the door.

The gun was in the marshal's hand, his voice quiet and placating when he said, "I want you to sit down, and I'm going to call my chief. Will you do that?"

"No," Maddie spat. "Call standing up. Do it now!" She swung the table leg, missing the gun in the marshal's hand by an inch. She stalked him in a crouch, her eyes murderous. She could see the worry in his eyes. "You aren't going to shoot me, so don't pretend you are. You people *need* me. You're supposed to be sucking up, doing what I want so I'll do what you want, but it isn't working that way. You have some major sucking up to do, Marshal, you and all those guys from the Big Apple, Justice, and the FBI."

Maddie's rage, which had begun to abate, rivered through her again. "Go ahead, make that call and be quick about it." She knew she was out of control and was going to do something terrible if her situation wasn't remedied immediately. She started to cry, her shoulders shaking, as the marshal made the call. Her grip on the table leg never wavered.

She started to scream again. "Tell that jackass you're talking to that it's at least a hundred and ten degrees in this cruddy room. I will not eat out of a paper bag again or drink out of a plastic cup. I want a bath and I want you out of my life. Get someone here or I swear to God, I'll break this leg over your head and then I'm going to get one of those *dull* knives in the filthy kitchen and slice off your balls! That gun doesn't scare me!" she shrilled.

Her tirade, she realized, had prevented her from hearing what the marshal was saying to the person on the other end of the phone. She whacked the cigarette-scarred end table with the table leg. The grimy lamp with its pleated shade teetered and then fell to the floor. The electrical outlet sparked as a puff of gray smoke eddied out to the center of the tiny room.

"Fire!" Maddie shrieked as she ran to the door. The marshal

dropped the phone, stuck out his leg to trip her, and still somehow managed to rip the lamp cord from the wall socket. Maddie stumbled and went down to her knees, her hand still clutching the table leg. She tried to roll out of the way, but the marshal was too fast for her. She saw his arm snake out, knew he was going to hit her. She tried again to roll, but the marshal's chair prevented free movement. She took the blow high over her left ear and appeared to black out.

"I hit her! Jesus Christ, I hit a woman," the marshal said into the mouthpiece. "You didn't say anything about hitting a woman." Sweat dripped from his face. "Now what?" he demanded. He listened, his face screwing up in disgust. "Since when do we treat witnesses like this? This woman is on the verge of a nervous breakdown, and no one told her about Wagoner. That's not right. She has a right to expect everything we promised. I don't like this, Bennett." He listened again. "I will not tie her up. I don't want a lawsuit. She's pissed, I can tell you that. I would be too if I was in her place. She's a goddamn human being. You want to sedate her, you come here and do it. The book doesn't say anything about tying people up and sedating them. I'll fucking quit before I do that!"

Maddie groaned, rolled over and puked on the floor. She tried to sit up, but fell backward. She tried shaking her head to clear her vision.

"Call me back," the marshal said. "Jesus, Miss Stern, I'm sorry. I'm really sorry."

"I told you, I'm not Miss Stern. You gave me a concussion. I belong in a hospital," Maddie whimpered as her stomach heaved a second time.

"I didn't hit you that hard. Look, I panicked, and I'm sorry. Let me help you. You need to change your clothes, you vomited all over them."

"It's all your fault. What did they say?"

"They're going to call me back."

"When?"

"Any minute now."

Maddie snorted to show what she thought of his response. "Get your hands off of me," she said as she wobbled to the bathroom.

The water from the tap repulsed her. The cold water ran warm and was light brown in color. It seemed to match the rust stains in the sink. She used almost a whole roll of toilet paper drying her face, neck, and hands. She tossed her T-shirt in the scummy bathtub and pulled a clean, wrinkled one from her bag.

Trembling, she sat down on the edge of the bathtub to sort out her thoughts. What had she accomplished? Nothing. Was she prepared to walk out of this cruddy apartment? Yes. Was she afraid? Yes. Petrified. None of this was right. She thought about Pete and Janny and started to cry all over again. The awful, sick feeling was back in her stomach. She had to stop vacillating and *do* something. She could no longer talk about it, think about it, or pretend she was going to do something. She needed to *do* something. She felt suddenly calm, sure of herself. "Anything," she muttered to herself, "is better than this."

The marshal was standing by the door when Maddie walked into the living room. "I'm leaving," she said. "I know you were trying to do your job, and I can accept that. Please, let me pass. Tell all those people I changed my mind. I heard you, you know. They want you to tie me up and give me sedatives. I heard you say you'd quit first. I don't deserve this. Please, let me pass."

"Miss . . . think about what you're doing. I won't stop you if it's what you really want to do. I couldn't live with myself if I did what they want. You need to know the consequences."

"I know them. Step aside, Marshal."

The marshal stepped aside. Maddie walked through the doorway and down three flights of stairs that smelled of everything under the sun and things that came from under the ground. Florida's August blanket-wet humidity slapped Maddie in the face the moment she walked through the grimy doorway that led to the street. The sound of the ocean waves across the street was music to her ears. The air smelled wonderful, better than any expensive perfume. She inhaled deeply.

Maddie looked around, seeing sunburned tourists carrying their straw mats, beach chairs, and plastic bags full of sun lotions. It was the most wonderful sight in the world. She smiled at a rosy-looking couple dragging two children who were just as pink-skinned as their parents.

People. Ordinary people going about their vacation business. A wave of giddiness rushed through her, to be replaced with a feeling of euphoria. She was *outside.* Walking down a crowded thoroughfare where no one paid any attention to her.

God, it was wonderful.

Maddie leaned up against the wall of a storefront to watch the busy vacationers. She knew the passersby were tourists, just the way she could spot the tourists in New York. In New York the tourists carried cameras and walked around with their heads stretched upward to look at the tall buildings. Here they wore flashy, colorful beachwear that reeked of newness. One man she noticed had a price tag dangling under his arm. A young couple passed close to her smelling of Noxzema and vinegar, supposed cures for sunburn.

Maddie waited until there was a break in traffic before she crossed the street. She ran up to the beach and down to the water. She removed her sandals and waded into the frothy water at the edge. How could something so ordinary be so wonderful? She was light-headed with feeling. She savored each moment. She would not ever, ever, take things for granted again.

She had to call Pete and find a way to place her ad in *USA Today* for Janny.

She flapped her arms and wasn't sure why she was doing it. She didn't care if people looked at her. She waded farther out into the water, up to her knees. It was warm, but cooling at the same time. She loved the feeling.

Pete. She had to call Pete. Pete would know what to do. He'd come and get her and somehow, some way, they'd find Janny. Pete wouldn't let them steal her life. No way, no how.

Maddie resisted the urge to look over her shoulder. She simply would not do that. She was *out*, and no one was going to drag her back. If *they* were going to kill her, let it be a surprise. Was surprise the right word? Maybe unexpected. Either way she'd be dead, so what did it matter?

Maddie waited for the traffic to slow before she raced back across the street, her sandals in hand. As far as she could tell, no one was paying attention to her. She looked, she thought, like anyone else walking around. On the strip she paused long enough to get her bearings. Her eyes were sharp in the blinding sun. The ocean roared in her ears, the salty air tangy in her nostrils. She remembered the smell in Mrs. Ky's store when she dropped to the floor, remembered the smell in the mean studio apartment she'd just left. She thought about rolls and rolls of toilet paper she'd used to dry herself with.

She was in front of a ricky-ticky store that smelled of mildew, new merchandise, and coconut-scented suntan lotion. She peered through the beach towels and T-shirts draped in the window, knowing it would be ice cold inside. In the transom on top of the door an air conditioner dripped water. She walked inside and checked the merchandise, which was the same as virtually every other shop on the strip. She passed up canned sunshine, cartons of orange bubble gum balls, and tables full of rubber-thong sandals. Cheap ashtrays and glasses, cups and plates, all emblazoned with the name Fort Lauderdale were lined up three deep on portable shelves. She knew stock was replenished at the end of each day. Tourists couldn't wait to buy cheap souvenirs to take home to family and friends. She headed for the back of the store, where the beachwear was displayed and picked out a dark blue baseball cap and a pair of oversize dark sunglasses. She also bought a long coverall in a rainbow of colors, to be worn over a bathing suit. She stripped down in the dressing room and put it on, ripping off the tags. She bundled up her hair under her cap, scraped the small white printing off the sunglasses, and hung them over her nose. It wasn't much in the way of a disguise, but for the moment it would do. On her way out she saw a huge straw bag with red flowers woven into the matting, and decided to purchase that too. Her purse went into it. Now she looked like any other tourist on the strip.

Outside, she walked aimlessly, looking in windows, trying to spot a pay phone. Her heart started to beat fast when she saw a blue and white modern-looking pay phone stuck on a pole along the beach. She crossed the road. In a minute she'd hear Pete's voice. The bills she'd exchanged for change clanked in the pocket of her beach coverall. She dialed Pete's number and felt lightheaded when his answering machine came on. Did she dare leave a message? Of course she dared, that was what this was all about. She waited for the operator to tell her how much change to deposit. She listened for the beep and then said, "Pete, it's me . . . they told me . . . it wasn't supposed to be like this. . . . They promised you'd get in touch. Janny and I believed . . . but only for a little while . . . I don't know . . . Pete, please, come and get me. I'm afraid. The marshal hit me when I tried to leave. I heard them say they were going to tie me up and sedate me. . . . I walked out. I'll try calling you again in a little while. . . . I love you, Pete." She choked up. "I'm moving around so they won't be able to find me. I have some money on me, not a lot. Pete, I didn't do anything wrong and they're treating me like a criminal. They say they're protecting me. I can't live like this. I can't eat or sleep. All I do is think about you and Janny. They took her away too. I don't even know where she is. That guy from the marshal's office said he would call you, and now they said he's dying. If anything happens to me, Pete, I want you to know I love you. Don't let anything happen to Fairy Tales. Keep it going, okay?" There wasn't anything else she had to say, so she hung up the phone. She waited a moment, and dropped in more change when the operator came on the line.

Maddie walked away, her eyes sharp behind the dark glasses.

God, it was hot. She needed a cool drink and some decent food. Sweat dripped down her body, but she didn't care.

A half mile farther down the beach she spotted another pay phone and decided to call Fairy Tales, hoping Pete might be there. She didn't recognize the strange voice that answered. She asked for Pete and identified herself.

"Maddie is that really you?"

"Yes, it's me. Who are you?"

"Annie. Pete's friend. He called me and asked me to come to the city and help out till you got back. He's combing the city looking for you. Where are you?"

"Do you know where he is now?"

"Out with a detective he hired to find you. Where are you?" she repeated.

"In Florida. I called his apartment and left a message. Will you tell him I'm trying to reach him? They have me in this . . . this program. I left. I'm on my own. How's the store doing?" she asked wistfully.

"Well, but probably not half as well as it would be doing if you were here. I'm doing my best to hold it together. Is there anything I can do?"

"Just tell Pete I called and I'll try and call him again."

"Are you all right?"

"That depends on what you mean by all right. I'm alive. I have to go now. Tell Pete I love him."

"I'll tell him as soon as I can. Take care of yourself, Maddie. Pete is worried sick about you. Maddie . . . are you talking about the Witness Protection Program?"

"Yes. I left it. I just walked out."

"Maddie, that's dangerous. Think about going back. They'll keep you safe."

"I can't do that. They lied to me. I have to go now."

She was crying behind the dark glasses when she entered a small restaurant. She sat down, ordered a cola and a full meal, which she consumed so fast she thought she would get sick.

Outside on the strip again she flagged down a cab and told the driver to take her to Miami.

She could get lost in Miami. She could also get herself killed. She didn't care. Right now she had the most precious thing in the world. The one thing most people took for granted, never thought twice about.

Freedom.

16

In New York, Pete headed for the busy delicatessen where he was to meet the private detective.

Simon Jakes was the most unlikely detective he could imagine. He was short, round, a one-size-fits-all kind of shape. He was dressed in walking shorts and a Fruit of the Loom undershirt. His Dock-Sides were older, more worn than Pete's. He was freshly shaved and smelled faintly of a woody glen. Sandy-colored hair curled around his ears and dripped onto his forehead. Pete guessed that the detective must have hated the curls, but had long ago given up trying to tame his wild mane. His eyes were sharp and piercing, his best feature.

"Pete Sorenson," Pete said, stretching out his hand.

"Simon Jakes. I'll have a pastrami on rye, double mustard, three pickles, a double side order of coleslaw, and coffee."

Pete flagged down a waitress and gave their order. "I need your help," he said to the detective as the waitress moved away. "You come highly recommended. They said you're expensive but worth the money."

"No two people put the same value on money. I'm good at what I do, if that's what you mean. I'm a graduate of MIT. I like to think I'm a bit of an electronics wizard. I have my MBA and I'm working on my doctorate. Something tells me you're either a CPA or an attorney. You have that look."

Pete nodded. "I'm an attorney, not that it makes a difference. My fiancée disappeared, and so did her friend. No, she did not get cold feet." He leaned over the table, made eye contact and started to talk. Jakes's eyes never wavered.

"I want you full-time on this," he concluded. "A bonus if you find both women. I filed Missing Persons reports. I had this . . . feeling the police were . . . sloughing me off. They had to take the report, but that's all they did. Don't you take notes?"

"Don't have to," Jakes said, biting into his sandwich.

Pete began eating his sandwich too. "I make lists," he said, and immediately wished he hadn't opened his mouth. Jakes stared at him over his sandwich. "In my business you can't trust your memory," Pete explained.

"In my business you don't put anything on paper," Jakes said. "At least I don't. Clients get nervous about things like that. I charge three hundred dollars a day plus expenses. Expenses can be high or low. Sometimes there are no expenses. I pay out whatever it takes, but I am always aware of my client's money. If that's going to be a problem, let's air it now. I'm not the kind of dick that calls for permission to grease someone's palm."

"Whatever it takes," Pete said, wiping mustard from the corner of his mouth. "Do you have any influential friends in the police department?" Jakes nodded. "How about higher places?" Jakes nodded again.

"I have a few," Pete said. "Let's call in our favors with the police. I have a feeling they know more than they're telling. It was this cop Nester's whole attitude. The guy didn't give a shit. That's not the kind of attitude a citizen is supposed to get from the police."

"Maybe he hates lawyers," Jakes replied. "Lots of people hate lawyers. Maybe you got him at a bad time. They put in a lot of overtime. I'm not playing devil's advocate here. I have some friends on the force and I know how it works. Do you have any pictures of your fiancée?"

Pete pulled his wallet from his hip pocket and withdrew a photo of Maddie he'd snapped in Central Park. She was smiling straight into the camera, her dimples showing clearly. He handed over a second shot of Maddie and Janny standing outside the apartment building. "I want you to find both of them."

"You're certain they're together?" Jakes asked, finishing off his sandwich.

"I think so. Check out the brokerage house where she works and see what they tell you."

"Then it's four hundred a day. I might have to hire operatives to run down possibilities where she's concerned. I can't be two places at one time."

"I told you, whatever it takes. Can you get on this now, after you finish lunch, and get back to me say around seven? My apartment. I'll even feed you. I have a friend from Boston who has taken over Maddie's shop. She'll be at the apartment, and I'd like you to meet her. She'll be our go-between in case I'm out checking something on my own. I have some office business I have to clean up too."

"I'll need an hour or so. I have to go back to my office and reassign some of my caseload. I charge overtime after six. Even if you do feed me."

"Look, Jakes, I don't care. I said whatever it takes. Just find Maddie for me."

"I like things cleared away up front," Jakes said, gulping what was left of his coffee. "Great lunch, counselor. I'll see you around seven. I'm partial to Chinese."

"Chinese it is." Pete found himself wincing when Jakes shook his hand. A moment later the detective was gone. Pete pushed aside his half-eaten sandwich and signaled the waiter for a coffee refill. Now what? He felt a groan starting to build in his gut. He needed to go home and make a list, but first he wanted to stop by Fairy Tales.

Pete paid the check and left a healthy tip for the overworked waitress.

"I'm going to find you, Maddie," he said under his breath. "Count on it." If it turned out she changed her mind and didn't want him, then she'd have to tell him face-to-face.

Four hours later Pete Sorenson listened to Maddie's message. She was alive and she was safe, for the moment. Jesus.

Maddie had every intention of following through on her plan to have a bite of dinner, pick up a copy of *USA Today*, and place her ad in the paper. A second call to Pete was number two on her list. Instead she showered a second time and washed her hair with the shampoo the small Miami motel provided. She turned on the television before she climbed behind the crisp, clean sheets. A moment later she was asleep. She didn't wake till noon the following day.

She was groggy and disoriented when she woke. In her life she'd never slept so long or so deeply. Even now she hated to get up because she didn't want to face the new day. She pulled the sheet up to her chin and curled into a ball. The soft whirring of the air-conditioning unit was comforting. The low voices on the television set made it seem like old friends were close by. She burrowed like a mole into the soft bedding.

She didn't like being alone because it made her vulnerable. Though more than capable of taking care of herself, the loneliness got to her. She'd put herself through college, got a good job, worked her way up to the position of buyer, managed to save money, and paid rent on a New York apartment. None of which was shabby. Pete always said he admired her perseverance, and it was the main reason he knew she would make Fairy Tales work. And it would have. She would have given one hundred percent.

Maddie showered, dressed, ate a huge breakfast. The moment she finished, she headed straight for the phone booth at the end of the motel building. She tried Pete's number for thirty full minutes. Each time she had the operator try it, she was told the line was busy.

Inside the motel office she asked for directions to a shopping center, where she bought a newspaper and some envelopes and paper. Before she went back to the motel, she called the 800 number of *USA Today* to ask for rates. She stopped at the coffee shop, copied down two messages for her ad, bought money orders farther down the street and some stamps. She mailed the letters feeling she'd accomplished something important.

At the motel she tried Pete's number. It was still busy. She couldn't make up her mind if she should call the Fairy Tales number or not. Pete should be sitting by the phone waiting for her to call. Instead he was talking on the phone. She wondered why that was. "Always go with your instincts," was one of Pete's favorite sayings.

She knew about Annie, Pete talked about her all the time. She was his compadre, probably his best friend in the whole world. After her, he was always quick to add. He admired everything about Annie, her quick wit, her super intelligence, her courtroom expertise, her humble beginnings, whatever they were. Annie's friendship was important to Pete. No matter what, Annie was always there for him, day or night. She'd never had the nerve to ask *exactly* what that meant. And, yes, she was jealous of Annie. Pete thought her jealousy was wonderful. She wasn't *really* jealous. She was more frightened of Annie, and she wasn't sure why she felt that way. Once she'd tried to explain it to Pete, and he just laughed and said, "Trust me, you are going to love Annie." In a pig's eye. Any time two women liked or loved the same man, it meant trouble and someone got hurt.

Maddie looked at the change in her hand. She had the operator try Pete's number one more time. When the answering machine came on, she hung up. Why wasn't he sitting glued to the phone? She started to cry as she made her way back to her room.

Inside she didn't know what to do. She paced, wringing her hands as a soap opera carried on with its daily tale of woe and calamity. The pleasant room was going to close in on her momentarily. She had to get out, enjoy her freedom and make some plans. Now. She should get out *now.* She didn't stop to think, didn't stop to use the bathroom or comb her hair. She slung the straw bag over her shoulder and walked out of the room.

Maddie walked back the way she'd walked earlier and then caught a cab that dropped her off on Biscayne Boulevard. She walked a few blocks and then hailed another cab to take her to Miami Airport, where she boarded a shuttle that took her to Palm Beach Airport. *Go with your gut instincts.*

She was almost afraid to look in her wallet to see how much money she had left.

In the airport, Maddie called the Chamber of Commerce and asked for the names of several small, inexpensive motels. She snitched a road map from the Avis desk to get her bearings, then moved on to the rental car pickup location. She waited until she saw a young man in his mid-thirties, then sauntered over, smiled, and asked if he could give her a ride to town. He obliged and gallantly agreed to drop her off at the first motel on her list.

Go with your instincts.

He was a salesman headed for Port St. Lucie, Melbourne, and Daytona Beach. When he finished his business in Daytona, he was going to stop in St. Augustine for a day to visit with his sister, drop the rental car off in Jacksonville, and fly home to New York. *Go with your instincts.*

"Do you mind if I ride along with you?" She blurted out a story she made up as she went along. Her tears flowed right on cue when she showed him the ring on her finger. "I have to sell it. He stole everything from me, my credit card, everything. I'm trying to get back home to Pennsylvania."

"Sure, miss. I'll be glad of the company. Bruce Holstein."

"I'm Jane Steinwitz. I don't know how to thank you."

"Hey, it's okay. I'd hate to have someone do that to my sister. I don't know what you're going to do when I'm conducting business, though."

"I'll walk around. It will do me good to see new places. I love visiting . . . churches and . . . local shops. Don't worry about me. When I get back home, I can send you whatever it costs for you to get me to Jacksonville. How many days will it take?"

"A day and a half. It isn't as far as you think. I'm visiting steady, old accounts that don't require a hard sell. I will have to take my sister out to lunch or dinner, though. You can come along if you like," he said magnanimously. Maddie demurred nicely.

It was a pleasant enough experience, Maddie thought two days later when Holstein dropped her off in downtown Jacksonville.

Maddie meandered down one busy street after another, trying to form a plan in her mind. The first thing she did was buy a copy of *USA Today.* She carried it with her into a luncheonette where she ordered a bowl of clam chowder and a cup of tea. She felt light-headed when she saw her ad and the one Janny placed.

When she paid the check she asked the cashier where the nearest library was. She needed to get back issues of the paper to see how many ads Janny had placed. She copied down the directions in a loose-leaf notebook she'd purchased back in Fort Lauderdale.

A bus ride later she climbed up the steps of the library. She looked around and headed straight for the magazine/newspaper section. Her heart thumped and bumped in her chest thirty minutes later when she realized she had a full set of numbers. Sweat broke out on her forehead and rolled down her cheeks. Did she dare call? Of course she dared. Nothing in the world could stop her. The sick feeling she was so familiar with of late settled in the pit of her stomach. For the life of her, she couldn't remember what it was they were supposed to do. It was supposed to be a pay phone somewhere, and they were supposed to be there at a certain time. *What time? Think, Maddie. Take your time and think. Get out of here, go someplace where it's quiet, where you can think.*

Maddie stopped to use the bathroom before she left the library. The small slip of notepaper with Janny's phone number went down her bra. As soon as she found out where the area code 801 was, she would know where Janny had been taken.

Maddie retraced her steps, took the bus that brought her to the library. When she got off, she was dripping sweat, but was so excited with the prospect of talking to Janny, nothing bothered her.

In the same luncheonette where she'd had the clam chowder, she ordered a tuna sandwich and a cup of coffee. She was in the last booth in the small but clean restaurant. Here she could shift her mind into neutral and think.

Maddie looked around and spotted the phone on the opposite wall. A thick phone book rested on the metal shelf. She was out of the booth in a second, flipping through the first pages of the huge telephone book.

Utah! Janny was in Utah!

Maddie swayed as her head buzzed. It took only a minute for her to realize she'd penetrated the oh-so-secret Witness Protection Program. In that one instant she felt more powerful, more in control than she'd ever felt in her life. She thought about Adam Wagoner and wondered if he'd really died, of Monroe from the Justice Department and Weinstein from the FBI. She remembered how they'd told her the program could not, absolutely could not, be penetrated.

Abruptly, she wondered if they were right about Pete's uncle. And then she almost laughed. They'd lied to her, they'd been wrong about everything! Why should she believe they were right about Pete's uncle?

Back in the booth, Maddie picked up the sandwich she didn't really want and started to chew. Her mind clicked as she chewed and sipped.

When she finished eating, she accepted one last refill on her coffee. She rummaged in her bag for a crumpled pack of cigarettes that was weeks old, lit up and looked around nonchalantly. The luncheonette was almost empty now, people lined up at the counter with their own coffee. A quiet time for the busy little restaurant.

This was nice, Maddie thought. Here she was, in Jacksonville, Florida, and she'd gotten here under her own power using her own ingenuity. They hadn't taken away her will or her mind. She knew Janny was in Utah because she'd listened to her instincts and made a plan early on. She knew if she could just relax enough, she would remember the details of the plan.

Maddie focused on the decor of the luncheonette. It was pretty in a cottage kind of way, with its black and white tieback curtains on the square-paned window. The place mats on the round, white tables matched the curtains, but had thin strands of red thread running through the material. Very pleasant and homey to the eye. Green plants in candy-apple-red pots lined the windowsills. Homey. Everything was homey and restful, and the service was excellent. Even though she couldn't afford it, Maddie knew she was going to leave a generous tip for the waitress.

She focused now on a domed cake plate housing a homemade carrot cake with thick vanilla frosting behind the counter. Thursday and then Friday, but for some reason that was tied into a weekly ad in the paper. They'd written on the steamed mirror and Janny wiped it off. Maybe she wiped it off. Eleven days. They'd been separated for eleven days, and Janny managed to get the whole phone number plus the area code into the paper. Utah only had one area code. Was that a plus or a minus? Lord, she couldn't remember what day it was. The beginnings of a panic attack started to form in the pit of her stomach. She couldn't give in to the feeling now, not here in a public place.

It was time to leave. Her best thinking was always done on the move when other things were under control. It would all come back to her, she just had to be patient.

Maddie paid her check at the counter, smiled at the waitress as she handed her back a quarter and took two licorice sticks from the crystal crock next to the cash register.

Outside she walked as though she had a purpose, up the street, around the corner, and then down a street to another corner. She refused to look over her shoulder. She was a free woman. When you were free, you didn't need to look over your shoulder.

Should she try to call Pete again or wait until she made contact with Janny? *Go with your instincts.* She paid attention now to her surroundings and looked for a drugstore. Drugstores sold everything and usually had phone booths. They were bright and shiny and smelled of expensive perfume and powder. Across the street, two doors down, she noticed a sign that said "Pharmacy" in bright red letters. She crossed the street when there was a break in traffic. Inside she bought two packages of cheap underwear and a package of men's undershirts marked Small. She added shampoo and a deodorant stick to her purchases as well as a comb and brush. When she paid for them, she asked for five dollars' worth of change.

In the aisle where the phone booth was located, Maddie waited patiently until two giggling teenagers finished their call. Lord, was she ever that young, that carefree? She felt like crying as she stared at the Revlon cosmetics lined up on the wall in little bubble packages.

Should she stay in Jacksonville or move on? She stared at a lip gloss that promised kissable lips the moment it was applied. She was tempted to buy a tube until she remembered there was no one to kiss her.

It was an old-fashioned phone booth with a metal seat. Maddie sat down and pulled the door closed. Should she leave a message for Pete or hang up when the machine came on? *Go with your instincts.* "Operator, if the answering machine comes on, I want to leave a message." She felt herself grow faint when she heard Pete's voice say, "Maddie, tell me where you are. I'm going crazy. I think I have a spin on what's going on here, but I need you to tell me how to get in touch with you. Maddie, listen to me very carefully. Do you remember where you got Tillie? Call them and leave a message. I'll be in touch. I love you, Maddie, more than life itself. I'll find you. I promise."

"Oh, Pete, I love you too. This is awful. I'll do what you say as soon as I can. I can't tell you where I am. I don't want them to . . . I love you, Pete, so much my heart aches."

Maddie left the drugstore, her purchases jammed into the straw bag. How long had she been on the phone? Three minutes? Calls could be traced in three minutes. If anyone was listening in on Pete's phone calls, they would know where she was. She had to leave.

This time Maddie hailed a cab and asked to be taken to the train station, where she again hovered near the rental car agencies. Her instincts or her sixth sense kicked in just as she was about to approach a middle-aged man with a worried look on his face. Not a good idea, Maddie, she cautioned herself. Time to hitchhike.

By using public transportation, walking, and taking one cab, she managed to get to the entrance of I-95, where she started to hitchhike. She knew it was dangerous, but she had no other options as far as she could tell.

Maddie pulled and yanked at the beach coverall until she had it over her head. She was soaked with perspiration when, after an hour of walking, a middle-aged woman on her way to Savannah, Georgia, picked her up. She learned more than she would ever need to know about Vidalia onions and green vegetation called kudzu.

The following day, after spending the night in a small motel in downtown Savannah, Maddie hitched a ride to Charleston, South Carolina. When she woke, she knew exactly when she was to call Janny. Saturday at noon. A day and a half to wait.

The bed was so comfortable she didn't want to move, didn't want to face the day and her uncertain life. She was going to have to give serious thought to selling her engagement ring. What she didn't want to deal with was Tillie's previous owner. How in the world had she forgotten to tell Pete that Mrs. Tillitson had retired from Bloomingdale's and moved with her husband and four cats to Texas, to be near her daughter and grandchildren? She'd been invited to Mrs. Tillitson's retirement party, had gone and had a wonderful time. Pete was in Europe at the time. There was no way for her to find out where Caroline Tillitson now lived. Pete was going to be in for a surprise when he called her old home in Queens. Would he go to Bloomingdale's and ask the people Caroline worked with for her new address? Would they know it, and would they give it out? She thought it unlikely. If she herself showed up in person, an ex-buyer of the prestigious store, maybe one of Caroline's closest friends *might* tell her. She knew they would never tell her over the phone if she were to make inquiries. A dead end.

Maddie rolled over and punched at the pillow. She thought about calling Nester to ask him if Pete had been to the police department asking questions. Annie said he'd hired a private detective. That had to mean Pete didn't know about the program, and obviously no one was telling him anything. Was his phone tapped? She snorted at the thought, then remembered Pete's message to her. Evidently he thought so or he wouldn't have changed his message. The question was, who tapped his phone, if it indeed was tapped? The good guys or the bad guys?

Maddie started to shiver and shake. What should she do now? Should she keep moving, or stay where she was until she spoke with Janny? *Go with your instincts.* Moving around was her answer. She yanked at the phone book under the night table and looked for a map of the United States. She ran her index finger from state to state wishing that she had paid more attention in her grade school geography class. Tennessee sounded good. No one would ever look for her in Tennessee. Maybe Kentucky. Or maybe she should try for Utah. She studied the states again. The only way she could get to Utah was to take public transportation. The ticket would probably be expensive. Did she dare? Of course she dared. But some changes would have to be made first.

Maddie hopped from the bed and ran to the bathroom. Dye her hair or buy a wig? Cut it? Both? A change of clothes, cheap slacks and maybe a windbreaker. Some sneakers.

An hour later she was in a discount store that sold just about everything. When she left, she had two shopping bags loaded to the brim. She rushed back to the motel, where she hacked at her hair until she was satisfied with the pixie cut. She bundled up the long dark tresses in the smaller plastic bags that she would personally deposit in the Dumpster when she left the motel.

She dyed her hair, and while the color was setting she munched on a bag of Oreo cookies. After rinsing the color off, she shampooed her hair and wrapped it in a towel.

She meandered out to the parking lot, where she called the airline from the phone booth and made a reservation on the four o'clock flight to Provo, Utah. She made the reservation in the name of Mrs. Andrea Monroe, and told the clerk she'd pick her ticket up an hour before flight time and would be paying cash. She went on to say she would be carrying her six-week-old baby with her, and no she didn't require an extra seat, and don't children fly free?

Back in the motel room, Maddie emptied out her second shopping bag. An oversize doll with a fuzzy fringe of hair stared up at her. She tied a cotton bonnet on the doll and then wrapped it in a blue blanket. If she kept to herself and didn't talk to anyone, she might get away with only a cursory glance from the other passengers.

The blue plastic diaper bag held two baby bottles filled with milk from the convenience store and a stack of Pampers diapers. She jammed as many of her own things as she could into the bag so she would have more room in her straw bag.

Maddie choked up when she remembered how hard it was to part with her engagement ring. She'd cried when she handed it over. The eighteen hundred dollars was safe in the bottom of her straw bag, along with the pawn ticket she knew she'd never be able to redeem.

She looked at her watch. At this time tomorrow she'd be in Utah trying to pass the time until she could talk to Janny. It was going to be a long night, with a stopover in Denver before she could make her final connection to Utah.

Three hours to kill before she could leave for the airport, where she could order lunch and walk around until her flight was called.

She paced, kneading her thighs with her fingers, praying she wasn't making a mistake.

Today she'd looked over her shoulder, paid attention to everyone she came in contact with. She hadn't seen anything or anyone that looked the least bit suspicious. No one had spoken to her and there were no footsteps behind her when she'd swivel suddenly to stare over her shoulder.

She felt safe.

The following day, after her flight, Maddie checked into the Holiday Inn a mile from the downtown area of Provo as Mrs. Penelope Barrister from Burlington, Vermont. She paid cash for her room, settled in, showered, ordered room service, and spent the remainder of the time sleeping and watching television.

At exactly five minutes to twelve, she exited her hotel room along with her make-believe child. Her body was shaking so badly, she thought she would drop the doll she was holding against her chest. By jiggling the doll, her quivering fingers located the stash of change she carried in her pocket.

God, Janny was going to be thunderstruck when she heard her voice, Maddie thought. She'd probably faint when she found out she was actually in Provo.

Maddie picked up the phone, the doll secure against her chest, dropped in her money and waited for the dial tone. She dialed the number from memory, waited for the operator, then dropped in more change. "Please be there, Janny," she muttered as she leaned against the pole the telephone was attached to. Her breathing was ragged, spurting from her mouth in hard, little gasps. "Please, God, please let her be there." The pay phone she'd dialed rang four, five, and then six times. With each successive ring, Maddie felt her heart thump. When it was finally picked up on the eighteenth ring, she was so dizzy her vision blurred. "Janny," was all she could manage.

"Maddie, is it really you? Oh, Maddie, Maddie, I—" Janny broke down, sobbing into the phone.

"Let's each take a minute to get ourselves together," Maddie said hoarsely, her own throat constricting with relief. When she was finally able to talk, she said, "Janny, I'm here in Provo. I cut and ran. I couldn't stand it. The place they had me in was so bad I couldn't eat or sleep. They didn't come through with my new identification and couldn't tell me when I'd get it. I blew up and walked out. They had me in Florida. I hitchhiked to Georgia and then to South Carolina and took a flight out of Charleston to here. I'm in *Provo*, Janny. Where are you?"

"Oh, my God, oh my God, oh my God," was all Janny could say. "You're really here!" she finally squealed.

"I'm here, and I don't think anyone followed me either. I bought this doll, pretended it was a real baby, and took a flight here under an assumed name. I cut and dyed my hair. I look awful. Oh, Janny, I had to pawn my engagement ring. I called Pete twice. They lied. I don't believe they contacted Pete, and I don't think his uncle is anyone to be afraid of. Where are you, Janny?"

"I'm in a small town called Saston, population 2223, if you count me. It's deadly. I'm not that far from Provo. If you're sure no one followed you, then it might be better for you to come here. I can't give you directions, you'll have to find out on your own. There's a café in town, if you want to call it a town, called Dumfey's. It has two booths and three tables. I'll be sitting at or in one of them. When can you leave?"

"Right now. All I have to do is pick up my diaper bag and I'm on my way. God, Janny, I can't wait to see you. How is it you can get away to use a phone?"

"Maddie, they brought me here, put me up in a boardinghouse for two days and said I had to find my own apartment. They gave me eight hundred fifty dollars and left. They said I'd be watched, but I haven't seen anyone out of the ordinary. I asked in town if there are any strangers other than me, and the local people say I'm the only new person they've seen in months. They aren't interested in me. I do have a case worker who checks on me once a week. My new name is Betty Gill. I'll never be Janny Hobart again," Janny said, her voice breaking.

"Oh yes you will. And I'll be Madelyn Stern again too. I don't know when, but we'll be . . . ourselves again someday. Let's hang up now. The sooner I leave, the sooner I can be there."

"Hurry, Maddie."

"I will. Just wait for me in case it takes me a little while. Promise."

"I'll wait forever. Well, until the café closes, and then I'll wait outside."

" 'Bye, Janny."

" 'Bye, Maddie."

17

"She called me, Jakes. She called the store too. She's running," Pete said desperately. He distractedly picked at the Chinese noodles on his plate. "Now what do we do?"

"Try and find her. I'm a detective, remember?"

"She told Annie she was . . . she walked out, in that Witness Protection Program. My God . . . did you find out anything, Jakes?"

"I don't have much to report. I checked out both girls' apartments. Nothing was left behind. Did you know," he said addressing Pete, "that a double murder occurred in Maddie's building?"

"The doorman at Maddie's building told me."

"Who?" Annie asked, her face full of shock.

"An Asian couple," Jakes replied. "They operated a store around the corner. Prior to their death there was a murder in their store. Two hoods. It was in all the papers. It was too late when I found this all out to do anything. First thing tomorrow I'll go to the papers and see if I can find back newspaper articles. This is just a guess on my part, but there were two eyewitnesses that Sunday afternoon when the hoods were gunned down. I'm not saying it was Maddie and Janny, but that's the way it looks to me."

Pete's legal mind kicked in. "If what you're saying is a possibility, then that means the police know something. It also means they lied to me. I'll sue the goddamn police department if that turns out to be true," Pete said viciously, his eyes murderous.

"And I'll be his cocounsel," Annie said spiritedly. Pete reached over to pat her hand, his eyes grateful for the support.

"I need more pictures," Jakes said as he shoveled the smelly Chinese food into his mouth.

Pete shoved the food cartons to the center of the table with the length of his arms. Seconds later Maddie's pictures were spread out so Jakes could view them.

"She's very pretty, isn't she?" Annie said, closing the carton in front of her.

"She's beautiful," Jakes said sincerely.

"She's beautiful inside too. Just like Annie here," Pete said, patting her hand again. Annie blushed furiously.

"How long will you be here?" Jakes said, addressing Annie.

She shrugged. "As long as it takes, I guess, or until Pete boots me out. I'm going to learn the retail business. You never know," she said lightly. "I might get tired of the law, and this way I'll have something to fall back on."

"There's no doubt in my mind that you can run Fairy Tales," Pete said warmly. "I wouldn't have asked you otherwise. This girl is one in a million," he said to Jakes. "Hell, I couldn't have gotten through law school without her. Someday some guy is going to be very lucky when he finds her. She's as perfect as they come." Annie turned crimson, but accepted the compliment with a smile.

"That was really good," Jakes said of the takeout meal. "Let's see what our fortunes are. It's the best part of all. Except for the food." The detective grinned wryly. He snapped his fortune cookie apart and withdrew the little slip of paper. "Ah, it says here I will meet a handsome woman who has grease on her sneakers and she will sweep me off my feet." He leered at Annie, who looked everywhere but at him.

"Mine says, it is not enough to persevere, you must prevail. Rather apt, wouldn't you say?" Pete said tightly. "Annie, what does yours say?"

"It says, you are almost there. These things are silly," she said, getting up to clear the table.

"So, what do you think?" Pete asked, jarring Jakes's thoughts.

Annie tossed the unused chopsticks into the trash basket. She stopped clanking the silverware long enough to listen to what Jakes had to say. *You are almost there.* Where? She turned from the soapy water to stare at Pete and Jakes.

"It would only be speculation at this point. Let's not beat a dead horse just yet. I'm going back out. I know a few guys on the force and where they hang out. I'll nose around and see what I can come up with. Thanks for the eats," he said cheerfully. "Nice meeting you, Annie."

"Same here," Annie said.

"You're coming back here, right?"

"Make up the couch, but don't wait up."

"Guess it's just me and you, fella," Annie said cheerfully. "We can watch some television, eat some ice cream, swig a few beers like the old days, and wait in case Maddie calls again."

"Jeez, Annie, I'm sorry. I'm going out too. I have people I need to talk to. You'll be okay here alone, won't you?" he asked. "By the way, I left a message for Maddie on my machine. Do the same at Fairy Tales tomorrow."

"Of course. Don't worry about me. I can eat ice cream and watch the pounds go on all by myself. This will be a good time for me to look over Maddie's business plan and make notes. I want to do it right. I don't want Maddie to come back and be upset with me, or you either."

"Annie, you could never upset me. I owe you so much. It boggles my mind that you dropped everything to come here and help me. I'm going to owe you big-time."

"Stop it, Pete. I know you'd do the same for me."

"You know what, Annie? You and I are like Maddie and Janny. We have the same kind of loyal friendship those two have. I want us all to be friends for all our lives."

Annie smiled weakly. "Go already, do what you have to do. I'll make up the couch for Mr. Jakes."

"Annie, I need to ask you something. Women have . . . a sixth sense—you know, intuition. Do you think Maddie is . . . you know . . . do you think they'll find her and do something to her?"

Love, Annie thought, was wanting the other person's happiness more than you wanted your own. "I think," she said carefully, her eyes on Pete, "Maddie is safe somewhere. I do not believe for one single minute that anything is going to happen to her. She's with Janny wherever she is, so they have each other. If there's a way for her to get to you, she will. Now, go get 'em, whoever they are."

"Annie, you always know the right thing to say to me." Pete kissed her lightly on the cheek. "No regrets about Dennis, Annie?"

Annie could feel herself grow light-headed. "Not a one. When something is meant to be, it will be. Like you and Maddie. It just isn't my turn yet."

"He damn well better be the best of the best, or I won't allow it. Don't wait up, Annie."

"Okay, Pete. Beat it now."

"Thanks. Turn the dead bolt when I leave."

Back in the kitchen after letting Pete out, Annie checked her domestic accomplishments. Everything she did, she did well. The kitchen counter was clean and dry. The table was free of crumbs and stains. The coffeepot was rinsed and filled, ready to be plugged in the next morning. The beer cans had been rinsed and stacked in a separate trash bag under the sink. She looked around to see if she'd forgotten anything. She snapped her fingers when her eye fell on a luscious green plant in the L corner of the counter. She was about to water it when she realized it was a silk plant. A Maddie present. Just like the one in the center of the table. She snapped off the overhead light and turned on the small light over the range hood and the one next to the sink. The last thing she did was straighten the braided rug in front of the sink. Another Maddie touch. Men would never think to put a rug by the sink to catch spills.

"What are you doing now, Maddie Stern?" Annie muttered as she made her way to the living room, where she made up the couch for Simon Jakes. She gave the pillow a vicious punch. Why did he have to stay here and intrude on the little bit of intimacy she was being allowed with Pete?

In the guest bedroom, Annie undressed and slipped into a warm robe that had seen better days, certainly not the kind of robe she thought Maddie Stern would wear.

It was a nice enough bedroom, Annie thought. Small, but cheerful. Neither manly nor feminine. Not a Maddie room at all. It was done in four shades of green and everything matched, right down to the ashtray on the night table.

Annie was sick with jealousy by the time she opened the dresser drawers and closet. Maddie's things. Maddie's scent. Maddie's spare cosmetics. She hated to touch Maddie's things, but she had to make room for her clothing. For the first time in her life she was faced with a dilemma she didn't know how to deal with. Did she take all of Maddie's things and put them somewhere else, which would mean she was taking Maddie out of this room? Or did she simply move everything into the bottom drawer and hope she would have enough room for her own things? And what about the jogging suits and the few dresses hanging in the closet? Would Pete be upset if she moved them? Probably.

In the end she carried a plastic trash bag in from the kitchen and carefully folded everything into it. She placed the bag in the back of the corner closet and proceeded to hang up her own clothing. She used all the dresser drawers, and had to put her panty hose in the night table drawer. Maddie's cosmetics and perfume went into a shoe box of her own. She set the box on the floor of the closet next to the large green trash bag. She didn't know if she felt good or bad about what she'd just done.

"Life sucks," Annie muttered when she sat down in Pete's chair, with Maddie's business plan in her lap. She wished, and not for the first time, that she was prettier, more stylish, less bookish, less business-oriented. She wanted to be more earthy, with sex appeal that drove men crazy, first for her body and then for her mind. She wished she didn't like the Maddie Pete spoke of so lovingly. Having never met her, and only heard her briefly on the phone, she only had Pete's glowing testimonials to go on.

Annie looked around Pete's apartment. There was no way she would ever have anything half as nice, not even if she worked twenty hours a day, seven days a week. Her eyes dropped to the business plan in her lap. A money maker. Maddie would be earning just as much as Pete in a year or so. Money to money, she thought sadly, while the rest of us bust our hump to get by from day to day. Sometimes it just wasn't fair. And who did Pete call when he found himself in a jam? "Me!" she said aloud. And she did mind, even when she said she didn't.

She flipped through the business plan, appreciating the work Maddie had put into it. She shifted into her legal mode and worked diligently until midnight, when she crawled into bed.

She was up early, perking coffee and frying bacon that she served alongside golden, fluffy eggs.

"Can this girl cook or what?" Pete said stuffing his mouth. "Maddie can't cook. Well, that's not fair, she takes a stab at it, but everything tastes the same."

Jakes blinked when Annie said, "It's hard going to work and then having to come home and cook for just one person. Anyone can make eggs and bacon. I'm not much of a cook myself. Most of the time I just eat soup or make a sandwich or eat a big lunch out so I don't have to cook. It helps when a client pays for lunch. Saves me money in the end."

Pete stopped chewing long enough to listen to what Annie was saying. "Are you having financial problems, Annie?"

"No. But it's hard on a single girl. Financial aid, rent is high, car payments are out of sight. You have utilities, and a woman has to dress in the business world. It don't come cheap, Mr. Lawyer." She forced a smile to cover her defensive tone. "Food is expensive."

"Tell me about it," Jakes grumbled.

Annie sat down at the table. She started to eat. Now her breakfast was spoiled, a meal she'd been looking forward to. She knew Pete was comparing her to Maddie and she was coming up short. Thanks to defending herself. She chewed methodically, knowing Pete was watching her out of the corner of his eye, sensing something out of kilter. Let him sense all he wanted, she thought irritably.

"So, Jakes, what did you find out last night?" Pete asked.

"More than I was prepared for. It's going to cost you. Five hundred." Pete waved the amount aside as if it were inconsequential. Jakes shrugged. "I spoke to one of the officers who responded to the call at the store around the corner from Maddie's apartment. There were two witnesses, and both fit Janny and Maddie's descriptions. The guy was feeling no pain. Because of that, and the money, he agreed to talk. I know, I know, you're thinking the cop is crooked. He probably is, but do you care? Hell no you don't. So I promised him the money and he talked. He said if word gets back, he'll deny it. So would I. I think he knows more. He said Nester has all the answers."

"Son of a fucking bitch! Nester is the guy I spoke to when I filed the Missing Persons report," Pete bellowed. "Are you sure that guy was telling you the truth?"

Jakes looked offended. "Do I look like a guy who can be conned? Trust me, he was telling the truth. I had another guy check out the duty roster for that shift. It computes."

"I'm going to speak to Nester today," Pete said, "and demand some answers!"

"Well, when you do," Jakes said mildly, "I'd forget where you got this information. The guy will deny it anyway, so there's no point."

Jakes looked at Annie after pushing his plate aside. "Good breakfast," he said.

Annie waited a moment to see if Pete echoed Jakes's comment. When he didn't, she carried her own plate to the sink. She felt like crying.

"You'd better get a move on, Annie," Pete said. "You need to be at the store at least thirty minutes before it opens."

Annie whirled around. "Pete, I only have two hands and two legs. You asked me to make breakfast. You didn't tell me I had to be at the store thirty minutes before it opened. And another thing, don't tell me to do something, ask me." She turned on her heel and marched out of the kitchen.

"Wha'd I say?" Pete demanded, his face stricken at Annie's words and tone of voice.

Jakes grinned. "I think it's that old, don't-take-me-for-granted crap. Sounds to me like you did. Take her for granted, I mean. I'll check back with Annie at noon as we agreed. Good luck with Nester."

Temperamental females, Pete thought. Shit. He marched down the hall to the spare room and knocked on the door. He found himself apologizing and pleading. Jesus, Annie was his friend. She was helping him and he'd . . . what the hell had he done? He'd been thoughtless, inconsiderate. Had he taken advantage of her? Damn, didn't she know how worked up he was, how worried he was about Maddie? Dennis's words rang in his ears. *She's in love with you, always has been.* "Oh, shit!"

Annie opened the door just as he was about to walk away. Her face was composed, her eyes wide and . . . *speculative*, for God's sake.

"Sorry I acted like a female back there," she said quietly.

Pete wrapped his arms around her. "I'm sorry too. Sometimes I don't think. If I was sharp with you or if I came across as bossy, I'm sorry." He could feel her stiffen beneath his touch. He dropped his arms and stepped back.

"No apology needed, Pete. I know how much stress you're under. It never happened, okay?"

But it had happened. Pete could see it in the way her jaw set and in the matter-of-fact way she asked, "Do you have any special instructions for me today? Is there anything in particular I should be doing, watching out for?"

"Just run the store the best you can. Check the register receipts, talk to customers, that kind of thing. I'll be checking in with you throughout the day. So will Jakes. You'll be our go-between. If business is brisk and you need to hire some people, go ahead. Maddie had a list of part-timers. I think she ran an ad in the *Times.* Whatever feels right, do it. Oh, by the way, my cleaning lady comes in today, so don't worry about the kitchen. I'll leave a note for her to make something for dinner. She's real good at cooking stuff in one pot." He wagged a playful finger in her direction. "Now, don't worry about the kitchen."

"I had no intention of worrying about your kitchen, Pete," Annie said quietly. "Is there anything else?"

Goddamn right there was, but he didn't know what it was precisely. He knew he was losing something, something he wasn't going to get back if his mind didn't come up with something real quick. Annie was watching him, waiting for that thing, whatever that thing was, that he was about to lose. He thought of a hundred things he could say, and knew instinctively none of them were right. What he settled for was, "You're a good friend, Annie," before he walked away.

Tears glistened in Annie's eyes as she closed the door.

• • •

The police station was just as busy during the early morning hours as it was at night. The only difference, Pete thought, was that the scent of Aqua Velva and Brut deodorant was a little fresher. He thought he smelled burned coffee when he approached the desk. "I'd like to see Detective Nester."

"So would a lot of other people," the officer behind the desk growled. "Detective Nester is on vacation. He takes his vacation at the same time every year. And, no, I can't get in touch with him. He's camping. In the woods," he said, by way of explanation.

"Does he call in?" Pete asked, his voice sounding desperate.

"If you were on vacation and camping in the woods, would you call in . . . sir?"

"If I had pending business I would."

"Well, I guess Detective Nester doesn't have any pending business because he hasn't called in."

"When is he expected back?"

"Next Monday."

"That pisses me off," Pete snapped.

"Me too. I'd like to be out in the woods about now," the officer snapped back.

"Who's in charge in his absence?"

"Finnegan." The officer pointed with his index finger. "His desk is the third one from the left."

He was a burly man, at least forty pounds overweight, with all the weight in his gut. He was chowing down on a box of Dunkin' Donuts and a large coffee that said Dunkin' Donuts on the side. Pete stared at the box. He knew from its size that it would hold a dozen doughnuts. Seven were gone, and Finnegan didn't look like the kind of guy who shared. He was licking his fingers when Pete introduced himself. He waved him to a wooden chair, sprinkles of sugar falling from his fingers.

Pete didn't like him, and he'd just met him. Finnegan had

mean little eyes in a doughy face, which stared at him. His thick lips were blubbery-looking and dotted with sugar. They pulled back from his gums to reveal small square, nicotine-stained teeth that seemed at odds with his overlarge mouth. He slurped at the coffee in the large container. Pete guessed it was laced with real cream and at least six sugars.

"I filled out two Missing Persons reports. I'm here to check on them, and . . . Detective Nester was the person I spoke with. The duty officer said he was on vacation."

"He's camping in the woods?"

Pete bit down on his tongue. He'd almost said, Where else do you go camping except in the woods? "I want to talk to your boss," Pete said belligerently.

Finnegan bit into another doughnut as he pointed to a glass-enclosed room. "He's in there."

Pete glanced down at the floor and saw Finnegan's feet. He was wearing one blue sock and one brown one. He must use the same laundry I use, he thought. The damn washer ate his socks.

The brass nameplate said the man behind the desk was Captain Joshua Markam. Pete introduced himself for the third time.

"What can I do for you, Mr. Sorenson?"

"Well, I wanted to talk with Detective Nester. . . ."

"He's on vacation. A camping trip." Pete waited for the words, in the woods, but the captain only folded his hands and leaned across the desk.

Joshua Markam was clean-shaven, dressed in a dark suit, the jacket hanging over the back of his chair. Someone had ironed his shirt, Pete noted. The collar didn't have those tiny little wrinkles near the point, and there were creases in his sleeves even though they were rolled partway up his arms. He wore a strap watch with a large face with bold numbers. One of those things that even gave sea-level readings, Pete surmised. He was older, possibly in his early fifties. In good shape, probably played squash or racquetball after work hours. He was lightly tanned, had all his hair, and the sharpest eyes Pete had ever seen.

"I have every reason to believe my fiancée and her friend were in your custody. I filed Missing Persons Reports with Detective Nester. What I want now is confirmation that my fiancée was put into the Witness Protection Program, and I want to know what's being done to find her."

"What makes you believe this, Mr. Sorenson?"

"Circumstances, and one of your men has a loose lip when he drinks. Plus, Maddie called me. She's out on her own. I told Nester and I'm telling you, I'm not going to let this drop. I'm going to keep at it until I have concrete proof that you people are covering up . . . whatever it is you're covering up. I strongly believe my fiancée and her friend witnessed that murder on First Avenue. I am not comfortable with all the coincidences that have happened. I hired a private detective who has the nose of a bloodhound. Now," Pete said, leaning toward Markam, "I'm the first to admit I don't know how you run this department, but I know how I run my life, and I know how Maddie ran hers and how we were going to run our combined lives after we were married. Maddie would never, as in ever, leave and not tell me where she was going, and why she was going. That's number one. Number two is she just opened what will in a very short time be a million-dollar business. Number three is Maddie would never walk away from her own wedding. Number four is of course me. I know Maddie loves me just as much as I love her. We planned a life together and now that's all gone. I want to know why. I want to see the police file. My fiancée is loose somewhere. I want her found."

"What police file? You need to be more specific. I cannot comment on any ongoing investigations."

"That's bullshit and you know it, Captain," Pete said, his voice rising. "You guys stuck her and her friend into the Witness Protection Program. Go ahead, look me in the eye and tell me you didn't do that. That's what you did, I know it. She told me when she called. I defy you to tell me I'm wrong." Pete was shouting now.

Markam jerked backward when Pete inched even closer to his face. "All I can tell you, Mr. Sorenson, is that I cannot comment on an ongoing investigation. I'm sorry about your problem, I really am."

"That's it! You're sorry!" Pete thundered. "That's not good enough. From this moment on I'm going to be this department's worse nightmare. I'm going to find Maddie, and when I do, it will be in every newspaper in the country. Police cover-up. I think the people are about ready to read garbage like that."

"Is that a threat, Mr. Sorenson?" Markam asked in a steely voice.

"No, Captain Markam, that is not a threat. It is a goddamn promise. You have no right to fuck with my life or Maddie's life or Janny's life. You can all go to hell," Pete stormed as he slammed out of the glass-enclosed room.

Outside, in the hot, humid air, Pete shook his head to clear it. "You just blew it, Sorenson. You let your temper get the best of you. You let them see you sweat," he muttered. Now what? When Plan A doesn't work, switch to Plan B. The only problem was, he didn't have a Plan B. "Shit!" he said succinctly.

Pete climbed into the Rover that was parked a block away. "I'm going to find you, Maddie," he muttered.

At Fairy Tales, Annie Gabriel was explaining for the twentieth time the reason for the store being closed so soon after its grand opening. For the most part, she made up things as she went along, never sticking to the same story twice.

It was only noon, and she was exhausted, her mind boggled with the amount of sales she'd rung up. In between sales and showing merchandise, she'd busied herself by dusting the glass shelves and rearranging displays that weren't to her liking, displays Maddie had spent hours working on. She'd called three suppliers to order additional stock, and placed an ad in the paper for part-time help. There was no doubt in her mind that Maddie Stern had a class operation in Fairy Tales, thanks to Pete's backing. She wondered if Maddie signed a promissory note or if the business was in both Maddie's and Pete's names.

She was eating a wrinkled, wilted apple when the phone rang. It was Pete asking if Jakes or Maddie had called in.

"Not yet. How did you make out?"

"The police won't comment on an ongoing investigation. I blew up, acted like a real ass. You know how good I am at doing that. How many times did you pull my chestnuts out of the fire?"

"More times than I can remember. I thought you were past that hothead stuff. Anger gets you nowhere. You have to learn how to outfox the foxes. That's the first rule, Pete."

"I know, I know. How are things at the store?"

"Fine. Business is great. You have a gold mine here. I put an ad in the paper and ordered some merchandise. I think it'll take me about a week to get the hang of merchandising."

"Don't get attached, Annie, I'm going to find Maddie and . . ."

Annie's voice turned to ice. "And . . ."

"Jesus, I didn't mean . . . what I was trying to say was I know the law is your first love, and you're doing this as a favor. Jesus, Annie, we don't seem to be communicating here."

"I wonder why that is, Pete," Annie said coldly. "You don't have to worry about me trying to take over Maddie's business. That's what you meant, isn't it?"

"Well, yes, but not really. Actually, Annie, it was a joke that laid an egg. I didn't mean anything by my comment, just the way I didn't mean anything this morning. I'm wired, Annie, cut me a little slack, okay?"

"Sure, Pete. I understand. I have to go now, I have a customer."

"I'll see you tonight. I'll call in around three if I get the chance."

Annie hung up the phone, her eyes burning unbearably. She tossed her apple core into the lace-edge wastebasket. A second later she removed it and carried it back to the plastic-lined pail in the kitchen.

She hadn't lied, there was a customer in the store. She walked up to her and asked if she could be of help.

"I was here opening day and literally bought out the store," the customer trilled. "Where is that pretty young woman who waited on me? She was so helpful. She seemed to know exactly what I wanted, and she had the nicest manner. Not pushy at all, like some salespeople. I adore those shopping bags. I'm just delighted the store reopened. What was the problem?"

"A death in the family. Unexpected death," Annie said coolly.

"I thought it was something like that. I've walked by almost every day since then. There were two strange ladies here one day, and then bang, the store just closed. No sign or anything." She wagged a playful finger under Annie's nose. "You should have put a sign in the window saying you were closed."

"Yes, we should have. I'll be in the back if you need my help," Annie said.

Annie walked back to her stool behind the counter. She shuffled sales booklets and pencils, stacked the charge slips next to the machine. Soooo helpful, such nice manners. "Hrumph," she snorted. "If this were mine I'd be ever soooo helpful and chock full of manners too," she muttered.

Annie reached for a slip of paper. She started to add a column of figures. She had her student loans, rent to pay back in Boston, and a utility bill to pay. Not to mention her car loan and charge accounts. She'd literally walked out on her job, and didn't know if she could go back when things were finished here. Pete hadn't said anything about how much he was paying her, and she hated to ask. He should have said something by now. She wondered *exactly* what the words "worth your while" meant, and when a check would be forthcoming.

Annie looked up to see the woman approaching the register, her arms full. She forced a smile.

"Make sure you wrap them pretty the way that other young lady did."

"I beg your pardon?" Annie said.

"You know, put those shiny strings of paper in among the colored tissue and add some of those rose petals. I just love the way everything smells when I get it home. The first time I was in here, people actually stopped me on the street to admire your shopping bags. I think that's a wonderful compliment, don't you?"

"Oh, yes. Yes, it is. I'm sorry, you see I'm new here and no one told me how to . . . wrap things. If you'll just be patient with me and help me as I go along . . ."

"Well, first you ring everything up, fold it, and then you layer the shopping bags with that rainbow tissue paper. Then you put the outfits in the bottom, crunch up more tissue, and throw in a handful of rose petals." The woman waited while Annie did as she'd suggested. "That's right, now you put the streamers in. They kind of fall over the sides. See how colorful it is? When you hand me my receipt you tie a purple velvet ribbon onto the handles of the shopping bag. . . . Oh, it's just lovely." The woman giggled.

Annie had to admit the woman was right. The few cents it cost, per bag, to decorate it with tissue paper, rose petals, and then colorful streamers was worth it. The bags were attractive. Packaging, she was finding out, was all-important. She also had to admit that if this store was hers, she never would have come up with the packaging idea. She was too analytical. Her mind would have been on costs, sales items, rent, and all that it took to operate a store. Frills and froufrous would have been the last thing she would have thought of. "And there goes one happy shopper," she muttered.

Maddie Stern was a businesswoman.

Annie Gabriel was a lawyer.

"And I'm jealous as hell of you, Maddie Stern."

18

Pete walked into his apartment, grateful he'd left the air-conditioning on. He was soaked to the skin with his own sweat. He opened a bottle of Gatorade, guzzling until the bottle was empty. He let out a belch that could be heard in the hallway.

In his bedroom he pressed the message button on his answering machine as he stripped off his sodden clothes. He listened to five full minutes of calls from friends and colleagues while he padded around naked, opening drawers for clean, dry clothes. He was about to enter the bathroom when he heard his uncle Leo's voice tell him a meeting was scheduled for September sixth at ten o'clock. He stuck his middle finger in the air before he turned on the shower. He was about to step into the shower when he heard Maddie's voice. He bolted from the bathroom, stubbing his toe on the marble doorsill. He listened, his eyes wide and disbelieving. He pressed Save, then Rewind, and listened to all the messages again until he heard Maddie's voice. He pressed Save again until he could repeat the message verbatim. He looked at the small digital calendar that not only recorded the date, but the time as well. August 29, 1983. The time was five forty-five.

Pete pressed Save one more time and dialed Fairy Tales.

"Pete, where have you been?" Annie said. "I've been waiting for you to call in all afternoon. Maddie called again. She said she needs to talk to you. She's safe, Pete. She said she was in Florida."

"Why didn't you call me?" Pete barked.

"Call you where? You said you were going to call in. You didn't tell me to call you. Those were your exact words, Pete, you said you would check in. You didn't. Neither did Jakes."

"You should have had enough sense to call here and leave a message. I came in here to change." He was being unreasonable, and there didn't seem to be anything he could do to stop his rambling tongue.

"What's the big deal, Pete? You weren't home, you weren't here. Maddie did leave a message and said she would call back. You should have stayed home and waited for her phone call if that's the way you feel about it. Don't take your hostility out on me. If I had known where to find you, I would have called you immediately. Is there anything else, Pete? If not, I have to close up."

"Annie—"

"I know, you're sorry. You know what, Pete, I am too. Sorry for you, I mean."

The click on the other end of the phone sounded ominous in Pete's ears. He'd pissed Annie off again. Jesus, couldn't he do anything right?

The displeasure he felt with himself, however, was short-lived. Maddie had called. She was still alive and well. Now all he had to do was hang around and wait for her call. He was lightheaded when he showered under the ice-cold needle spray.

He managed to shower, dress, and comb his hair in seven minutes. He spent the rest of the time listening to Maddie's voice until Jakes and Annie arrived for dinner.

The hostility at the dinner table was thick as mush. Pete repeated Maddie's message for the benefit of Jakes and Annie. Annie repeated hers, reading from a slip of paper.

"That explains why no one from the department is talking," Jakes said. "Cops are touchy about the feds."

"What about all those friends you have in high places?" Pete grated.

"What about *your* friends in high places?" Jakes shot back.

"They're all sitting on lofty perches the same as yours. I'm having a hard time dealing with this," Pete said, slamming his fist on the kitchen table. The salt shaker skittered to the edge, teetered, and then fell on the floor, the top shaking loose, allowing the millions of minuscule granules to shower down onto the floor. Three sets of eyes stared at the gray and black tile. No one made a move to clean it up.

Annie bit into her pepperoni pizza while Jakes popped a can of Budweiser beer. Pete scuffed at the salt-littered floor with his foot. "This shit is for the birds," he grated.

"I agree," Jakes said. He drained the last of his beer in one long swallow. He aligned his bottle alongside the other five in the center of the table. "I have here," he said, opening his briefcase, "every article, every word, that has ever been written about the program. I have the address of the agency. We can take the shuttle to Washington tomorrow and from there rent a car and drive to Arlington, Virginia, and do some talking. I skimmed through most of it, and the one thing that sticks out in my mind is you can write a letter and the marshals will forward it to the person in the program, though since Maddie said she escaped . . ." Jakes shrugged and left the thought hanging.

Annie laid her pizza down on the paper plate in front of her. "I did some research today too. I called the library today and had the reference desk check out a few things. If I understood everything correctly, once you're in the program, you're in. You can, of course leave, but the program can no longer protect you. To date, no one who is in the program has been harmed. Maddie must be in very grave danger for her to have been put in the program so quickly. Now . . . if she left, what does it mean? To me it's the only thing that makes sense. She didn't give you up, your wedding, or the store because she wanted to," she said to Pete. "She gave it up because she was petrified and afraid she would be killed. Self-preservation is right up there at the top of the list. I don't see that she had any choice. And from what you told me about Maddie, she wouldn't have wanted to place you in danger either."

"What she says makes sense," Jakes said.

"Pete, you need to give some thought to something else. If Maddie was in the program, she was safe. Now . . . it could be dangerous for her. As far as the librarian knew, no one has ever penetrated the program. The odds of you finding her on your own are about nil," Annie said glumly.

"She's right about that too. It's all in there," Jakes said as he pushed a stack of photocopied papers across the table to Pete. "By the way, what did the Attorney General have to say?"

"Nothing but bullshit," Pete snarled.

"Whose turn is it to clean up?" Jakes asked.

"Not mine. I have the day's receipts to go over, and I need to make a list of . . . not mine," Annie said, getting up from the table. Pete waved the printed matter Jakes had turned over to him.

"Guess that leaves me," Jakes grumbled.

"Guess so," Pete said, already devouring the articles Jakes had given him.

"Pete, I won't be coming back tonight," Jakes said. "If you need me to do anything else give me a call. Stay close and wait for Maddie to call."

In the living room, in order to take advantage of the television and read at the same time, Annie sat on the opposite end of the sofa so she wouldn't disturb Pete, who was poring through the material Jakes had given him, the portable phone on the middle cushion of the seat.

A Mickey Mouse calculator that she brought home from the store was in Annie's lap. She punched in numbers, tried not to show emotion as the numbers mounted. Fairy Tales was indeed a gold mine. She set aside bank receipts and started on the one-of-a-kind merchandise she'd ordered. She mentally subtracted the running totals from the bank receipts. Merchandise was to be paid on delivery, even though the bills said payment due in thirty days. Maddie's way of doing business. The day you took delivery, you paid, if the merchandise was up to par. She shrugged, set aside those bills.

Annie rummaged in her briefcase for a brochure a salesman had dropped off earlier in the day. His pitch had been professional, and she'd agreed to display his line of herbal teas in colorful tins. A straw basket with a lace-trimmed doily that draped over the side would look extremely attractive and in no way take away from the decor of the store. The line of flavored coffee was just as tantalizing, and she did love the smell of coffee. The salesman had left two of the decorative baskets, and by the end of the day she'd sold seven of the tins of tea and five tins of southern pecan coffee beans.

Now she was having second thoughts about the decision she'd made. Even though the money was kept separate, was it hers or was it Maddie's? Should she tell Pete or keep the sideline to herself? Maybe splitting the profit with Fairy Tales would be more fair. Damn, now she was getting a headache and she could feel the tension start to mount between her shoulder blades. It was going to be a migraine, and there wasn't anything she could do about it. Stress always brought them on.

Small, old-fashioned coffee grinders. The profit was outrageous. The salesman had left two of them, and when she had a break, she'd tried it out in the kitchen. The coffee was delicious, but it was the aroma that sold the grinders. She'd explained to the last customer of the day that she'd used the grinder once, and the woman said she didn't care, just wrap it up. She immediately placed a call to the salesman and ordered a dozen, three-dozen tins of tea and a like amount of coffee. Damn, should she tell Pete?

The coffee and tea business wasn't really what was bothering her. Pete's insensitivity to her financial situation was starting to nag her. She needed to say something now before she let her feelings get out of hand. Maybe the headache would dissipate if she aired her unhappiness.

"Pete?"

"Hmm?"

"I need to talk to you about something." She hated the look of annoyance on her friend's face. She tried to bolster her courage when Pete finally met her gaze.

"Is something wrong?" The annoyance was in his voice too.

"Not *really* wrong, but there is something bothering me. When you asked me to come here, you said you would make it worth my while. My rent is due back in Boston. I have bills and insurance payments, my loans to make. I do have a savings account, but I promised myself I wouldn't dip in to it. I did buy two plane tickets on my charge card, and that bill is coming due too. I feel terrible asking you, with everything you have on your mind. . . ." she finished lamely.

"My God, Annie, I'm sorry. You should have said something sooner. I did forget and I'm sorry. Is this what's been bothering you?"

"Not really. I guess it's the newness of everything and seeing you so uptight. Right now I feel a migraine coming on. . . ."

"Don't move, Annie, I'll be right back." Pete was as good as his word. He handed her a check for five thousand dollars. For some reason, she'd expected more; "worth your while" meant more. She didn't try to hide her dismay.

Annie laid the check on the coffee table. "What does this cover?" she asked bluntly.

"Well . . . it covers your plane tickets, working at the store. You are managerial, and if you were a regular employee you'd be getting a commission. I guess it's for running the store."

"Well, for what time period?" Annie persisted.

"Jesus, I hadn't thought about it, Annie. This is important to you and I screwed up. Did you have a figure in mind?"

How anxious he looks, Annie thought. "Well, I was making

eighty thousand a year. Actually, we should have discussed this prior to me coming here. I hate diddling over money. We're friends. It shouldn't be like this."

"No it shouldn't, and you're right, we should have discussed it. I took advantage of you and I'm sorry. Give me a number, Annie."

"I was making eighty thousand a year. To me, the words 'worth my while' have to mean a great deal more than my salary. I wouldn't have taken the job for less than $150,000. You don't go down, you go up. We both know that. And there's the sign-on bonus. I think you did take advantage of me. That's why I'm getting this migraine headache. This check," she said pointing to the blue square on the coffee table, "should be a quarterly payment of around $28,250, and that counts for the extra month. You know, September, October, November, and December. I'm not even counting the sign-on bonus. If you want a number, then I think this check should be seventy thousand, and that includes the sign-on. If you have any trouble with the numbers, you should tell me now."

"Hell no, Annie. If that's what you want, then that's what you're going to get." Pete ripped up the check on the coffee table and scrawled a second one. "Now will you smile? I miss that, you know. We've been like snarling cats this past week. Now, what else is bothering you, besides your headache? And I'm going to remedy that in a minute. If you remember, I'm the guy that gave you middle-of-the-night shoulder rubs while we were cramming for exams. You said I was the best shoulder rubber you ever met."

"That's true. And yes, something else is bothering me." She told him about the coffee and tea. "How do you feel about me keeping the profits?"

"Jesus, Annie, like I really care. Do what you want. I'm leaving it up to you."

"Then what I propose is to give Fairy Tales ten percent of the profits. Are you sure it's okay?"

"Yes, it's okay. Tell me now all this crap is behind us."

"It's behind us, Pete."

"Good. Pin your hair up and I'll do your neck and shoulders. Thirty minutes of bliss. If your headache goes away, will you do mine?" he asked wistfully.

"Your neck rubs always put me to sleep. That's what makes the headache go away. I'll get the quilt."

Pete could see the pain in her eyes when she returned to the living room. He thanked God he'd never been cursed with migraine headaches. She'd changed from her work clothes to a lightweight sweat suit. Her hair was piled on top of her head, giving him free access to her slender neck. He watched her spread the quilt and then lie down.

"You might as well give me a back rub too," she said. "If I don't fall asleep, you get one too. Deal?"

"Deal," Pete said.

"Did you find anything in the material you were reading?" Annie mumbled as Pete's fingers started their magic.

Pete spoke slowly, his voice a low monotone as he kneaded, rubbed, and massaged Annie's shoulders and neck. He could feel the tension start to leave her body.

"Hmmm, that feels so good. More, more, more."

Thirty minutes later Pete said, "I'm tired."

"You're whining, Pete," Annie replied, rolling over.

She wanted it to happen, but hadn't expected it ever would.

One minute they were friends who were antsy with one another, and now . . . this. She wanted to tear her gaze from him, but she couldn't. She'd waited so long, hungered forever, it seemed, for this moment when Pete would look at her with . . . desire. She wouldn't give up. A hundred reasons raced through her mind. All one hundred reasons were named Maddie Stern. She had to do something now before it was too late. If she didn't, Pete wouldn't be able to live with himself. Love meant putting the other person first.

Annie sat up and looked away. The simple head turn took every ounce of willpower she possessed.

"I had no idea it was so late," she said. Lord, was that her voice sounding so normal, so nonchalant? Of course it was, she was the only female in the room. Her legs almost failed her when she got to her feet, but she managed to walk away. She called over her shoulder. "My headache's gone. You give a good neck rub, Pete Sorenson."

Then, blessedly, she was in the guest room with her back to the door, her hands fumbling for the lock. Her knees gave way and she slid to the floor. Tears spilled from her eyes.

In the living room Pete stared at the television, his mind as blank as the dark screen. Maybe he should turn it on so he could hear sound, see make-believe people walking around doing make-believe things.

Jesus, he'd almost . . . If Annie hadn't . . .

Annie. What was she thinking? Usually he could just about read her mind. Annie's feelings always showed on her face, except when she was in court, and then she was completely unreadable, just as her face had been unreadable when she left the room. Annie only presented an inscrutable face when something was important to her. He thought: And that makes you, Pete Sorenson, a first-class jerkoff.

Hell, he couldn't even pretend a memory loss or pretend he thought he was with Maddie. He'd known it was Annie from the get-go, and still he'd . . .

He was so goddamn frustrated. Excuses, Sorenson.

Pete reached for the stack of papers on the couch. Could he really keep reading this crap? Did he really believe in his heart of hearts that somehow he was going to get Maddie back? Not if she signed the memorandum of understanding. By now, if she was in the program, as she'd told Annie, she would have gone through the screening orientation. But she's out, he thought. She walked out, she's not in the program now. They were probably searching for her too. Was Maddie any match for the federal marshals?

In the morning he was going to Virginia and present himself at the U.S. Marshals Service. He was prepared to raise all kinds of hell if he had to. "Who the hell do they think they are, mucking up my life? I have the right to know if she's in or out of the program," he sputtered. "I deserve to know what's being done."

Jakes had advised him to write a letter and bring it with him. To what end? How in the hell was he supposed to write a letter now, after what he'd almost done? *It didn't mean anything.* He knew it was a lie. It meant something to Annie, otherwise her face would have been readable. God, he knew her so well. Better now than he ever thought he would. The question was, what did it mean to him?

"I love you, Maddie. Someday I'll tell you about this. But not for a very long time."

Then he thought about Barney. What would Barney do? What would he think?

Pete woke from a series of dreams that were so terrible he dripped sweat, his face fearful as he remembered brief snatches. He could feel his stomach start to churn when he swung his legs over the side of the couch. He'd slept here because he felt too guilty to sleep in the bed he'd shared with Maddie from time to time. It didn't matter that he hadn't done anything. He'd contemplated it, and that made him feel guilty. He looked at his watch; 4:57. Almost five o'clock in the morning. He slumped back against the deep, comfortable cushions. His bare feet scuffed at the papers near his feet. He bent down to search for the one that most affected him at the moment. He knew the words by heart, but he read them again.

> From the marshals' point of view, permitting mail to be forwarded both limits the client's abdication of old responsibilities and decreases the distress associated with abandoning past life. Such procedures are offered as long as the witness requests them or wants them. In essence, the witness agrees to complete a change of address order so that all mail addressed to the old name is routed to a post office box number by the Marshals Ser-

> vice. Although notified of the availability of mail forwarding, the "Memorandum of Understanding" goes on to point out that the witness acknowledges the necessity to terminate correspondence.

And on and on it went.

Surely Maddie would have told the marshals to expect mail from him. Well, by the end of today, he promised himself, he would know for certain if she was still out on her own or if they'd picked her up.

Should he write a letter? Would other eyes read it? Would it be an exercise in futility? His legal mind clicked into gear. He should talk it over with Annie and get her opinion. She was an observer, and could be analytical. And then he remembered Annie's inscrutable face when she went to bed.

Damn, he didn't want to think about Annie now. He had enough problems without compounding them. Jesus, he loved Annie, would walk through fire for her. Next to Maddie, she was his one true friend in the whole world. How was he supposed to live with what they'd almost done last night?

In his turmoil he decided to write the letter. What did he have to lose?

Pete padded into the kitchen, turned on the lights and made a pot of coffee. While it perked he sat at the table to compose the letter to Maddie.

> My Dearest Maddie,
>
> To say I don't know what is going on is the understatement of the year. I suspect I know what is going on, but cannot as of this date get a solid confirmation that you are in the Witness Protection Program.
>
> When I got home today, I received your message. I played it so many times I probably wore out the tape. I really don't understand a lot of your message.
>
> I fear for you, Maddie . . .

Pete ripped the paper to shreds. What was the point of writing a letter if the marshals didn't know where Maddie was? How could they forward it to her?

"This is bullshit," he snarled.

As he drank the scalding coffee, he wondered if he was missing some vital piece of information in regard to Maddie. Between Jakes and himself, they'd covered miles of ground during the past few days. Bull Balog and John Naverez were still in jail without bail. He hadn't been totally surprised to discover that Leo's law firm represented the men in jail. Leo's firm had the best criminal legal department on the East Coast. "Everyone," Leo said when he'd called yesterday, "has the right to their day in court and the best legal representation possible." He'd gone on to say client attorney records were sacred. As if he didn't know that. Leo had also said he wouldn't interfere in any way other than to look over the case as any senior partner would do. "If there are any irregularities, they will be taken care of." At that point he'd been dismissed.

Pete poured himself a second cup of coffee and carried it into the bathroom, where he showered and shaved. He was dressed for the day when he walked back to the kitchen to start breakfast. Bacon in one frying pan, scrambled eggs in the other. Deftly he slid toast into the toaster and somehow managed to juggle everything so that breakfast was done when Annie entered the kitchen. The new pot of coffee bubbled comfortingly.

"Just in time," Pete said, setting a plate in front of her. "Annie, I want to talk to you. I don't want either of us to leave this apartment until we . . . until we talk about last night. It was all my fault. I don't know what happened to me. I'm sorry, it never should have happened."

Annie eyed him over her coffee cup. It seemed a smile tugged at the corners of her mouth, or was it his imagination? She appeared to be staring into the core of his being. "Sex," she said coolly, "is a participatory event. Neither of us participated. I think we should put it behind us and not worry about what we didn't do. Today is a new day. Yesterday is gone. I'm not the type of person who carries tales, if that's what's worrying you. These are good eggs, Pete. You're a better cook than I'll ever be. Listen,

I have to run. I called the coffee man's eight-hundred number last night before I went to bed, and hopefully he'll show up at the store before I open for business. Will you be home this evening?"

"I'm not sure. I'll call." Pete looked at his watch. No damn wonder she was such a fine attorney. You couldn't ever sidetrack Annie. Black was black and white was white. Just the facts. You deal with facts and go forward. If she was prepared to do that, how could he do less?

"Annie . . ."

"Yes, Pete?"

"There's nothing in the world I wouldn't do for you. You believe that, don't you?"

"Of course, Pete."

Damn, she had that inscrutable look on her face again. He waited for her to say, "Vice versa," but she didn't. Dennis's words rang in his ears. *Annie's been in love with you forever. You're the only one who doesn't know it.*

Jakes arrived at ten-fifteen dressed in a lightweight summer suit. "Good impressions and all of that," he said. "I have news. We'll talk on the way to the airport."

Pete nodded. Whatever he found out today was going to affect the rest of his life. He crossed his fingers the way he had when he was a kid and wanted something good to happen. He wished for a grown-up Barney to confide in.

What good was all the money in the world, and what good was a job that provided that money, if you didn't have someone to share it with? What good was life without someone to share it with? He voiced the thought aloud to Jakes, who stared at him with undisguised pity.

"You're free, Mr. Sorenson. You can move about, do as you please. None of us has any idea what freedom really means until it's taken away from us. To be alive and free has to be the greatest thing going. You're thinking about yourself now, and I'm not saying that's wrong, but if we're right and Maddie was in the program, think about what she's given up. Now that she's left it, we have a new set of worries. Just to be alive. Think about *that*, Mr. Sorenson. We better get moving," he said, looking at his watch.

Freedom. Pete rolled the word around and around his tongue.

Everyone's inalienable right. Except for Maddie and the others he didn't know about.

Pete was about to lock the apartment door when he said, "Wait, I have to leave a new message on my machine for Maddie. I want her to know. . . ."

19

Saston proved to be twenty miles from Provo according to the taxi driver. To call the dry, dirty dustball a town was being kind. Maddie paid the driver and stepped from the cab. Dust swirled up her sweaty legs. Her skin started to prickle, but not from the dust. She looked over her shoulder, checked the pickups in front of Dumfey's Cafe. Everything looked normal.

Maddie delayed the moment when she would walk through the fly-speckled glass doors of the café. God in heaven, she thought, looking around, Janny must be bored beyond belief. There wasn't one single thing that could be called pretty about the town. Maddie was reminded of a western movie with flat storefronts and wooden sidewalks. Across the street was a store whose sign said, GENERAL STORE. Next to it was another building that said DRUGSTORE. The two buildings on each side read, HARDWARE STORE and BARBERSHOP. Obviously no one in town suffered from an identity crisis. All the windows in the buildings had dark green shades that were aligned evenly. The merchants must check them in the morning to be sure they all met some invisible line, Maddie thought irritably.

Maddie stepped up to the short walkway that led to the entrance of the café. Two black pots that looked like caldrons held flowers that had gone to seed. Weeds dripped down the sides. A sheet of paper with blue lines was Scotch-taped to the door. In black crayon it said, NO CREDIT. DON'T ASK FOR ANY!

Maddie pushed at the door. It wouldn't budge. She gave the bottom a kick with her foot. The door shot open at the same moment a huge cowbell overhead bonged to life. Startled, Maddie ducked and skittered to the side until she identified the sound. She was shaking when she shifted her straw bag from her left shoulder to her right. She stared through her dark sunglasses at the few customers sitting at the counter. The stools were red and patched with gray electrical tape. Three tables were against the far wall. Janny was sitting at the last one. Her face lit up when she saw her friend. Maddie quickly put her finger to her lips. She didn't want to call attention to herself or Janny.

Maddie's chair wobbled so badly, she changed to another one, which wobbled even more. "Custom interiors by Bubba and Leroy," she muttered. "God, I'm glad to see you, Janny. Look, don't laugh or cry, don't do anything that will call undue attention to either one of us. I've only been here a few minutes and already I hate it. How's the food?"

"If you don't mind the roaches and the flies, I guess it's okay. I didn't think you'd make it. Unitec is up five bucks. All I do is cry. I hate it, Maddie. I can't stay here. I don't want to stay here. They gave me eight hundred fifty dollars and told me it had to last all month. I have a little apartment that makes my skin crawl. I can't find a job. In order to work in Provo, I have to get a car, and how am I going to do that when they took away all my credit history? There's one bus a day from this dump if the driver feels like making the run. If he doesn't, you don't go anywhere. The one activity comes from three churches. Nothing is the way they said it would be."

Maddie nodded. "You know, Janny, I've had nothing to do but think since I've been on the run. I don't think this program is geared to people like you and me. It's for criminals who cop pleas and stuff like that. They're grateful, I guess, to go anywhere as long as they're safe." She told her friend about the apartment in Fort Lauderdale. "A man could tolerate that, could tolerate those people and the excuses they came up with. For me, it was different. It was like they didn't give a hoot about me. They thought they could bamboozle me and I'd take it. They sure wanted us to do what they wanted, when they wanted it done, but try asking them to move a little faster and see what happens. You had your identity, why wasn't mine ready? They moved quickly and let me sit sucking my thumb. It's not right and it's not fair."

"What are we going to do?" Janny asked.

"Does anyone check with you? Do you report to someone? How does it work? I had a twenty-four-hour guard. I had to tell him when I was going to the bathroom."

"Once a week I check in. No one has bothered me. Why should they? What's to do in a place like this? I guess it's because you're the one who's the real witness."

"Where do you call?" Maddie asked.

"A number in Provo. My contact is a person named Steven Maloy. He seems nice enough. I don't know what he'd do if I didn't check in on time. I don't have a phone because I don't have enough money for the deposit and connection charge, and since I've never had a phone in Utah before, they won't hook one up unless I can produce a credit history. The utilities are included with the rent, so I didn't have to worry about that. I suppose if it was an emergency, my landlord would let me use her phone. I haven't gotten friendly with her," Janny said tightly.

"How do you spend your time?"

"Believe it or not, this town has a traveling library. A guy drives through every Thursday, and you can take out books. I now have a library card with my new name," she said sourly. "But to answer your question, I read and drink ice tea because it's cheap."

"It is *so* good to see you, Janny," Maddie said, gripping her friend's hand on the table and squeezing it. "Listen, do we order and hope we don't get ptomaine, or do we leave and go back to your apartment? I assume it's within walking distance."

"Let's leave. I'll give the waitress a tip. Come on," Janny said, getting up from the table.

Maddie watched and listened as Janny handed the waitress a dollar bill. "My friend has a bad headache so we won't be staying for lunch. Guess I'll see you next week." The waitress pocketed the dollar and nodded, her expression uninterested. No one at the counter paid any attention to either one of the women as they walked out the door.

It was a short walk to Janny's small second-floor apartment. It was clean and neat, but incredibly hot. The furniture was worn, the carpet threadbare in places. The kitchen was old-fashioned. The stove had legs, the oven was on the side. It also had a large overhead warming oven that Janny pointed out. The sink had a paisley skirt that was tacked to the wooden frame around it and matched the kitchen curtains. "How about a sandwich? I have baloney and cheese, or you can have canned Spam. I even have a jar of pickles. I eat a lot of soup and sandwiches. I just don't want to do anything, Maddie. What's my incentive? There isn't any," she said through clenched teeth. "We're going to leave, right, Maddie?" she said, her face full of despair and hope.

Maddie put her arms around her friend and hugged her, then stepped back and regarded her with a smile, despite the tears in her eyes. "I'll take that sandwich and two pickles. Ice tea, if you have it. I need to talk this out, Janny. We both agree nothing is the way it was presented to us. Right?" Janny nodded. "That stupid orientation they presented didn't in any way indicate you would be living like this or that I would be in the kind of place I was in, waiting for a new identity that never materialized. Right?"

Janny nodded again, and said, "Nester seemed like an okay guy. At least to me he did."

"As long as it was just the police, yes. As soon as Justice, the

FBI, and the marshals got involved, it all changed. Nester is just a hardworking cop trying to make the city a little better. At least that's how I perceive him. Those other men, they're the big guns. They . . . they took over. Nester is out of it for now. All along I've been thinking that I got away so easy. In the beginning I refused to look over my shoulder. I think I was trying to prove something to myself. That marshal could have followed me. I don't know that he didn't. They're professional. I'm just a scared, dumb woman who doesn't know the first thing about crime and what all it involves. Look at me, Janny. I cut and dyed my hair. I look like a witch that's been on her broom too long. I bought a doll and a blanket and thought that would be the perfect disguise. As we speak, there's probably some damn marshal hiding in the bushes out there just waiting for the perfect moment to make his presence known. I wonder if they'll ever give me back my belongings—you know, that box of treasures I had. My dad's pictures, my baby pictures, all the things I love so much. I understand you have to start fresh with nothing but your clothing, but what harm could there be in having a few momentos of your past, things that don't speak of a specific time or place? It would make survival so much easier. They robbed us of everything. I hate them for that," Maddie said bitterly.

"I've come to love Spam," Janny said, setting Maddie's sandwich in front of her. "The mustard kills the taste, and when it's fried, it's not too bad. I can eat three days on a can of Spam."

Maddie bit into the sandwich. "It's tasty," she said, washing it down with a swig of ice tea. "Somewhere along the way we both lost sight of how important we are to the authorities. I think we need to fall back and regroup. By that I mean we should decide what we want and what we don't want. The fact that I managed to get here scares me. I am scared, Janny, make no mistake about that. We're no match for professionals, and it doesn't matter how many crime shows you watch. Those programs always ended in sixty minutes and the good guy invariably won. This is real, and that's why I'm so scared. I know you are too.

"Now, this is what I want," Maddie went on. "I want those men to take us to some safe place. I want them to bring Pete to that place. I want to talk to him face-to-face. I want us to be allowed to live someplace where it's clean, nice, and safe. Someplace where there are people, places, and things for us to do. They need to help us find jobs that pay us a decent amount of money so we can live with some semblance of our old lives. I want my box of treasures. If Pete can't or won't join us, that's okay, I can live with that, but I want to hear him say so. Trials can be postponed for months, years. If we were going to be in hiding for a short while, I'd go with everything they set up. We don't know for a fact the trial won't be postponed, and they don't make promises. Is there anything I said you don't agree with?"

"We were scared, Maddie. Those men played on our fear. I think, though, we gave them a run for their money, don't you?"

Maddie smiled for the first time in days. "That's part of it, Janny, we have no control. Our lives are in other people's hands. Well-meaning, I grant you, but as I said, this program is not geared to people like you and me. Now, what do you want to do?"

"The same thing as you. I'll go along with anything you decide. I think you should call Pete again. Late at night, to be sure he's home."

Maddie nodded. "We need to pick a place where we can go now. Someplace where there are a lot of people. I have enough money for us to take a bus to where we decide to go. I have a bad feeling about this place, Janny, and I can't explain it. I feel like we've been here before or we went through all of this before. We keep going . . . and doing what we said we weren't going to do. We need a firm, hard plan we can stick to. Do you have any ideas?"

"We need to accept that if we can make a deal and stick with that deal, with the government people, for the short term only, that it will make all the difference to us," Janny said. "Did what I say make sense?"

Maddie nodded.

"It's that unknown, that time thing, that's jerking us off. If they would say, 'Okay, ladies, you're going to be in this program for twelve months and then you're free to go once the trial is over,' I could accept that. No one ever said that to us. We've been thinking in *forever* terms. That's what's driving me out of my mind. God, can you picture me living here for the rest of my life?"

"No. And I'm not going to live this way either. We didn't do anything wrong. We need to think in terms of supply and demand. They want us because we have what they want. So for them to get us, they have to meet our demands too. I've had a taste of being on the run, and I don't like it. We can't afford to be on our own. We don't have to tell them that, though. If you sold Unitec, how much would you have?"

"Not enough for us to live off for any length of time. Besides, I haven't received the stock certificate yet. My savings account hasn't been transferred either."

"I guess we have to scratch that idea. I called Nester, but he was on vacation."

"Why?"

"I don't know why," Maddie said miserably. "If I had to take a wild guess, I'd say I called him because he represented some kind of stability in my mind. Pete's friend is running Fairy Tales. Pete said she's very nice. I got angry when I heard her answer the phone at the store. I never met her, but Pete invited her to the wedding. He said he couldn't get married without his best buddy there to cheer him on."

"Are you jealous of her?"

"Sure. Wouldn't you be?"

"Guess so."

"I know Pete's feelings for her are those for a sister and a close friend, but I don't know what hers are for him. Everything is suspect these days. I hope we all live to see the day when we can laugh about all of this."

Janny cleared the table. "Now what do you want to do?"

"What do you want to do?"

"Let's go for a walk. I'll show you the town. By the time you blink, you're through it. Twenty-two hundred people are supposed to live here, but I'll be damned if I know where the houses are. On the outskirts, I suppose."

"Do you have a straw bag like this?" Maddie asked.

"Sure. I got it at the general store to carry my groceries. Why?"

"Pack it up and let's go. We'll walk as far as we can and then hitchhike. The fine hairs on the back of my neck are starting to bother me. Don't take more than you'll need. Wear sneakers. When do you have to call in again?"

"I called in yesterday. That gives me six days before I have to check in again. They aren't interested in me, Maddie. It's you they can't afford to lose."

"It's hard for me to believe they just plopped you here and left you. You do have freedom. You can go into Provo, you can do pretty much what you want. They've been treating me like a criminal. Get your things, Janny. The sooner we get out of here, the better I'll feel," Maddie said, an edge to her voice.

"Maddie, what about my stock certificates and my bank account?"

"No one else can cash them in. Don't you have to sign for them when they arrive in the mail?"

"Yes. They haven't notified me that my savings account was transferred. Will I lose it all if I leave?" she asked nervously.

"I wouldn't think so, Janny, but I'm not sure. If they're in your new name, you can prove you're Betty Gill. I would think you could come back any time and claim what's yours. You have to decide, Janny, I can't make the decision for you. As it is, just because you're my friend, your life . . . You don't know how sorry I am about all this. I wish it was just me and that you were back in New York setting the financial world on fire."

"In your dreams." Janny guffawed. "I'll just be a few minutes.

The bathroom is off that little hallway by the pantry, in case you want to use it."

Maddie was washing her hands in the tiny sink when she heard Janny's anxious voice in the kitchen. "There's someone coming up the walk," she said, running to the bathroom doorway. "I saw him from the bedroom window. He's coming around the back now. No one has come here since I moved in. What are we going to do, Maddie?"

Maddie stuffed her hairbrush and comb into the straw bag. "Maybe it's someone for your landlady," she said, not believing her own words for a minute.

"My landlady went to some kind of festival with her sister. I heard her talking about it yesterday. When the kitchen window and door are open, you can hear everything that's going on. What should we do?"

"Quick, close the kitchen door and lock it. Is there someplace for me to hide?" she whispered, her eyes rolling back in her head.

Janny snorted. "Here? A mouse couldn't hide in this apartment. Wait a minute. Under the sink. Get behind the curtain. You'll have to crouch down. There's nothing under there but a bottle of dish detergent. Hurry, Maddie, he's on the steps, I can hear him."

Maddie parted the curtain, tossed in the straw bag, and crawled under the sink. Janny adjusted the curtain just as a knock sounded on the back door.

"Don't open it, Janny, talk through the glass. He'll be able to hear you," Maddie cautioned. She huddled back, her knees against her chest. God, where was Janny's straw bag? Did she leave it in her room or was it in the kitchen? Who was at the door?"

"Yes?" Janny said, her voice carrying clearly to Maddie under the sink. She could hear sound from the other side of the door, but the words weren't distinguishable.

"How do I know you're who you say you are?" Janny said, her voice quivering. "Where's Mr. Maloy?"

"He's at the hospital, his wife is about to have their first child," the voice on the other side of the door said. He flashed his ID.

Janny squinted to see the words clearly. The picture matched the face of Marshal Hendriks. "What do you want?"

"We're going to move you. We want you to pack your things. You are to come with me. Now."

Janny's heart thumped crazily in her chest. "Oh, no. No, no. I'm not moving again. My stock certificates haven't arrived and my bank account hasn't followed me either. I don't even know you. You tell them . . . tell them I said no. You can't do this to me. Everytime I come in contact with you people, I lose a year off my life. This is hard enough as it is. Your people said when I was relocated it would be until after the trial. You just go back there and tell them I said no. I don't like it here, but you aren't going to uproot me again."

"Miss Gill, please, open the door and let's sit down over a glass of lemonade and discuss this. I'm not here to hurt you, I'm here to help you."

"You say. Hrumph," Janny snorted. "Furthermore, you don't give me enough money to buy lemons, I have to drink ice tea because tea bags stretch further. I'm not interested in discussing anything with you. I checked in yesterday with Mr. Maloy. Until next week I am free to do as I please, and it does not please me to open my door to you. Annnnnd," she said stretching out the word, "you have not told me why you want to move me. Your organization is beginning to sound more and more like a Mickey Mouse operation. You people haven't followed through on anything you promised. That's not fair. You have two sets of rules, one for you and one for people like me. I don't like double standards. Now, are you going to tell me why you want to move me?"

Janny sucked in her breath when the marshal said, "Your friend left the program. We think she might be trying to find you."

"And because of that you want to *move* me!" Janny shrieked. "You're nuts! She walked out on you and you lost her. That's why you're here," she continued to shriek. "Get off my porch, now, do you hear me? I'll open this door and slam you over the railing. You lost my best friend in the whole world. If Maddie left, she left for a reason. You don't keep your promises. I told you to get out. I mean it, I'll slam you right over the railing!" She made a move to unlock and open the door. She knew in that one instant she would have pushed the marshal over the railing if he hadn't stepped down onto the first step.

When Janny was satisfied the marshal was indeed leaving, she opened the door and screamed, "How can Maddie find me, she doesn't know where I am, you people took care of that! Oh God!" she cried dramatically. "Now the case goes down the toilet!" She scurried back up the steps and into the kitchen, slamming and locking the door behind her.

Janny yanked at the curtain stretched around the sink before she dropped to her knees. "I'm sure you heard all that. You can come out now. Maddie, what's wrong with you? Maddie, look at me!"

Maddie was curled in the fetal position in the corner, her eyes glazed and blank. She shrank back from Janny's outstretched arms. "Maddie, you're scaring me," Janny said. "What's wrong? He went away. I told him I wasn't moving. He knows you left and thinks you're trying to find me. He's stupid. Maddie, please, come out of there. Let me help you. Maddie, we have to . . . God, we have to leave, go somewhere. Maddie, you were always the thinker, the one who solved our problems. Don't . . . don't quit on me now. Maddie, look at me," she wailed.

Janny sat back on her haunches. She tried a new tack. "Maddie, we have to call Pete. Pete will know what to do. Maddie, I need you to make some decisions here. That man said he was a marshal. He showed me ID. It could be phony, but I don't know that for a fact. It doesn't make sense to me that they would want to move me if they thought you were trying to find me. They should . . . wouldn't it make more sense to stake out this house and snatch you when you showed up? None of this makes any sense. They did lose you. Somehow you eluded them. Maddie, please, look at me. I don't make good decisions, I need your input. Damn it, Maddie, you're scaring me. Come on now, come out of there. We have to call Pete."

Janny's hands went to her temples. She rubbed at them furiously. Common sense said you didn't run from the good guys. She hunkered down again and pleaded with her friend. "Maddie, I think we should leave here. There's a cellar to this house, and Mrs. Isaacson never keeps anything locked. We can go there and hide until we get in touch with Pete, but you're going to have to help me. There's a phone in the cellar and one in Mrs. Isaacson's kitchen. She went to some festival with her sister and won't be back for three days. He's going to come back, I know it. You said they were going to tie you up and sedate you. What if they come back and do that to both of us? Maddie, what's wrong with you?"

Maddie was slobbering, her knuckles kneading her lips. Tears splashed from her eyes and rolled down her cheeks. "It was all for nothing," she singsonged. "I was stupid. I always do stupid things. You never do anything stupid," she continued to say in a singsong voice.

"That's because you don't let me do anything stupid. You've always been there for me, Maddie. And it wasn't all for nothing. How can you say that? We're together. That's the most important thing of all. There's strength in numbers. You penetrated the Witness Protection Program. It's never been done before. *They* told us it could never happen, but you proved them wrong. You did it. You found me."

"Because we broke the rules after we agreed not to."

"No, we did that before we signed their damn paper. We made a plan and we stuck to it. They screwed up. They lied to us. For our own safety, but it was still a lie. I'm piss-ass scared, Maddie. I really am." Janny cried hysterically.

Maddie ignored her, her eyes still glazed and blank.

"I'm going downstairs. I'll be right back."

Janny hurried down the back stairway to Mrs. Isaacson's kitchen door. She tried it, found it unlocked. She loped through the kitchen to the stairway that led to the cellar. Why couldn't they hide out here for a day or so until they got in touch with Pete? No reason at all. And by doing so, they were leaving the program. Well, she could live with that. Anything had to be better than living the way she'd been living since entering the program. It was better for Maddie too.

Janny surveyed the cellar with the aid of a dim forty-watt bulb hanging from the ceiling. The small windows were painted black, fine wire was tacked over them. The outside door was steel, and locked from the inside with a two-by-four that fit across two heavy-gauge-steel brackets. She struggled on the moss-covered steps, in the near dark, to slide the piece of wood firmly into place. If she could get Maddie to the cellar, no one would ever know they were here. She could bring down some food, a large wattage bulb, open up the rusty aluminum chairs, and voilà, all the comforts of home. Temporarily. Until Pete could get here and make things right.

Satisfied with the condition of the cellar, Janny raced upstairs to Mrs. Isaacson's kitchen, where she rummaged for paper and pencil. She scribbled off a note, signed Mrs. Isaacson's name to it, and slid it under the lid of the milk box. If anyone came snooping around, they would see the note, read it, and not bother with the rest of the house. They'd go through her own apartment, though, so she had to make it look as if she'd left in a hurry.

She checked on Maddie, who was still curled in a fetal position under the sink. In her room, Janny pulled out her suitcase and scattered her clothes about. She folded a few shirts neatly and placed them inside the suitcase.

In the kitchen she filled a paper sack with food, which she carried down to the basement along with hers and Maddie's straw bags. She returned to the kitchen, dropped to her knees. "You have to come out now, Maddie. If you don't, I'm leaving. You can stay here and take your chances. At best, I think you have about an hour. Right now that man who was here is probably talking to everyone in town, and the waitress at Dumfey's is telling him we were there. He's making calls and he's coming back, Maddie. I won't say they're going to harm us, but they'll try to split us up again, and God knows where either of us will end up. They know we know they lied to us. So, my thinking is they'll promise us anything to get us to go along with them. I'm going, are you coming?" Maddie didn't stir. Words like shock, comatose, withdrawn, filtered through Janny's brain. Angrily she reached out, grabbed Maddie under the arm and pulled her out onto the kitchen floor, where they both landed with a thump. Maddie immediately curled into her position again.

"Suck your thumb, damn you," Janny hissed. "That will make this all just perfect. When I call Pete, I'll tell him you reduced yourself to a vegetative status and don't want to go on with life. If you aren't killed, they'll lock you up somewhere and throw away the key." When there was no response from her friend, Janny said, "Oh, damn you, Maddie. Talk to me. Okay, you asked for it. Don't blame me when I finally get you to the cellar and you won't have an inch of skin on your ass." Her words were razor sharp, startling her, but they had no effect on Maddie.

Using all her strength, Janny dragged Maddie under the arms, out through the doorway and to the top of the steps. She propped her up against the post as though she were a rag doll. Maddie's blank stare petrified her.

Each time Maddie's rump hit the wooden step, Janny winced. Her friend's tush was going to be black and blue for months to come. Janny could hardly breathe when she leaned up against the wall at the bottom of the steps. Out of the corner of her eye she saw Maddie move, struggle to a sitting position. "Are you trying to kill me?" she barked.

"Yes," Janny barked back. "You scared the daylights out of me.

You've been out of it for almost an hour. Look, I'm sorry about your rear end, but it was all I could think of. Can you get up? We have to get inside. I don't think we have a whole lot of time. I'll explain when we're safe inside. Can you walk?"

Maddie struggled to her feet, groaning and moaning as she did so. With Janny's arm around her shoulder, she made it into the kitchen and down the cellar steps. The moment Maddie collapsed into one of the rusty aluminum chairs, Janny raced back upstairs to lock Mrs. Isaacson's kitchen door. She spent another five minutes locking all the windows as well as the front door before she rejoined Maddie in the cellar.

"Would you mind telling me what we're doing here in this dungeon?" Maddie asked wearily.

Janny sat down, her breathing labored. "I'm not sure. You know me, I'm not an idea person. You are, but when you . . . when you . . . did what you did, I didn't know what else to do. What made you . . . why . . . you scared me out of my wits. When Hendriks—that's what he said his name was—left, I knew he was coming back. They want to move me again. If you can believe this . . . because you up and left them. I think they lost you somewhere along the way. He as much as admitted it. Now, you tell me why they want to move *me* if they think you're on your way here? It doesn't make sense."

"I think what it all comes down to is they didn't know how to react to us, how to treat us," Maddie said wearily. "They thought we would put up with anything. They didn't figure on either one of us having a mind of our own. We keep talking about this, saying the same things over and over. Why are we here, what do we hope to gain by hiding out in your landlady's cellar? I'm not sure this is one of your better ideas."

"It gives us a chance to call Pete," Janny replied. "Look, there's a phone over there at the bottom of the cellar steps. We can use it, make as many calls as we want as long as we leave money to pay for them. Pete will help us. He will, won't he, Maddie?"

"I don't know anything anymore, Janny. I think I screwed everything up for both of us. Because I can't live without my identity doesn't mean you have to feel the same way. I'm me, I'll always be me. Why couldn't those men see that, why couldn't they make provisions for us? I was born Maddie Stern, and if and when I die, I want to die as Maddie Stern, not some Jane Doe person. I should have paid attention to my instincts, but I didn't. And those people fed on our fears. Now look at us. We're running and hiding from people who, misguided or not, are trying to help us. I'm sorry about before, Janny. I guess I reached my breaking point."

"Look, it's over and done with. The question is, what do we do now?" Janny asked.

"What you said, we call Pete. But we don't leave a message and we don't talk to anyone but Pete."

"That sounds okay to me. Can I get you a drink, Maddie? You look kind of white and drawn."

"A drink would be nice. I'm tired to the bone, Janny. I hate it when I can't handle something, and I hate it even more when I botch things up."

"I think of it as a learning experience," Janny said airily.

"You know, Janny, we've led a colorful life these past few weeks. Now we can add breaking and entering to our list."

"We did not break in. Yes, we did enter. We didn't . . . enter with the intention of doing harm or to steal. We entered to stay safe. We're going to leave money for the phone calls we make. The door was open. See, that makes all the difference. Are you ready to make your phone call?" she asked as she handed over a paper cup of water she'd drawn from the faucet over the laundry sinks.

"God, yes. Where's the phone?"

"By the steps. I brought a larger light bulb down with me, but I'm not sure we should put it in. Even though those windows are painted black, there might be some cracks in the paint and light will show through. I know I'm paranoid," Janny said, anticipating Maddie's comment.

But Maddie said, "We don't need a brighter light, and you could be right."

Maddie sucked in her breath and dialed Pete's number. Her watch said it was four forty-five. She slammed the phone down after the third ring.

"We'll try calling every twenty minutes. We aren't leaving here till I speak to Pete."

When the hands on Maddie's watch read seven forty-five and Pete still hadn't answered the phone, Janny placed her index finger next to her lips. "I hear something," she whispered. "Voices." She pointed to the small window on the opposite side of the cellar. "That window is near my steps." The girls ran to the window, crouching underneath. "They're going up the steps to my apartment," she whispered. "If they're talking, I can't here what they're saying. It sounds like there's three different voices."

Maddie rocked back on her heels when she heard a clear, distinct voice bellow, "Where the fuck did they go? She didn't stop to take her things, so that has to mean she left in a hurry. Probably hitchhiked. I told you all along the other one was headed here, but did anyone listen? *No!* The curly-top was seen in the café with another woman. It could have been anyone, but I know in my gut it was her. Doesn't matter if she had short blond hair or not. Women are forever changing their hair, my wife does it once a week. This is all your fault, Hendriks, and you'll answer for it."

"Wait a minute, what's this?"

"What's what?" The second voice said.

"There's a note in the mailbox and it's addressed to . . . someone named Anna. Maybe our girl put it here?"

"Eat shit, Hendriks. It says Mrs. Isaacson went to the festival with her sister and won't be back for three days. Everyone has gone to the damn festival. She'll be back in time for her gin rummy game with this Anna. Now I suppose you're going to tell me this is some kind of code." The disgust in the man's voice was apparent to everyone within earshot.

Maddie clapped her hands over her mouth. Janny gave her a thumb's up salute.

"They could be hiding in the house somewhere. There's a cellar to this house," Hendriks said defensively.

"I told you to eat shit, Hendriks. Old ladies lock up their houses, and this old lady probably locked her cellar door too. You do that when you're old so you'll feel safe. You want to check, be my guest."

The girls ran to the bottom of the moss-covered steps and waited, both of them holding their breath.

"Perps often do the obvious to throw you off the track," Hendriks said, his voice clear and still defensive.

"This lady is not a perp. She is a federally protected witness. So is the other woman we've been tracking. Thanks to you, Hendriks, this one got away. I say they're long gone, but if you want to break into this house, you take the flak. The damn house is dark and locked tight. Decide."

A third voice spoke. "I agree with Cunningham, the woman is gone. She's probably in Provo by now. We don't have the manpower to put a man here to watch over things. I can call the sheriff and have him do some ride-bys."

"Do that," Hendriks snapped.

"Call it in, Martinson. I'm going to call the Provo police and have them put out an APB on both women. This isn't going to look good for any of us. We aren't supposed to lose people. Now we lost two. How's that going to look? Let's get on the stick and get moving."

Janny clenched both her fists before shooting them in the air.

Maddie smiled from ear to ear. She laughed. "We're famous."

"Infamous," Janny shot back.

"Time to call Pete again," Maddie said.

Maddie's watch said it was eight-ten when she dialed Pete's number. There was no answer. She tried it again at eight-thirty and again at eight-fifty. "Maybe I should leave a message."

"No. I don't think that's a good idea, Maddie."

At nine-twenty, when Maddie placed her call, Annie Gabriel answered the phone. Maddie sucked in her breath and mouthed the words, Pete's friend Annie. She hung up the phone without saying anything.

"I don't think Annie would answer Pete's phone if he was there, do you?" Janny shook her head from side to side.

Jealousy reared its ugly head. Maddie chose her words carefully, her voice neutral. "It doesn't look like Pete is at home waiting for my call. I guess he isn't too broken up over my absence."

"Maddie, you don't know that. For all you know he could have been in the shower or taking the trash down to the first floor. He could have gone to pick up a pizza. I don't want you thinking like that. Pete loves you as much as you love him. He could even be out combing the streets looking for you."

"Janny, remember when we were little and we feared something? We thought about it so much, worried ourselves sick that what we feared would happen, and then it did happen because of that fear. This is like that. I can't explain it any better."

"I think you need to keep an open mind."

"I think," Maddie said, sitting down gingerly, "we need to call Nester."

"Nester! For God's sake, why?"

"He's the one who got us into this mess, and he should be the one to get us out of it."

"But Maddie, that means we . . . that means we have to go back into the program. I thought we were going . . . oh, hell, I don't know what I thought."

"That's just it, Janny, neither one of us can think clearly. We've been fooling ourselves. We know what works for us and what doesn't. My thinking is, Nester can convince the service to work with us, to bend and give a little. I know that I'm personally as close to a nervous breakdown as I'll ever get. People aren't meant to live this way. I cannot give up my life, I just can't. If I do that, there's nothing left. It doesn't mean you have to do it too." Her tone of voice was listless, an I-don't-care-what-happens-either-way statement.

The rusty aluminum chair squeaked when Janny sat down across from her friend. They were to the left of the hanging forty-watt light bulb that bathed both of them in a sickly off-yellow color. Maddie didn't look right, and it had nothing to do with the low wattage from overhead.

Janny watched as Maddie tried to curl herself in the chair, but the rotting weaving and rickety aluminum legs prevented comfort of any kind. Her stomach started to knot up, a sign that upheaval was eminent. She wanted to say something cheerful, something witty and brilliant, but what came out of her mouth was so unexpected she leaped off the chair and started to pace.

"Maddie, I have this feeling you're going to wipe out and leave me stranded. We need to pull together. I gave it all up. And you know what bothers me the most, the one thing I haven't been able to talk to you about because you are so . . . intense about all of this. They're relaxing the child adoption laws, and one of the attorneys I spoke with from the company said it was more than possible I might be able to find my natural mother or she might be able to find me. It's not impossible, Maddie," Janny said brokenly.

"I didn't say it was," Maddie mumbled.

"Look at you! Just look at you!" Janny said, jabbing her hand in Maddie's direction. "You're withdrawing, I can see it, feel it. You don't want to deal with this anymore. Well, we have to deal with it. Going into this . . . damn program, I gave up the possibility of ever finding my mother or her finding me. So, what I'm saying here is, I gave up just as much as you did, and you don't see me . . . wilting . . . and throwing in the towel." She broke down and started to sob, expecting Maddie to offer the right words, give a comforting hug that would take away the loss she was feeling. When Maddie made no move to comfort her, Janny cried harder.

Maddie dozed in the chair while Janny continued to cry. She hadn't caved in, she'd gone along with everything Maddie said. Now what was going to happen to them? She risked a tearful glance at her friend. Maybe she should try Pete's number again. Maybe she should call Nester like Maddie suggested. Maybe, maybe, maybe.

Janny looked at her watch. Ten-fifteen. Time to go to the bathroom. She inched herself off the lawn chair and made her way to the staircase that led to Mrs. Isaacson's kitchen. She was on the top step when she saw the blue flashing light of the sheriff's patrol car flash through the dotted Swiss curtains in the kitchen. A moment later she saw a round circle of light dance across the kitchen. She heard the doorknob rattle. She sucked in her breath and backed down another step. She listened, heard the top of the milk box crash down, heard heavy, booted steps as the sheriff climbed the stairs that led to her apartment. It was a good thing she hadn't gone into the bathroom. She'd be flushing by now, a sure giveaway to the sheriff, with the house's outdated plumbing.

When she thought she couldn't wait another moment, she heard the steps again, then the sound of the car's engine. The blue light flashed against the refrigerator. She waited another minute before she bolted for the bathroom. Flush or not flush? She flushed, washed her hands and dried them on her shorts, not wanting to disturb the whiteness of the unwrinkled towels hanging on the rack.

At the bottom of the steps she stared at the phone. Without hesitation she picked it up and dialed Pete's apartment. The phone was picked up after the third ring. "Is Pete there?"

"No he isn't. Can I take a message?"

Janny's eyes were glued to the second hand of her watch. "This is Janice Hobart. Where is Pete and when will he be home?"

"Janice! Good Lord. Where are you? Pete isn't here. He left early this morning and isn't back. Where are you?"

"We left the program. We're together. Maddie found me. I'll call again. Tell Pete to say home and wait."

"I'll tell him."

Janice broke the connection in case the wire was bugged. A minute and a half. Safe.

Should she call Nester or shouldn't she? She drummed her fingers against the hard black plastic of the phone, trying to make up her mind. If this were a crime show, what would the star do? Janny dialed New York information and asked for the home phone number of Otis Nester. Thank God she remembered his first name. She was referred to the Staten Island area code and redialed. Luckily, it was listed. She repeated the number four times before she dialed it. A sleepy voice said Detective Nester was on duty. "Tell him . . . tell him Miss XYZ called," Janny said dramatically before she broke the connection. Her fingers tapped furiously before she made up her mind to call the police precinct where Nestor worked. She dialed again, said she was Adele Newcomb and needed to talk to Detective Nester on an urgent matter. The voice on the other end of the phone said the detective was about to go off duty. "Hold on, ma'am, I'll see if I can catch him for you."

Janny watched the minute hand on her watch. When the small hand reached the two minute mark, she hung up, redialed, and said she was cut off. A moment later Nester's voice rang over the wire. "Detective Nester, this is Janice Hobart. You do remember me?"

"Very well. Where are you?"

"Listen, okay? Don't ask questions. Maddie is with me. She's . . . acting funny. I think she's going to have a nervous breakdown. She said as much. Before Maddie started . . . she said she thought we should call you. All of you lied to us. Nothing is the way those people said it would be. I need to hear you say you all lied. About Pete and his uncle. You have thirty seconds and then I'm hanging up. Did you or didn't you?"

"Miss Hobart, listen to me, I just take orders. I do what I'm told. You could be in danger, whether Pete or his uncle are involved or not. What in the hell made you two leave the program?" His voice was that of a chastising big brother.

"Time's up. I guess that means it all was a lie, that's what I'm getting out of what you said. Shame on you. You've ruined our lives, and it's on your conscience." Breathlessly, she hung up the phone. "Servant of the people, my ass," she muttered.

"Who were you talking to, Janny?" Maddie said, stretching her legs out in front of her.

"I called Pete's apartment and then I called Nester. That's what you wanted me to do, isn't it?"

"I guess so. Did you talk to Pete's friend?"

"She said he wasn't there and doesn't know when he'll be back. She asked me twice where we were, but I didn't tell her. I also forgot the time difference here."

Maddie's eye's sparked momentarily. Janny ran with the spark and started to babble. "Nester almost admitted he lied . . . they lied . . . someone lied . . . they all lied . . . whatever. He said he just followed orders. To me that's an admission. He said we could be in danger, even if not from Pete's uncle, and wanted to know why we left. Sometimes people are so stupid. I told him you were on the verge of a nervous breakdown. Are you?"

Maddie stirred, her eyes full of tears. "I've never felt like this before. There's no incentive to make me want to move, to do anything. I don't even want to think. That's what's scaring me, so if that means I'm having a nervous breakdown, then I guess I am. I want to go to sleep and never wake up."

Janny's eyes filled with panic. "Are you telling me," she said carefully, "that we should sit down and wait for the marshals to come back and get us? If you're telling me that, then you're going to sit here by yourself because I am not going to sit around and wait to go someplace more deadly than this. I made a mistake listening to you. I thought you had all the answers, and now you're sitting there sucking your thumb. You don't care that I gave up my life, gave up hope of ever finding my mother. You gave up Pete and your business. Big, fucking deal. I gave up my *mother.* Do you hear me, Maddie? Until now I just diddled with the idea of finding her, it was something to dream about, something to hang on to. Now that I know I can't ever do that, it's suddenly the most important thing in the world to me. So you just go ahead and sit here and do whatever it is you're going to do. I'm getting out of here."

"Where are you going?" Maddie asked, fear seeping into her voice.

"I have no idea, but I'm going. As far away as I can go or until my money runs out. Good luck, Maddie."

Maddie was out of her chair running after Janny a second later. "Wait. Cut me a little slack, okay. Let's sit here on the steps and try to formulate a plan."

"Maddie, that's what we've been doing. Neither one of us is any good at this. We need to admit to ourselves and to each other that we are not cut out to . . . live on the run. You know it too, or you wouldn't have told me to call Nester. At best we have a day, maybe a day and a half, until Mrs. Isaacson comes home."

"When did you get so uppity and persnickety?" Maddie demanded.

"When you curled into a fetal position," Janny shot back. "Now, what's it going to be?"

Maddie picked up the phone and dialed Pete's number. It rang five times before it was picked up on the other end. "Annie, this is Maddie. Has Pete returned?"

"No, Maddie, he hasn't."

"Is Pete's phone bugged?"

"It was. Mr. Jakes said he removed the device. I personally don't know much about things like that. I understand your reticence in disclosing your location. I don't know what to tell you. I think you should know Pete's going to be leaving shortly on a business trip. His uncle called earlier. What do you want me to tell him?"

"Tell him," Maddie said, her eyes locking with Janny's, "that Janny and I are back into the program. Tell him I did everything I could to reach him so he could help me. I needed him. Tell him . . . tell him I don't need him anymore."

Janny watched her friend hang up the phone. "Why did you say a thing like that?" she hissed.

"It's true, isn't it?" Maddie's voice was flat, devoid of any emotion.

"Now what?"

"Now you call Nester back. Tell him to call the marshals to pick us up. Our only stipulation is we go together. If he can't agree, then we start to hitchhike."

The United States Marshals picked up Maddie and Janny at four o'clock in the morning. They climbed into the backseat of a maroon sedan. They huddled together and were asleep almost instantly.

The driver headed north.

The hour was early. The room was in shadows cast by the overhead light fixture, which was missing two bulbs. It was a dusty room, a room in the narrow basement at 600 Army Navy Drive. Mostly an unused room that now hosted six angry, belligerent men.

Otis Nester looked around at the faces staring at him. He knew the resentment he felt at this middle-of-the-night summons showed clearly on his face. He'd driven all night to make this particular meeting. He felt irritable because his clothes were wrinkled and he needed a shave. And he had to drive all the way back to New York shortly.

There was no doubt in anyone's mind that Otis Nester was pissed-off. Big-time.

Introductions were made by a young man who, Nester thought, still hadn't shaved: the Attorney General, the Security Chief of the U.S. Marshals Service, William Monroe of Justice, and Carl Weinstein of the FBI. Three marshals in uniform stood against the wall. All their eyes were on Nester. His own eyes were narrowed, mostly because they were full of grit as he gazed at first one man and then another until he completed his scrutiny of the room's occupants.

"I told you it wasn't going to work," Nester said. "Did you listen? Those young women suspect we lied about Leo Sorenson to get them to cooperate. Sure you have them now, but you aren't going to keep them. I'd bet my pension on it. Just because you agreed, which you should have done in the first place, to let them be together, won't keep them in hiding. You screwed up, and I for one don't blame them for bolting. *They found each other. Maddie got away and you lost her.* What the fuck does that say for you guys? Not much to me, and even less to them."

"They trust you," the Attorney General said quietly. "They called you."

"And called me a liar. They aren't stupid. They're going to remember all this, and when they get antsy again in a month or so, they're going to do the same thing. Jesus Christ, you took Miss Stern's lover, her wedding, her business away from her. Your program," he said, eyeing the Chief of Security, "is not designed for people like Maddie Stern and Janice Hobart. You needed to make concessions, and you didn't. What you're doing now isn't going to work any better. Those women are *intelligent.* And Maddie Stern is on the verge of a nervous breakdown. If that happens, Janice Hobart will be your worst nightmare come to life."

"We have rules," the Security Chief said.

"Fuck your rules. They didn't work the first time out, and they aren't going to work this time either. Get that through your head," Nester snarled.

"We don't have the money for first-class hotels, and we can't provide the kind of jobs they desire. We can't give them cars and privileges. We aren't set up that way."

"Exactly!" Nester shot back. "You can find the money to do what has to be done. Keep them happy and content, tell them the truth, and you might have a chance of keeping them in the program. If you don't, I'm going to get another midnight call. Jesus Christ, don't you get it? They got away from you. Maddie Stern is in love, and you didn't have the decency to bring about a meeting so Sorenson could be told what was going on. Well,

let me be the first to tell you he's on their trails. I know Maddie Stern called him. She didn't tell me that, I figured it out for myself. This guy loves her too, and he isn't going to let it die down. You ripped all that out from under her and then you didn't follow through on what you promised," Nester said, his voice as chilly as his eyes.

"What do you suggest?" the Security Chief asked quietly.

"Be good to them. They don't deserve anything less. I realize you can't give them back the life they had, but you can come damn close. Pull strings, make calls, do what it takes, for Christ's sake. With Maddie Stern's testimony, she's giving you what you only dreamed about. Without her you have no case."

"They trust you. Why is that, Detective Nester? You lied to them too."

"Yes, but under orders. I told you they were smart. They saw through that once they had time to think. They know cops follow orders. That was the first thing they asked me last night."

"And your reply was . . ." the Attorney General said.

"My reply was, I do what I'm told, I follow orders. If I had lied, they would have hung up. Give me some credit, sir."

They talked among themselves for the next thirty minutes, arguing and snapping and snarling at one another. Nester sipped at his coffee, which tasted like his running shoes smelled.

"Adam Wagoner promised Maddie Stern a meeting with Pete Sorenson," Nester said when he finished the coffee.

"Adam Wagoner passed away," the Security Chief said quietly. "That promise is not binding to the rest of us."

"I'd rethink that if I were you. Maddie Stern is going to be thinking about it a lot. If there's nothing else, gentlemen, I'd like to get on the road and out of Washington before rush-hour traffic."

Outside in the early morning air that was clear and fresh, Nester contributed to the day's pollution by lighting a cigarette. He wanted to kill someone or something at that moment.

As Nester headed for I-95 he wondered when the muckety-mucks would tell Maddie and her friend it would be at least three years before the case came to trial. Not for a year at least, and then it would go on a month-to-month basis. He consoled himself with the fact that both women were safe and they were together.

For the moment.

20

Pete dated the check September 4, 1983, scribbled an amount, signed his name, and handed it to Simon Jakes. "Thanks for everything, Jakes. Have a nice weekend," he said wearily.

"What are you going to do, Pete?"

"Well, I thought I'd drive up to Connecticut, meet with a new broker and see if I can move things along a little faster. I'm going to sublet the apartment to Annie, and I'll move into a new house. I have a few days to get things in order before I have to make another trip. Jesus, Jakes, I can't believe Maddie said . . . said she doesn't need me now. How could she say a thing like that?" Pete said brokenly. "Christ, I did everything I could think of. For days, I tried to get a line on that woman who sold Maddie her cat Tillie. Zip. Fucking zip. I was so sure that was the answer. She was in, then she was out, now she's back in. Maddie I mean. Annie said she sounded disgusted. What the hell does she want from me? Disgusted. Jesus."

"Look, Pete, it was meant to be this way. Accept it and be grateful that Maddie and Janny are in safe custody. That should be your main concern. How long does it take a trial to come to court?"

Pete snorted. "A trial like this? At the very least, a year. They'll want to make sure the case is as airtight as they can make it. Time . . . time doesn't always make things right. When this is all over, if it's ever over, none of us will be the same as we are now. I'm changing already, and I know Maddie is too."

Jakes nodded. "Well, if you need me, you know where to find me," he said. "Good luck, Pete. Say good-bye to Annie for me."

"I'll do that. Stay in touch."

"That trip you mentioned—where are you going this time?"

"Montana," Pete said. "The consortium I work for decided they want to buy up cattle ranches. I'm actually looking forward to this job. I can't wait to smell the great outdoors and eat home-cooked food. That was one of the promises they made to me. They tell me ranch life is good for the soul. I'll send you a postcard."

"Do that."

When Jakes left, Pete wandered around the apartment feeling lost. He thought about Maddie until his vision blurred. He wished he could blink his eyes and have Barney materialize. Barney would have answers for him.

In a fit of something he couldn't define, Pete stomped his way to the hall closet and yanked out his surfboard. He carried it back to the living room, where he laid it on the floor. He had wax, polish, and a bag of old rags. He started to work on the board, not knowing if what he was doing to it was right or wrong. He worked for two hours before he threw down the rags in disgust. Who was he fooling? He didn't want to do this. He didn't want to do anything. But most of all, he didn't want to be alone. Annie. Annie always made things better. Good old Annie.

The surfboard went back into the closet, the rags and polish placed on the overhead shelf.

It was ten-thirty according to the clock on the mantel. The long day stretched in front of him. Did he really want to go to Connecticut? Not alone he didn't. A moment later the phone was in his hand. Annie answered on the third ring. "How'd you like to go to Connecticut with me? Close up."

"I'd love it if you can manage to work a little enthusiasm into your voice. I can't close, though, I have the Labor Day sale going on and business is very good. I expect it will slow down around three or so. How about if I give you a call around two?"

"Okay. I'm going out, so if I'm not back, leave a message. Oh, Jakes said to tell you good-bye."

"Pete, I'm sorry you couldn't make things work for you. I know you don't want to hear this, but you have to think about what's best for Maddie."

"You're right, I don't want to hear it. I'll talk to you later." Maddie doesn't need me, he thought. Maddie sounded disgusted.

An hour later Pete was driving through Saddle River Park on his way to his uncle Leo's. He loved the park, had come here often on foot and then on his bike the first summer he spent with Leo. As he made his way down Ridgewood Avenue he wondered if he should have called ahead. Leo could have gone away for the holiday weekend. In the end it didn't matter. He liked driving, it was a way to pass the time. Besides, this talk was long overdue. It was something he'd put off for years and wasn't sure why. So why did he feel it was time to do it now? Because, he answered himself, if I'm to go on with my life, I have to go with no excess baggage loading me down.

Leo himself answered the door. He managed to cover his surprise with a weak smile. "Peter, it's nice of you to come by. Is anything wrong?"

Suddenly Pete wanted to cry, to sob into his uncle's shoulder, to feel the older man pat him on the back and mouth soothing words of comfort. "There's a lot that's wrong. There isn't much that's right these days. I need to talk to someone. I guess you think you're a last resort . . . and in a way, you are."

"Come in, Peter. Let's go out on the patio and talk. I've been closing up the pool. Can you stay for lunch? I gave the staff the weekend off. I made pickled eggs this morning. My cook made a tray of vegetable lasagne and a pot of stuffed cabbage, all the things I'm not supposed to eat."

"Why is that? Sure, I'll have lunch with you."

"Because my heart isn't so good. I cheat once in a while."

"I didn't know that. You never said anything," Pete said.

"A man doesn't go around talking about his . . . weaknesses. Our family was always robust and . . . healthy. Well, your father wasn't exactly robust, but he was in good physical shape."

"I think you should have told me," Pete said with annoyance.

"Would you have been nicer to me? Is that what you mean, Peter?"

"Yes . . . no. I'm your only living relative. You should tell me things like that."

"Shouldn't that work two ways? You weren't going to invite me to your wedding. I don't want us to argue, Peter. I'm just glad you stopped by. I don't even care what the reason is. Why don't we . . . visit for a bit, and then you can tell me why you're here."

Pete settled himself in a padded lounge chair under a gaily striped, oversize umbrella. His uncle handed him a glass of ice tea.

"Tell me about my father, and don't bullshit me," Pete said. "Tell me all the things you *didn't* tell me when we first met. I know he didn't like you. My dad liked everyone. Everyone but you."

Leo sipped at his ice tea. "Harry was younger than me by three years. When we were young, we were inseparable. I looked out for him. I was the robust-looking one, big for my age, and I was also a bit of a bully I suppose. Harry was tall and thin. Very thin. Children picked on him, in the beginning. He wasn't much of a fighter. I'm not saying that was wrong. He didn't do all that well in school because he was a bit of a dreamer. He didn't want to go to college, so he did all manner of things. For a while he was a mechanic, and then he was a salesman. He was also a house painter and a roofer. He managed to keep himself going. I wasn't in much of a position to help him because I was working my way through college and law school. We stayed in touch, though. Harry wrote faithfully, and I did too. In the beginning."

Pete held his glass out for a refill. He noticed the way his uncle's hands shook when he poured from the heavy cut-glass pitcher.

"The year I graduated from law school I met a lovely young woman and I invited her to go home with me for the Memorial Day weekend. I loved her dearly. She became my reason for getting up in the morning. I introduced her to Harry, and it was love at first sight for both of them. I didn't take it well and neither did Harry. We had a fistfight, and of course I, in my anger, beat the crap out of him. The object of both our affections called me every unthinkable name she could think of. I watched her kiss away every bruise, every cut, every mark on your father. She wanted to spit on me, but she was too much of a lady to do that. Calling me names was okay, though.

"I left, my heart in shreds. I sent a wedding present, and at one point I offered to loan your father money for a down payment on a little house, the one you grew up in. Your father refused the offer. There was no contact after that for a long time.

"Then, when I found you, it all came back. Now you were mine, and I didn't know the first thing about kids. You were a sassy, arrogant boy, and I didn't know how to handle that. I'm not making excuses here, I'm telling you how it was.

"I thought if I gave you everything under the sun, it would make things right. It drove you further away. I gave you every advantage, and you still thumbed your nose at me. I likened that to what your mother did to me. I wanted you to be everything your father wasn't. And you are. You're bright, you're successful, you're rich. I made you what you are today, Peter."

"For all the wrong reasons, Leo. What good is all that if I can't have the woman I love? I never married. You never forgave my father. You didn't do it for him, you did it all for yourself. You wanted to prove—and I don't know how you prove things to dead people—but you wanted to prove to them you were the better one. When my parents were alive, we were happy. You never once made me happy."

"I didn't know how, Peter."

"Damn it, couldn't you learn? Listen, I'm not blameless here. As long as we're in a confessing mode, I need to tell you a few things. I thought, believed, that you were searching for me. I honest to God believed that. Just the same way I believed Barney would come for me when I was sixteen. In the beginning I wanted to go to you so many times and bawl my head off. I ached to have you hug me and take me in your arms and thump my back. You know, guy stuff.

"Another thing, I don't hate the law. I know I say I do. It was a way of jamming it to you. I truly don't know if I would have made a better engineer. I guess what I'm trying to say here is nobody gets it all, and I am grateful for everything you've done for me."

"And I'm grateful you allowed me to do it," Leo said quietly.

"I guess neither one of us tried hard enough," Pete went on. "I'm sorry for the years we lost. I think I turned out to be a pretty nice guy." Leo beamed. "Okay, you had a little to do with it." Leo kept on beaming. "I really don't *like* the law, though," Pete blurted.

"I know. Explain to me how you can do so well at something you hate so much."

"I think I've been trying to prove to you that I'm better than you are. At what I do," Pete said hastily.

"Spoken like a true lawyer. I'm so proud of you I could burst."

"Where do we go from here?" Pete asked quietly.

"One day this will all be yours," Leo said, gesturing broadly. "It ain't shabby, kid. I busted my ass to get it, and it isn't tainted, if that's your next question."

"What about all those sleazebags your office represents?"

"Those sleazebags, as you call them, are less than one percent of our clients. Sure, I know members of the crime families. Hell, your father and I went to school with them. I call them by name, they call me by name. They do what they do for a living, and I do what I do." Leo paused for a moment and eyed his nephew speculatively. "Are you trying to find out from me if there's a way I can intervene on your behalf?" he asked quietly. "Is that where this is going?"

"Yeah, I guess so." Pete brought him up to date on the past several weeks.

"My advice is to wait it out, let the authorities do their job, and you, Peter, sit back and wait. It's the only sensible, logical, reasonable thing to do. To do anything else would be very foolhardy."

"I haven't had the time to go back and read up on what happened. The detective I hired gave me highlights, enough to go on. How good a case do the authorities have? How long before it comes to trial?"

"From what I've read and heard, they have a very good case. My best guess would be two years before this case sees a courtroom, maybe three. They can't afford to make any mistakes."

"Is this where you tell me to keep busy, work my ass off and the three years will go by like lightning?"

"In a manner of speaking. You cannot penetrate the Witness Protection Program, Peter. It's never been done."

"There was a tap on my phone."

Leo made an ugly sound in his throat. "There's been one on my phone for years. The feds are experts at things like that. Don't pay any attention to it. I don't. When you don't do anything wrong, they can't do anything to you. That alone should answer any questions you have about me. Now, how about those pickled eggs?"

"My mother used to make pickled eggs, but only on Easter."

"I know. That's where I acquired the taste. I make them every week. I'm not supposed to eat them. Yolks are bad for you. When it comes right down to it, nothing's good for you. Sex is up for grabs, smoking will kill you, alcohol will rot your liver, eggs will bust your veins, and cake and pie will blow your heart right out of your chest. You know what I say to all those greedy doctors? I say fuck you, if I'm meant to die, then I'll die. When

God's ready for me, I'll go, kicking and scratching, but not eating bean curd and brussels sprouts. Jesus, the gas alone can kill you."

Pete laughed, and his uncle smiled in response, his face merry and relaxed.

His uncle, Pete noticed afterward, was at home in the kitchen, setting fine china on place mats, folding napkins, setting the bowls of food in two separate microwave ovens. "I like things to be ready all at the same time," Leo said, pointing to the four microwave ovens lined up on the counter. "It's decadent, right?"

Pete laughed, then changed the subject: "Tell me what you know about cattle ranching."

"Red meat is bad for your arteries," Leo said, and roared with laughter. "We want to buy up as many of the ranches as we can so the Japanese can't buy them. That's the bottom line. The Japs are trying to buy up the ranches so they can ship the beef to Japan. We don't want that to happen. That's the extent of my knowledge. I'm along for the ride. My money is in the pot. You'll make a bundle, if you can pull this off. You know, Peter, you can retire after this job. I know your contract has four months to run, but that contract also says if you are in the middle of negotiations, you'll carry through until the deal is consummated. If I'm right on the three-year trial, you'll finish up for the consortium, take a year off, and wait for your fiancée to come back to you. You're young, you're healthy, and you're rich. Think and plan how you want to spend the rest of your days."

"Bell's Beach," Pete said without a moment's hesitation.

"Now you see, that's something to shoot for. How many of these pickled eggs do you want?"

"Three, if you trade me your yolks for my whites." Peter ate one of the yolks, then looked up and said, "I heard from Maddie, indirectly. She said she doesn't need me."

"Give her time, Peter," Leo replied. "No doubt she's under a lot of strain right now. If it's meant to be, it will be. If Maddie isn't the one you're meant to spend the rest of your life with, it won't happen. Everything is ordained or preordained or something like that."

"Or something," Pete said.

"Something good came out of all of this," Leo said shyly as they ate their eggs. "We got to know one another a little better."

"Yes we did. I wish I'd had the brains to come to you a long time ago. My dad was an okay guy, so was my mom. She had the sweetest smile, and she baked the best cookies in the world."

"Let's drink to your parents," Leo said, pouring wine into two fragile long-stemmed glasses.

"Are you allowed to drink wine?"

"No. It does something to your blood pressure. I have a whole list of things, you know, do's and don'ts." He held his glass aloft. "I think you should make the toast, Peter."

"To my mom and dad and Bell's Beach."

"Tell me about that surfboard and Bell's Beach."

"It was my father's dream. I made it my dream. I know as much about surfing as you know about cattle ranching. I'll take that year you spoke of to learn while I wait for Maddie, and hope she changes her mind about me. I can make the dream come true. If I want to. Sometimes it's better to just dream. I guess it's the same principle as saying, be careful of what you wish for because you might get it. We can talk about Bell's Beach and the surfboard another time."

"Yes," Leo said sadly. "Another time."

Pete was on his way back to the city a little after two o'clock. His handshake was firm and hard when he said good-bye at the door of Leo's mansion. Pete blinked when Leo said, "Son, don't let the Japanese get the upper hand on this deal. Whatever it takes is what we'll pay. The little cruds already own half of Hawaii if not all of it."

"Maybe we should spread out. Montana isn't the only state that ranches. If they have a foothold, they'll spread out. It may pay us to beat them to the punch. Let me do a little research. I'll be in touch in a few days."

"In the meantime, I'll see if there's anything I can find out about Maddie for you. I have a few friends who have a few friends who are owed favors. No promises, Peter."

"I understand. Do what you can."

"I appreciate this visit, Peter. I hope we can do it again soon. Drive carefully, there are a lot of drunks out there. This is a holiday weekend."

"Do you know what I liked best about this visit?" Pete called over his shoulder.

"What?" Leo said, drawing in his breath.

"I stuck you with the dishes!"

Leo laughed so hard his eyes watered. He watched his nephew until his car wound its way down to the long, meandering road that led to the gate of the estate.

"I think," Leo murmured, "this was one of the nicest times in my life."

Annie was waiting for Pete when he returned to the apartment. She was dressed in pink slacks and a pink and white pullover. Her hair was pulled back into a ponytail and tied with a pink, checkered ribbon. A wicker picnic basket was open on the kitchen table. He recognized the basket as the one the Range Rover people gave him when he bought the heavy-duty truck. He'd shoved it in the hall closet and forgot about it.

"Things slowed down around one o'clock," Annie said, "so I left the shop in charge of Ada. I came home and made all this food." She pointed to potato salad, fried chicken, boiled eggs, and several cheese balls decorated with green peppers, bits of bacon, and finely minced onion. "If you're ready to go, I can leave the dishes to soak. Where did you go?" she asked casually.

"I'm ready. I say let the dishes soak. I went out to visit my uncle and stayed for lunch. We had a long talk. Cleared a lot of stale air that's been hovering over us for years. We parted with a better understanding of one another."

"Then let's hit the road," Annie said, snapping the lid shut on the picnic basket. "Where to, Mr. Sorenson?"

"Darien. It's not that far. I told the realtor I was backing out of the house deal in Stamford. I lost my deposit, but that's okay. That house would haunt me. When Maddie gets back—if she gets back—we can look into that again. In the meantime I'm going to check out this house in Darien. It's on a lake, has a dock, all that good stuff. Four bedrooms, two fireplaces, gorgeous kitchen—or so I'm told—great landscaping, and the price is right. Darien isn't that far from New York, so it will be ideal for me when I get back from a trip. You need to bring your car down here, and then you can drive up on the weekends if you want to get out of the city."

"Sounds wonderful," Annie said lightly. "Maybe I can get one of my friends to drive it down next weekend."

"Garage space is expensive," Pete said, reaching for the picnic basket.

"Everything in this town is expensive. Now might be a good time for me to tell you I can't afford to sublet this apartment. It's out of my reach. I'll look for something more reasonable."

Pete stopped in his tracks. "We never discussed the rent, so how do you know it's out of your reach?"

Annie grew flustered. "Well, I just assumed . . . you did tell me you were paying twenty-seven hundred a few years ago. That's outrageous, Pete. I might even move to the Jersey side and perhaps buy a house of my own. I don't want to give up my apartment back in Boston, in case Maddie comes back. I don't want to pay two rents, no matter how much I'm making. I'd rather build equity someplace and know it's mine. I'm surprised you never wanted to buy before this."

"I did. I do. It's just that I travel so much. Leaving a house empty for long periods isn't good. I'm not home that much, so apartment living is fine for me."

"I like all those things, raking leaves, planting flowers, trimming the hedges, mowing the grass. I like anything to do with the outdoors. Maybe it's because I grew up doing things with my parents. We all had our chores, and yard work was part of it.

Hey, I'm ready, the dishes are soaking. I feel like I'm skipping out on something really important."

"Soaking dishes?" Pete said, a stupid look on his face.

"Uh-huh." They both laughed about it on the way down to the first floor.

The trip was made in companionable silence for the most part. The radio played softly, mostly romantic tunes of the fifties. Annie felt excited, buoyant. She was going to spend the weekend with Pete and share a picnic supper. She was going to be part of his decision on the house in Darien.

They were almost to the Darien turnoff when Annie said, "Are you okay with the . . . with Maddie's situation?"

"No," Pete answered curtly, "but I'll live with it. I really don't want to discuss Maddie, Annie."

"Do you mean forever . . . or just now?"

"For as long as she's away. Don't bring her up. It sounds corny to say it hurts too much, but that's the way it is. And Annie, about the rent, I never expected you to pay the full amount. Why don't you come up with a reasonable figure, what you can afford, and I'll pay the difference. I know you'll take care of my things and treat the apartment like it was your own. That's important to me. I'll clear out all my personal things so they won't be in your way. Is that okay with you?"

"Well, sure. What about Maddie's things?" she asked carefully.

"What about them?"

"Well, will you take them with you?"

"I guess what you're saying is you want me to take them out of the apartment. Okay, I'll take them, if you pack them up for me. I could put them in storage in the basement I suppose."

"Oh, Pete, don't do that. People only store things in the basement when they . . . don't want them or don't know where else to put them. It's okay, I can keep them. I'll be using the main bedroom, so I won't need to use that spare closet."

Pete made a funny sound in his throat. "You have enough junk to sink a ship. I'll take them. It's settled," he said firmly.

"Keep your eye peeled for Route 124. The directions are in the glove compartment. Read them off to me."

After she read, Pete said, "Annie, do you remember the time we left the campus at one o'clock in the afternoon to go to that strange woodland wedding of those two kookie undergrads and didn't get there till nine o'clock at night and then got so hopelessly lost we had to sleep in the car?"

Annie laughed. "I remember. You, Mister Know-it-all, refused to ask for directions. Do you remember the time we went ice skating and I broke my ankle and you had to carry me for two miles when the car wouldn't start?"

"God, of course I remember, my back still aches." Pete chuckled.

They played Do You Remember until Pete steered the Rover onto the overgrown shale road that led to the lake house. Annie gasped. "This is beautiful. Are we going to be able to see inside?"

"The realtor said she'd leave the key under the mat. She's going to a family party today. She said all the people around here are nice and not to worry about putting the key back under the mat when we finish. She'll pick it up tomorrow. I don't think she'll mind if we picnic on the dock."

When they got out of the car, Annie looked around, her eyes full of awe. "Pete Sorenson, do you have any idea how lucky you are that you can buy a house like this? I would kill to be able to do what you're doing." She walked around the side of the house, exclaiming over this and that, things Pete wouldn't take a second look at. "Hollyhocks!" he heard her shriek happily.

Pete walked down to the boathouse. He'd get a cabin cruiser and dock it at a harbor on the Long Island Sound, he thought. And maybe a sailboat for this lake.

"Let's go inside." Annie chortled gleefully. "Oh, I can't wait to see the kitchen and the bathrooms. Do you know, Pete, that almost all the houses sold are bought because of the kitchen, the bathroom, and fireplaces? I read that. That's what a woman looks at. What do men look at?"

"The amount of the mortgage, the cellar, the roof, the drains."

"How boring. Come on, I'm dying to see the inside." Inside the house, they went their separate ways, Annie to the kitchen, Pete to the basement. They met later in the wide central foyer.

Pete stared at Annie. He'd never seen so much animation on her face before. "I just love this house. Pete, you're going to be sooooo happy here. The kitchen is a dream, an absolute dream. God, you could throw some parties here, I can tell you that. Did you say there's five thousand square feet?" Pete nodded. "Lordy, lordy," Annie exclaimed as she scampered up the circular, oak stairway. Pete laughed as he heard her shout, "Come see this, you aren't going to believe it! Cedar closets. A Jacuzzi! Triple vanities! A fireplace in the master bedroom! An office, Pete, you lucky stiff! A dressing room! God, I cannot believe this. Tell me you're buying this house," she yelled, leaning over the banister on the second floor. "Come up here, you dodo, and look at everything."

"I saw the basement. The roof looks good. The boathouse appears to be in good shape. I think I'll buy a boat," Pete said, climbing up the circular stairway. "It's nice," he said, looking around.

"Can you see yourself living here, Pete? I can see you living here. Tell me you're going to buy it."

"I guess so. Do you think it's a good buy at $850,000?"

"In today's market? Absolutely! Snatch it up. If you can afford it. I closed deals on houses that cost more than this and weren't half as nice. What are the taxes?"

Pete shrugged. "Is it a good investment, Annie, in your opinion?"

"You can't go wrong with property, Pete. It will only rise in value at some point. You're on water. Water always increases the value of a house."

"Do you think Maddie would . . . is it a woman's house?"

Annie's heart skipped a beat. "Yes, Pete. Who are you going to get to decorate it?"

"The woman who did my apartment, I guess. I don't know anything about decorations and buying furniture."

"Pete, can I do it? I know your likes and dislikes. I'll check everything with you first, though. I can do it on Sundays. I mean I can drive up here or I can commute while the work is in progress. I'll do a super job for you. You liked what I did with my apartment, and I furnished it on a shoestring and from garage sales. When are you leaving for your business trip?"

"Soon," Pete said vaguely, his eyes wandering around the huge first floor of the house. "I like everything open, and the half walls. I like to be able to see outdoors."

"You can go skating when the lake freezes in the winter," Annie said.

"Okay, I'll buy it, and yes, you can decorate it. If, and this is a big if, you aren't bogged down with the store and your own life."

She wanted to say, What life? But she didn't. "I can handle it."

"Okay, we have a deal. I'll call the realtor tomorrow and get things moving."

Annie moved off to make a second tour of the house. Pete stared into space. Would Maddie like this house? Would she be as excited as Annie was? Annie hadn't said one thing about who was to clean it, and she hadn't brought up the business of a maid or a housekeeper. He remembered Maddie's excitement about hiring help for the Stamford house. She'd liked it, but . . . He tried to remember what she'd said, if anything, about decorating the house. It was not a move-in-with-your-toothbrush kind of house.

He thought about Maddie then, the way he'd thought of her every day since returning from Hong Kong. She didn't need him anymore. He'd failed her in the worst possible way, and now she didn't need him. The only thing he should be concerned about, according to Jakes, was Maddie's safety. His face turned stubborn. "What the hell am I supposed to do in the meantime?" he snarled as he made his way out to the redwood deck. Keep busy,

Leo said. As if that was the answer to life's problems. Maybe in a way it was, he thought glumly. His shoulders started to slump, and then straightened when he heard Annie move into the kitchen.

He moved to the little alcove off the kitchen. He felt like a spy as he watched her walk around. He could hear her murmuring to herself, but the words didn't carry to where he was standing. He watched as she moved to the window over the sink, watched as her hands marked off sections of the sill. She was measuring it for the little red pots she would someday have on her own windowsill. He felt his throat constrict when she turned and walked to the fireplace. She backed up, advanced, and positioned an invisible rocking chair and then a second rocking chair. He saw her sit down on the hearth and drop her head into her hands. His heart flopped in his chest. His feet itched to move. He wanted to run to her, to put his arms around her. Then his eyebrows shot up when she got up and twirled about the middle of the floor. He clamped his hand over his mouth when he heard her say tearfully, "If I can't have this, then I'm glad Pete's going to have it." He did move then, and was standing in the living room when Annie scooted past him.

He looked around, *really* seeing the house. Annie was wrong. This wasn't a Maddie house at all. It was an Annie house.

Suddenly he wanted to bawl. He wished Barney was here so he could run to him and tell him of his discovery. He was buying an Annie house and not a Maddie house. What's it mean, Barney?

"I bet the stars are brighter up here at night," Annie said a while later, as it was getting dark. "Bet the moon is brighter too. During the day I just know you'll see cotton-ball clouds and blue sky. When was the last time you saw blue sky, Pete?"

"You going to pin me down on that one?" Pete grumbled.

"Nah, let's eat, I'm starving."

The tablecloth and napkins, compliments of the Range Rover people, were checkered green and white. Annie spread everything out on the dock. "Help yourself," she said, reaching for a golden-fried chicken leg.

"Look, that's a fish. Did you see that, Pete? A fish jumped out of the water. You have fish. You can sit here on the dock and dangle your feet in the water and fish. God, how lucky can one person get? Trust me, Maddie is going to love this. Ooops, sorry I forgot."

"Do you really think she'll like it, Annie?"

"Pete, what's not to like? It's perfect. It has everything."

"It's pretty big."

"That's true. You clean one room at a time. How dirty can two people make a place? I guess you can get a cleaning woman to come in one day a week to clean the kitchen and bathrooms and dust. It's no big deal. When you have something this pretty, you want to work to keep it that way."

"Do I need a housekeeper or groundskeeper?"

"Jeez, Pete, I don't know. I think that's one of those if-you-don't-want-to-do-it, get-someone-else-to-do-it things. I have to pay attention to money. You don't."

"You make me sound like Moneybags himself," Pete said tartly.

"Well, aren't you?" Annie's voice sounded just as tart.

"Does that bother you?"

"No. I merely made a statement. Let's dangle our feet in the water. I used to wade in the creek in our town when I was a kid. We caught tadpoles by the dozen.

"You know, Pete," Annie said, her feet in the water, "if you decide to buy this property, it will be, in a way, starting over. A temporary setback until Maddie gets back. Setback is probably the wrong word. I guess what I'm trying to say here, Pete, is these next months are going to be whatever you make of them. For you, this is a new start, because your options are limited right now. I'm babbling here. Did anything I say make sense?"

"Of course. I get on with my life, you get on with yours, and Maddie does what she has to do. We're just doing it in different locations."

Annie laughed. "I knew you'd get it." It was fully dark now. "It's a beautiful evening, isn't it?" Annie said. "I don't think I ever saw stars this bright, and it's almost a full moon. Have you ever wished on a star, Pete?"

"When I was a kid. Barney and I made a wish every evening. I wished for everything under the sun back then. Now, if I wanted to, I could buy each and every one of those wishes that dealt with material things. I used to hurt so bad, Annie. I cried more than six girls. Every goddamn day, after my parents died. I don't think I stopped until I was seventeen. I haven't cried since. Men aren't supposed to cry. Men aren't supposed to show weakness."

"That's bullshit," Annie snorted. "God wouldn't have given you tears if he didn't mean for you to use them. That's why He gave emotions to both men and women. He didn't say anything about holding tears and emotions in reserve. For what?"

Pete guffawed. "I knew I liked you for a reason," he said, slapping her on the back. "You always make so damn much sense. I feel better already."

"I'm glad, Pete," Annie said, pulling on her socks. "Let's walk around the property one last time. Don't you love the sound of the crickets?"

"Is that what that sound is?" Pete said, tilting his head to the left to hear better.

"Yep, and they're all going to be yours. They're making love. They rub their legs together, that's what makes the sound."

"Jesus, you know everything," Pete said in awe.

"I wish."

It was all so perfect, this wonderful outing. Pete was trying hard to be companionable, trying so hard to make things right between them, trying to restore their old friendship, which at best was fragile.

Pete reached for her hand. They walked together, swinging their hands like two young children as they made their way back to the house.

"What do you think about me getting a boat?"

"Don't expect me to go out in open water with you. I can barely swim."

Pete grinned. "Actually, I was thinking more along the lines of us picnicking while tied up at the dock. I don't know starboard from aft. Front and back."

Us. He'd said us. He'd said something else, but whatever it was, it didn't matter. Annie dropped his hand and ran, her sneakers slapping at the dewy grass until she was on the front walkway lined with bright yellow chrysanthemums. She was breathless when she dropped to the brick steps under the small overhang.

"Who lived here before, do you know?"

"The realtor said it was a middle-aged couple who were getting a divorce. The wife wants her share, so it has to be sold. Can't say I blame her. What's your feeling on prenuptial agreements, Annie?"

"Depends on who's doing the prenupting. In a way, it's an insult. The flip side of that is, why should one side have to share property and wealth that was earned prior to the marriage? My personal opinion is, it's a lousy way to start off a marriage. Getting a divorce is too damn easy. In our parents' day you stayed married and you worked at your problems. Couples today are too busy, so they part, squabble, we as attorneys make money, and they end up never speaking to one another. What's your feeling?" she asked cautiously.

"Pretty much the same as yours. We do think alike on so many things. Sometimes I find it scary."

She didn't want to ask, wished she could bite her tongue so the words wouldn't come out, but they did. "Did you and Maddie have one, or were you thinking about it?"

"We talked about it. Maddie was the one who brought it up, but the truth is, I was thinking about it, but not clearly. I'm sure I wouldn't have gone ahead with it. Most of my money is locked up pretty tight. Trusts and all that. What bothers me the most is, you're talking about getting married, swearing to love one another into eternity, and then you have to be practical and think about what-if. What-ifs are a bitch. The kids have to be protected, if there are kids, that is. Maddie wasn't keen on the idea of having children."

"You never told me that," Annie said, her eyes wide. "I don't mean you *had* to tell me. But why not?" she finished lamely.

"Maddie is a career woman. Her own childhood wasn't all that happy. She wants . . . wanted guarantees, and no one can give you that. We agreed to think about it and talk about it down the road."

"But the store . . . it doesn't make sense."

"If you think about it, it does. Everything in the store is the best, top-of-the-line, one-of-a-kind. Outrageously expensive. Priced out of most people's reach. Things she only dreamed of having. In a cockeyed way, it makes sense. She knew it would work, and she was right. You're running the store, do you see a time in the future where a family might come into being? We talked about opening a chain of stores. She was so excited."

"I think you're wrong, Pete. I'm sure Maddie would want to have children as soon as the business started paying for itself. If she didn't have a happy family life, she'd want one when she married. We all want to leave footprints behind. I know I do. You said the same thing to me many times. Flesh of my flesh, that kind of thing. You're thinking too much. We agreed not to talk about Maddie today, and it seems that's all we're doing. You're going to eat yourself alive if you don't reconcile all of this. For now. Just for now, Pete."

"It's not easy, Annie. I had my whole life planned out, and now this. Of all the things that could possibly go wrong, this was . . . is the last thing that would have entered my mind."

"Pete, can I ask you a question? It's okay if you don't want to answer it, but I think it's something you yourself need to give voice to."

"Shoot."

"If the people who run the program Maddie is in came to you

and asked you if you wanted to join her, for however long it takes, would you go? Would you give up your life?"

"Jesus, Annie, don't you think I've been asking myself that for weeks now? The answer is, I don't know. That's what's bothering me. And you're absolutely right, it will eat me alive until I resolve it in my mind."

"One day at a time, old friend," Annie said, reaching for his hand. "Let's go find a motel or hotel and call it a day. What's on the agenda for tomorrow?"

"See the realtor, give a deposit, sign the contract, ride around the area, check the boat places if they're open on Sundays, eat, we could probably go swimming in that lake if we wanted to, eat some more, and then either head back to the city or stay through Monday. We can wing it."

"I'm open to everything except the swimming part. I didn't bring a suit, and I can barely dog paddle. I can watch you, though. Today was nice, wasn't it?"

"Yes it was. Thanks for coming with me, Annie."

"Hey, I had a nice time. You have no idea how lucky you are, Pete. I'm going to remind you every chance I get."

"Pushy broad," Pete said fondly.

Annie smiled. She was still smiling when Pete kissed her cheek as she fit her key into the lock of her motel room. "Sleep well," she said.

"You too."

"I'm going to be decorating your house in my dreams," Annie gurgled. "Tomorrow I'll be able to tell you, over breakfast, what the color will be. Does Maddie have any favorite colors?"

Pete gaped at her. He should know the answer to that question. He thought about her apartment. There wasn't much in the way of color. Now that he thought about it, everything was more or less neutral, except the kitchen with its red accents. The Red Skeleton clown picture was the only bright tone in the whole apartment. "She likes yellow sheets. And yellow blankets. There's red in the kitchen."

"Okay, that's a start. You're a green and blue person, or has that changed?" Annie said seriously.

"I like red too." He felt stupid, out of his depth with the pitying look on Annie's face, which she couldn't hide.

"I like red myself. Red is a good accent color. We can talk about this some other time. 'Night, Pete."

"Good night, Annie," Pete mumbled.

In his room as he prepared for bed, Pete thought about Annie's apartment back in Boston. It was in an old building on the second floor and very large. Two bedrooms, a large living room, with an L-shaped dining room with a big, sunny kitchen loaded with green plants in bright yellow pots. The kitchen table was oak and had huge claw feet. And it had to weigh at least three hundred pounds. How she'd ever gotten it up the steps, he'd never known. He should ask. The chairs weren't an exact match, but they did go well with the table. They had comfortable green-and-white checkered cushions on the seats. He remembered a bright red teakettle on the stove. The salt and pepper shakers were red and had handles. They matched the teakettle. Strange that he should remember that. Maddie didn't have a teakettle, and she had cardboard salt and pepper shakers from the supermarket.

Annie's refrigerator was always loaded with food, good food. Leftovers and cheeses, lots of fruit, and she always had munchies and beer and soda pop. She even had a spice rack any gourmet cook would envy.

Once when he was in Boston he'd stopped to see Annie and had taken her out to dinner. They'd returned to her apartment and at midnight decided to make cookies to pacify his sweet tooth. She had every condiment, every flavoring, every nut, every kind of sugar needed. At one-thirty when the cookies were done, all three dozen of them, they'd sat on the living room floor devouring them. Then they'd curled up with gaily colored pillows from the sofa and slept next to one another. It was one of his nicest memories.

Pete slid between the cool sheets, drew up the spread. He felt alone, bruised and wounded. He thanked God for Annie. If she hadn't agreed to come with him today, he'd probably be outside baying at the moon.

He needed the nourishment of a good sound sleep, needed to wake full of piss and vinegar, needed something to propel him through the coming months.

What if, what if, what if . . .

21

Pete looked around. "Looks like someone is moving." He grinned. "Are you sure you don't mind taking care of all this?"

"Pete, the moving company will be here by nine o'clock on Sunday morning," Annie said. "I'll count the boxes, they'll sign the manifest, and I'll sign it. Your belongings will be delivered to the lake house by noon tomorrow. How did you get the owners to agree to let you store your things before the closing?"

"The deal is going through, they had no problem with it. You also have the go-ahead to proceed with your decorating plans. The key is under the mat. I have a written consent form from the owners. I made it all a condition of the sale."

"I'm going to miss you, Pete. Promise to call often. I really am going to worry about you driving out West. I wish you had a dog or something."

"Look at me, I'm all grown up. I'm looking forward to driving the Rover over country roads. I might even do a little four-wheeling if the occasion arises. This is going to be good for me, Annie."

"I know that, but I'm still going to worry."

"I left my itinerary in the kitchen. I don't want you worrying about me, Annie. You have the number for the super, all the numbers I left for you in case anything goes wrong."

"Look at me, Pete Sorenson. I'm a big girl. Did you pack your warm clothes? Even though it's mild for the first of October, it's going to be cold where you're going."

"I can't believe it's October already," Pete muttered. "Has your Halloween merchandise come in yet?"

"It's due today, as a matter of fact."

"I like your theme idea a lot. With Halloween a few weeks away, I can see that you're going to be busy. I know a place in Jersey that has the biggest pumpkins, the best scarecrows, the best of everything for Halloween. When I was a kid, my mom and dad made a big production of taking me there to pick out the pumpkins and the outfit for the scarecrow. I think they enjoyed it more than I did. How about if I give you directions and you check it out over the weekend? Oh, I almost forgot, they have cider that is to die for." Pete scribbled, drawing a crude map for Annie's benefit.

"I'll do it this weekend. The best part is, we can write it all off."

"Atta girl, Annie, now you're thinking like a businesswoman. Okay, guess it's time for me to hit the road. I know I'm leaving everything in good hands."

Pete drew Annie to him, hugged her tightly and then kissed her lightly on the cheek. "I owe you so much, Annie. I know I don't tell you often enough how much I appreciate you. I do. Someday I hope there's something I can do for you that will make things even for us."

"This isn't a contest, Pete," Annie murmured.

"Annie . . . if . . ."

"I'll call you immediately if Maddie calls. Regardless of the time of day. Now get going. Make lots of money, because it's going to take buckets to decorate that house, and remember you want to buy a boat."

"Scratch the cabin cruiser on the Sound. I'm not ready for

that yet. But I'll get a big sailboat for the lake. You can sleep on it too."

"Go already!" Annie shouted.

"I'm gone. I'll call every other day."

Annie walked with Pete to the elevator. A lump the size of a walnut seemed to be stuck in her throat. Just as the door was about to close, Pete stuck his tongue out at her and wiggled his ears. She laughed as she made her way back to the apartment.

Inside the apartment she stared at the packed boxes. Pete's things. The colorful surfboard was leaning against the wall. Maybe she shouldn't send it with the movers, maybe she should take it up herself the next time she went to Darien. The surfboard was too important to Pete to leave it in the hands of an unknown person. She carried it back to her room. Pete's room.

Would she really be able to move her things into this room? Would she really be able to sleep in the same bed Pete made love to Maddie in? No, a thousand times no. She carried the surfboard to the guest room and leaned it up against the wall. She closed the door to Pete's room. It would always be Pete's room, Pete and Maddie's room. Nothing would ever change that.

Annie ate a sketchy breakfast, her thoughts far away. She knew in her heart she should run as far and as fast as she could. No matter how thoughtful she was, no matter what she did for Pete, no matter what she felt, Pete belonged to Maddie. All she was doing was postponing the moment when she would have to cut him out of her life. Later it was going to hurt more. She knew she was making Pete's life easier, taking responsibility for so many things. But at what cost to herself? She was thirty-four years old, and it was time to make a life for herself. A life that didn't include Pete Sorenson. She'd been doing that until Pete asked her to drop everything and help him. She'd even diddled with the idea of moving to California to put as much space between them as possible, and that way she could gradually wean herself away from the soul-wrenching phone calls, occasional visits that had become a ritual with her and Pete. Now she was more mired in his life than before. Who but a fool would offer to decorate a house another woman was going to share with the man she loved? Who but a fool would take over and run the other woman's business and put her own life on hold? Who but a fool would gladly give up her life back in Boston to move into a sublet of the man she loved, who in turn loved someone else?

Pete counted on her. Depended on her. And she fed on those dependencies like a fool.

If Pete was right, it would be two years, maybe three, before Maddie testified in court. If she stuck around that long, she would be thirty-six or thirty-seven, the best years of her life gone, at least the three years that really counted. She'd be almost past the child-bearing stage. She'd be gray-haired with bridges in her mouth, wearing bifocals and fighting a losing battle with flab when her kids went off to college. Providing, of course, there was a man out there who would want a woman who was in love with another man.

"And that, Annie Gabriel," she said aloud, "makes you just about the biggest fool walking on the face of the earth."

Annie choked back a sob as she dressed for another day of work that would make her rival richer for her efforts. *Don't think about that, Annie, you're doing this for Pete because you love him heart and soul.*

At first, the days crawled by, and then they picked up speed and literally seemed to whiz by.

Annie eyed the calendar on her desk. Ten days until Christmas. The house in Darien was finished. She closed on it the day before Thanksgiving with Pete's power of attorney. Now that she had experienced, full-time help at the store, she had some time to herself. She used it to oversee the last minute decorating. This weekend the drapers were coming to hang the curtains, verticals, and shades in all the rooms. The carpeting and tile had been completed by the closing date, thanks to the owner's willingness, the bank's approval, and her own spare time to allow the renovations to be done. Pete's sizable down payment, of course, made all things possible. The furniture arrived the past weekend and everything was in place. This weekend she was going to put up a huge Christmas tree and decorate it, so when Pete arrived on Christmas Eve, the house would be fragrant, and hopefully, just what he wanted. Plus the grand surprise if it materialized.

She thought about the surprise, a smile of pure happiness on her face. Her present to Pete, which she'd planned months ago. In fact it had come to her the day she first met Simon Jakes. Find Barney Sims. Find him and bring him to Pete's house. His special Christmas present.

Just yesterday Jakes had called to report on his lack of progress. "It's like he dropped off the face of the earth. Every lead fizzles on me. I'm trying, Annie, I need you to believe that. If I don't find him for Christmas, then we'll concentrate on Easter. And if Easter doesn't work, we'll go with the Fourth of July and on through every holiday. I won't give up. I'm gonna find that guy. It's a challenge now. I think they changed their names, though not legally. That's what's making it so hard."

The perfect present, and it might not materialize. It's the thought that counts, Annie, she told herself, and sighed mightily.

For days now she'd been praying for snow. Every night she watched the long-range forecast, the weatherman teasing her, saying yes and no. Whatever, it would be cold, and that was a plus. The past weekend she'd carried in firewood so it would be dry and ready to burn. As far as she could tell, she hadn't missed a thing. She was taking Friday off so she could get a head start on the grocery shopping, stocking Pete's freezer, cooking extra meals that could be frozen.

And what would Pete do? Why, Pete would hug her, his eyes would light up, and he'd say, "Annie, you are amazing!" He'd hug her again, her heart would swell and her eyes would mist over. All because she was a fool, and fools acted with their hearts instead of their brains. Now, if her special surprise came into being, well, Pete would just about die.

Somehow Annie managed to get through the days until Friday, when she rose at four-thirty and was on the road to Darien by five-thirty. She was antsy, impatient to get there so she could start on all the last minute details that would make Pete's homecoming special.

Pete was as good as his word, calling every other day. The first question he always asked as soon as he said hello was, "Any news?" Since leaving, all he'd said about the house was, "How's it going?" She hadn't told him how much time and effort she'd put into his house, and she wasn't sure why. The big surprise! The special pat on the back. The special smile that reached his eyes.

It was a beautiful day, crisp and cold, fireplace weather. Annie immediately set the thermostat to seventy degrees before she took off her shearling jacket. As she filled the coffeepot, she kept saying over and over, "This is going to be a wonderful day." She believed her own words.

The perfect house, the perfect setting, the perfect holiday. But most of all, the perfect man. The absolutely end-all of surprises.

By noon the drapes, shades, and vertical blinds were installed. They matched the furniture perfectly. Annie clapped her hands in delight after she wrote out the check.

In town, before she shopped for groceries, she stopped in a quaint tearoom for lunch, which she gobbled, impatient to be on her way.

At two-thirty the new refrigerator and freezer were stocked to overflowing. She made fresh coffee while she worked on a menu list. At four o'clock she was in her Volvo heading out to the main road once again, in search of a Christmas-tree farm. It was dark when she picked out her tree and ready-made wreath for the front door. For five dollars extra the owner promised delivery of the tree by noon the following day. For ten dollars this man would set the tree up in the stand. She parted with thirty more dollars.

Everything was under control. The only thing she'd forgotten to do was carry in the Christmas decorations, specialty items she'd been picking up since Thanksgiving. She had wide red satin bows for the wreath and the mantel garland, unique Christmas balls, tiny strings of lights in the shape of stars, and the most glorious Christmas angel she'd ever seen, made especially for her by one of Maddie's suppliers.

Annie's mood darkened to match the night around her. Where was Maddie? What kind of Christmas was she going to have? Would she spend the holiday thinking about Pete? But more important, would Pete spend the holiday thinking about Maddie? If so, then all her work was for nothing. Instead of making Christmas special for Pete, she might be making him miserable. Damn, she couldn't do anything right.

Her mood shifted and she cried the whole evening as she prepared a tray of lasagna, made spaghetti, a pot roast, and fried chicken. When the food cooled, she portioned it out into trays that she wrapped and slid into the freezer. She went to bed with tears on her cheeks. Her pillow was damp when she woke, and she had a terrible headache she knew was going to turn into a migraine.

The tree arrived at mid-morning. It took the delivery man ten minutes to set it up and hang the wreath on the front door. It was huge, Annie thought, craning her neck to see the tip of the tree, and it was so fragrant she was transported momentarily back to her childhood, waking to see the magnificent tree in her parents' living room.

"Don't decorate it till tomorrow," the man who brought it said. "The branches need time to fall, and they're still a little wet. Don't forget to add water. The stand holds a quart, but the tree will suck up the first quart real quick. I made a deep X in the trunk. The tree will stay fresh till the middle of January if you do that. Try and keep your thermostat set around sixty-eight. That's ideal. Beautiful house, ma'am."

"Thank you."

Her headache raged. There was nothing for her to do but lie down and pray it would go away. She went out to the kitchen, her head pounding with each step she took. She swallowed four aspirin with a glass of water before she made her way back to the brand-new sofa. She slept until noon the following day. She still had a headache, but it was bearable.

Annie decorated the tree, placed the angel on top, vacuumed the pine needles, set the timers for the tree lights, the foyer light, and the kitchen light to come on at four-thirty.

She was on I-95 heading back to the city by six o'clock. Pete's homecoming had been taken care of, right down to the three presents she'd placed under the tree, all done up in sparkly silver paper with huge red velvet bows. There was no way she could wrap her special, superduper gift, if Jakes came through for her.

What was she going to do for Christmas? Who would she share the holiday with? She hadn't had time to make friends in New York, and all her old friends in Boston were married and usually spent the holidays with parents or in-laws.

"God," she said, "I didn't even buy myself a Christmas tree." She laughed so hard her eyes watered. Her head started to pound again, but she was home, so it didn't matter. She'd get one of those table trees fully decorated from the florist. She could buy herself a present and stick it under the tree, she decided.

Annie fixed some soup, ate it, showered, and got her clothes ready for the following day before she curled on the sofa with the phone book and telephone in her lap. She called six churches before she found one that said they would be delighted to have her help serve the needy and the poor on Christmas Eve and Christmas Day.

The decision to open or close Fairy Tales on Christmas Eve, one of the biggest shopping days of the season, was hers to make. She opted to close it. There were more important things in life than making money . . . for one's rival. She immediately had an attack of conscience. This wasn't like her. All her life she'd been an honest, forthright, tell-it-like-it-is person. She'd lived her life under the banner of honesty, and here she was, throwing it all away for a lousy day of sales.

Annie looked at the clock. It wasn't too late to call her two full-time employees. If she agreed to pay them overtime or double time, out of her own pocket, she wouldn't be compromising herself. She punched out numbers, waited for Ada Rollins to pick up the phone. She spoke quickly, ending with, "I need to know, Ada."

"Double time, close at four-thirty, and I'll do it," the older woman said. "Don't worry about Caroline. If I agree to work, so will she. What about the day's receipts?"

"Oh, I forgot about that. Tally up and I'll pick up the receipts on my way home. Ada, if business is slow, use your best judgment about closing earlier. I know you and Caroline want to be with your families."

Annie made a mental note to be extra generous with the women's Christmas bonus.

Now she could go to sleep.

At the end of the day before Christmas Eve, Annie was reaching for her purse when the phone rang.

"Pete! Where are you?"

"Anaconda, Montana. Lots of snow here. It's as cold as a well digger's ass, I can tell you that. I'm heading out to Butte and should be in Darien late tomorrow evening. Any . . . word?"

"No, Pete, I'm sorry."

"I thought . . . the holidays and all. It was supposed to be Maddie's and my first Christmas as a married couple."

"I really am sorry, Pete."

"I know you are. How's business?"

"I don't think it gets any better than this. I think you'll be pleased. Did I tell you a lady came into the shop after Thanksgiving and wanted to know if she could sell, on consignment, Victorian lace sachet balls made in the shape of Christmas balls? I said okay. I sold eleven hundred! Is that amazing?"

"Yeah, amazing. Maddie would be proud of you. Listen, my driver is here so I gotta mush on out of here. See you, Annie."

" 'Bye, Pete."

Not Merry Christmas. Not a word about inviting her to Darien. Not a word about stopping by the apartment, not a word about the Darien house.

Annie wiped at her eyes. Getting one's hopes up only allowed for disappointment. "Damn." She should have known better. What was it the poets said? Hope springs eternal. Yeah, right, for other people, not for the Annie Gabriels of this world.

The following morning Annie arrived at the Good Shepherd's soup kitchen at five A.M. She introduced herself, donned a tattered apron, and became one of a dozen volunteers. Breakfast was the first order of the day. Afterward there were dishes to wash and lunch to prepare. Her job was to cut the vegetables and pick through the beans that went into the hearty soup that was served every day.

At ten-thirty, when the minister told her to take a break, she did. "You need more volunteers, Reverend," she said wearily. "I had no idea you had *families*. For some reason I thought . . ."

The minister smiled. "It is a shock, isn't it? We take care of roughly twenty-three families, and we have thirty-seven children. It's going to be a very . . . lean Christmas for the children."

"Don't you get donations? Don't your parishioners give toys and clothing?"

"This is a very poor parish, Miss Gabriel. This month the church barely had enough money to pay the electric bill. If you trust in the Lord, He comes through. He sent you to us, didn't He?"

"Well, yes, He did . . . but—"

"There are no buts, Miss Gabriel. You're here. We need you. It's that simple. Now, if you could just figure out a way to turn meat loaf into turkey, you would have my eternal thanks."

"Well, Reverend, if you can spare me for a few hours, I just might be able to do that." Annie had her coat on before the minister could say yes or no. "Do you by any chance have a vehicle I can borrow?"

The minister tossed her a set of keys. "It's the van parked in front. Don't let the exterior fool you, the engine is in perfect condition, one of my flock sees to it. Can you use some help?" he asked. "For whatever you have in mind?"

Annie grinned. "Reverend, an extra pair of hands would be wonderful. Let's go, but first can I make a phone call?"

"Of course."

Annie sprinted into the makeshift office and dialed Fairy Tales.

"Ada, it's Annie. Listen to me. Close the shop *now*. Say there's a gas leak, say anything you want, but get whatever customers you have in the store out. Hang the sign in the window and close the shutters. Don't open the door for anyone but me. Pack every single thing in the store in boxes. *Everything.* Toys, clothes, baby gear. Everything. Have Caroline call the market and tell them to have a dozen turkeys with all the trimmings ready for me by noon. One o'clock at the latest. I want cranberry sauce, sweet potatoes, vegetables, stuffing mix, dinner rolls, and salad greens. Pumpkin pies too. I need enough for . . . seventy people. I have to go now."

An hour later Reverend Tobias said, "I can't believe this! I do believe it! You see, Miss Gabriel, God sent you to us for a reason."

"Wait, wait, we forgot the wrapping paper and all the other decorations. Ada, Caroline, help me, please."

"Miss Gabriel, do you know what you are doing?" Ada asked, her face puckered in worry.

"Of course."

"The store's empty. There's nothing left but the shelves."

"I know, isn't it great?"

"Well . . ."

"Have a wonderful holiday. Spend your bonuses wisely. I'll see you next week."

"But . . . how can we work, we have no stock?"

"That's true," Annie said happily. "We'll think of something. Come in on Monday as usual."

"Miss Gabriel—"

"Call me Annie, Reverend."

"If you agree to call me Albert."

"All right, Albert, what were you going to say?"

"I was going to say I don't think there's room in the van for the food."

"Albert, I learned a long time ago not to sweat the small stuff," Annie replied.

Annie wrote a check for the food. Later, she thought, she would have an anxiety attack over the amount. Later she would think about what she'd just done to Maddie Stern's shop. Later she would think about the flak she was going to get from Pete. Later she would worry about paying for everything.

"God will truly bless you, Annie," the reverend said when they were in the van, weaving through traffic.

"Albert, I need a friend. If—"

"Child, I was your friend the moment you called me. I'll always be here for you, and it has nothing to do with what you've just done for my flock. You're happy right now, aren't you?"

"Yes I am. My adrenaline is pumping. Why is that?"

"Because you are doing for others materially as well as physically and mentally. You are giving of yourself."

"I hear ya, Albert," Annie said as she careened around a taxi, her foot bearing down on the gas pedal. "If I call you in the middle of the night to bitch and moan, will you talk to me?"

"Absolutely."

"If I told you I was in love with a great guy who's in love with someone else . . . ah, forget it."

"We'll talk about it when we aren't so . . . wired up. My bishop is not going to believe this. I'm having trouble adjusting."

"Albert, I didn't see a Christmas tree. Don't you have one?"

"No one donated one. The children were going to make one this afternoon with crepe paper and a broom handle."

"What?" Annie said, slamming on the brakes. Everything in the back shifted to the front, then shifted backward again when

Annie surged forward. "Well, we're going to get one right now," she said, swerving into an Arco station. "C'mon, Albert, we're getting the biggest and the best tree this gas station has to offer."

"Annie, there's no room," Albert fretted.

"Of course there's room. We'll have them tie it to the door handles, and you can hold the top part through the window. Where's your faith, Albert?"

"A mile back up the road. You drive like a demon."

"That's true," Annie said agreeably. "Look! They're selling Christmas ornaments. It won't hurt to buy a few boxes. The children can string popcorn and cranberries. They have tinsel too. We are one lucky couple, Albert." God, she couldn't remember the last time she'd been so happy.

"I think," Albert said, "this is going to be the best Christmas ever."

He looks like he's just removed a hundred-pound yoke from his shoulders, Annie thought. She watched him as he walked among the trees, trying to find just the right one. He was so homely he was beautiful. One of God's chosen few. She wondered if anyone ever noticed that his nose was too big and his ears didn't quite seem to fit his head. What they probably saw was his warm, kind eyes, which always seemed to sparkle, and his smile, which stretched from ear to ear. She closed her eyes and all she could see behind the closed lids was Albert's kind face. He was too thin, though. He probably didn't eat enough, or if he did have food, he gave it to others, she thought.

"Are you sure this is going to work?" Albert asked.

Annie laughed. "Oh ye of little faith. Of course it's going to work." Annie paid for the tree, the three boxes of ornaments, and the tinsel with a credit card. She needed to hang on to the cash she had in her purse to put in the collection plate during Christmas services.

"I think we should sing, Albert. Do you know 'Jingle Bells'?"

"Of course."

"Then let's hear it, Albert!"

Albert sang at the top of his lungs, Annie joining in. Both of them were so off-key, people turned to look at the loaded-down van, shaking their heads in disbelief.

Later, when all the stock from the store was safely secured in the parish house, the food in the kitchen, Annie accepted a cup of tea from one of the volunteers. In her life she'd never felt so peaceful yet emotionally charged up. She watched as the children played around the tree, their little faces alight with happiness.

"We'll be serving meat loaf for dinner this evening," the volunteer who handed her the tea said. Annie smiled weakly. She hated meat loaf. She would never, ever, take anything for granted again.

She rinsed and dried her cup. "If you don't need me for the cook detail, I think I'll go over to the parish house and wrap as many presents as I can. Thanks for making me the name and age list."

"Thank *you.* It took me just a minute to make the list. I know the families so well."

Her name was Rose and she was in her late sixties. She was the most efficient, in-charge person Annie had ever met. It was impossible not to warm to her smile. Hands on ample hips, she said, "What are you doing here, Miss Gabriel?"

Annie knew instinctively that nothing but the truth would do for this woman. "At first I came for myself. I didn't have anyone to spend the holidays with. I came here with bitterness in my heart and a tremendous amount of jealousy. Like most people, I didn't take the time out of my own busy life to think about those less fortunate than myself. I'm sorry about that." She told Rose about Fairy Tales, Pete, the house in Darien that she'd decorated, and the special surprise. "Suddenly, none of that is important."

"Can I call you Annie?"

"If you let me call you Rose."

"We'll be friends. Now you have two, Albert and me. When you leave, everyone in this place will be your friend. And let me tell you something else, they can all, myself included, spot a phony a mile away. I could use some extra help on weekends if you don't have anything better to do."

"Sign me up, Rose. I can give you Sundays. I work six days a week."

"Every other Sunday. No one should work seven days a week."

"You do," Annie said.

"That's because this is my family. Get along with you and start to pretty up those presents. Oh, I can just see the tykes' eyes tomorrow when they see all those gifts. God will reward you, Annie."

"And on that note I'll leave you."

It was five-forty on Christmas Eve when Annie started to wrap the Christmas presents, with Albert's help. They sang "Jingle Bells" again, off-key, and "Rudolph the Red Nosed Reindeer," making up the words as they went along.

Annie was happy and at peace.

Pete drove his rental car over the shale road leading to the lake house. He was home. Home being a house he was going to set foot in for the second time. That's bullshit, Sorenson, he told himself. It isn't a home. It's a damn house with furniture. He was driving at a slow crawl when he saw, through the pines, the outdoor lights. He didn't realize he'd been holding his breath until it exploded from his mouth with a loud swish. Annie was here. "Thank you, God," he murmured. It was going to be a nice Christmas after all. Annie would cook, they'd eat, they'd open presents and sit in front of the fire and talk about old times, and he'd tell her all about the past months. She'd want to talk about the store and how well it was doing. He loved to reminisce. Annie preferred the here and now, but always agreed to the Memory Lane talks.

Pete tapped on the horn, three light taps and then one longer blast. That should bring her on the run. The wreath was pretty. He loved big red bows. His mother always used to put red bows on his birthday and Christmas presents. He heaved the sack of presents for Annie out of the backseat along with his bags. He wondered if Leo had received the Federal Express presents he'd sent out two days ago from Montana. Damn, he was going to have to make two trips. Where the hell was Annie?

Pete struggled to the door, tried it. Locked. He set everything down and looked under the mat for the key. He frowned when he fit it into the lock. Maybe Annie was snoozing. He looked around for her car, realizing for the first time that it wasn't parked in front. Stupid, she probably put it in the garage, that's what garages were for. Without noticing it, he kicked the Federal Express envelope that had been propped against the door as he entered the foyer.

"I'm home," Pete shouted. "Where's the wine, the welcoming hug? Annieeee!"

Jesus, was this the same house he'd walked through with Annie back in September? He kicked at the door with the heel of his shoe to shut it. His jacket dropped in a heap on the floor.

He saw the Christmas tree, drew a deep breath to inhale the fragrant fir. There were three presents underneath, with huge red velvet bows. He clapped his hands like a kid. He whirled, wanting to see it all at once. Un-be-liev-able!

The sofa was large and could seat six comfortably. It was one of those deep, curl-in-a-ball sofas that welcomed sleep. Deep hunter-green fabric with a thin string line of beige running through the nubby material. The easy chairs were beige with hunter-green stripes, and were picked up in the soft, luxurious carpet that was two shades lighter than the furniture. The drapes looked like they were made from burlap sacks, with wide, dark green stripes.

All his personal belongings had been unpacked and placed around the room. Everything was exactly where he himself would have placed it if he'd done the unpacking.

The fire was laid, all he had to do was spark it. He did. When he was on his feet, his eyes were drawn to the wall over the fieldstone fireplace. He sucked in his breath before the tears rolled down his cheeks. In a bright red frame was a blown-up picture of himself and his parents. He was holding on to his surfboard. "Annieeee!" He backed away, staring at the picture from every angle. The frame matched the red shirt he'd been wearing that day. "Annieeee! Goddamn it, Annie, answer me!" he shouted. Maybe she was taking a bath and couldn't hear him.

In the kitchen he cursed. Annie must have gone through his photo album. He closed his eyes. It was so like his mother's kitchen it was scary. Shit, he couldn't handle this. He backed out the door and headed for the steps, calling Annie's name as he went along.

He opened one door after the other. Each room was decorated to perfection. He knew his room immediately when he saw the huge four-poster. He'd had a bed like this once. The spread was plaid with red stripes running through it, and it had fringe all along the bottom. Just like this one.

His favorite picture of himself and Maddie was on his night table. His and her chairs with ottomans were side by side. Two magazine racks were along each side of the chairs. An exquisite Tiffany lamp separated the two chairs. Here too a fire was laid in the fireplace. The wall above held a second blown-up photograph of himself and his parents. His father was holding a huge catfish, he had a three-incher on his line, and his mother was making a face. He loved the picture. Jesus, Annie. "Annieeee!"

This was for *now*. It wasn't a Maddie room and it wasn't a Maddie and Pete room. He knew instinctively that Annie had done her best to make it his to ease his aching heart.

Son of a bitch, where was she?

Pete ran down the steps and out to the garage. The emptiness stared back at him. "She's not here. She fucking well isn't here!" How could that be? They were supposed to spend the holiday together. Who said so? he asked himself. Did you invite her? Did you specifically ask her here? "Never presume, never assume, Sorenson," he seethed, back in the kitchen.

Because there didn't seem to be anything else to do, Pete

opened the refrigerator. Food. All kinds of food. He opened the freezer. Frozen dinners. "I'll be dipped in shit if I'm going to eat a frozen dinner by myself on Christmas Eve," he snarled. His clenched fist banged down on the kitchen table. He recognized the legal folder. The closing papers on the house. His arm swept them onto the floor.

His chest hurt and his eyes were burning unbearably. His pain eased slightly when he thought about the store. Annie would arrive late. He was so relieved with the thought, he felt lightheaded. He dialed his old number. He listened to Annie's message, his throat constricting.

"Pete, welcome home. Merry Christmas. I hope you like the house. Be sure to water the tree every day. A quart should be in the stand at all times. This message is for you, Maddie, in case you call. Pete's new number is 203-555-4632. . . . Call me before you leave, Pete." He cried then for all the would-haves, the should-haves, and the could-haves. His throat hurt when he finally blew his nose in a wad of paper towels.

Never assume. Never presume. He thought about Maddie and Annie and wanted to cry all over again. *Barney, I need you.*

Pete picked up the telephone and called his uncle. Leo picked up on the second ring. "Leo, it's Pete. Merry Christmas. Listen, I know it's late, but if you aren't doing anything, why don't you have your chauffeur drive you up here. I don't want to be alone. I'll explain what happened when you get here. If you want to come." He listened to his uncle's voice and knew he was doing the right thing. "I'm sorry the invitation is last-minute. Can you make it?"

"I'm on my way, boy."

Pete felt like a hot air balloon with a slow leak when he sat down on the kitchen chair. He stared at the phone, willing it to ring, but it didn't. He was off the chair searching for a local phone book. When he found it in one of the kitchen drawers, he flipped to the section on churches. He called every number until he found one that was reasonably close and was having a midnight service.

Leo was going to be his first guest. Christmas dinner. But first he had to carry his bags upstairs to his new room, and after that he had to put all of Annie's presents under the tree. He'd even brought presents for Maddie. He would put those in his dresser drawer. He even had a present for Leo, which he'd planned to take to his uncle the day after Christmas. "You are a shitful person, Pete Sorenson. If you can't give a present on time, what's the point?" he said aloud. It would be on time now. Upstairs, he dumped his bags in his room, then came downstairs again. He was about to pick up the bags of presents when he spotted the Federal Express envelope. Maybe it was from Annie. Maybe it was from Maddie. He picked it up to see the sender's name: Leo Sorenson. He ripped at the tab and withdrew a long red envelope. A Christmas card. He hadn't sent out cards, even to Annie or his uncle. It was a simple card. A baby seal with a tear in its eye stared up at him. Inside the card said PEACE and was signed by Leo. Airline tickets fell out of the card. Two tickets to Australia with an open date going and coming. Land reservations with open dates to Bell's Beach. He bawled like a baby. When his shoulders finally stopped shaking, Pete walked over to the tree to put all his presents under it. Leo was going to get a kick out of the Stetson. He'd probably get a huge belly laugh out of the red reindeer socks and the soft shearling slippers.

"Get it together, Sorenson, this is Christmas. It's going to be whatever you make it." Damn it, he'd been counting on Annie, looking forward to spending his favorite holiday with her. *Where was she, what was she doing?* He refused to think about Maddie.

Pete wiped his eyes on his sleeve the way he'd done when he was a kid. "This is now," he muttered as he selected a Christmas tape for the stereo. Bing Crosby's mellow voice rang through the house. Pete's thumb shot in the air. "I have a turkey to defrost, stuffing to make, and a pie to bake. And a Merry Christmas to one and all!" he bellowed.

• • •

It was a snowy fairyland, the kind of setting artists captured on Christmas cards. Evergreens, their branches bowed with feathery light snow, gave off a heady, pungent aroma. The moon, a silvery half circle, bathed the snow-covered mountains in a glorious, shimmering spectacle of delight.

Spirals of smoke spewed upward from the squat row of bunkhouses. The barn, a magnificent edifice, stood square and dark amid the plowed mounds of snow. Dim yellow light from the frosty windows spilled outward to create a patchwork quilt.

The main building—or the big house, as the ranch hands called it—stood sentinel as though guarding the outer building from the silence that surrounded the ranch spread.

It was Christmas Eve.

Inside the bunkhouse six ranch hands and two "city slickers" played cards and drank Johnnie Walker red. Most of the hands, with the exception of the six remaining men, were in Cheyenne for the Christmas holiday. These six playing cards would go to Cheyenne for New Year's when the others returned. The "city slickers" would remain.

Everything was battened down for the night. The special furnace and the warm pipes inside the monstrous barn kept the animals warm and snug.

The perimeters of the ranch appeared to be at peace.

The big house was also quiet, but well-lighted. It smelled of wood smoke and fragrant pine. It was a drafty old house full of leather, open-beamed ceilings, and wide-planked floors.

Inside, cuddled near the open fire, Maddie and Janny toasted the holiday with homemade wine that had the kick of a mule.

"To Christmas and heavy receipts at Fairy Tales," Maddie said, holding her glass aloft. "And to your Unitec stock, may it go up, up, up."

Janny drained her glass. "Don't you ever think about anything but money?" she said sourly.

"What would you suggest I think about? Pete? His old dear

friend Annie? Nester? Those killers? Besides, didn't anyone ever tell you Christmas Eve is one of the heaviest-selling days of the year? Sales during the Christmas season can keep a retailer alive and well when his year sales are soft."

"I wonder if there was a Christmas party at Merrill Lynch," Janny mused. "I would have bought a new dress and hit on the broker I told you about. He made my toes tingle, and he believed in Unitec too."

Maddie gulped at her wine. "I've noticed something, Janny. You seem to be taking this all very well. Why is that?" Maddie asked bitterly.

"Because I have no other choice. I could have held out back in Utah, done my time, so to speak, and I can do it here too. After the trial I'll make my decisions. You're fighting it, Maddie. Give in already and accept that things are the way they are."

"We're slaves," Maddie shot back. "We cook three meals a day for ranch hands. We're so tired at seven o'clock, we go to bed because we have to be up at four to make bread. We're getting a hundred dollars a week, and we have yet to be paid, and even if we were paid, there's no place to spend the money. There's no phone, no television, and there's a radio that plays on Sunday morning. Deliberately, I'm sure. We're snowbound and have to wait for a thaw. I've read *Field and Stream*, all nine issues, at least a dozen times each. I am on my second reading of *Moby Dick*. I can recite whole paragraphs by heart. Another thing," she spat, "I hate the name Olive Parsons."

"I wish you'd lighten up, Maddie. All we do is go over the same old things, day after day. I'm getting tired of it. I want to go to sleep. It's my turn to make the bread in the morning. Maybe you should take my turn and you can punch out your hostility on the bread. It's Christmas Eve, Maddie, peace on earth, goodwill toward man. We're alive, we're healthy, and we're safe. We have a roof over our heads and our stomachs are full. I wasn't going to say anything, but if you don't—if you can't—cope, then I'm going to ask to be moved."

"After what we went through?" Maddie screeched.

"After what *you made us go through.* The answer is yes."

"But Fairy Tales . . . Pete . . ."

Janny sat up and wrapped her arms around her knees. "Maddie, you did not own Fairy Tales. Pete put up the money, paid for the stock, paid the rent. Yes, your retail background was put into use, yes, you got it ready. Pete will keep it going somehow. He's a money person, like I am. He knows it will be a thriving business someday. Anyone with a brain can run a store. As for Pete . . . we talked about this so many times, I don't know if I can go through it again. One more time, Maddie. He's going to wait it out. No one in their right mind would expect someone like Pete to cave in and . . . join us in this godforsaken place. Use your head. He loves you. You love him. If that love is strong enough, he'll be there for you when you get back."

Maddie's face turned ugly. "I requested a meeting, a face-to-face, because that's my right. Obviously, he turned the request down. He's not going to screw up his life. That's love all right. Who needs him?"

Her voice was so bitter, Janny cringed. "Does all this have something to do with Annie Gabriel?"

"Of course. They're probably exchanging presents as we speak. They're curled up in front of the fireplace drinking fine wine. They might even go to bed together. How do I know what's going on?"

"I'd say your imagination is pretty vivid."

"Well, what would you think?"

"I think I would give them both the benefit of the doubt. You are turning into a very hateful person, Maddie."

"Justifiably so," Maddie shot back. "I wonder if he went through with the deal on the Stamford house. What do you think, Janny?"

"I think he backed out because it would remind him too much of you. Is that what you want to hear?"

"I asked you what you thought. That means you personally. It's your turn to throw another log on the fire."

Janny felt like screaming. "It's always my turn. Starting tomorrow I'm going to start keeping track of *my turns* at everything. You are so damn lazy, Maddie. I answered your question. If you don't like my answer, then that's your problem. Another thing, I'm sick and tired of coddling you, deferring to you, listening to you bitch and moan, and I'm not going to put up with it. I'm doing everything I can to make the best of a bad situation. I don't need to hear you making it worse on an hourly basis."

"Janny, I'm sorry. I . . . I can't reconcile . . . I love Pete. You don't know what it's like. You've never been in love."

"That's it! That's it!" Janny said getting up. She ran to the coatrack by the front door. "I'm going out to the bunkhouse and . . . and well, I don't know what I'm going to do, but at least I won't have to listen to you. For the record, Miss Madelyn Stern, a.k.a. Olive Parsons, I was in love once, and I know exactly how it feels, and I even know how you're hurting because I hurt the same way when he dumped me for someone nineteen years old with silicone implants. If you decide to have a nervous breakdown, do it when I'm not around. Merry Christmas, Maddie."

"Janny, don't go. I'm sorry. It's the holiday . . . it's everything."

An artic burst of air whipped through the room when Janny opened the door. It swirled around Maddie. "You didn't put the log on the fire," Maddie shrilled.

"Ask me if I care!" Janny shot back. "If you want to talk about slaves, I've been yours since we got here. Start doing for yourself. You can make the bread in the morning too. I did it the last two days." The door closed with a bang.

Maddie curled into her heavy quilt. "Merry Christmas, Maddie," she whimpered.

22

Pete stood at the entrance to 600 Army Navy Drive, his thoughts in a turmoil. Nothing seemed changed since he was here a year ago. If things hadn't gone awry, he would have celebrated his first wedding anniversary a few weeks ago.

What the hell was he doing here? Why had he come back here to talk to the marshals? He knew what they were going to say, so why was he tormenting himself? Hell, they might even boot his ass out the door.

He was a man with a purpose when he identified himself, stated his business, and said, "I'm not taking no for an answer. Either you people talk to me or I'm going to the newspapers. Furthermore, I have a letter here I want sent to Miss Stern. And I damn well want a reply."

The marshal Pete spoke to was as tall as he was, middle-aged, with a lot of gray in his hair. Formidable. Pro ball in his prime, Pete thought. He worked out, had just the right amount of suntan. He also had the sharpest, keenest eyes he'd ever seen. Pete extended his hand in a bone-crushing grip. The marshal didn't flinch. If anything, he was amused.

"Sandor Neville," the marshal said. "Call me Sandy."

He didn't look like someone named Sandy, he looked like his name should be Duke or Chuck.

Pete's belligerence spilled over. This guy knew where Maddie was or knew someone who knew where she was located. His eyes narrowed. "Look, it's been a year, and I've had no word from Maddie. You will never convince me she doesn't want an arranged meeting or that she won't write to me. I believe in my gut that people are keeping us separated, that you aren't cooperating. I've read everything there is to read about your program, and it says you people can arrange a face-to-face meeting and you forward mail. I want to know why that hasn't been done."

"Who told you it hasn't been done?" Neville asked curiously. He sounded like he was discussing the weather.

"I'm not a fool. No one has contacted me. I haven't had any mail and . . . what else do I need in the way of proof?" Pete said angrily.

Neville shrugged. "What exactly do you want?"

"I want you to arrange a telephone call or a face-to-face meeting. Don't give me any crap that it can't be done. I've researched this up the kazoo. I want this letter forwarded," Pete said, extending a long white envelope. "I expect a response."

"I'll pass the information along. That's all I can do."

"That's what your people said last time. And here I am, one year later, almost to the day," Pete said bitterly.

"Has it occurred to you, Mr. Sorenson, that Miss Stern doesn't want any communication with you?"

"Yes it has occurred to me, but I want to hear her say so, and I want to know the reason. Is that so hard for you to understand?"

"Not at all, Mr. Sorenson. As I said, I'll pass it along."

"Well, here's something else for you to pass along. Either you people get back to me in a few days or I'm going to every single newspaper in New York and Washington, D.C. It's not a threat, it's a goddamn promise. Now, what I want to know before I leave here is, when will you get back to me? I want a date and time."

"At this moment I can't give you a date and a time. I will, however, call you as soon as possible. Give me a number."

"Be sure," Pete said, scribbling the telephone number for Fairy Tales on a slip of paper, "that you tell those people you're going to talk with that I mean exactly what I said."

"You need to understand, Mr. Sorenson, you could be endangering Miss Stern's life by doing what you suggest."

"I'll take that chance. Maddie would want it this way. I know her. There's something funny going on here. If I find out, when this case comes to trial, that you people are not giving her my messages or giving me messages from her, the shit is going to hit the fan, and I don't care what it does to this organization. Enough is enough. You people have ruined my life. Maddie's too."

"You look hale and healthy, Mr. Sorenson. I'm not disputing that your ego and your heart may be bruised, but you cannot categorically state that we have ruined Miss Stern's life."

Pete stormed out of the office rather than venting his fury at the marshal's cool response.

Three days later, after two preliminary calls, Pete was advised that Maddie would speak with him at six-thirty Eastern Time at the Fairy Tales number.

Pete arrived at the store during the tail end of the Labor Day sale. He watched in amazement as merchandise literally flew off the shelves. Annie was good with the customers, smiling, going out of her way to check stock, promising to order and reorder. She kept meticulous records, he noticed. The store sparkled with enthusiasm. Maddie was going to be so pleased. He wondered if she still needed Fairy Tales, or if she was disgusted with it, the way she was with him.

The store was closed and empty when the phone rang at precisely six-thirty. The receiver was clamped to Pete's ear after the first ring. His voice was so gruff and hoarse, he didn't recognize it as his own. He could hear Maddie crying on the other end of the line.

"Pete, is it really you?"

"Jesus, Maddie, I can't believe I'm talking to you. Did you get my letter?"

"Not yet. They told me it takes time for it to be routed . . . to . . . however they do it. How's Fairy Tales doing, Pete?"

Not, how are you, Pete, I love you, Pete.

"Fantastic. How are you, Maddie? God, I miss you!"

"I'm fine. Well, I'm alive, safe and well. Did you get the house in Stamford? I've been trying to imagine you living in it. What did you do about your apartment?"

"I sublet the apartment to Annie, and I didn't get the house in Stamford."

"Oh . . ."

"I would have agonized in it. . . . I did get another one in Darien, though. It's closer and . . . it's on a lake. It's on a wooded lot. I think you'll like it. I miss you, Maddie. Listen, I did everything I could think of. I'm sorry I wasn't at the apartment when you called. I was out trying to find you. I guess that sounds pretty ridiculous since no one has ever penetrated the program. You need to believe I did everything I could think of. Do you have any news of the trial?"

"No. It's going to be a while yet. Janny is with me. We fight all the time," Maddie said, choking back a sob.

"I'm sorry, Maddie. You were closer than sisters. Don't let this awful thing come between you."

"Pete, they said I could ask you if you want to . . . join me. Do you?"

Here it was, the question he'd been dreading. Did he want to or didn't he? "I can't Maddie. I want to, but I can't. I will wait for you, no matter how long it takes. When this is over, we'll make a life together, better than the one we used to talk about. I want to hear you tell me you understand."

"I understand," Maddie said flatly.

"No, I don't think you do. I'm in the middle of a monster deal. It's going to take me at least another eight to ten months to wind it down. There's Fairy Tales to think about. All of that is almost incidental to the real reason I can't join you. Leo is in the hospital. He's had a serious heart attack. They tell me he'll recover. We more or less patched up our differences. I can't leave him to go into hiding."

"That sounds to me like everything is more important than I am."

"No, Maddie. It's a question of priorities. I know you're alive and safe, and I thank God for that. Leo needs my help. Annie needs me for Fairy Tales. I have a business. Leo has a business. I'm being stretched too thin. I'm committed, Maddie."

"I thought you committed to me, Pete."

"I did. I am. Maddie, did you hear what I said?"

"I dreamed about this phone call, prayed daily that I would get to hear your voice again, and now all that I prayed for is . . . why did we even bother with this call?"

"Because I love you," Pete said. "People are separated all the time for different reasons. Men go to war and women wait for them to come home. This is something like that. I'll be here for you, Maddie, no matter what. Is there anything I can do?"

"No. My time is almost up. I knew you wouldn't agree to come and be with me. I knew it."

"Maddie, do you still love me?"

"I thought I did . . . I don't know anymore. You should have been there for me, Pete," she howled tearfully. "They took everything away from me. Now you're telling me you gave up the Stamford house, and Leo, an uncle you professed to hate, is suddenly more important than I am. Your business deals come first. What am I supposed to think?"

"I can't tell you what to think. All I can ask is that you try and understand. I'll wait as long as it takes for you to return. We have the rest of our lives."

"You're a fool, Pete. I could be . . . it could take forever. Didn't anyone tell you that?" Maddie shrilled. "Don't tell me to think positive either. There is not one damn thing about my life that's positive. I might as well be dead. Do you hear me, Pete, I might as well be dead!"

"Jesus, Maddie, stop talking like that. Listen to me, ask . . . ask for a counselor. You need to talk . . . Maddie, are you listening to me?"

"You think a counselor is going to help me? Well, you're wrong. Nothing is going to help me. I want my life, I want yesterday. You all robbed me of my life, and yes, I'm blaming you too. I have to hang up now. Don't ask them to put through a call again, Pete."

Pete stared at the phone receiver in his hand. The dial tone was the only sound in the quiet shop. His eyes were wild when Annie tried to pry the receiver out of his hand. "Easy, Pete, take deep breaths. We'll talk about this. But not here. I promised you dinner and a good stiff drink. Let's go."

"Where?" Pete said stupidly. That wasn't the Maddie he knew and loved.

"Follow me," she said, taking his arm. "We aren't going to talk about this until we have a drink in front of us. Pete, snap out of it. It's not the end of the world."

Pete made an awful sound in his throat. Annie's grip on his arm tightened. "When did Leo go into the hospital?"

"Last night. I spent the night and almost all of today at the hospital. I think he's going to be okay. You should have seen the look on his face when I told him I would stay. I felt . . . I felt . . . it was like when my parents died . . . that awful, sick feeling because you don't know what happens next."

"You did the right thing, Pete. Family is very important. Leo is all you have left. You patched up your differences. You can't cast all that aside."

A few minutes later Annie guided him through the open doorway of a restaurant called Samantha's. She pointed to a back booth. The hostess led the way to the rear of the long, narrow restaurant.

"Two double bourbons on the rocks," Annie said. She held out her pack of cigarettes. Pete took one, lit up and drew deeply. "Relax. When you're ready to talk, I'm here to listen."

Annie was on her second cigarette, her glass almost empty, when Pete said, "She didn't even ask how I was." Annie winced at the pain in her friend's face. "I can't believe the person I spoke to was Maddie. She sounded so . . . selfish . . . so . . . was I wrong about her, Annie? No, don't answer that."

"Start at the beginning, Pete."

Pete ran the entire conversation through his mind before he shared it with Annie. He stared across the table, his face clearly expecting some magical words from Annie that would make things right.

"Pete, you have to understand what's she's going through. I don't know if I could handle what she's going through, and neither do you. Maddie's thinking is all mixed up. Of course she wants yesterday. Yesterday means you. Suggesting a counselor was a good idea. When she gets your letter, I bet she requests another phone call."

"Do you think so?" Pete asked flatly.

Annie didn't think so, but she lied and said, "How could she not want to talk to you? She loves you."

"She wants yesterday. She said everything was taken away from her. She didn't understand about the Stamford house. I could hear the anger in her voice. Maybe she was hanging on to that. You know, we were going to live there and be happy."

"Do you believe that, Pete?"

"No," Pete said miserably. "I don't think Maddie liked the house that much. She tried to get excited about it for me. She's a city girl. A house is responsibility, and Maddie . . . I don't know, Annie, I'm second-guessing her and probably coming up with all the wrong answers. What do I do?"

"Well, I think you need to wait and see if she responds to your letter. Obviously, she's permitted to write you, and the marshals check it out and take care of the mailing. You do what you have to do where Leo is concerned, and you get on with your life. If there's anything I can do for your uncle, just ask."

"Like you really have the time. Are you still donating your time to your friend Albert and the Church of the Good Shepherd?"

"Are your mocking me out?" Annie said stiffly.

"Jesus, no. You're getting as touchy as . . . no, Annie, I was not mocking you out. I think what you're doing is great."

"That's not what you said when you found out I donated all the stock to the church at Christmastime. I paid it back."

"So I was a jerk about it all. You screwed me up. There I was, expecting you to spend Christmas with me, and I'm all hopped up about the holidays and you were gone. I thought something happened to you. I didn't give a hoot about the merchandise. You could have left me a note, Annie."

"You could have invited me, Pete."

"Touché. I'll let you know about Leo. I feel like shit, Annie."

"I know, Pete."

"She's squabbling with Janny. That's not good. Can't they see she needs help? You know what hurts the most, Annie?"

Annie rotated the glass in her hands. "What, Pete?"

"She was more interested in how Fairy Tales was doing than in me. Doesn't that strike you as odd?"

"Pete, you're closing your mind to what she's going through. She was talking to you, hearing your voice. She knew you were okay, knew you initiated the call. She didn't know anything about Fairy Tales, so it was natural for her to ask. She responded to your news about Leo out of frustration. You need to have more of an open mind, Pete."

"She said she might as well be dead." He stared at Annie, a strange look on his face. "You would never act like that, you'd never say a thing like that."

Annie sucked in her breath. He was making comparisons. She felt light-headed. "She didn't mean it, Pete. Nobody wants to be dead. She's angry, and I don't blame her. Actually, it goes beyond angry. I don't know what the word is, but whatever it is, she's it. When she has time to think about things, she'll realize you're hurting as much as she is. Who's to say how I'd react in a similar situation?" She looked away, avoiding Pete's eyes.

"She's never going to forgive me for not jumping at the offer to join her. I could hear it in her voice. She doesn't want me to initiate any more calls. What does that tell you? Another thing, I think . . . I lied when I said I'd wait . . . forever. I lied."

"She's disappointed, unhappy, trying to cope, and you do not know for a fact that she is not going to forgive you. You are assuming again, Pete. If you lied, as you said, you were under stress, just as she was," Annie said lamely.

Pete stretched out his hand to take her hand in his. "Thanks, Annie, you're a true friend. If you hadn't been at the store, I probably would have walked straight into traffic without a second thought. My life wouldn't be complete without you." His thoughts rolled back over the years. His feelings and emotions threatened to suffocate him.

"Let's talk about something else. Did you send flowers to the hospital?"

"No, but I will. Do you mind if I go back to your apartment to shower and change before I go back to the hospital?"

"Of course I don't mind. Talk to me about Leo, Pete."

He didn't want to talk about Leo, and he wasn't sure why. Maybe it had something to do with mortality. If Leo died, he'd be staring his own mortality square in the eye. All the buffers would be gone. Leo wasn't *that* old. Christ, he was thirty-six himself. If he went by Leo's number, half his life was over. The thought was so chilling, he swallowed the bourbon in his glass in one long gulp. He sputtered, to Annie's amusement.

"Do you realize, Annie," Pete said when his sputtering was over, "that half my life is over? Right now, at this point in time, I'm half shot down."

"Guess that puts me in the same category," Annie said lightly. "Does that mean we should start stewing and fretting, or should we do something wild and crazy? Like that time we went cow tipping." She started to giggle. Pete laughed so hard, tears rolled down his cheeks.

God, he loved this woman sitting across from him. They had so many memories. They had so much. It struck him then that he loved Annie Gabriel the way a man is supposed to love a woman. His stomach curled in fear at the realization. Maddie Stern was an interlude in his life to get him to this place in time. Jesus H. Christ. Annie was saying something, he had to pay attention.

"It's harder for women to get older. Men grow distinguished, and women just seem to get older. Why is it that men want young, nubile females when they get to their forties and fifties? They think nineteen is . . . don't they realize how foolish they look with a young thing like that hanging on their arm?"

He needed to think, to talk to Barney. His foot moved jerkily and he grabbed his kneecap and twisted it. Later, when he felt the pain, he wondered why he'd done such a dumb thing. He broke out into a sweat. She was waiting for him to say something. "I guess . . . I suppose they're trying to recapture their youth," he said. "I would never do that." Jesus, what a stupid thing to say, he thought.

"You can't stop the clock," Annie said quietly. "You can work out till you're ready to turn blue, you can get cosmetic surgery, you can dress like you did when you were nineteen, but you're still the same age."

She was pretty. No, she was more than pretty. She was somewhere between pretty and beautiful. Hell no, she was beautiful. He loved the way her eyes crinkled up when she smiled. He loved the wide smile that always reached her eyes. He loved her energy, her intellect. He loved Annie Gabriel. He leaned across the table, his eyes intent. "Annie, why didn't we ever . . . you know, get together?"

Annie's stomach churned. She wanted to scream. She needed to say just the right thing. "I guess we didn't want to spoil a wonderful friendship."

"Nah, it was Dennis. You were the first one to go into a relationship. I think I was just hanging in there waiting for you to make a move in my direction." Pete stared into the amber liquid in his glass. This wasn't the right time or place. He needed time. Time to . . . time to . . .

"Why was I the one who was supposed to make a move?" Annie asked. "Isn't it the man who's supposed to do that? Besides, you never gave me any encouragement. I might have . . . you know, but who wants to be rebuffed?"

"Aren't . . . didn't you do the same thing you are always accusing me of?"

"What's that?"

"You always say I assume and presume. That's what you did, Annie, you assumed I would rebuff you."

"Well, wouldn't you have?" Annie said tightly.

"I don't know that and neither do you. That was then. You can be a real hard-ass when you want to be, do you know that?"

"I think we're on dangerous ground here. I think we should order, since we've been drinking on an empty stomach. The only thing I had to eat today was cottage cheese."

"Jeez, Annie, that's terrible," Pete said, his eyes rolling from side to side. "I'm going to buy you the biggest steak this establishment has to offer," he added magnanimously, his arm narrowly missing the glasses on the table as he gestured with a wide flourish.

"No. This is my treat," Annie said. "I'm buying *you* the biggest steak this establishment has to offer. And lots of black coffee. They serve good apple pie here."

"It can't be half as good as yours," Pete said loyally. He wanted to say something meaningful, but he felt numb.

"That's probably true, but for a restaurant it's good," Annie said with no trace of false modesty.

"We get along very well, don't we, Annie? How long have we been friends? Forever, right?" Forever meant forever. He'd fucked up. Big-time. He wanted to tell her . . . needed to tell her.

Annie signaled the waitress. "It seems like I've known you forever," she said carefully.

"Maddie and I were never . . . we went right into the relationship. We should have been friends first. That's what happened to you and Dennis. You need to be friends first or you have no foundation for a relationship to grow on. Isn't that right, Annie?" That was meaningful, wasn't it?

"How do you know that's what happened to me and Dennis?" Annie said crossly.

Pete did his best to widen his eyes. "Because, Miss Smartass, you told me. How else would I know? You should have told me that when I met Maddie. What kind of friend are you?" The kind of friend, he answered himself, who . . . who . . .

"The kind that minds her own business. I didn't see you sticking your nose into my business when I started dating Dennis."

"That's because I'm not as smart as you. You're smart, Annie. You even have common sense."

She was in a prickly mood now. He knew her so well. What the hell did he say to put this strange look on her face?

"You always have the right answer, or you point me in the right direction," he said. "You've never failed me. Except for Christmas."

"You didn't invite me. Let's drop it, Pete." To the hovering waitress she said, "Two porterhouse steaks, baked potatoes, sour cream and butter, creamy Italian dressing, string beans with almonds. Coffee. Bring the coffee now, please."

"You're supposed to tell me what you want, and I'm supposed to order it. That's the man's job. You screwed up, Annie."

"I'm paying the bill, so I can order. It would have taken you an hour to decide." She giggled. "You're half drunk."

"It's your fault, you brought me here. I want blue cheese."

"You hate blue cheese dressing," Annie snapped.

"Maddie likes it. She said I would learn to like it. You're right, I hate it."

"If you don't mind my asking, what exactly did you and Maddie have in common?"

"Is this one of those trick questions?" Pete asked, slurring his words. When he saw the disgust on Annie's face, he made an attempt to straighten his slumped shoulders and look Annie in the eye. He wanted to tell her he loved her, had always loved her but was too damn stupid to know it.

"We . . . well . . . sex was good. We like . . . liked the same kinds of movies, you know, murder and mayhem. We both like to read in bed. We both like . . . stuffed peppers with a side order of sour cream cucumbers. What else do you want to know? Ah, I see by your expression you don't think those are good enough reasons to get married. I didn't like her friends, she didn't like mine. I did like Janny, though. Well, are you going to say something?"

"No."

"Does that mean you're pissed off?"

"It doesn't mean any such thing. I think, Pete, you need to go into what you used to call your 'think tank,' and not come out until you have things straight in your head. This might be none of my business, but what did she think about you guys going to Bell's Beach?"

"She said she'd go. Sometime. I'm going, did I tell you that? Leo gave me an open ticket. He wants me to go. The surfboard is all ready. All I have to do is decide the time and the date. If I wanted you to go with me, would I have to send you an engraved invitation? I don't want to make another stupid mistake like I made at Christmas time." He sucked in his breath, waiting for her answer.

Annie felt herself grow light-headed. "A verbal invitation would suffice. Look, here's our salads."

It was the look on her face that smoothed out the wrinkles in his heart.

"Thank God it's creamy Italian," Pete said, staring at his salad bowl. "Jesus, you have no idea how much I hate blue cheese."

"Eat."

"Nag, nag, nag," Pete said. Time, he thought, would make it right.

Annie stared at the phone in her hand, then hung up. She felt almost dizzy as the breath she'd been holding swooshed out of her lungs. Her knees wobbled as she made her way to the couch to sit down. Jakes had said he had a lead on Barney. "I've dropped everything to concentrate on it," the detective told her. "I know it's taken a long time, but I did tell you I wouldn't give up. Keep your fingers crossed. I feel in my gut we're going to make Pete Sorenson one happy man soon. Thanks to you, Annie. I'll call when I have more news, and don't worry, I didn't forget, he's to show up with a big, red bow on his head. Pete's gonna love you forever for this, Annie. See you."

Pete's gonna love you forever. She wished. God, how she wished. Tears brimmed in Annie's eyes. *This is the last thing I'm doing for you, Pete Sorenson. I need to start over without you in my life. Knowing I was able to do this, with Jakes's help, well, that ends it for me. Am I being noble here, a martyr, or what? I don't know. What I do know is I can't go through another holiday season. Thanksgiving, yes. Because I have so much to be thankful for. Then it's good-bye, Pete, hello world.*

Sniffling and hiccuping, Annie made her way to the kitchen. What she needed was a good strong cup of coffee laced with something, and whatever that something was, it was going to be one hundred proof. Maybe she'd get snookered all by herself so she could have a good crying jag. The kind where her eyes puffed up and got red and she got hoarse from sobbing. Her nose would get red from blowing it and she'd use up a whole box of tissues. Her good-bye salute to Pete Sorenson. Damn straight it was her good-bye salute.

Some things just weren't meant to be.

Pete left the hospital. Thirty minutes later he was ringing Annie's doorbell.

"I didn't know where else to go," Pete said brokenly. "Leo . . . passed away. I don't know if I can handle this, Annie."

Annie gritted her teeth and tried to bring her friend's countenance into focus. She tried harder and managed somehow to usher him into the apartment. He seemed oblivious to her condition. Pete needed her. She was supposed to respond in true Annie fashion. She was supposed to make things better for him. What about me? she screamed silently. She took a deep breath. Thank God she hadn't had that last drink. If she'd consumed it, she'd be lying under the table right now.

"Pete, God never gives us more than we can handle. You thought you couldn't handle Maddie's disappearance, but you did. Leo wouldn't want you to cave in now. I'll make some fresh coffee."

"Tea. Annie, make me tea. My mother always used to make tea for my father when things weren't going right. Tea and toast. Something light. Nourishment. The only reason I was able to handle it was because of you. Only you, Annie."

"Tea's good."

The early sunrise crept through the kitchen window. "This tea and toast must be an old wive's tale," Pete muttered after he ate. "I don't feel one damn bit better." Suddenly, he noticed Annie's drawn face. "Are you crying?" he asked.

"No, not really. It's sad when someone leaves this earth. I'm sure your uncle had a good life, but it's still sad. We take so much for granted, you, me, all those people out there," Annie said, pointing to the kitchen window. "We're alive, we're healthy, the world isn't such a bad place. It's whatever we make it. Life is going to go on no matter what. Now, is there anything I can do for you? I still have your power of attorney. I can handle the legal matters. I don't think it's a good idea for you to do that."

"If you don't mind. You always make such perfect sense, Annie."

"I accept the compliment. Do you want me to handle the funeral arrangements?"

"No. I have to do that. I'm going to shower and . . . head out to New Jersey. Close Fairy Tales, Annie."

"Okay. Do you want me to go with you?"

"If . . . are you sure you want to? Yeah, yeah, I do need you to come with me. I need that level head of yours."

An hour later Pete picked up Annie's small bag. "How come you don't use the big bedroom?"

Annie looked away. "I don't know. Too much trouble to move my stuff from the guest room. I'm only here temporarily."

Later, I have to think about what she just said, Pete thought. It did mean something, he was sure of it.

The afternoon of the funeral found Pete in Leo's study. Annie sat behind the desk with Leo's will in front of her. "I'll skip the legalese and get to the heart of things."

Pete nodded.

"You inherit everything, Pete. Requests to the servants. A large lump sum, a hundred thousand dollars to his secretary, and of course her pension of two thousand a month. She's to retire now to take care of her cats. This house, and everything in it, goes to you. There's a provision here for the perpetual upkeep of your . . . mother's and father's graves. His own too. All stocks, bonds, bank accounts go to you. He's got six trusts here that have to be gone over. His life insurance will pay the estate taxes. His share of the firm, which is half, goes to you too. That's about it. There's a sealed envelope here for you. You might want to read it in private. He took care of everything. I'll file the claims with the insurance companies. I'd say, Pete, you are one hell of a wealthy man. Oh, I forgot, money has been set aside for the upkeep of this estate, and Leo asks that the servants all be kept on until retirement. There's a fund set up for that too." Annie folded the will, snapped the rubber band around it, and handed it to Pete. "I think I'll go for a walk."

Outside in the warm September air, Annie reflected that Pete looked so vulnerable, so lost. Instinct warned her not to go back inside. Pete would pull up his socks and get on with his life, and she had to do the same.

Just now, going through Leo's will, handling legal details, made her realize how much she missed the practice of law. Running Maddie Stern's business, enjoyable as it was, simply wasn't for her. The problem was, did she tell Pete now, when he was so whacked out, or did she wait for a more opportune moment? Or she could formalize it and send a letter of intent?

Annie sat down on an iron bench and stared at her surroundings through misty eyes. It was beautiful here. She wondered how many people it took to keep the estate intact. Had Leo Sorenson enjoyed this lovely place, or had he been too busy to smell the proverbial roses? Probably the latter.

She thought about the funeral and the hundreds and hundreds of people who stopped to pay their respects. Flowers, tons of flowers, had arrived and were still arriving as the funeral procession made its way to the cemetery. Large sums of money had been donated in Leo's name to the hospital, to the Heart Fund, to the Cancer Fund, and one incredibly handsome donation in his name had been sent to a children's year-round camp, a camp the donor said Leo endowed many years ago. A camp called the Harry and Jane Sorenson Camp for Handicapped Children. Pete's eyes had rolled back in his head when he heard about that.

Annie swatted at a bluebottle fly bent on attacking her ankle. Would Pete tell her what was in the letter with the gold seal?

If only . . .

• • •

Pete sipped at the cup of coffee he carried into Leo's study. This was his now. This shiny mahogany desk, this rich leather chair Leo had broken in, all belonged to him. His eyes burned when he stared at the framed picture of his parents that sat on Leo's desk. His desk now. The picture was his too.

He ripped at the envelope in his hand. There were four sheets of paper and a letter on crackly paper. He read the letter first.

Dear Peter,

If you're reading this letter, it is obvious I am no longer of this world.

I want to say so many things to you, but I don't know the words. I feel I have to leave you with something besides material things.

In life, Peter, we have choices and options. I missed out on so much by never marrying. I guess you could say I am a one-woman man. I loved your mother dearly and I could never find anyone to fill her shoes. After a while I simply stopped looking. I don't want that to happen to you. If I can leave this earth knowing you are going to find someone with all those wonderful qualities your mother had, I would die happy. She was warm, generous, kind, considerate. She would never harm a living thing. She used to open the screen door so the flies could go outside. She would never think of swatting one like the rest of us do. When she smiled, the smile came from her heart and reached her eyes. Rather like the way Miss Gabriel smiles. She was so loving, Peter.

There was one minute there, when I first met your friend, that I thought I was seeing your mother all over again. I don't mean in appearance, but more her inner qualities.

I'm wandering here. I guess it's because I hate writing this letter, knowing I'll be gone when you read it.

Attached is a list of the numbered bank accounts in Geneva.

Take care, Peter. Go on with your life and don't look back. Do what's best for Peter and those you love, especially those you love. That's what it's all about.

Thank you so much for that wonderful Christmas we shared

together. Imagine what it would have been like if Miss Gabriel had been there. After all, she made it all possible. Open your eyes and your heart, Peter.

Much love and affection,
Leo

The crackly letter dropped to the floor as Pete's hands closed over the arms of the chair he was sitting on. He was having trouble breathing and his mouth felt dry.

23

It had been a terrible week, as far as Maddie was concerned, beginning with the dissatisfying phone call to Pete, and then coming back to this prison and going through the motions of living. She'd also gotten a letter, which arrived after the phone call.

"Aren't you cold?" Janny asked curiously as she snipped at the evergreens on the side of the front porch. She herself was dressed in a heavy jacket and wore gardening gloves with a fleece lining. They probably weren't gardening gloves at all, but workmen's gloves. She'd found them in the barn and confiscated them.

"Do you mean me personally or just my heart? How can you be cold when you're dead? I am, you know, I just don't have enough sense to lie down and get it over with. What *are* you doing?"

"Trimming these bushes. Or are they shrubs? It's something different to do, and I like to keep busy. You should try doing something besides feeling sorry for yourself, Maddie. This isn't going to go away, and we need to make the best of it."

"Like you do with those ranch hands," Maddie snapped.

"Yeah," Janny drawled. "I enjoy playing cards with them and talking. That's all we do, Maddie. I hate being around you because you depress me." There, she'd said it and it was out in the open.

"Is this where you start to blame me for what happened?"

"No. All I said was you depress me. You never speak to me unless I speak first. You grumble and complain, and I can't stand your constant crying and whining. We have to make the best of this and look forward to the day it all comes to an end."

"And when, pray tell, do you think that's going to happen?"

"I don't know, Maddie. All I know is it will, and I don't intend to sit here and suck my thumb."

"That's easy for you to say. When it comes right down to it, what did you give up? A job, that's it. I gave up Pete, the business, my marriage. Everything," Maddie said bitterly.

"It wasn't just a job. It was my career. I know with a lot of hard work I could have done very well. And, Miss Stern, I had to put my dream of finding my real mother on hold. That counts, Maddie. A lot. It's something I dreamed of doing all my life, and now I can't. Someday, when this is all over, I hope I can find her. I can't let that stop me from living. Life goes on, Maddie. We're alive and well." She'd gone through this same speech so many times, she was sick of it. Who *was* this person sitting on the porch shivering in the cold because she didn't have the good sense to put on a jacket?

"So blame me, I can take it," Maddie said wearily.

"No you can't, that's the problem. You need help, Maddie. I think we should ask the caseworker to get you a shrink to talk to. We could probably both use a little counseling. I'm game if you are. I'll even do the asking. You need help, Maddie, and I'm not saying this to hear my own voice."

"Do you think I'm crazy?" Maddie shouted.

"No, I don't think you're crazy, but I do think you need to talk to someone before you go over the edge. You need professional help. So do I. I realize it, why can't you?"

"Stuff it, Janny. Do you think every time a guy dumps a girl she should go to a shrink? That's what you're saying. People lose their businesses every day of the year, and do they seek professional help? I doubt it. What makes me different?"

"Our situation. You aren't accepting it."

"You have?" Maddie said bitterly.

"A lot better than you have. I don't know you anymore, Maddie," Janny said quietly. "And you know something else, I don't blame Pete one bit for not coming here. You are so selfish, you'd let Fairy Tales go under, you'd make Pete give up his business, just so you can have what you want. Grow up, Maddie, that isn't the way the real world operates. This is going to be over, and I believe Pete when he said he'd wait for you. It's something to look forward to, but you took care of that, didn't you? If he does what you told him to do, it will be your fault. At the risk of repeating myself, grow up, Maddie."

"I quit," Maddie said quietly, Pete's letter clutched in her hand. She'd read it five times, knew the words by heart. She could throw it away when she went into the house.

Inside, Maddie flopped down on the sofa.

Olive Parsons. The marshals had screwed up on that too. Six months ago they found their mistake and came to give her another identity, saying that in their haste to try and satisfy her the wrong numbers were put into the computer. It seemed there was a real Olive Parsons, her caseworker had said sheepishly. Janny told her she'd lost it that day, screaming and yelling, her eyes rolling back in her head. There had been a regular parade of people for several days after that, apologizing, trying to explain she needed this new identity and she *must* turn over all the old papers given to her. She'd refused, and that night after Janny was asleep she'd buried everything in the backyard in a five-pound lard can. Someday she was going to fuck them all over the way they fucked her over. God, she was starting to think and talk like a criminal.

In the house she fixed herself a cup of tea and carried it to the living room, where she smoothed out Pete's letter and read it again.

My Dearest Maddie,

I don't understand any of this. The marshals told me you were given permission to write me. Why didn't you? I need to know. If the marshals follow through, I will probably speak with you before you get this letter. Hopefully, we will be able to sort things out.

There's so much I want to tell you, I don't know where to start. Anywhere, I guess. I gave up the house in Stamford. I didn't think I could be happy there without you. It was just a house, Maddie. I bought one in Darien. Annie decorated it for me and it's quite nice. She calls it my pad. I had to do something because she needed a place to stay, and giving up my apartment to her was easy, since it held memories of us. It was absolute torture to walk into it and know you wouldn't be there when I was in town.

My uncle Leo and I made peace. I invited him for Christmas. I didn't want to be alone. It would have been our first Christmas as a married couple. We had a nice time and got to know one another.

You would not believe how well Fairy Tales is doing. Annie is a magician. It runs so smoothly. She's got a fine business head and customers seem to like her. She's not trying to take your place, Maddie, she's standing in for you until you get back. I guess what I'm trying to say is, the store is in the best of hands so you don't need to fret about it.

God, I wish I knew where you were. I wish so many things lately. All I do is think about you and how I failed you by not being home for your calls. But Maddie, I was trying to find you. The police wouldn't tell me anything. I hired a private detective, but the marshals are as close-mouthed as clams. I did everything I could possibly do. I just found out about the letter writing and phone calls a short while ago. They told me you had to initiate them. It makes me wonder, Maddie, why you didn't. Didn't you have faith in me? Don't you trust me?

I'll wait for you, Maddie. As long as it takes. If our love is as strong as I believe, then we will weather this. I need to hear from you, Maddie. I need to know what your feelings are.

From the things I've been reading in the papers and from my contacts in the D.A.'s office, it seems they have a pretty airtight case and it's getting tighter. They expect to go to trial by the middle of next year. That's not long, Maddie, less than a year. If they bring down the family, your life will be your own again. We can pick up where we left off. It seems, according to one of my sources, the rats are rolling over trying to make deals. What that means is there won't be anyone left to harm you after the trial. In my opinion.

I know you probably don't want to hear this, but because of you, this town will be a lot safer for all of us. Because of your bravery, others will have the guts to come out and say what they know. It's hard, but it's for just a bit longer. Hang in there, Maddie. It will be over soon.

My love for you is constant. Take care of yourself and think about me and how bright our future will be when this is all over.

All my love,
Pete

"And I thought lawyers were supposed to be smart," Maddie muttered. "If you believe for one minute we are going to have a bright, wonderful future, you're crazy. If you loved me, you'd be here right now, telling me these things in person. I might believe you then. Letters don't count. What counts is being here with me. So there, Pete Sorenson. So there."

"I'm worried about you, Maddie," Janny said that evening when she'd finished the dishes.

"Well, don't worry about me. By the time this thing gets to court, I'll be declared incompetent and my testimony won't be needed."

Janny's eyebrows shot upward as her jaw dropped. "Is that what this is all about?"

"They won't need me then. Pete said in his letter that all those criminals, the ones that belong to the crime families, are . . . rolling over and making deals. Don't you get it, Janny, this is all for nothing. When it's time to go into court, I won't even be needed. And for that they ruined my life. Yours too, but you refuse to accept it."

"The way I look at it, Maddie, my life is on hold for a while. Personally speaking, I think you're in a very bad emotional state right now and you aren't thinking clearly. I'm sorry you won't ask for professional help because I think you need it. My suggestion to you right now would be to ask if you can call Pete. It might be nice to wish him a happy Thanksgiving. You know, be grateful for what you have because the alternative isn't something I want to think about."

"Butt out, Janny," Maddie said nastily.

Back in the kitchen, Janny pulled at Marshal Parker McNally's arm.

"Parker, I need to talk to you," she said quietly. "Let's go outside and take a short walk."

He was okay for a marshal, Janny thought. He missed his family and he hated this particular job. He was tall, broad-shouldered, fit and trim. She pretended not to see the gun stuck in the back of his trousers. Instead she concentrated on his dedication, his homely face and the big ears he said were his personal curse to live with the rest of his life. He was married to the sweetest girl in Texas, he said, and had three of the most beautiful daughters in the whole world. His assignment was six weeks on and three weeks off.

"I hope you aren't going to tell me Unitec nose-dived," McNally grumbled good-naturedly.

"Nothing that interesting. I'm worried about Maddie. She needs help, Parker. You have to call somebody, and you need to do it today. I'm no psychiatrist, but I know Maddie and she's mentally teetering on the edge. Will you call someone?"

"Are you sure, Janice? I talked to her yesterday and she was her usual nasty self. I didn't pick up on any . . . mental problems."

"You don't know her like I do. Like I *thought* I knew her. If I'm wrong, what harm is done? Some shrink gets to mush through all this snow and eat my cooking. I don't want . . . later to know I missed some signals and Maddie . . . went over the edge."

"How is it you can handle this and she can't?" McNally asked for the hundredth time.

"I wasn't engaged. I didn't have any wedding plans. I didn't open up a million-dollar business, and . . . and I don't have a fiancé, a fiancé who doesn't want to join me. That's Maddie's explanation. And I still have the same identity I was given at the get-go. They dicked her around, and you know it. I agree with her, we don't belong in this program. Your people didn't take the time to figure that out, and yeah, I know, things moved quickly and you did the best you could. It wasn't good enough. It still isn't good enough. Promises were made. Promises were broken. It wasn't fair and it still isn't fair. I hate this as much as she does."

"But you're handling it."

Janny wiped at the tears in her eyes. "I guess my expectations weren't as grand as Maddie's. I'm a simple person. I'd like to be rich someday, but more than anything, I want to be contented. I want a family because I never had one. To me, that's a very high expectation, but not a monetary one. Maddie equates everything with dollars. Will you call, Parker?"

"Yes. I don't know who I'm going to raise on Thanksgiving eve, though," McNally said, a frown building between his brows.

"Maybe you need to get tough. I happen to think this is crucial. If anything happens to Maddie, I swear to God I will personally walk all the way to Cheyenne and spill my guts to the first reporter who will listen. And all those ranch hands in there, they'll help me. You know that, don't you?"

"Yes, I do know that."

"So . . . tell them to get the shrink here by tomorrow. They can fly in by helicopter and land in the field."

McNally felt out of his depth. He believed everything Janice was telling him, but he knew there were going to be hundreds of questions, and he didn't know if he could answer them. "Does that mean I should ask them to send a woman or a man?"

"I don't think a woman would be good, Parker. Maddie will see that she's dressed well, free to work at her profession, free to come and go as she pleases. That will work on her mind. At least I think it will. I think a man will be better. Yes, I think it should be a man. Do you have any opinions?" she asked.

"No I don't. I'll tell them what you said, what you suggested."

"Maybe it should be a fatherly figure, you know, an older man."

"That sounds good," McNally said, relieved that he now had something to say that made some kind of weird sense, even to him.

In the offices at 600 Army Navy Drive in Arlington, Virginia, Sandor Neville was participating in a three-way conference call with the Attorney General and Manhattan's District Attorney. He repeated Marshal McNally's phone call word for word. He fired up a cigarette while he listened to the two attorneys hash out the pros and cons of the request. His mind wandered. Was his wife going to serve pumpkin and pecan pie tomorrow or would it be apple? It probably wasn't going to make a difference because, from the sound of things, he wasn't going to make it home for a few days.

Neville thought about Maddie Stern. He felt sorry for her. He wished there were something he could personally do for the young woman. He wondered if Pete Sorenson was going to be alone for Thanksgiving or if he had someone to share it with. The whole thing sucked as far as he was concerned. He fired up a second cigarette. He was stubbing it out in the ashtray when the Attorney General gave the okay to send a psychiatrist of Neville's choosing to Jasper Springs. And where in the goddamn hell was he supposed to find a shrink on Thanksgiving eve? The Yellow Pages? Well, yeah, it was a place to start.

Neville called his wife, told her not to hold dinner for him.

The following afternoon, with a light snow falling, a blue and white helicopter set down in the cornfield on the ranch outside of Jasper Springs. Parker McNally, in a four-by-four, waited for his passenger, who he thought looked meaner than a castrated bull. "Oh shit," he muttered.

He wasn't fatherly-looking at all. Grandfatherly would be more like it. Maybe even great-grandfatherly. He expected his voice to be brittle and raspy, like dry leaves rubbing against each other in the fall. Instead it was warm and gentle-sounding. A chuckle crept in when Dr. Phillips said, "I'm as cold as a well digger's ass. Tell me about my patient."

"Well, we didn't tell her about you. That's for starters. Did they really swear you in as a marshal?"

"At the airport. I felt important," Dr. Phillips said. "It was necessary to maintain the secrecy. In a way, it wasn't necessary because I'm bound by the Hippocratic oath, but I took it anyway to make everyone feel better." He chuckled again as the four-by-four sped through the snow-covered fields. "Now, tell me everything you can about the patient."

McNally told him everything he knew. Out of the corner of his eye he saw the doctor nod several times. His voice full of awe, McNally said, "She can tell you what's on every page of the Sears catalog."

"Amazing," was all the doctor said. "How shall I address her, as Miss Parsons, or have you given her a second name?"

McNally shrugged. "That's part of the problem. They told her she couldn't be Olive Parsons anymore because the computer made a mistake. It seems there's a real Olive Parsons somewhere. She refused to accept a new name. She's very angry."

"Justifiably so," the doctor said.

McNally continued to talk, and Dr. Phillips continued to listen. He didn't ask any more questions. McNally thought it strange, but what did he know about psychiatry?

The house, when they arrived, smelled of cinnamon and apples. Janny was baking pies with the apples from the root cellar.

McNally made the introduction and discreetly withdrew to the kitchen with Janny.

"Are you a psychiatrist, Dr. Phillips?" Maddie said, marking her place in the catalog by turning down the page. She was on sleds, Flexible Flyers.

"Yes I am," Phillips replied, taking a chair near the fire. "I was told you needed someone from the outside to talk to. I'd like to help if I can. If you aren't ready or if you'd like me to leave, I will. The decision is yours, Miss . . . Stern."

"Didn't they tell you I'm not Maddie Stern anymore?" Maddie asked flatly.

"Yes, and they told me you aren't Olive Parsons either. At my age I get confused easily, so I prefer to go with who you *really* are." Phillips chuckled.

Maddie stared at the sleds in the catalog. "If you're just here to talk to me, I don't think you can help me. I'm tired of talking. No one listens. No one cares. I don't belong here. You aren't going to change that, so what it means to me is we're wasting each other's time. What does it mean to you?"

"I think it's too early to make that kind of an assessment. I'm certainly willing to give you the benefit of my years in practice. I'm happy to say I've never lost a patient yet."

"To what?"

"To that netherworld that closes out the rest of the world."

"There are days when I think I'm losing my mind. Maybe I already lost it and don't know it," Maddie said quietly.

"That's a start." Phillips smiled.

"I know this catalog from front to back," Maddie said.

"What is that going to do for you? Next year there will be new items and the page numbers will change."

Maddie stared at the doctor. He reminded her of someone, but she didn't know who. Maybe a movie star. That was it, Fernando Lamas. Distinguished, with pearl-gray hair and matching mustache. His eyes held a smile that was hard to ignore. "I never thought about that. Hopefully, by next year I won't be using this catalog to entertain myself."

"Oh, why is that?"

"By then the trial should be over and I'll be . . . someone else. I guess. I don't know that for certain. There are no certainties. You know that, don't you, Doctor?"

Phillips chuckled. "Death and taxes."

Maddie closed the catalog. "I lost my way, Doctor, and I can't find my way back. I want to. I need to."

The words tumbled out then, in a torrent. From time to time Phillips nodded to show he was following her. He watched as she sipped from a cup of tea, and watched as she wiped at the perspiration dotting her brow. If he were alone, he would have cried for her anguish.

It was dark out when Maddie halted and looked around. The room was dark, the only light coming from the fireplace. She got up and turned on the lamps. "I think we missed dinner."

"That's all right. We can eat later. Tell me, what do you want? What would make you whole again? If you could do it right now, today, what would you do?"

"I want to put on my coat and walk away from here."

"As?"

"As Maddie Stern."

"And?"

"Go back to New York. Pick up my old life. Take my chances."

"The trial?"

"I'll go through with it."

"What about the danger you'd be in?"

"What about the danger I'm in now? As a psychiatrist, I think that's a rather foolish question. I'm in danger now of losing my mind. I know that, I'm not exactly stupid. That netherworld you spoke of, I can't think its preferable to death if death is the end result of my leaving here. Now, let me ask you a question, Dr. Phillips. I want a straight-out answer, don't take time to think, just blurt it out. If you were me, what would you do?"

"The same thing I know you're going to do. Leave. Be who I am."

"You aren't supposed to say that, you're supposed to try and talk me into staying."

"Wherever did you get an idea like that?" the doctor asked.

"Isn't that why they sent you here?"

"I can't say what was in *their* minds, but it wasn't in mine. A very nice gentleman named Sandor Neville called me on the recommendation of the AMA and told me about you. He said he'd never met you personally and he wished there was something he himself could do for you. He said something I totally agreed with."

"Which was?" Maddie said breathlessly.

"To have to stand by and see your life taken away from you through no fault of your own had to be the worst thing in the world. I reviewed my own life and came to the same conclusion. Well, I'm glad we settled all that. I thought I was going to be here for weeks."

"I beg your pardon?"

"If we tell Mr. McNally to call the airport, we'll have time to eat that wonderful dinner I smelled earlier and be on our way."

"To where?"

"I'm heading back to Atlanta, Georgia. I thought you said you wanted to go to New York."

"You mean I can . . . leave?"

"Maddie, you could have left anytime you wanted. You did it in Fort Lauderdale and again in Utah. You made the decision. This is probably the most important decision you'll ever make in your life. If you can live with it, and there's no pun intended, then let's get the phone call out of the way and some dinner under our belts."

"Not so fast, Doctor. How do I handle Pete and the store and . . . all that?"

"Oh, no, Miss Stern, we don't supply the answers, we just help you down the road. You must make your own decisions."

"I've changed."

"That's understandable."

"Pete has too. Changed, I mean."

"Can you forgive that change?"

"I don't know. I had all these preconceived ideas about him."

"Do you think he had the same preconceived notions about you?"

"I think so, Dr. Phillips. I guess it wasn't meant to be."

"Relationships have to be worked at. Absence doesn't always make the heart grow fonder."

"That sounds like an answer to me."

"I like the word 'observation' better."

"Before we go into dinner, Doctor, I have to show you something."

Maddie opened the Sears catalog and withdrew a long white envelope. Pasted on sheets of blank paper was a birth certificate, her first communion and baptism certificates, and a copy of her driver's license and Social Security card. The last sheet of paper contained replicas of her credit cards.

Tears blurred the old doctor's eyes. "It must have taken you a long time to do this, to cut out those letters so painstakingly and then line them up. These," he said, holding up the papers, "are works of art."

"No, Dr. Phillips, they're who I am. I want the originals back. I deserve to have them returned. I won't settle for anything less."

"Then, Maddie Stern, I suggest we do what we have to so we can be on our way."

"They won't try and stop me?"

"No. You have my word."

"Then, Dr. Phillips, let's go eat that turkey and apple pie. I have a lot of catching up to do."

In the kitchen Janny reached out to her. "Good for you, Maddie," she whispered.

"Janny, I'm sorry. I mean that. Are you coming?"

"No. I'm going to stay here. I kind of like it, and the guys are depending on me to keep their affairs in tip-top shape. I'm going to go out on my own when it's all over. I wish you the best."

"Do you want me to write?"

"No. I think this chapter of our life is over. I have things to do and places to go. I'll try and find my mother. McNally said he has some sources he can help me tap. I'm going to be fine."

"So am I."

"I know you will, Maddie. Good luck."

"The helicopter will be here in forty minutes," McNally said quietly.

"Guess you're glad to see me go, McNally? I can't apologize, you need to know that."

"None expected . . . Miss Stern."

"Thank you for that, McNally."

"Can we eat now?" Phillips grumbled.

Maddie laughed. "Absolutely."

She'd walked through this door hundreds of times, but today it was different. She wasn't going to walk back into the cabinlike house again.

She was taking nothing with her but the clothes on her back, the envelope with her homemade credentials, and the little money she'd saved.

She was Maddie Stern again. She had papers that said so.

She laughed then, a sound of pure joy, her eyes sparkling with her freedom. She skipped through the snow and then dropped to her knees. She made a snowball and pretended to throw it at the doctor, who dodged as if she had. He laughed with her. All his cases should be this easy, this satisfying.

Dr. Phillips smiled. "You'll be in New York before midnight."

"I can't believe it!" Maddie squealed. "I'm free. I'm not Miss Nobody, I'm not Miss XYZ. I'm Maddie Stern. I'm me again. Me. God, I really am me.

"Me!"

Her shrill cry of pleasure carried in the clear, frosty air and came back to wrap itself around her.

She was going home. *Thank you God. Thankyouthankyouthankyou.*

24

"It was a wonderful dinner, Annie. I think I can truthfully say this was the best pumpkin pie I ever ate."

Annie smiled. "You say that no matter what kind it is."

"And now it's time to talk, is that it?"

"Yes, Pete, now it's time to talk. I think you even know what I'm going to say."

"Then maybe you shouldn't say it."

"I have to say it, Pete. I'm leaving. The store is in good hands. You've come to terms with Leo's letter. I'm no longer needed here anymore. I want my own life back, Pete. The store, as much as I love it, isn't for me. I'm a lawyer, it's what I do best. So I'm leaving you with the dishes and heading back to the city. Tomorrow is the biggest shopping day of the Christmas season. Saturday will be busy too. I want to get that set up and under way. This way I can leave knowing I did my best. Oh, don't look so glum, Pete. I'll stay in touch. I'm going to take a vacation first, though."

"Annie—"

"Shhh," Annie said placing her finger against his lips. "You'd have done it for me. It's time to move on. You're going to be fine, Pete. Before you know it, the trial will be here and then it will be over. Maddie will come around once it's all over, and then you two will live happily ever after."

"And you, Annie?" Pete said with a catch in his voice.

"Me!" Annie said in mock horror. "Have you ever known me not to come out on top?"

"A time or two," Pete said in a funny-sounding voice.

"That doesn't count." She swooped down, bussed him on the cheek, and was out the door before he could get up from the table. He heard the car's engine, saw the headlights arc on the kitchen wall. Total silence wrapped itself around him.

"What the hell. . . ?"

Good old Annie. His best friend. His pal. His confidante. His moral conscience. Good old Annie. Best cook in the whole world. Best goddamn store manager he'd ever seen. Best fucking overall lawyer. Best of everything. Annie was the best.

And now she was gone. Just like that. He shook his head to clear it. At that moment he would have driven after her, but he'd consumed over a bottle of wine all by himself. Annie had only a few sips. He was in no condition to drive.

She said she'd stay in touch. She would, because Annie never lied to him.

Annie was his best friend. Annie was his conscience.

Annie was the best.

And he loved her.

The following day the remains of the scrumptious Thanksgiving dinner were still on the table. At breakfast he'd picked at the turkey stuffing. At lunch he'd gnawed on a wing and ate some dried turkey breast. For his dinner he was going to finish off the pumpkin pie and drink another bottle of wine. Maybe two, maybe three. For sure he'd be able to sleep. But first he needed some sound. Bob Marley's "Stir It Up" ricocheted off the walls. "That's more like it," Pete said, dusting his hands together before he uncorked his first bottle of wine. Before he passed out on the couch, he decided he'd listen to Marley's "I Shot the Sheriff" sixty-two times.

He woke the following morning a little before noon when a horn blared in his driveway.

"Shut the fuck up," Pete groaned as he covered his head with one of the sofa cushions. The horn blared again.

"Annie!" Pete bounced off the sofa and hit the door at a dead run, his head pounding like a jackhammer. He blinked when the doorbell rang. He yanked it open and cried "Annie" at the same time.

"Sorry, Pete, it's just me, Maddie."

"Maddie! Jesus Christ, it's you, Maddie?"

"In the flesh. Can I come in?"

"In the house? Well, hell yes." Pete took a backward step, still startled. "Maddie, how did . . . what . . ."

"Coffee would be nice."

"Coffee? Oh, coffee. Yeah, yeah, I'll make some coffee." He stumbled twice on his way to the kitchen because he kept looking over his shoulder. "It really is you, I'm not dreaming. Am I dreaming, Maddie?"

"No. It's me. Looks like you had a party. Is this still from Thanksgiving?" The amusement on her face wasn't lost on Pete.

"I didn't feel like cleaning it up. Actually, I've been . . . sort of snacking on the leftovers. Why don't you clean it up while I make coffee?"

"I beg your pardon. I don't do . . . okay, if that's what I have to do to get a cup of coffee, okay. Should I just throw everything away?"

"That sounds good. Dump the dishes in the sink. Maddie . . . how . . ."

"Sit down, Pete, and I'll tell you."

Pete sat down. He listened, and when she was finished with her story and her coffee, he poured her another cup. "Isn't it dangerous for you?" he asked.

"You know what, Pete? I'm not who I thought I was. I truly believed I could handle anything. I was wrong. I was wrong about a lot of things. That's why I'm here. I realized in my captivity—and that's how I thought of it, captivity—that I didn't love you. Not the way a woman is supposed to love a man. The way I think Annie Gabriel loves you. And I don't think you love me the way a man is supposed to love a woman. If you did, you would have joined me. If I really loved you, I would not have asked you to join me. We need to talk about all of this openly. I do love you, but in a different way. I did love your money, though. Once I lost everything, I started to think differently. Something happened to me. When you said you'd wait for me forever, were they just words or did you mean them?"

"At the time, I think I meant them. If you were to ask me the same question now, I'd have to be honest and say they were just words."

"We're not the same people anymore, Pete."

"In a way, that's hard to accept."

"Not if we learned something about ourselves in the process," Maddie said softly.

"I never . . . what you're doing takes guts. I don't know if I could do it."

"No one knows until it's all taken away. If I'm going to die, I want to die as Maddie Stern. Promise me, Pete, if anything does happen to me, that my . . . tombstone says Maddie Stern on it. Can you do that for me?"

"My God, Maddie . . . yes, yes, I'll see to it."

"Good. Now, about Fairy Tales—"

"Wait a minute, Maddie. Just like that you walked away?"

"Not quite. On my own I wouldn't have had the guts. They sent this shrink to talk to me. He gave voice to my wants. He understood what it meant to be in hiding, losing everything. If those others understood, they didn't tell me, and they didn't help me either. By the same token, I didn't do much to help myself. All I know, Pete, is I'm going to enjoy my life for however long it lasts. I will do my duty and testify, because it's the right thing to do. I'll keep my word. That's important to me, that I follow through. Do you understand any of this?"

"Every word. To answer your question, the store is yours. It was always yours and it will continue to be yours. Annie was keeping it intact for you. By the way, where do you get off saying Annie loves me?"

"Oh, Pete, sometimes you can be so dumb. Why do you think she dropped everything and came here? Women know these things. I think you love her too, but you're just getting around to admitting it to yourself. Do you remember how hyper you used to get when I would ask you about her? I was jealous, and I'd never even met her. Nobody puts their life on hold, to do what she did, unless they care deeply for that person. I'm going to miss you, Pete."

Pete found himself at a loss. He felt both relieved and yet anxious. "More coffee?"

"One more cup and then I have to leave. Can I have the keys to the store?"

Pete reached up to an array of hooks on the wall and took down his set of keys for the store. "Do you like Bob Marley, even a little, Maddie?"

"Not even a little bit."

"How about sailing? I bought a boat."

"Not even a little bit. Hate the wind in my hair."

"Would you have gone to Bell's Beach with me?"

"This is one of those important, trick questions, isn't it?" Maddie said quietly.

"No, it's just a question."

"I'd have gone to Australia and probably found a way to avoid the beach. I don't like sand up my butt and getting my hair all mussed up, and for sure I wouldn't take surfing lessons. Do you still have that board?"

"Yeah, I still have it. What do you suppose would have happened to us if we'd gotten married?" Pete asked curiously.

"In the beginning we'd have done okay. Then you would have started to travel more, and I'd start planning a second store, and we wouldn't see too much of one another. We'd probably drift apart. Neither of us would do anything about it. We'd start to lead separate lives, and eventually we'd probably divorce. This is me talking now, Pete. Back then none of this occurred to me. I'm trying to be honest for both of us. Do you concur?"

Did he? "At this point in time, yes. But, like you, not back then."

"Maybe something good did come from this," Maddie said sadly. "Well, I have to be leaving. I've got to start looking for an apartment. And I need a loan."

"My pleasure," Pete said, reaching into a kitchen cabinet for his household checkbook. "Look, Annie is leaving tomorrow. Moving out. You can use the apartment as long as you like. I can sublet it to you."

"Thanks, Pete, I appreciate it, but that's kind of going backward. I need a new place to go with who I am now. I wish you all the best and I'm truly sorry if I gave you a bad time. I can't take that back, as much as I want to."

"And I wish you the best too. Let's stay in touch."

"Only in the business end. What are you going to do with your life, Pete?"

"Well, much as I hate certain aspects of the law, I don't think I'll switch professions. It's what I do best. I think I'm past due for a vacation. I think I'll go someplace."

"Someplace? That's not good enough, Pete. Do it all. Go for it. Do it now. Don't wait. There might not be a tomorrow. I guess I shouldn't have said that, huh?"

"Hell no. You're right. Maddie, if there's anything I can do, all you—"

"I'll ask. Take care, Pete." She kissed him lightly on the cheek.

"By the way, how'd you know where this house was?"

"I memorized it off the letter you wrote. Hey, guess what? I memorized the entire Sears catalog. Surfboards, page 486. The entire catalog, Mr. Sorenson. The index too. Try and top that."

Maddie was laughing as she backed the car around. Pete had come outside to see her off. "Take care of yourself, Pete."

"The *whole* catalog?" Pete said.

Maddie tapped the horn, five notes of zippy sound as she drove away.

"I'll be damned." In the house he sat down to think about what her visit meant to him personally. Maddie was taking charge of her life. For better or worse, she was going to do what was best for her.

Without thinking twice, Pete called the precinct and asked for Otis Nester. When his voice came over the wire, he identified himself and told him Maddie's story. "Will your people look out for her, Nester?"

"Around the clock, and she won't even know we're there."

"That's good." He didn't say thanks. They owed her that much. More, but they'd never be able to make up for what they'd taken away. He hung up the phone, did the dishes, threw away the wine bottles, and put Marley's tunes on the stereo again.

Upstairs, he showered, shaved, and packed his bags with enough clothes to last him a month. He carried his cases out to the Rover. His last trip into the house was spent turning down the thermostat, turning off the stereo, and locking all the doors and windows. He grinned broadly when he pulled the surfboard from the closet. He wiped at imaginary dust, his eyes brimming. Inside his breast pocket was his open-end ticket.

He had one stop to make, Fairy Tales, where he was going to swoop Annie off her feet and take her with him.

It didn't work out that way. Pete charged into the store a little after four, his eyes raking the sales help and customers. When he didn't see her, he bellowed her name.

"Annie isn't here," he was told by Ada Rollins. "She left around two. She had a plane to catch."

Pete's jaw dropped. "Where did she say she was going?" He should know that. He should have asked.

"She said good-bye, that's it, Mr. Sorenson. She said she wouldn't be back. Last week she said she was thinking about moving to San Francisco. Maybe that's where she went. I'm sorry I can't be more helpful."

"I'm sorry too. Listen, the owner of the shop will be in tomorrow. She'll be taking over from Annie. 'Bye, ladies," he said to all the curious sales help looking at him.

Fall back and regroup.

Outside in the brisk air, the surfboard in the backseat of his Rover, Pete felt suddenly stupid. Always the last one out of the gate, Sorenson. Too much, too little, too late. Time to go back to Darien and think this through.

And that, Pete Sorenson, is the story of your life.

Well, hell, if Maddie had the guts to come back and take on life, then he had the guts to use Leo's ticket and go for his dream.

"Yeahhhhh."

It was dark when he drove down the shale road to his Darien home. He swerved to the side when a tow truck pulled alongside. The driver tapped his horn, slid over to the passenger side and rolled down the window. "Hey, are you Pete Sorenson?"

"Yeah. Who're you?"

"I'm your last year's Christmas present eleven months late. I'll back down the drive."

"What the hell . . ."

He must be lost. But the man had called him by name. Pete shrugged when he climbed out of the Rover. Last year's Christmas present?

The man got out of the truck and approached. "Pete?"

"Yeah?"

"Do I look that different? Aside from this red bow on my head. I'd have known you anywhere."

"Nah, it can't be. How . . . Jesus . . . Barney! Barney, is it really you?"

"In the flesh. Pete, I don't know what to say," Barney said, gripping Pete's hand in his. "This guy Simon Jakes, he tracked me down in Woodbridge, New Jersey. Someone named Annie

Gabriel hired him to find me. Jakes told me he's been looking for me for over a year. I was supposed to show up last year for Christmas, but he couldn't find me. Until three days ago. The shop's closed today. This was the first chance for me to drive up here. I tried to find you, kid, for years and years. I don't want you thinking I'm the kind of person who makes idle promises.

"My mom lit out right after they took you away. She changed our names. Lord, I cried for days. For you. I was glad, though, we were getting away from David Watkins. We went to North Carolina and my mother got remarried and my stepfather adopted me. Guess that's why Jakes had so much trouble finding me."

Barney looked at Pete for a long moment, his eyes watery. "Pete, I prayed for you every night. On the day of your sixteenth birthday I got drunk with some buddies. I kept seeing your face. Maybe I should have tried harder, but there was no money for private detectives. They wouldn't tell me anything at Child Welfare, and Social Services booted my ass out the door.

"I swear on my wife and five girls that a day didn't go by that I didn't think of you. I just wanted you to know that."

"Barney, Barney, Barney," was all Pete could say. Suddenly the two men embraced and Pete was wrapped in a strong pair of arms that were crushing him. He didn't care. He was blubbering like a baby; so was Barney.

Arms around each other's shoulders, Pete marched his friend up to the house. He opened the door and turned on lights, leading Barney inside. "Jesus, this is the best day of my life," Pete said, blowing his nose lustily.

"Mine too, kid. Mine too."

"Sit, sit. How about something to eat? A beer? You name it, I got it."

"Peanut butter and jelly with mashed banana sandwiches, just the way your mom used to make them. Chocolate milk."

Pete beamed. "You got it."

They talked until the sun came up, and then they had breakfast.

"So, you're the best foreign import mechanic in the business, huh?" Pete said.

"Yeah, but that's just my opinion." Barney laughed. "And you're a hotshot attorney. I never would have figured you for an attorney, Pete."

"What happened to horticulture, Barney? Hell, I wanted to be an engineer. I'm good at what I do, but it's my own opinion too."

"Are we screwed up or what?" Barney drawled. "I had no money for college."

"Listen, I have an idea. You don't have to get back right away, do you?"

"Nope, my wife gave me the whole weekend. Her family's visiting, so she's okay. What do you have in mind?"

"Well, since you're my surprise, it's only fair I show you *my* surprise. We're going to Jersey. Follow me in your truck. This way you won't have to come back for it. I have some things I have to load in my truck. I'm not coming back here either."

"Pete?"

"Yeah."

"If you never believe anything else the rest of your life, believe me when I tell you that Simon Jakes made my world right-side up. I've always felt like something was missing in my life, that I had unfinished business to take care of. I can go back home to Woodbridge and tell my wife she's never going to have to listen to me bellyache again about you. Only in a good sense now. We won't lose touch, will we? Hey, I'm just a mechanic, and you're this fancy attorney with a degree and all."

"Kiss my ass, Barney Sims!" Pete exploded. They whooped with laughter, kids again as Pete loaded his bags into the Rover.

"Lead on, oh fearless leader, I'm right behind you, and if that fancy truck gets stuck or breaks down, I'm the guy who can fix it."

"I love you, Barney," Pete said unashamedly.

"I love you too, kid. You wanna know something? My daughter Jessie says kiss my ass all the time. I really have to wallop her. I can't make her understand you only say that when all else fails."

Pete smiled all the way to Ridgewood, New Jersey. He gunned the engine the moment the gates of Leo's estate swung open. He roared up the drive, cut the engine, and was out of the truck in the time it took him to blink.

"Some fancy digs you got here, counselor."

Pete watched as Barney ran from bush to bush, tree to tree, his grin stretching from ear to ear. "Listen, if you ever need a gardener, let me know."

"I need a gardener. It's yours, Barney," he said, gesturing to indicate the entire estate.

"Huh?"

"It's yours. I'll work out the legal details when I get back. Here're the keys," he said, tossing a key ring at Barney. "Do you think your family will like living here?"

"Are you putting me on, Pete?"

"Hell no. I have my own house in Darien. This place . . . this place doesn't hold fond memories for me. I think Leo . . . would approve. You can fire the gardeners and do the gardening yourself. There's a fund set up for that. Hell, you can live off what Leo was paying that crew. You're set, Barney. I want to do this, don't say no."

"Pete, I appreciate this offer, but it's too much. My wife is kind of funny about taking. Me too . . ."

"What would you say if I told you there was a string attached?"

"I'd say let's hear it."

"Okay," Pete said, drawing a deep breath, "the string is, this is all yours providing you take in a couple of foster kids and . . . love them. Do you think you could do that, or is having five kids too much for you to take on more? A couple of dogs too. That's the deal."

"Then it's a done deal." Barney grinned. "I'm sure my wife will okay it. The girls will for sure."

"If you need extra income, rent out the carriage house. You can probably get a couple of thousand a month for it."

"A couple of thousand a month!" Barney said in awe.

"Yeah. Prime location. Take a trip to New York and put an ad at the U.N. Look, stay as long as you like. I got some traveling to do and I don't want to waste any more time. My destiny awaits," Pete said grandly. "Listen, when I get back, we'll get together. I want to meet your wife and kids. It's a deal, then."

"How do I say thanks?"

"No need, Barney. Just seeing you, just knowing you didn't forget me, is all the thanks I need."

"You take care of yourself, you hear me?" Barney said gruffly.

"Yeah, yeah, I will." Tears puddled in Pete's eyes as he embraced his old friend.

"Get going before you have me blubbering," Barney said, blowing his nose. "I can't cry, I'm older."

"Kiss my ass, Barney," Pete hooted as he climbed behind the wheel of the Rover. Barney howled, wiping his eyes until Pete was out of sight.

"Thank you, God, thank you for everything." Pete said as he sailed through the opened gates. "For Leo, for Annie, and for Barney."

Maddie sat in the taxi, her face pressed against the window. Fairy Tales.

At last.

She paid the driver and was suddenly overwhelmed at what she was seeing. Shoppers by the dozen, in and out, carrying the spiffy bags she'd designed. She felt light-headed when she made her way into the store.

It was decorated to perfection in shiny white and gold, and with glistening make-believe snowflake mobiles hanging from the ceiling. "Ahh," she sighed as she walked around the store, touching this and that, her eyes trying to take in everything all at once.

Perfection.

Hers.

Tears brimmed in her eyes as she made her way to the back of the store, where busy salesclerks were wrapping gifts and smiling at the happy shoppers.

Hers.

She twirled around, a megawatt smile on her face. She was free. She was alive. She was going to get on with her life. Here in this wonderful place called Fairy Tales.

"Thank you, Pete. Thank you for everything."

Epilogue

It was chilly, the sky overcast. Maybe rain before the end of the day. So what? Pete thought. I'm here. I waited all my life for this. I'm going to run down the beach and slam this board onto the water and then jump on it just the way they do in the movies. If I fall off, so what, I'll get back on. Tomorrow I'll sign up for lessons, but today is mine. If I get myself killed, I won't have to take lessons.

There was hardly anyone on the beach, a few kids and a couple of teenagers working on a six-pack. Beyond the children a lone figure sat huddled in a beach robe. If he made an ass of himself, Pete thought, did he care if some tipsy teenager saw him, or some little kids who would giggle and laugh? Not likely. The only problem was, he would have to sprint in front of the huddled figure. He or she would probably laugh their head off. So, who the hell cares? This was his moment.

Pete hefted the surfboard as he dug his heels into the sand. His heart thumped in his chest as he started off down the beach. He was almost abreast of the huddled figure when he heard a voice say, "What took you so long?"

"Annie!"

"Yeah, it's me. Who else would be stupid enough to try and follow someone else's dream? I've taken root. I've been here for five days."

Pete dropped the surfboard.

"Annie, it's really you. I went to the store to ask you to come with me, but you were gone. Maddie's back."

"I know. She called me. She's the one who told me to come here. She said . . . she said, 'Just go and wait for him. He has to find his own way, the way I did.' "

"She was right, Annie."

"I know."

"I guess I always loved you. I was just too stupid to know it," Pete said, hugging her.

"I know that too."

"You always were smarter than me."

"That's true too, but we still make a good team. Are you going to kiss me now?"

"Hell no I'm not. I'm going to hit that water, and then I'm going to kiss you and never stop."

"Then you'd better get moving because I've waited long enough for this moment."

"Ah, the hell with the water. C'mere, Mrs. Soon-to-be-Sorenson."

She wasn't stupid, she did as she was told. "I *like* that. Do it some more."

He obliged. He wasn't stupid either.